MURDER OF CROWS

MURDER OF CROWS

BOOK ONE
OF
THE PILLARS OF DAWN

Athena

Dedication:

I'd like to dedicate this book to all the Muses who touch our lives and create our daily stories. They may look like children, or teachers, family or friends. They may wear the guise of a stranger, or a lost passerby.

Muses may take the shape of books, movies, songs...even a poem. They may appear in lightning brilliance or as a slow, sensuous awakening. They may touch us in nature, move us to tears with a well-timed chord, or leave us to our weighty ponderings before a loving memorial. They may cloak themselves in an overheard fairytale, or whisk us away with the bloom of an autumn rose, or crack open our deepest wounds with the glory of an arctic sunrise and pour molten revelation therein.

A Muse may even grace us with a lover's caress, flooding our very souls with luminous abundance.

Muses flutter in and out of our lives as seasons, keeping artistic rhythms, the very cycle of creation and re-creation, a dazzling master-clockwork in the tending of *Our Story*. And the Muses ask only one thing in return for their gifts of inspiration. One fee for their blessings.

Creation.

Create the life you want, for which you've been given ample inspiration. Create the future you desire, the love you've wished for, and the healing you need. Create the reality your dreams have imagined, and the worldview of your deepest yearnings. Create your bliss.

For in this contract with the Muses, to create from cosmic dust and the amniotic fluid of arts and sciences, mathematics and histories, your creations bring forth the light of dawn. Your creations bring evolution. They bring…*revolutions*.

So sing, dance, and write. Raise your fist and shout. Compose, paint, and sculpt. Tell a story. Reach out to your neighbor. Weave, study, and act. Always *act*. Hypothesize, fail, and rethink, but keep imagining. Keep creating. Keep filling the world with the radiant fruit of the glorious human experience.

Because without you and your fierce, beautiful chaos and your magical, frail humanity….

Without you, we would not have a *Story*.

Trust the Story.

With Heartfelt and Special Thanks to:

Jason Brown, Robert Chiniquy, Jay Collins, Jeff Croft, Sara Croft, Jim Davison, Jordan Devereaux, Charity Heller, Stephanie Kompkoff, Judy Lara, Maria Spiering Locatell, Erin Mahony, Alison Moore, Jessica Page Morrell, Brett Nielson, Craig Nielson, Jace Nielson, Trevor Nielson, Diane Elizabeth Schaeffer, Andy Wells, Dylan Wells, Loey Werking Wells, Amy West, Sondra Winters, Ambria Wood-Saucier, and Gordon Taylor.

Thank you for all your generous and loving support to help *Murder of Crows* fly.

Thank you also to Amanda M. Sartor, for the brilliant cover illustration and artwork.

Prologue

The Prophecy of Crows
Page 239

I always thought it would be easy to kill in self-defense, believing the line between right and wrong straddled a sea of black and white, and that self-preservation was the obvious, easy truth.

Kill or be killed.

Yet in that moment when someone has their hands around your neck and your windpipe is failing, your hands slapping helplessly at their face, kill or be killed doesn't even cross your mind. Instead, you want only to live. It's not about killing. It's about seeing the face of the man you love. It's about listening to Vivaldi, or tasting honey, or feeling your family in your arms.

It's about one last chance to say "I love you."

Groping to the right, my hand slid along the ground to where the gun landed. My fingernail scraped the grip. I choked on a sob as my pinky slipped helplessly over the cool metal. So close, but it may as well have been the moon.

My lungs burned. The knife wound in my side ached. My entire body was swamped with pain, and I didn't want it to stop. As long as there was pain, I was alive.

In one last surge of adrenaline, I gave up on the gun and wriggled my fingers around the throat of my attacker. I fought for my life. I fought for all that would be destroyed if I died and the world lost the power of Story.

How the hell did my life come to this?

Darkness swallowed my vision. My muscles buckled and my arms dropped to the grass.

I should have told him.

How much of my life have I wasted not knowing the truth?

Then I felt the gunshot.

Chapter One

Beware Destiny cut loose its tether
Birds of a feather murder together

"Miss, we're here."

I jolted awake at the cabbie's voice. My jaw throbbed from clenching my teeth. Images from my dream evaporated in a whisper of black feathers and a pool of blood running into the gutter, washing a dried oak leaf toward the drain. My throat ached. I swallowed and rubbed my neck.

"Um, thanks." I gathered my purse, shaking off the fog even as remnants of the dream-voice called out my name. Rubbing my eye left a half-moon mascara blotch on my knuckle. I sighed, still disoriented from the 12-hour, cross-country plane hopping.

"Need a hand?" he asked.

"I got it, thanks."

I paid the driver and hauled my bags out of the back seat. He sped away, leaving me curbside in front of my aunt's giant Victorian home. The quiet, tree-lined neighborhood rested at the end of Thurman Street. Hers was the last house before the road gave way to Forest Park, 90 acres of woodland in the heart of Portland's metropolis.

The unsettling feeling of the dream lingered. I wheeled my suitcases up the walk, and for the first time in memory Auntie Celeste didn't meet me on the front porch, arms wide to welcome me home.

A sharp *caw!* startled me.

A dozen crows were perched in the front yard maple tree, observing me with beady eyes. One crow, slightly larger than the others, hopped off a branch. He landed in the damp grass and took a few daring struts forward.

I stepped toward him, waving my purse. "Shoo!"

He tilted his small black head, then flapped his wings, rustled his feathers, and screamed, *Caw!* Unbothered by my command, he went about posturing on the lawn.

I continued up the steps to a house that no longer seemed like home.

The skeleton key rusted under the potted fern on the porch, as it had since I was a child. I struggled with the lock before turning the knob, and pushing open the door. The scent of my childhood washed over me like a monsoon across parched land.

I'd kept it together on the flight from New York, ever since the call from her lawyer. But as soon as I smelled the deep, earthy fragrance of Celeste's life spill out as though I'd released her spirit, my knees gave out and I leaned against the doorframe, sobbing.

"Murdered," Mr. Grosskopf had told me over the phone, his metallic voice delivering the news. "A random act of violence."

Mom died when I was six. Then I traveled with Dad around the world on digs. After my 12th birthday, he accepted a director of antiquities position on a dig in Siberia. Auntie Celeste begged him to let me live with her in Portland, Oregon. Then my childhood had begun in earnest, with a true sense of home for the first time.

It will never be home without her.

I leaned against the door wishing I'd come home more often. Wishing I'd called more or sent more updates. We talked on the phone every week, but what excuses had seemed important enough to miss the last four Christmases?

Murdered.

Multiple lacerations.

Hefting my luggage into the entry, I swatted at the light and kicked the door closed. The room was a blur behind a glaze of tears, but I doubted much had changed.

Auntie Celeste's house always smelled like the forest. Not the edge of the woods where the trees meet civilization, but the deep woods where trees are hundreds of years old and the bracken is nourished by layers of undergrowth and moss. The aroma that lingers when living things flourish on the remains of what thrived before.

The fragrance enveloped me as I stumbled into the living room. I collapsed onto the couch, and it was as though Auntie Celeste wrapped her soft arms around my body, welcoming me back from a long journey.

Mutilated. No suspects in custody.

Gazing over the room, I found things to be much like I remembered. Floral print couches. An area rug faded to light pink from wear. The fireplace mantle crammed with tiny figurines of fairies and woodland elves, collected for as long as I could remember. The late-Victorian architecture included built-in shelves, bookcases, and picture-window panes with the original 1920s hand-rolled glass. Every color choice, every doily, exuded Celeste and her life.

It was growing dark outside. I hadn't eaten since grabbing a cup of coffee and a shrink-wrapped doughnut during the layover at Chicago's O'Hare airport. I tripped over the rug on the way to the kitchen, staggering, exhausted. I didn't think I could actually stomach much but hoped for a bottle of wine in the pantry.

At the threshold where dining room hardwood gave way to kitchen area rugs, I patted along the wall for the light switch.

Something rustled in the darkness.

I froze, waiting for my eyes to adjust, but didn't hear it again.

Then I flipped the light—and screamed.

Something the size of a fist, iridescent and lightning fast, flashed across the countertop. Tufts of white flour puffed along its trail as it blurred past. It leapt off the counter in a white plume—and flew under the refrigerator.

I shrieked an ungodly banshee wail, sure I was about to be attacked by a rabid creature. I bolted back through the house, catapulted onto the sofa, and hopped up and down, shuddering.

When the panic wore off, I inched off the couch and fumbled through the living room for a weapon. Strange muffled bumps and skitters echoed from the kitchen.

Grabbing the ash-shovel from the fireplace, I crept back toward the sounds, brandishing it like a baseball bat.

It looked as though a small bomb had exploded in the kitchen. A bottle of maple syrup lay on its side, spilling amber ooze through a swath of scattered flour and sugar. Raisins—at least I hoped they were raisins and not mouse leavings—were strewn haphazardly through the syrupy gruel.

"Please, god, let them be raisins," I whispered.

I tiptoed through the flour, righted the bottle, and surveyed the disaster. Then I yanked a stretch of paper towels off the roll and plopped them down in the goop.

Something caught my attention, so I leaned in closer to a spot on the tile where the flour appeared…well…*sculpted*.

There on the countertop was what appeared to be a snow angel, or rather, a flour angel, no larger than the palm of my hand.

I squinted.

Something crashed behind me. I spun around, screeching as a box fell off the fridge, spilling granola across the floor.

"Oh, my god!" I yelped. "They're everywhere!" I jogged in place, shovel high, ready for the killing strike.

When it seemed like I might actually be okay and my heart stopped racing, I turned back to the flour angel.

It was gone. Dusted away or never was, I couldn't be sure.

Suddenly, I needed to get out of the house. Snatching my purse, I hurried out into the Portland drizzle to the bar down the street for a cup of coffee, or better yet, some straight-up whiskey.

The next day the exterminator came. To my utter astonishment, he claimed I didn't have mice, rodents, or a vermin problem at all!

I called for a second opinion.

The second exterminator was a rugged old man with deep folds and creases in his face. He looked strong enough, but something about his gait urged me to shuffle behind and prepare to catch him if he should fall.

Deloy, read the embroidered nametag on his blue jumpsuit. He wandered around the house, opening cupboards, crawling around, digging at the bottom of cabinets and closets. Then he stood in the kitchen, surveying the mess I'd left in an effort to preserve evidence.

"Is this the only place you've seen the mice?" His voice rolled out like a puttering motor.

I grimaced. "Yup. See? They left droppings." With a shiver, I clutched the pendant of my necklace, finding comfort in the warm green stone.

He knelt on the floor and picked up a small brown, roundish thing.

I frowned.

"Well, Miss, it seems that you have a raisin infestation." The old man glanced up. "But I haven't seen any signs of rodents or insects."

"Can't you spray around the house, just in case?" I reasoned.

"I could, but I won't." Deloy stood and looked at me with a warm, grandfatherly expression. It was as though he could see my grief, and he wanted to put a comforting arm around my shoulder and ask if I wanted to go for ice cream. Instead he said, "If it'll help you feel better, I'll lay a few traps around the place and check on 'em next week. If there're any critters in the traps, I'll exterminate for you. But I wouldn't suggest filling your home up with chemicals for no good reason."

"But…" I motioned to the mess. "Where did that come from?"

"My grandkids make messes like that all the time." He smiled, flashing dentures. "Maybe one of the neighbor kids has a key."

He laid mousetraps and little rodent "hotels" around the house before scheduling a time to come back. I couldn't shake the feeling he was humoring me because I reminded him of someone.

As I walked him out, a thundering *bang* reverberated off the sliding glass door.

"What the hell?" I mumbled, edging toward the back door to see if a kid had thrown a ball into the glass. I hoped the window wasn't cracked.

Deloy pushed past me. He peeked out onto the porch then quickly turned and said, "Don't look. A bird flew into the glass."

"Oh, no! Is it okay?" I hurried forward to see for myself.

On the back deck lay a crow. Several black feathers were scattered about the wood. The bird's neck was obviously broken.

"Do you have a paper bag, or a grocery sack? I'll clean it up and put it in the trash on my way out."

"It's dead?" I asked, feeling sad, even oddly guilty.

"I believe so."

Fetching a trash bag from under the sink, I watched in detached horror as Deloy picked up the limp bird and dropped it in the sack.

"Thanks, Deloy." I followed him through the house to let him out.

"No problem at all." He made his way down the front steps and stopped at the trashcan near the driveway to dump the crow. "I'll be back to check those traps."

I closed the door and sighed. I'd need to bleach the sliding door and clean up the mess in the kitchen. It all seemed like too much. All I wanted to do was sleep.

Two separate exterminators found no evidence of critters.

I must be nuts.

The flour and syrup might have been there for days, maybe even before Auntie Celeste died. Between grief and sleep deprivation, I could have imagined the whole thing.

A bird committing suicide on the window. How weird is that?

Back in the living room, my gaze fell upon a small figurine on the end table. I didn't remember seeing it there the night before. The tiny fairy was much like the others Celeste collected.

The figurine was the size of my palm and wore black and white striped stockings and had a fuchsia bob. Her little black dress was carved to look like a second skin, and her wings were painted with shiny iridescent glaze.

White powder covered her left wing and face. Flour. I must have had some on my hands. I carefully dusted her off with my shirt and placed her on the mantle.

The fairy collection was one of Celeste's favorite treasures. Thinking of the time she spent arranging them, finding the perfect little nook for each sculpture, I felt her loss again.

Her body found by two teenage skateboarders.

As I turned from the fireplace, I caught a glimpse of a reflection in the window.

Celeste's heart-shaped face smiled at me from the wavy glass.

I gasped, staggering backward until I bumped into the rocking chair. I glanced down, wrestling with the furniture.

When I looked up, she was gone.

After a shower, I wiped the steam off the mirror. It was only Wednesday, five days since Celeste's murder, and already I looked thinner, older. My curly hair hung limp and sad. I looked more pale than usual and my eyes seemed more dull than green. I glanced away, unable to muster the energy to care that I appeared to have been cored out.

A lot had happened in the past week. I lost Celeste the day after my fiancé, Erik, admitted he'd been cheating. He wanted to call off our engagement to be with his "true love." Just a week earlier, my boss at the magazine told me they were closing my section: "No more need for inspiring stories of triumph over tragedy in a cosmetics and fashion periodical."

I could always find another job, even waiting tables. And as much as Erik hurt me, I couldn't say he broke my heart. I was actually more relieved than burned.

But none of it even compared to the pain of losing Celeste.

Random act of violence.

Exsanguination.

I crawled into bed as the plastic stars on my ceiling glowed in the darkness. Resting my head on the pillow, holding her picture close, I drifted off to sleep.

My dream began with the sensation of being sucked backward. Tremendous pressure in my ears and the sound of windy surf and then…I was sitting in the backyard of Celeste's house.

The garden was at peak bloom: abundant rose bushes, dahlias, a vibrant green lawn edged with flowers of every variety guarded by six-foot stone walls laced with ivy. I lounged at the table in the center of the yard, surrounded by lush flora. I poured the tea, Earl Grey as usual, then added two lumps of sugar and a dollop of cream before placing the cup and saucer across the table as Auntie Celeste eased into her chair.

"You're late," I teased.

"A lady is never late, Fable. She arrives precisely at the moment she arrives." She smiled.

It was our game. The ritual of tea-time began before I could remember. Every Sunday at four o'clock, we sat to tea in the back yard with a fresh-baked batch of cookies. Per the rules of the game, we were only allowed to speak in our very best (but usually worst) British accents for the duration of the ceremony.

I watched her from across the table as I sipped. She looked divine, a vision of classical beauty in lilac chiffon. After a moment, I cleared my throat and spoke in my best British accent, which sounded more like a Southern drawl.

"Dearest Auntie, the police insist it was a random act of violence."

She smiled. "The tea is quite delicious, my dear." Her cup tinked gently against the saucer. The gold edging around the porcelain was chipped. "Tell me, my lovely, have you been writing?"

I frowned. "I write for *Fashionista*, Auntie. Have you forgotten?" I stirred my tea idly, glancing at the flowerbed where bumblebees hovered over the roses.

"That's not what I heard, Rosebud. A little birdie told me you were fired from the magazine. No matter," she said cheerily. "Now that you're home, you can devote yourself to writing full time, fiction, as you always dreamed."

As she spoke, a trickle of blood escaped the edge of her broad summer hat and dripped from her eyebrow onto the table.

"Celeste…?"

"Hush, my dear girl. If you don't wish to write, you must only say so. Remember when you would tell me your fantastical stories? Do you remember the game we used to play when you were a child?"

"Yes," I admitted, confused.

"Let's play it," she insisted. "You're never too old to play the imagine game." She sipped her tea and said, "Okay, I shall start."

Glancing around, she spotted a bee near a blooming iris. "I do not see a bumblebee; I see a fairy in a striped dress teasing a daisy nymph."

Once named, the bumblebee popped, revealing a pixie in a black and yellow dress and none too happy for being noticed.

The pixie zoomed to the table with a high-pitched buzz and sat on the edge of the tea caddy, pouting. "No fair, Celeste! You always see me!" The little creature folded her arms across her chest and glared.

"Well, Agatha, you always choose the most obvious disguise."

"It works on everyone else," she mumbled.

"Your turn, Fable." Celeste nodded to the yard.

I looked around, finally spotted one, and said, "I don't see a dandelion in the rose garden bark; I see a nymphet."

"Aww," a tiny voice whined. The dandelion head tilted and the leaves turned down as though pulling up the hem of a skirt. The little nymphet lifted her roots, which turned to shapely legs, and skipped to the table. "No fair! Dandelions always stick out in your garden, Celeste!"

All the while I observed my dead aunt, noting blood appeared to be dripping from several different spots on her head, seeping under the brim of her hat, pooling in a scarlet warning on the table and saucer, and leaving splotches on her gown.

The nymphet nibbled a small piece of shortbread cookie.

I wondered aloud, "Auntie Celeste, were you in pain? Was it…" My throat choked up, forcing me to swallow to continue. "Was it quick?"

Red stains oozed through her dress. Her skin paled, and yet she sipped her tea as though it were any other beautiful summer day. "It was quick, the time I had you as my own. You grew up so fast. I always meant to tell you the truth. You must believe that."

"Auntie Celeste, are you at peace?"

"Good lord, Rosebud! Am I at peace?" She sniffed and smiled with blood-stained lips. "I am always at peace when you're with me."

"I mean—"

"Tell me what else you see," she prompted.

I sighed and looked around the yard. This was wrong. All wrong. I spied a black spot at the edge of the fence near the park. Squinting, I made out a crow.

"I don't see a crow; I see..."

The creature looked directly at me. Another crow landed on the fence above him, and more on a tree limb, and another on the grass, and on the edge of the roof, and on the wisteria lattice.

"I don't see a crow; I see dozens of crows!" Like a cloud mass at the edge of the forest filled with black feathers and squawking beaks.

They cawed, flapping their wings.

Startled to my feet, I bumped the table, spilling the tea. The fairy lunged into the air. The nymphet jumped to the ground, promptly turning back into a dandelion.

"Be still, Fable. They cannot see you if you don't draw attention to yourself."

Panic stricken, I turned to my aunt, who was no longer the Celeste I remembered. She was older, auburn hair turned flat gray. Heavy lines marked her features. Ghastly bruises and blood smeared her skin and clothes. Yet she continued to lift the delicate porcelain cup with chipped gold edging to her mouth—unaware she was dead.

Murdered.

"Listen carefully," she said. "I'm not there to protect you from them anymore. You need to remember. Remember how to see. Remember the languages and songs. Above all, remember who your true friends are."

Hordes of glassy black eyes peered out from the woods. The cawing grew louder. I barely heard her add, "I left a gift for you with Mr. Lincoln. Remember, Fable. Remember."

The shriek of crows sounded strangely like ringing. Then squawking. Then ringing. The noise was deafening, grating right to my bones. I grabbed the nearest teacup and launched it at the murder of crows.

I woke in my bed, stars glowing on my ceiling, my phone ringing from where I'd thrown it in my sleep. In a daze, I stumbled out of bed toward the green blinking light. It screamed from an open suitcase, lodged in my laundry.

"Hello?"

"Fable? We called as soon as we heard. Are you okay? Where are you?"

"Eleanor?"

"LeeLee and Biddy are here, too. We're on our way. Where are you?"

"I'm at Celeste's." I rasped and coughed. "I just had the weirdest dream."

"We'll be on the next train. We'll call you tomorrow from Zurich at a more reasonable hour. We love you. Be strong."

The NaNas are coming. Thank god. The NaNas are coming.

I hung up, head throbbing from dehydration. Groaning, I shuffled to the bathroom for aspirin and drank two tablets with a handful of water from the tap before ambling back to bed.

I stepped on something near the edge of the doorway and flipped on the light.

Several loose black feathers were scattered around the carpet, mingled with a handful of larger brown feathers.

Chapter Two

Betwixt the Midway,
Neither here nor there,
Waits the witch with oaken hair

The Multnomah County Coroner's Office was not as sterile as I'd imagined it would be. The reception area, though small, was almost funeral-home-like in its décor. I stopped at the desk managed by a woman with more wrinkles than skin.

"You Fable Montgomery?" She looked me up and down.

"Yes. I'm here to see Dr. Westermill."

"Sorry to hear about your loss. Celeste was a good woman." She continued to squint at me. "Dr. Westermill will be right with you."

"Thanks." As I walked toward a waiting-room chair, I felt her eyes on me and turned back. "How did you know Celeste?"

"We belonged to the same Aerie. We played bingo, bridge, and gates, from time to time." Her smile was more of a grimace.

"Oh, like the Eagles Auxiliary or something?"

"Something like that." She turned back to her computer screen.

The only other person in the lobby was a tall, muscular man sitting in the corner by a potted geranium. His face was lit by the window.

He stared at me boldly.

I shifted my weight, uncertain, not wanting to sit in the waiting room with him or hover by the front desk. As if sensing my discomfort, he smiled, revealing crowded teeth. The sun highlighted a half-missing ear on the left side of his bald head and a small gold hoop in his right ear.

I made up my mind not to sit near the thickly muscled, creepy Mr. Clean. I didn't care how ridiculous I looked standing awkwardly near the reception desk.

"Miss Montgomery?" a smoky, masculine voice inquired.

"Yes, that's me."

I immediately identified Dr. Westermill, the deputy state medical examiner, by his lab coat, but I had little attention for him as my gaze focused instead on the taller man beside him.

"My condolences," Dr. Westermill said and greeted me with a handshake. He was a middle-aged man with a paunch and bushy charcoal eyebrows.

"Thank you."

"This is Agent Drake of the FBI. He's been working on your aunt's case."

"Miss Montgomery." Drake shook my hand, mindful of my smaller fingers. I could tell he had a lean, powerful build beneath his jacket. He wore dark slacks, a blue button-up shirt, and a cell phone that hung on a clip at his belt.

"If you'll come with me, I have papers for you to sign." Dr. Westermill said.

In his office, he ushered me to a green leather chair before sitting behind his desk. The room held a surprising note of warmth in a place that dealt with daily death and bereavement. The desk was piled with stacks of files and a cheap gold-plated lamp. A handful of pens were stuffed in a mug that read, *You can always outrun taxes.*

Agent Drake leaned against the huge mahogany desk, the grip of his gun showed. I glanced away, trying to find interest in the collegiate placards on the walls. I couldn't seem to look at him again until he adjusted his posture and the handle of his weapon was hidden by his jacket, but it was too late. I already knew it was there.

"Why is the FBI investigating my aunt's murder? I thought it was a random act of violence."

"Miss Montgomery, what I am about to tell you must remain confidential, as we're in the middle of an ongoing investigation," Agent Drake said.

"Actually, I'm about to step out and let you talk," Dr. Westermill said. "But if you don't mind, I'd like to get your signatures on these first, so I can release your aunt's body to the funeral home." He stood and offered me two sheets of paper with large print at the top reading *Multnomah County Coroner Release to Cremate*. He handed me the pen from his lab coat.

I recalled making the arrangements over the phone with the coroner's assistant and the funeral home attendant, but I only remembered the vaguest of details. Auntie Celeste had been very adamant about cremation. She'd left a file of paperwork I was to go through if anything ever happened. "Fable, I will not have you mourning a grave for me. Make my body into ashes, but do not settle my bones in the earth."

I signed, fingers stiff, awkwardly gripping the pen.

"I appreciate the use of your office, Doctor." Agent Drake moved to the chair beside me as Dr. Westermill left with the papers.

The door clicked shut. The room felt unbearably warm.

"As I mentioned, the case I'm working on is an ongoing investigation."

"I understand," I said.

Leaning forward, elbows on his knees, he continued. "Celeste Augustine was assisting the FBI in the missing person's case of Harmony O'Brien, who disappeared from Los Angeles, California, two months ago. I am currently investigating the possibility that Celeste's murder was not a random act of violence but is instead a link, possibly a murder in connection with Harmony O'Brien's abduction."

I couldn't breathe. The eggs I'd managed to eat for breakfast drifted up the back of my throat in a cloud of bile.

"Miss Montgomery?" Agent Drake grasped my upper arms. "Do you need a trash can?"

I inhaled with a gulp and struggled for air as the room spun for a moment.

"I'll get the doctor."

"No, I'm okay. I'll be okay." I swallowed hard.

The pressure of his grip on my arms offered a point of focus. I sucked a deep breath, clutched my pendant, and pulled myself together.

"Sorry about that," I said. "I've been feeling a little off lately."

"Understandable," he said, releasing me. He sat back down. "Do you feel up to continuing? I hate to press, but a woman's life is unaccounted for."

"Of course." I sniffed and took another deep breath. "Can we please back up to the part where Auntie Celeste was helping you? What does that mean?"

"Do you know a woman named Harmony O'Brien?"

"No, I don't think so." The name didn't register.

"Celeste said she was a friend of the family, a very dear friend. Are you sure you've never heard the name Harmony O'Brien before?" His hazel eyes drilled me, dark brows imploring.

"Not off the top of my head…but, Agent Drake, I'm not at my best right at the moment. Memory is pretty crystal where Celeste is concerned, but I can't remember the obvious things, like where I set things down, or phone numbers…or how I even got here."

Agent Drake's eyebrow arched.

"Well, obviously I drove my dad's Jeep. But until I force myself to think, I can't recall which turns I made or if I even left the keys in the ignition."

He drew a small notebook and pen from his jacket pocket. "Okay. Then let's go with Celeste. When was the last time you saw her?"

"Nearly two years ago. I flew through Seattle and she drove up to meet me and hang out for a few days. But we talked on the phone every week. Every week! How is it even possible she wouldn't tell me about this?"

"Did she mention this girl to you?" He held up a picture of a beautiful young woman in her early twenties with dark glossy hair and light brown eyes.

I shook my head. "No, she doesn't look familiar."

"Did Celeste ever talk about a man named Vojhane?"

"Not that I recall. I'm pretty sure I'd remember a name like that."

"Did Celeste have any known connection with religious cults?"

I snorted. "She didn't dance around naked under the full moon or drink Kool-Aid, if that's what you mean. What does this have to do with her murder?"

"Celeste was informing for us."

"What? Like...snitching? On who, her writer's club? The old ladies she played bingo with?"

"At first it started as anonymous tips through a source line. Then as leads for Harmony dried up, Celeste came forward as an informant, but part of her agreement to help us was she would keep the anonymity of her source. Her tips were helpful enough that we were able to pinpoint a human trafficking ring. We were set to sting a location in the suburbs outside Seattle. We weren't even aware Celeste was in Seattle until I got the call from the local police." He shook his head and ran a hand through his hair before continuing.

"Evidently, she was scheduled to speak at a writer's conference the day she was murdered. Two teenagers found her body under the overpass by the ferry terminal dock, an hour away from her speaking engagement."

I was hearing it, but none of it made sense. Not a single thing made any logical parallel to the woman who raised me.

"I don't understand any of this." I kept shaking my head. "Are you sure you have the right body? I mean, I never saw her. She was identified by the serial number on the plate in her hip from the car accident years ago. But maybe it was a mistake." Suddenly filled with hope, I sat up. "I should see her."

"Fable," Agent Drake said in a gentle voice. "I double, triple checked. Dental match. Fingerprint match. I even offered a conclusive ID for the local police in Seattle, since I was the only one who knew what she looked like."

He paused then added, "Miss Montgomery, it was a brutal attack. There's no reason for you to see her. If you would like to see for yourself, however, for closure, I can take you in before they release her body."

Silence. I couldn't feel anything, not even my legs. It went on for an unbearably long time before I shook my head. "I can't. I know that makes me a bad person. But I can't see her the last time with no life in her eyes."

I saw my mother one last time.

"I understand." Agent Drake stood, offering me a hand. "May I look through Celeste's things? Her office or workspace, anything that might lead me to her tip source? Harmony O'Brien's life depends on a break in this case."

"Do you need a warrant or something?"

"Only if you say I need one," he said flatly.

"I don't know why you would. I only hear them say that on TV." I shrugged.

"Please allow me to give you a ride home, then, and I'll take a look around."

"I'd appreciate the lift."

"Anything?" I asked as I set a fresh cup of coffee on the desk in Auntie Celeste's study.

Agent Drake stretched in the chair. "Your aunt was an amazing writer." He spied the Winnie the Pooh mug. "Thank you."

"She has 23 published novels to her name," I said, glancing at the bookshelf where her books were lined up in order of their release. I'd read them all at least half a dozen times. "I mean *had*."

"You're a writer, too?" He sipped at his cup, coffee with cream and no sugar. The second since he'd arrived five hours earlier.

"Yeah, I write—wrote—for *Fashionista*, but I got re-organized recently."

"Do you intend to follow in your aunt's footsteps? Write some novels?"

"I planned to when I was younger, but I got sidetracked."

"By what?"

I frowned. "I don't know exactly. It's weird. I just—stopped doing it."

"Well, it's not too late to start again."

Smiling, I glanced away. "So you want me to order some take out, or something? You haven't really eaten all day."

"Neither have you, Miss Montgomery."

I couldn't help but be charmed by his dark hair, tanned skin, and cultured charisma seeping from cracks in his professional demeanor.

I opened my mouth to deny that I was hungry, but thought about sitting across the table from Special Agent Drake and said, "I guess I could eat."

He grinned. It was contagious. "Excellent. How about I order the food, since I have an expense account…if you'll let me stay a few more hours and work on this file that seems promising."

"Sure. What is it?"

"It appears to be an encrypted file. You wouldn't by chance know her password, would you?"

I shook my head. "Sorry. If it's locked, I figure it's a new manuscript she was working on and didn't want me to read before it was ready to be seen. Is that the only locked file?"

"Yeah. Do you mind if I take a copy to one of our specialists?"

I shrugged. "If you think it will help."

He retrieved a portable jump drive from his pocket, plugged it in to the side of Celeste's laptop, and made a copy. "Let's eat. What sounds good? My treat."

"Thank you, Agent Drake."

"Call me Julius," he replied. "My co-workers call me Drake; my mother called me Jules."

I smiled.

It was nearly midnight when I walked Special Agent Julius Drake to the door. He left with a notebook scribbled in Celeste's shorthand code she used when she was working on a new plot. I tried to tell him it wasn't related to what he was looking for, but he seemed to think it would help save a woman's life, so I sent it with him. The only other things he took were the copied file on the jump drive and a copy of her most recent novel from the give-away box in the closet.

His headlights pulled away from the curb, and I remembered I'd need to call a cab to retrieve the Jeep from the coroner's office tomorrow. It was Dad's Jeep for dig locations in the States, but for years it had stayed in Celeste's garage as a backup car.

I still couldn't wrap my brain around Auntie Celeste's involvement in a kidnapping case, as an informant or otherwise. It didn't make sense. I wanted to help, for sure, but I also wanted to understand.

How could she hide something this big from me?

I gathered up the take-out Thai boxes and dumped them in the trash, pondering the possibilities as I hit the start button on the dishwasher and wandered back to the living room to flop on the sofa. There on the end-table near the couch was the little porcelain fairy I'd moved to the mantle yesterday. Julius must have moved it.

Julius.

I thought it interesting I was thinking of him on a first name basis already.

A week after being dumped by Erik for a stripper in pigtails...

I gently moved the figurine back to the mantle and returned to the sofa to sort through the box of odds and ends I'd gathered through the day.

While Julius had searched Celeste's files, I'd fussed and tried to help, awkwardly getting underfoot. At length I picked up on his occasional sigh and stiff shoulders and finally offered to leave him alone.

His obvious relief embarrassed me a little. So I'd done my own search while he was busy. I gathered a pile of Celeste's belongings to go through. It was a much easier task going through her things with someone else in the house. While he was sorting papers in the study or digging through the library, I compiled odd bits and pieces of interesting things to review.

I'd added a miniature brag book of photos that should have been in a larger album to the box. A teal sweater. A baggie of random keys I figured might come in handy. A piece of gaudy costume jewelry caught my imagination. It was a bronze heavy-link chain with a palm-sized medallion depicting a rearing centaur.

When I'd picked it up, testing the weight in my palm, a sudden rush of wind through my hair and the tremor of hooves on the floor startled me. I dropped the medallion, nicking the hardwood.

I stood in the attic, stunned, disoriented. Light flooded the packed room with motes of dust. There were no galloping herds, no breezes. I shook my head, feeling stupid. The weird jewelry was both hideous and beautiful, and I couldn't make up my mind if I liked it or not. But I'd picked it up anyway and added it to the box, along with a stack of notebooks containing poetry snippets in Celeste's meticulous penmanship.

The object that had captured my curiosity the most, however, was a heavy book constructed of thin walnut panels and hemp binding. It was the size of an overgrown coffee table book and must have weighed at least ten pounds. The wooden panel on the front was expertly engraved with ivy florets and the word *Angelica*.

My mother's name.

I retrieved the book with my mother's name from the box and settled onto the sofa to examine it. The craftsmanship of the binding was crude, at odds with the intricacy of the engraving. The title page was painted on age-tinted paper, an elaborate watercolor scene of nine little girls holding hands, dancing around a sapling.

Beneath the picture was my mother's delicate scrawl: *Sacred Nine and Nine Shall Be.*

Each page, and there were perhaps 200, contained a watercolor painting of advanced technique; and below the images were phrases, poems, or a few lines that said nothing, really, but somehow managed to give the picture a context.

One watercolor image was of an autumn-bare tree, each limb full of dozens of black crows. The words beneath read, *Murder of Crows! Murder of Crows! Murder of Crows!*

It wouldn't have caught my attention, but there were what appeared to be spatters of blood on the ground, mixed with dried leaves and black feathers. The level of detail in the watercolor was remarkable. I had no idea my mother was such an artist.

I got up and poured a glass of merlot before returning to the book. I had to lay it on the floor to look at it in detail.

As I turned through the heavy pages, another image caught my eye. A field of red flowers with a towering oak tree. On closer inspection, the tree had a woman's face, and, depending on how I tilted my head, the tree was either a woman dressed in dark robes or wrapped in bark.

My eyelids grew heavy, and the wine did its work. I didn't have the energy to get off the floor. Using my toes, I gripped the edge of a stack of afghans on the rocking chair and pulled them down atop myself, where I curled up and fell asleep looking at my mother's picture book.

Again, my dream started out with the sensation of rushing backward through a pressurized noise.

Then I was in a marshy field that stretched as far as I could see before the horizon crashed against a cloudless turquoise sky. My bare feet were covered in reddish-brown muck that clung to the bottom of my pants.

Mud squished like thick, dark blood through my toes. Eventually I succumbed to the monotony of being shin-deep in slime, and moaned aloud, "Is anyone out here? Hello?"

It was then that I noticed a mark on the faraway horizon: a scraggly black etching against the perfect blue. I stepped twice, the distance to the horizon folded, and I suddenly stood before a massive oak, burned and gnarled, its trunk wider than my Jeep. Ten feet up it split into two limbs, each with hundreds of naked blackened fingers grabbing at the skybowl above.

In dream logic, the only thing I thought upon examining the tree was profound grief.

"Oh, Loughnag! What has happened to you?" I threw my arms around her great trunk.

A dry crackled voice replied, "Dear Child! It is true! You are alive!"

The tree lurched sideways. A deep groan ricocheted through the marsh, and the mud snapped and burbled as Loughnag's roots lifted from the ground. I watched in mute awe as the tree swelled, stretched, and contorted before hunching over.

When the bare branches lifted skyward, they were the oak-limb antlers of Loughnag's crown, and she stood before me as the Oak Crone I recognized.

"You wear the black robes," I said. "I am saddened by this, but I can't remember what that means."

Her frail limbs reached for me. Her pointed fingers ended in scorched twigs, arms sagging with the weight of folded black robes. Loughnag took me into her embrace, pressing her wizened face against my long, dark curls. "Oh, Child, we thought you too had perished with your aunt! We are so relieved."

Her face was human-ish, but the rest of her body bore the characteristics of a tree: an awkward bend in her hips, a crooked tilt in her neck, and the unevenness of her half tree-half human arms. Her cascade of wild white hair was a gnarled cocoon, patchy with red mud nesting atop branches in a haphazard bundle amidst a crown of charred limbs.

"The black robes are a banishment." She held me at arm's length, appraising my person. "Goddess! You have truly grown into the beauty we always knew you'd be. Right, Sage?"

A feline nose emerged from the mess of hair and sniffed me. I had the vague sense that I knew this creature as well.

"Now, Fable, how did you make it to the Midway?" Loughnag asked.

"Midway?" I wondered.

"The Midway: the place neither here nor there. I am banished until the rebellion wins, or the Phoenix rises, or the Crest falls. Hell's pretty tinkling bells, Child, I might be here till the convergence destroys us all… But what I would like to know is how did *you* get here? Did someone bring you?"

"I don't think so," I replied, puzzled. "I just fell asleep on the floor, reading."

"Interesting," said Loughnag. She stretched her back to the tune of cracking tinder. "Interesting." Ticking her chin with a twiggy finger, she frowned. "Just exactly what were you reading?"

I thought about it but couldn't seem to remember. "I don't recall."

"Well, when you wake up from this, mind you pay close attention to that book, and to all Celeste's books." She reached up to her mass of hair. "Sage, would you please be so kind?"

Sage's black and white feline body emerged from the bramble and climbed into the arms of her mistress. "Please go with Fable and keep an eye on her. See that she comes to no mischief. Well, nothing serious anyway."

Sage purred, kneading Loughnag's chest with delicate white paws.

"Fable, you found your own path to the Midway, the halfway point between two worlds. Neither yours nor mine. You will perish if you stay too long. Please, take Sage with you. She was not banished as I was and should not be punished for my crimes."

Reluctantly, I reached up and took hold of the cat. Sage stiffened at my touch and although I tried to carry her next to my body, her white-tipped limbs went rigid, splayed outward. She hung awkwardly in my clutches, groaning.

"Come visit soon. I have news of Aria," Loughnag said, her voice shaky.

"Aria?" I wondered.

"You have much to remember, Fable. Remember."

"Loughnag, why do you have Auntie Celeste's crochet needle in your hair?"

Then I was staring at Auntie Celeste's crochet and knitting basket on the floor next to the couch. Strands of yarn spilled over the basket onto the carpet. I'd knocked over my glass of merlot and my feet were soaked in red wine, the rug tragically stained.

I thought I heard cackling laughter from a distance. I sat up, wiping my mouth and straining my ears. It was only the wind clicking tree branches together. Not laughter. Not a witch's cackle.

Just the wind in the trees.

Chapter Three

Mnemosyne, goddess of memory,
Grant my mind moonbeams
That I might remember thee

The trailhead smelled of turned earth, full of iron, minerals, and sweet layers of green: ivy, cedar, and temperate rainforest. Small threads of water trickled across patches of the trail, soaking into pools before seeping out to dribble downhill and merge with small streams throughout the 90-acre park.

I had grown up on the trails, climbed them barefoot—often in my pajamas, after taking my Saturday morning breakfast out the back gate into the woods. I'd disappear into my fantasy world until I got hungry enough to come home for lunch.

Cedar trees formed the columns of my palace, supporting a canopy of leaves, and branches swathing moss and ivy through the woods, like so many fine draperies. It was easy to believe myself a fairy queen or heroine or great adventurer.

Further into the forest, the smell changed. Gone were the earthy scents of forest dirt exposed to air and sunlight, replaced by the dank, ever-changing aroma of the cycle of decay and rebirth. Mold and rot mixed with budding greens, mushrooms, and soil so rich with minerals it left the air moist, heavy, and delicious enough to chew.

• • •

I saw the mound of ivy from the trail crest and knew it could only be the remains of my fort. Scent memory overwhelmed me completely, and I leaned heavily against a nearby tree, recalling something from deep in my past that lay buried in the bracken of my mind.

It was only a fuzzy memory of costume wings fashioned from paper and dancing around…with someone whose face I couldn't see. No one but Celeste knew about my hideout in the woods. I strained my thoughts, pushing against what felt like a pebble in my memory. Who had I been dancing with?

But the harder I taxed myself to dig up the memory, the faster a fringe of lights bloomed at the edge of my vision.

"That's just great," I grumbled, knowing I needed to get home and take some painkillers before the blur turned into a full-blown migraine.

I knew I could reach Little Avalon, my fort, and get back to the house just in time to take something for the pain and crawl into a dark room. I'd have to postpone my trip to pick up the Jeep from the coroner until after the migraine passed.

A branch snapped, and I flinched, hands flying to my chest, heart jumping. Peering into the forest depths, I held my breath, waiting for something or someone to move. A full minute passed and no more snaps or rustles echoed.

I cautiously stepped forward and shifted a low-hanging limb, squinting into the woods. A shaft of sunlight pierced the autumn-rough canopy, filtering down to the brushy trail winding back upon itself. I expected, or rather, hoped, to see a deer, or raccoon.

But instead, in a trick of light and shadows, I saw the outline of giant wings.

I gasped. Blinked.

And it was gone.

A rare configuration of cascading light, tree boughs, and ivy made it seem, for just a moment, that angel's wings stretched across the trail. I waited, hoping to fool my eyes into seeing it again. But once I'd made out the actual objects of the illusion, I couldn't repeat the experience.

The upside-down kiddy pool lay buried in braided ivy as thick as my thumb. Someone would have to sit on it before they even knew it was there. I smiled, remembering when I snuck the pool out of the garage, then dragged, rolled, pulled, and finagled the stupid blue plastic tub over the back fence, up the hills, down the trails, and over fallen trees. Once there, I'd nailed it to a few pieces of wood to make a framework from the crates I'd used to carry up supplies, such as canisters of foods, sandwich baggies, and a few pieces of waterproof Tupperware I didn't think Celeste would miss. (Turned out, of course, she did.)

After nailing the roof to my frame, I dubbed it *Little Avalon.* I had just enough space to sit on a makeshift chair with my few rudimentary supplies and write, read, sketch, and play. While other kids went to church on Sundays, I was happily worshiping in my temple of imagination, sheltered in my faith that the woods and my characters would protect me from all harm.

I tugged at a bundle of ivy but it wouldn't budge. I got down on my hands and knees to peek under the shelter. Something scrambled beneath.

I shrieked, lunging backward into the bramble.

A raccoon bolted out the side of the enclosure through the thicket.

When I could breathe again, I stood up and faced north. Thirty not-so-adult paces from the cedar holding up the fort, I knelt beside a large rock. The top of the stone just beneath the ivy was marked with a symbol I'd etched with a nail: a spiraling piece of calligraphic lettering similar to an *S.* It was a protection and sealing symbol I'd read somewhere, and as a child I put it on everything. My journals, my box of trinkets, my bedroom door.

I rolled the stone over and dug under it with a stick. The dirt was soft and pliable, and I reached my treasure quickly: an old Tupperware container Celeste used for casseroles; a horrid avocado green plastic remnant of the 1970s. It was just big enough to hold a few of my notebooks, favorite items, and the leather-bound book of *Sacramentum* I'd come for. Wriggling it out of the ground, I climbed to my feet, clumsily dusting off my jeans.

The shimmery lights in my vision from the on-coming migraine were much worse. I couldn't tell if it was the pending headache, but I felt like I wasn't entirely alone.

Glancing around, I expected to see someone but the only other creature was a solitary raven, watching me from a low cedar branch with beady eyes. The raven's body was larger than his crow brethren's, his shoulders marginally wider. I shifted a little to the left, and its black head followed my movement. It screamed once: *Caw!*

They're everywhere.

With a shudder, I quickly made for the house and the welcome relief of some painkillers.

The migraine was in full swing as I came in through the back door. I was long past the point of being able to medicate it, and, worse, someone was banging on the front door.

I ran to the front door and jerked it open. Agent Drake and a strange woman stood to the side of the mat.

"Hello," I groaned.

"Fable? Are you okay?" Agent Drake asked. His eyes scanned the living room behind me as if he expected someone to be inside.

"No, I have a headache. Come in," I said, ushering them inside.

"Are you alone?" He didn't wait for me to answer but moved past me and into the living room.

The woman, dressed in a gray suit, stepped over the threshold. "Your cat brought you a little gift," she said. "Mine does that, too."

Glancing at the dead brown mouse on the welcome mat, I frowned. "I don't have a cat," I murmured.

"Fable, are you here alone?" Agent Drake asked. "This is my partner, Agent Mendelson. Please stay with her. I need to do a sweep of your house. I'll explain in a minute. Don't move."

Buried under the pain and heat of my head, I was astonished when Agent Drake drew his weapon and disappeared around the corner into the kitchen. I stood near the door with Agent Mendelson who was pointing her weapon at the hardwood floor. A bewildering sense of urgency in the air prevented me from speaking or even moving, like whatever had them worried should worry me, too.

While we waited, my migraine shifted from bright fuzzy lights to a firestorm with a marching band accompaniment in my skull.

"Clear," he said when he finally came back. He clicked his gun back in the holster under his jacket then took my arm and led me to the couch.

"What the hell is going on?" I demanded.

"Miss Montgomery. You don't look well." He studied my face. "I have some bad news, and then some really bad news. I think you should sit down. Can I get you something to drink?" He seared me with hazel eyes.

There's something different about him.

"I need something for my head." Even as I said it, Agent Mendelson walked past me to the kitchen. She was pretty, with olive skin and high cheek bones, an exotic Latin flair about her features. Just seeing her sleek black hair pulled tight in a bun made my head hurt even more.

"Where is it? I'll get it for you." she asked over her shoulder.

"Top of the cupboard on the right side of the sink. Blue and white bottle," I replied and glanced at Drake then settled on the sofa.

"I'm sorry you aren't feeling well, but I have some bad news, and it can't wait. Didn't you get my voicemails?" Agent Drake asked.

He's definitely different.

I checked my phone—six missed calls. "I was in the woods."

Agent Mendelson returned with a bottle of migraine-strength painkiller and a glass of water. She set them on the coffee table where I helped myself. They watched me expectantly until I said, "Okay. Let me have it. Really bad news first."

"Your aunt's body has disappeared," Agent Mendelson said as she sat on the couch beside me.

"What? They lost her?"

"We believe she was taken," Agent Drake said.

"Someone took her body? Why? How do you know she was taken?" My lungs ached.

Drake rubbed his neck. "Because of the other piece of bad news. Worse news."

"How can anything be worse?" I wondered.

"Worse is when we arrived at the coroner's office first thing this morning, we found your Jeep had been vandalized and a note left behind. The vinyl windows and rag-top had been slashed, the interior trashed and the seats cut open. We've been trying to reach you all morning on your cell. When you didn't answer, well, I got worried." He pulled an evidence bag from his jacket pocket.

A comforting calm enveloped me.

This is not real.

I don't have to be upset, or hysterical, or cry, or even be sad.

Because it's not real.

"Does this note mean anything to you?" He held out the clear bag containing a piece of paper.

I stared at it, then despite myself, I reached for it.

Grasping the plastic, I read the note contained inside. One word in perfect hand-lettered calligraphy.

NINE.

"Does it mean anything to you?" asked Agent Mendelson. "Strike any thoughts?"

"Nine what?" I asked.

"We're working on that, but the 'worse' part of that news is you are now officially part of this investigation, Miss Montgomery." Agent Drake took the evidence bag from my slack fingers before it could fall to the floor.

"What? Why?" I felt like I spoke from outside my body.

"Because very similar notes have appeared in three other abduction cases." Agent Mendelson gazed at me with dark brown eyes. "We believe you are the next target, Miss Montgomery."

Their voices seemed far away as Drake and Mendelson talked to one another and then to me, but I didn't allow any of their words to sink in. A pervasive sense of déjà vu gave the room a stagnant heat. I heard words like *surveillance, van, protective custody, street,* and *guard*.

I stood with wooden limbs that belonged to someone else. "May I get you something to drink? Maybe some tea?" I asked.

They looked at me with slack faces.

"Have you heard anything we just said?" Drake asked.

"You're taking my Jeep for evidence. Keep phone close. Protective custody around the clock. Something about a cat. Van across the street. One of you here at all times."

Agent Mendelson tilted her head. "Except for the cat part… yeah." She stood and gripped my shoulders. "It's gonna be okay, Fable. You'll be safe with us. We're going to get this guy."

"What about Celeste?" I asked, picking up the fairy figurine from the end table.

"We'll let you know as soon as we have something," Agent Drake said. "But for now we ask that you stay here, where it's safe."

Absently, I carried the fragile sculpture to the mantle where I replaced it, vaguely wondering how many times I'd returned it to the same spot.

Then I asked, dazed, "Is that a yes to the tea, then?"

• • •

The next two days were spent in constant anxiety. A detail of cops patrolled my neighborhood every hour, and a black van with government plates sat parked on the street out front, around the clock.

They sure aren't trying very hard to be inconspicuous.

Agent Drake came by the house during the day to relieve Agent Mendelson, who stayed at night. I didn't have a sense of real protection so much as the constant presence of strangers invading my last safe haven.

Every day I struggled with the awkwardness of people in my house and the natural instinct to hostess. I kept wanting to fill drinks, cook food, and make sure they were comfortable.

Mendelson didn't seem to mind, but Drake put a stop to it the second day with a sharp "Please go about your normal life as though we aren't here."

I didn't understand his much colder attitude but was pleased to be able to ignore the constant sense of intrusion. I kept mostly to my room or Celeste's office.

Logically, I knew the plan was to keep me protected, as I appeared to be the center of a kidnap plan—but as of yet, no one could tell me who I was supposed to be afraid of. Therefore, I was suspicious of everyone.

When I needed groceries—Agent Drake insisted on taking me to the store himself—I was afraid of the old lady with a shopping cart on the bread aisle, and the checkout clerk, and the pimply teenager who offered to carry my bag.

Agent Drake did little to help me relax as he insisted on walking ahead of me, and constantly eyed men and women alike. His broad shoulders must have ached from the tension.

He cut an intimidating figure with his height and suit, and the bulge of a gun under his arm. I started thinking I'd imagined we had a great connection the first time we met. Maybe he was just being nice because I'd been grieving.

He was polite, nothing more. Get over it.

"Next time, make a list and we will send someone to the store for you," Agent Drake said as he led me down an aisle.

I paused in front of a wall of tampons. "There are just some things I don't want another person picking up for me, you know?" Grabbing a box of super absorbency, I found a small measure of enjoyment as Agent Drake grunted and looked away, pretending to be scanning an empty row.

However fearful I was of the threat that had no face, it'd be a cold day in hell before I let some FBI intern pick out my plugs.

As we walked out of the store and into daylight, Drake walked ahead as usual, scanning the street for who-knows-what. I was staring at the broad plane of his back when a shadow on the asphalt caught my attention.

In the patchy autumn light, I saw the shadow of someone on the roof with enormous, outstretched wings.

An angel?

I spun and peered up at the roof. The glare of sun between clouds was just enough to blind me, and I shielded my eyes. "Julius! The roof!"

It happened so fast. Drake's gun was in his hand and he was dragging me behind him as he aimed upward. My heart hammered in my chest like sonic booms. The clouds shifted just enough to cover the glare. The top of the building was empty.

"Did you see someone?"

"I thought so," I answered lamely.

Drake rushed me into the car without another word, his silence and sharp movements alienating me even more.

The ride home from the grocery store was quiet, uncomfortable. When we got to the house, Agent Drake did another sweep while I tried to avoid stepping on the newest dead mouse on the mat.

I stood on the porch thinking maybe I'd be better off if I just went to Siberia and stayed with my father at his dig site for a while. It couldn't possibly be colder than in Drake's company.

"It's clear." Drake holstered his weapon and motioned me in from the porch.

"No, it really isn't. Nothing about any of this is clear," I said as I followed him back into the house and left him alone as I made for the kitchen.

As much as the temperature between us had shifted, altered by his unknowable distance and the factors of ever-present danger and uncertainty, at least it was only awkward. Awkward is still livable.

In the evenings, I got to know Agent Mendelson better. A Los Angeles native, she had a lot to say about the darkness of our Portland autumn. She was 32, had been with the FBI for five years, and a special agent for less than one. Mendelson was from a large Latino family with five sisters. I envied her. I couldn't imagine what it would be like to have a sister.

She'd never read Auntie Celeste's novels, so once I pointed her to the first one, she spent most of her time reading.

On top of it all, I wasn't sleeping well. I dreamt of strange creatures and groggily went about my days in a fog of disbelief interspersed by bursts of impotent fury. I was angry that my father was unreachable in the wastes of Siberia; I'd left a dozen messages with his company's service in New Mexico but had yet to receive a response. I was angry about being fired from my job. Angry at Erik. Angry that some damn cat continued leaving dead mice on the front doormat. Angry that Auntie Celeste had left me. Angry that some lunatic was snatching women. Angry that my life had become a frenzied blur of questions without an end in sight.

• • •

37

"You really don't need to cater or cook or take care of me, Fable." Even as she said it, Agent Mendelson accepted the plate of spaghetti and we sat at the table.

"It's nothing fancy, just spaghetti." I shrugged. "Besides, I'd feel weird not feeding a guest."

"I'm not a guest," Mendelson said around a mouthful, "but I never turn down hot food on a stakeout."

"Is this a stakeout then?"

"Protective custody, actually."

I nodded, unsure what to say.

Mendelson swallowed and licked her lips. "Can I ask you a question?"

Twirling my spaghetti on a fork, I shrugged. "Sure."

"Do you like Julius?"

"What?"

"Agent Drake—do you like him?"

"Um, well, I…"

Something about her question felt like a trap. She flashed me a conspiratorial smile. Sudden pressure built behind my shoulder blades. The air in the room grew thicker, more difficult to breathe, and I found myself wanting to tell her anything she wanted to know.

"I just got out of a relationship," I answered as though my tongue were on fire and I couldn't talk fast enough to cool the flame. "Kind of a breakup that needed to happen for a while. I mean, Erik wasn't such a great guy, but I thought, you know, what if no one else gets around to asking me to marry them? It's stupid, you know, because I realize I didn't really ever love him, I was just afraid of being alone. Then my aunt just got murdered, and it's possible I'm on someone's twisted kidnap agenda, but, yeah, I guess I'm attracted to Drake, but I don't have the headspace to think on it much more than that."

When it was all out in one long rush of disjointed explanation, I couldn't believe I'd just said it. I shuddered and sucked in a deep breath.

Why did I just blurt all that?

Mendelson shrugged, smiling. "I only ask because he's different around you." She forked another bite of slippery, red noodles and sucked in the last stray strand.

The pressure left and the air in the room felt normal again. All I could taste was the garlic in the sauce and I blinked rapidly. "Different how?"

"Just different."

Monday night, rain slammed against the antique glass of Auntie Celeste's writing room, hammering the roof with a ferocity that would have worried me if I hadn't grown up in the Pacific Northwest. As it was, I stared uselessly past my computer screen and zoned out at the rivulets—or more accurately, small rivers—running down the window.

Auntie Celeste, murdered.

I sighed, glancing around for a clock to see how long I'd been staring out in space without writing a single word, but Auntie Celeste kept no clocks in her writing room.

Well into my high school years I'd read in the window seat, nestled on cushions next to sun or rain or clouds, and listened to her typing away on her newest manuscript. She said I was her good-luck charm. Her muse.

Gone. She is gone.

I glanced around her writing room. The trinkets. The stained-glass Tiffany lamp on the desk. The file cabinets full of stories and partial manuscripts. Her desk still had the dish of sea shells we'd gathered at the coast, and a framed picture of us on our trip to a convention in New York for her work, both of us smiling.

I couldn't stay in her room anymore. There was too much of her and not nearly enough. So I turned out the light and closed the door.

• • •

Agent Mendelson sat in the rocking chair by the hearth, totally engrossed in Celeste's first book, *Earth Song,* when thunder began and clusters of lightning lit up the windows. With a start, she put the book down and sighed. "Your aunt was an amazing writer! I'm hooked."

I silently agreed as Mendelson stood and walked down the hall to the bathroom.

I filled a glass with cool water and set a pot on for tea, then took the Tupperware container I'd dug up in the woods and carried it to the table. I flipped through the stack of loose papers with snippets of rhyme, and filed through old pictures of my mother I'd kept safely hidden with odd bits of string, ribbon, and a child's stamp with a smiley face. Then I pulled out the leather-bound book of *Sacramentum.* It was really one of my father's old dig journals. He'd only used a few pages, so he let me scribble in it.

Skimming through the first few pages, I struggled to read my handwriting. I couldn't help but smile, remembering fondly all the tales of fairy worlds, of a mythical place I called Aria, or the Song of Earth. I wrote about cultures of centaurs, a city of bird people called Avians. Pixies, sprites, and mermaids. There were dragons and their Ryders and serpents and a race of people who grew antlers from their heads. Mixed with it all along the margins, I'd sketched—endless doodles of wings.

I got up when the tea kettle whistled. As I walked past the sliding glass door, a particularly bright flash illuminated the back yard.

There, in the lightning illumination, was an enormous birdman. His giant wings outstretched and his head tipped back to feel the rain on his face, his gloriously naked upper torso ribbed with muscle to the top of his jeans.

He held his arms out, clearly lost in the delight of the pouring sky.

Outside went dark and I stood shaking, waiting with my heart in my throat for the next flash, unsure whether I wanted the back yard to be empty or not.

The flash didn't come. Thunder pealed nearby.

I crept forward and pressed one hand against my own reflection in the sliding glass door, the other clutched my pendant.

When the lightning finally flared again, the back yard lit up like day as a streak of fire from the sky struck the oak tree in the neighbor's yard.

White light.

Sparks exploded.

Flames shot across the branches, catching the trellises. Thunder simultaneously shattered the air, rattling the windows. The ground shook.

Yet I noticed none of it at the moment, for there before me, on the other side of the glass, stood the Avian, his hand pressed against my own on the opposite side of the glass.

It happened so fast that I saw his face, the intensity of deep-set blue eyes, dripping strands of curly blond hair to his bare shoulders—and umber wings, arching behind him in an angelic display. He tilted his head, smiling.

My mouth fell open.

My god.

My heart stopped and started again.

And the neighbor's tree was on fire. The trunk groaned, leaned, and its flaming wooden weight fell sideways. I turned in a brief moment of horror as the blazing oak toppled over, crushing the wall between our houses, smashing the rosebushes and spraying burning rubble across the yard.

When I looked back he was gone.

I didn't have time to wonder if I imagined it all. There was fire.

Fire!

Launching myself out the sliding glass door into smoke and reeking ozone, I grabbed the hose and started spraying in the rain. I had the vague awareness Agent Mendelson was not far behind me, and soon we were joined by agents from the surveillance van across the street.

Some of the men used pots from the house filled with water. Agent Mendelson and I both used the hoses. The fire was mostly out by the time the fire department arrived. Thankfully, the rain kept the fire from really catching or spreading beyond the super-heated strike zone.

Someone shook my shoulders, or was I shivering?

I stood in the rain wearing nothing but a tank and yoga pants. Soaked. Tinted blue from cold. I glanced up at Agent Drake.

"When did you get here?" I wondered.

"Mendelson called me. I got here as fast as I could." His hands were scalding hot against my freezing skin. "Are you okay?"

The back yard looked like a charred construction zone. The wall would need to be rebuilt; some of the roses might make it. Celeste's house was full of mud and strangers, and fire hoses crushed the flowers. Red and blue lights flashed in the darkness from the street. Charred oak remains covered the lawn, and a streak of black burn damage shadowed the left side of the house from the heat blast. It was lucky the house hadn't caught fire.

"Are you okay?" he reiterated with a gentle shake.

Am I okay?

Then I started laughing. Not a chuckle or a ladylike giggle. I laughed like a tortured donkey. A braying, heaving ass. And once I started, I couldn't stop.

I walked through the yard to the flowerbed to check on Celeste's roses, slipping in the deep imprints left by firemen's boots in the slick, grassy mud, and fell to one knee. People stared, yet pulling myself together seemed beyond my strength. I stopped at Mr. Lincoln, Celeste's favorite, only to realize the bush was crushed, the stalk split right down the middle.

My laughter halted abruptly. I stared at the crippled plant.

A vivid memory flashed of Celeste walking in with a handful of long-stemmed blood-red roses in one hand and her shears in another. "Mr. Lincoln sends his regards!" She'd put them in a vase and pressed her nose to the petals. That vase of roses marked the centerpiece of our last breakfast in this house together.

"Icarus' wings!" I shouted. "Damn it, Mr. Lincoln, *fuck you!*"

I kicked at the broken stalk, then kicked again. My foot flared to life with pain, and I liked it. I liked that something outside my body hurt for a change, and I just kept kicking until my footing skidded in the mud and my legs slipped out from under me. The full weight of my body came down on my back with a grotesque squelch. I lay in the muck staring up at the sky as rain pelted my body, foot throbbing.

Then Drake stood over me, holding his hands out to stop the rain from hitting my face. "Who's Mr. Lincoln?"

I pointed at the rosebush.

He turned to speak to someone. I heard voices in the chaos but didn't care. I knew I looked like an idiot, and I just couldn't be bothered to give a damn. The rain masked my tears, baptizing me in cold waters.

Celeste, I need you.

"No. I've got this," Agent Drake was saying to someone as he returned to my line of sight. He reached down, and despite my petulant desire to stay in the freezing mud, my hands reached for his. Contact. A way out.

He pulled me to my feet. I hobbled, unable to put weight on my right foot.

"You probably broke a toe," he admonished. "We should get you to the hospital."

"No. I'm fine. I can bend it, it just hurts." I couldn't look him in the eye, so I glanced around and saw the last of the firemen carrying hose out the side gate. The back yard was a ruin.

"They're all done here. Mendelson went to file the report." He shifted my arm over his shoulder to help me walk. "We'd better get you warm and cleaned up."

"I really miss her, Julius."

"I know," he said, wrapping his arms around my muddy, wet, sooty body.

Chapter Four

Champion and Hero
Bled by the thorns
Both saved by a rose
Both saved by a rose

I stood in the shower, hot waves sluicing over chilled skin. When the water finally ran clear and my flesh pulsed with heat, I dried off and changed into clean stretchy cottons. It hurt to step with my right foot as I limped toward the first aid box down the stairs.

Drake stood from his seat on the couch with his case files and laptop. "Do you need anything?"

"No. Just gonna grab a wrap for my foot."

"I still think you should have it checked."

"I'm fine," I said with a wince.

"Then at least let me help you." With sturdy arms he helped me down the last few stairs and across the room to the sofa. "Where's the bandage?"

"In the kit on the top shelf of the hall closet."

He went to fetch it, and I admired his strong forearms revealed by rolled-up sleeves and the shape of his body defined by his holster. His dark hair was mussed as though he'd been running his hands through it. Noting his gun, I realized I wasn't as uncomfortable around the weapon as I used to be.

"Put your heel up on the coffee table," Drake said as he returned with a beige roll, two silver clips, and tape. He sat on the coffee table and placed my foot in his lap. It was the same foot I'd broken in the accident six months earlier.

"I can do it," I said.

"I can do it better and faster."

His hands were warm and gentle as he wrapped two of my tender toes together with tape then bound them to a third toe that felt fine. I clutched the cushions of the sofa and bit my lip, studying his face, which was a mask of focus: eyebrows pulled together, mouth a thin line.

When he finished with the tape, he wrapped my foot with the stretchy, beige strip.

"Julius?"

He looked up and his eyes were haunted, far away. "I'm sorry I wasn't here earlier," he said.

"Why are you sorry for that?" I wondered. "Is that why you're angry with me?"

"I'm not angry"—He blinked—"at you." He held my foot captive, a small bundle of bones in his large hands.

He exhaled before continuing. "Fable, I need to stay alert and clear-headed. I need to get this guy, and I need you not to get hurt as I do that." His hazel eyes seemed greener, his voice wavering between asking and commanding. "Can you please just do that?" He paused. "For me?"

Stunned, I could only nod and whisper, "Okay."

He met my eyes a moment longer, then with a sigh he lifted my heel off his lap and stood. The shielded eyes returned, his posture hardened.

"I'll be here tonight. I told Mendelson to get some rest." It was nearly three in the morning. He walked back to his spot on the other couch and picked up a file he'd been reading. "The house is secure. Two more agents just relieved the surveillance team in the car. You should be able to sleep safe."

Dismissed in my own house.

"Thanks for taking care of my foot," I said and brushed against him on my way to the stairs.

"Fable?" He looked tired in the lamplight, a scruffy shadow tinting his jaw. Whatever he was about to say evaporated, and he shook his head, finishing with, "'Night."

"'Night," I replied.

The familiar feeling of backward sucking and the rush of pressurized sound preceded my dream. A marble corridor stretched before me, impossibly long. Flying buttress ceilings arched far into the sky. The walls were only 15 feet high, leaving the rest of the wall unfinished till the stained-glass canopy above that seemed to drift unattached from any structural support. Stepping forward, I wondered where I was. Evidently, some new dreamscape. Not a church, though it was cathedral-esque; the structure dwarfed any cathedral I'd ever seen. Certainly beautiful. A place of some reverence.

My bare foot slapped the floor in an uneven tempo with my bandaged one.

Then from the ceiling in the distance, a figure drifted toward me. At first it was difficult to tell exactly what it was, as it was backlit by the stained glass windows casting azure light. A winged angel in flowing robes?

I didn't feel fear. Even for a dream, the location felt powerfully sacred. Like danger simply wasn't welcome in such a place.

As the creature neared, I saw it was one of the Avian creations of my childhood imagination. "Fable?" she shouted. "Icarus' wings, am I happy to see you!"

I could not have been more astonished. Her umber wingspan stretched nearly 12 feet. She was easily the most beautiful woman… bird…bird-woman—Avian—I had ever seen. She had a veritable tower of shiny red hair in both curls and feathers atop a face as pale as moon-lit bone. Wide blue-green eyes, more round than a human's, were centered above exaggerated cheekbones.

She landed in a gust of wind fluttering the many layers of her black gown. Her face glowed with happiness, as though she were seeing someone dear for the first time in ages.

I glanced back, but I was alone, save the rushing arms and voluminous dress of the bird-woman sweeping toward me. "Fable! Fable! Fable!"

Then I was swallowed in her embrace, swaddled by giant wings. It felt like being enveloped in silk sheets. "Goddess, I am glad the ban is lifted! I have missed you like I'd miss a wing!" She rocked us to and fro, letting out a schoolgirl shriek. "I'm so happy I could crush you!"

I smelled the sun on her skin and the crisp edge of wind. Her feathers tickled my nose. I sniffled.

How can a dream feel so real? How can I smell sunlight in my sleep?

She was talking so fast I could barely keep up as she stepped back, held up my arm, and turned me in a circle.

"You've grown up!" she cried, clasping her hands to her mouth. "Did Liam or Gabe tell you where to find me? What a foolish question! *You* of all people would know how to find me."

She led me down the corridor as she talked. "I can't wait to hear everything. How long can you stay? I must finish this session with the Norns. You know, politics, but afterward we can fly home and you can see mother and father. Can you stay the night? It'll be just like old times."

I jogged, limping, to keep up with her stride. Suddenly, she stopped and turned. "When was the ban lifted?"

"Um." I looked around, desperate for a clue to the right answer, because it somehow seemed important. I liked her. I liked everything about her, and she felt familiar, almost familial to me. "I don't know."

Her smile faltered, wings drooping. "Then how did you get here? Did Liam come with you?"

I opened my mouth but nothing came out. I had no answer.

"Shit," she said flatly. "Fable, I love you. You know I do, but why do you have to do everything backwards?"

She pulled my face in close. "Go back. You must do it the right way. The legal way. We'll get to catch up and tell stories and braid each other's hair soon enough. You're my best friend and we are going to grow old together—but not if you get us both killed or banished because you are taking shortcuts and rifting the veil. I love you, but go home."

She kissed my cheek.

"Wait! Wait a minute, please wait." Clutching at her desperately, I begged, "Please tell me one thing: Is this real or a dream? Am I crazy? "

"Fable Rose Augustine Montgomery," she said, cupping my face in her hands. "You are not your mother. You are a Muse. And yes this is all real, but to get back here, you've got to follow the rules like everyone else. Find my brothers. They will help you." She smiled, showing even white teeth against lush rose lips.

"Go," she said, and gave me a gentle shove.

I sat up wide awake. It was light outside, but only just; autumn clouds hovered, waiting for any excuse to pour. Throwing the covers back, I couldn't remember when I'd last woken feeling…alert. As if something had clicked on, and the fog in my brain was lifting. Clarity. How long had it been since I felt clear?

I stood at the back window surveying the damages from the fire and storm. Despite the events of the night before, I'd slept like the dead and remembered only parts of one dream. It took a few moments to recall why my back yard was wrecked. I hobbled downstairs to see if it looked any better by daylight. It actually looked worse.

The coffee mug warmed my hands while I looked out at Celeste's beloved roses, most of them crushed. Much of what was left had been seared by heat. Muddy footprints marred the lawn, leaving patches of green showing through the muck here and there. The neighbor's oak tree was a pile of black char scattered through lumps of stone and jagged pieces of the wall.

It would need a lot of work.

Yet the damage wasn't what bothered me. Time and again, my thoughts side-railed back to the birdman in the rain.

Did I imagine him?

I stared out to where I'd seen him basking in the storm. The more I thought about him—his hand against mine on the glass—I became convinced he was in fact a character from a traumatic incident that took place six months earlier, on the other side of the continent. The birdman in the rain was familiar to me.

I wriggled my bandaged foot and the memory came rushing back.

It had happened six months earlier.

People crowded shoulder to shoulder on the subway platform. The train was late, and folks eager to get home continued to push their way down into the stairwell as the spring rain hammered above. It just happened to be one of those New York days when the weather drove from above and commuters elbowed toward the platform, hoping just one more would fit, and a jostling frenzy ensued.

I fought to maintain my footing at the edge of the platform. The pressure from behind forced my heart into my throat. Sweat popped out on my face and neck. I heard the train coming. The crush of bodies smelled like wet asphalt and cheap cologne. When the rest of the crowd heard the train, the shoving and shuffling took one last heave, and I was flying.

It happened in an instant.

Not flying, I realized. Falling.

I hit the track eight feet down. My right foot twisted and cracked as I tumbled across the rails. I landed on my right shoulder and smacked my head.

Lights from the train rounded the bend. Raw terror surged through my limbs as I struggled to sit up.

People shouted. The commuters at the front of the line stretched out their arms, screaming for me to grab on. Blood pulsed in my ears.

My broken ankle throbbed. Agony. It hurt to breathe. I tried to roll to the edge of the platform, hoping to be close enough to the wall that the train might miss me, but as I moved onto my right shoulder, I screamed. It was dislocated.

In that instant, when I knew I wouldn't make it, I saw faces. A Hispanic woman with a brown leather purse, her coat folded over one arm as she knelt on the platform reaching for me. She looked nice, I thought, like someone's mother, screaming at me in Spanish. Next to her, a middle-aged executive was lying on his belly, throwing his trench coat for me to grab.

Other commuters waved at the coming train, flashed the lights on their cell phones. They flapped jackets, umbrellas, whatever they had, to get the attention of the train.

I managed to position my left foot under my body and totter to a stand. The noise was deafening. The horn of the train rang out as it finally saw me in its lights, too late. The mass of commuters roared as they realized the shoving had pushed someone onto the track.

Metal hummed under my foot, and although I knew it was too late, I hopped and grabbed for the executive's coat.

Then wind surrounded my body with a *whoosh*.

Hands crushed my upper arms so hard they bruised, jarring my injured shoulder. The gust from the train lifted my hair off my neck as it screeched past where I'd stood just a heartbeat before.

I was flying for real. Flying over the heads of the people who'd reached for me. Flying over half the platform, before I collapsed onto the crowd, who rushed to gather around my body.

Shouts and hands and people touching me. I gathered that I wasn't dead but didn't understand why. It took some time to piece it all together, and what I could fathom still didn't make sense. I should have been dead.

Later, I remembered him. As I lay on the platform stunned and in shock, his face was one of the faces I remembered while waiting for paramedics.

He bent over me, curly blond hair escaping a knot at the base of his neck. He shrugged out of a beige trench coat and draped it over my body before reaching a hand out and brushing hair away from my face. The reason I remembered him was because he appeared worried. More worried than I thought a stranger should look—but that memory came later, much later, as I recovered in the hospital.

Police reports were varied. They told me eye witnesses couldn't agree on what happened after I fell. Some claimed I jumped back onto the platform fueled by super-human adrenaline. Others swore on their lives an angel jumped onto the tracks, picked me up, and threw me back onto the platform. The Hispanic woman and the executive who were closest to me when I fell both claimed a blond good Samaritan jumped in after me and lunged back onto the platform with me in tow, with so much strength that he flew us both over the first five people at the edge—like a comic book hero.

The Hispanic woman followed my gurney up the steps with the paramedics, claiming she'd seen wings: "The wings of god working through an ordinary man. An angel." She kissed the delicate gold cross hanging around her neck then kissed my hand and mumbled something like a prayer in Spanish as they loaded me into the ambulance.

As the police questioned me at the hospital, I asked, "What about the security cameras on the platform? What did they see?"

"The cameras went down the second you fell onto the track, Miss Montgomery," said Officer Baker, chewing his gum, looking bored by the whole conversation.

I pestered them with questions, desperate to find the man who rescued me and give him my thanks. Onlookers described the good Samaritan as being of every race and hair color. The only two people who could agree what he looked like, were the man and woman who had both tried to pull me back up. Based on their descriptions of blond hair, tall, and deep-set eyes, I imagined my rescuer was the man I'd seen with the worried expression brushing hair away from my face.

I was in the hospital for two days with a broken ankle, mild concussion, three bruised ribs, and a dislocated shoulder. Who knew you could get so broken up falling less than ten feet? Evidently, I'd landed just right. At least I didn't land on my head.

But painkillers, sleep, and being propped up in front of the TV for the next week couldn't shake his face out of my memory. The worried face of a man I didn't know. I'd asked about the beige trench coat at the hospital but was told I came in with only my own clothes and purse. So much for a wallet in the coat pocket that could lead me to him.

I rubbed my arm where someone, maybe him, had left a clear five-fingered handprint on both of my upper arms; thumbs pointing inward, so he was obviously behind me. I played it over and over in my head, but there simply wasn't a logical reason for the outcome. It was a mystery even my imagination refused to fill. Maybe I needed it to be a mystery.

Celeste called every day from London, where she was touring, insisting, "I should be there with you. Not that useless boyfriend. What's his name?"

"Erik. And I would love to have you, but you know how cramped and small it is in this apartment, and now with crutches and me lying around it's even worse. There wouldn't be anything you could do, and besides, if you were here I'd be depressed that we couldn't go off and do fun things. Best just to let me heal up so I can come home for Christmas this year."

"Christmas! It's about time!"

"Oh, don't start that again. I promise if you stay there and let me get all patched up, I will be home for Christmas. Deal?"

"Why not both?" she asked.

"Auntie Celeste."

"Okay. Okay. It's a deal."

I thought of the good Samaritan a lot. His face drifted into my thoughts at the most inopportune times. During work, on the cab ride home, while grocery shopping—even while having sex with Erik. One minute I'd be looking at Erik's dark complexion and eyes above me, and suddenly I'd be imagining the Samaritan's blond hair and angular features.

Two weeks after the accident, Erik proposed. I was still on crutches. We were at the restaurant where we'd met three years earlier, a little hole-in-the-wall Italian spot in Queens. I'd wondered about the date, since he'd been so wrapped up in his book lately, writing night and day. He hadn't even been to the hospital to see me until the morning after I was admitted. He said his phone was off and no one could reach him. The date was supposed to be a sort of quality time and make-up for our recent fighting.

"You've been distant," he'd said over our fettuccini.

I opened my mouth to accuse him of the same, but he held up a hand and said, "But I've also been really caught up in this manuscript. I've been pre-occupied and haven't exactly been there for you."

Understatement.

"I'd like to turn a new page, and I want you to know I will always be there for you in the future."

He stood, took my hand, and knelt on one knee beside the table.

When I was about to be hit by the train, my life didn't flash before my eyes. I didn't think of all the things I still wanted to do. I didn't imagine what my children would have looked like, or what it would feel like to have a best-selling novel on the shelf at my local bookstore. I didn't wonder what regrets I'd have, or what countries I still wanted to see. I only thought of reaching for safety.

But when Erik uttered the words "Will you marry me?" and held a simple silver band toward me, my life flashed before my eyes.

My efforts to write a best-selling novel would always be usurped by his need to create. My hope for a family would be dependent on my earnings until he could support us with his writing. Traveling with him wasn't an option, as he refused to get a passport.

But isn't this what I've always wanted? A chance to settle down and have what every woman is supposed to want? A family? What if this is as good as it gets?

Then I saw his face—the man who jumped in front of a train to save my life, who looked at me with the kind of concern Erik had never shown. A man who would risk death for a stranger. Then before me with a ring and a proposal was a man who wouldn't heat up a can of soup for me if it interrupted his writing and I was on crutches.

Erik cleared his throat. "Fable, I'm asking you to be my wife. Be my muse forever."

I glanced around the tiny restaurant full of expectant faces.

Erik shifted his weight, hands shaking slightly. "Take your time. I'm just out here hangin'," he joked. Sort of.

This is what I want. Right?

Maybe having a normal, bland life would give me a sense of belonging, a place to fit.

I took the ring and whispered, "Yes."

The room erupted in cheers as Erik and I embraced. I cried.

That night in bed, Erik settled next to me chattering about how much money we could save if we just eloped. "Most weddings start couples in debt. We don't want to start that way, do we, babe?"

But as usual, he didn't wait for an answer, just kept talking while I stared up at the ceiling, wondering what I'd just done. Does everyone with a near-death experience feel like they dodged one bullet only to take another?

I reached over and turned out the lamp so I could picture my Samaritan in the dark. Erik continued rambling until I fell asleep, thinking of another man.

I sat at the kitchen table with my coffee, staring out at the ruins of the back yard, remembering the time six months earlier when I'd nearly died gruesomely in an accident in the subway. Wishing I'd told Celeste to come to New York. Wishing I'd known she'd be gone before I could make it home for Christmas. Wishing I hadn't said "yes" to Erik…for all the difference it would have made. He admitted to me five months later that he was seeing someone else, and he'd proposed only because he thought it would help him focus on the "right thing to do." And, quote: "to keep you close, because I do my best writing when you're around."

All of it circled around and around, and at each turn I saw his face, the face of the Samaritan on the body of a creature from my childhood imagination. Swirling coffee in my mug, I couldn't shake the feeling I'd really seen him last night.

For sure, it could have been a hallucination. I could be crazy. I wouldn't be the first in my family.

He seemed so lifelike.

Well, except for the wings and taloned feet. That part, not so much. But that easily could have been the power of suggestion; the woman on the platform swore she saw the "wings of god." Maybe I was seeing his face and imagined the wings.

Just what if? What if I wasn't imagining it? What would the Samaritan be doing on the opposite side of the country—at my house?

• • •

Agent Drake was bent over his laptop when I walked into the living room with my coffee.

"Good morning," I said.

He barely looked up.

I sat in the loveseat opposite the coffee table where his work was spread out.

"Agent Drake, I need to ask a favor."

"Okay." He met my gaze. He looked awful, exhausted. His clothes were rumpled, eyes baggy.

"I need you to hear me out and not think I'm crazy until I'm done."

"Uh, I'll do my best."

Close enough, I guess.

Then I told him everything about the subway accident six months earlier, leaving out the details about Celeste and Erik. Just the part where I saw the Samaritan's face. Then I told Agent Drake I thought I'd seen the Samaritan again last night at the sliding glass door. I also neglected to mention the wings and talons.

When I finished, Drake was silent for a moment. "You only just now decided to mention this?"

"Well, I thought I was imagining it. Last night, I just thought it was a hallucination, and it took till this morning to put it together that it really might have been him, and even as I say it, I think it's stupid. Crazy. The kind of crazy I don't want to be, ya know? And last night was utter chaos. So I was thinking the fastest way to know if he was real or my imagination would be if you check the glass door for his handprint. That way, if it's all in my mind, I will only have to worry about my sanity and not a potential stalker, right?" I clutched my malachite pendant.

Agent Drake stood, pulling keys from his pocket.

"Are you leaving?"

"No. I have a print kit in the trunk."

I didn't know what to say. He was a focused flurry of motion, shutting his laptop and rushing out the front door.

I sat in a hazy surprise, wondering what to do if there wasn't a handprint. And wondering what to do if there were.

What would it mean either way?

Drake returned with an aluminum carrying case.

"Where were you standing and where was his hand?" he asked.

I led him to the sliding glass door and put my hand on the glass where I thought it was the night before. I told him the Samaritan had touched the window on the opposite side.

I watched from the warmth of the house as Drake went outside, put on gloves, and carefully applied a purple-black powder to the glass. It stuck to something, but it wasn't a full handprint.

He pulled out sheets of clear sticky tape and used the tape to pick up three spots on the glass. Luckily, the roof overhang had protected the door from rain and the spray from the hoses we'd used last night.

"Did he touch anything else?" he asked through the door.

I shook my head, and Drake returned with the kit and a few slips of sticky tape folded onto white paper.

"It looks like the corner of a palm and portions of a thumb and forefinger."

My heart pulsed in my throat.

"What does that mean?"

"It means you didn't imagine it. It also means your house isn't safe for you anymore, even with us here. It means you need to get dressed and come down to headquarters with me, and we're going to talk about everything you might remember about this guy." Drake began packing everything into his kit.

A weight pressed on my chest. For months I'd fantasized the Samaritan was a good guy. Someone looking out for me.

"But he saved my life," I said.

"Fable, how do you know he wasn't the one who pushed you off the platform? You said yourself it was crowded. And why would he be in your back yard, half a year and thousands of miles across country? If it's even the same guy." He gripped my shoulder. "Either way, it's sketchy, and right now you can't be too careful. Go change. We need to go get these prints in the system and see if there's a match. I'm going to call it in. We need a full print sweep of your house."

I climbed the stairs to my room. My legs felt rubbery, limbs slack. I realized underneath everything that had happened, I'd been keeping a little place in my heart a secret that maybe an angel was looking out for me. But he wasn't an angel, just a man.

A man with fingerprints.

A man on the wrong side of the country, and in the wrong back yard, to be just a coincidence.

Chapter Five

Oh, Shape-shifter. Trickster!
You damned old Crow.
What mischief you've started!
What trouble you sow!

Agents Mendelson and Drake were set up in a temporary taskforce space at the FBI office downtown. According to Agent Drake, due to the recent events involving both Celeste and me, the headquarters of this particular investigation were temporarily relocated to Portland.

I stood in the converted conference room. A whiteboard covered one wall, tagged with notes, a timeline, and full-color glossy photos, one of which was of me. I stared at the picture of myself that had been taken as I stood on the porch of Celeste's house sometime in the last couple of days, when I went outside to carry another dead mouse to the trash.

Agent Mendelson asked questions while I stood in front of the whiteboard looking at the pictures of the missing girls. They all had stats listed below their images, but as far as I could tell, none of the women had much in common.

"Can you describe the guy for me again?" Mendelson asked.

"Tall, blond, blue eyes, smile with a dimple on the left. Nice body," I replied.

"Seriously?"

"Yeah. Why?"

"You sound like you're attracted to him," she said. "You sure this guy is a stranger?" She sat at the end of the table with her legal pad. She looked like she hadn't slept. Her dark olive skin was patchy and dry. Her hair slicked back in the usual bun was less taut, and her left eye had a mascara smudge.

"Yes. I only saw him the one other time, on the subway right after the accident."

Agent Mendelson went back to her notes. "Anything unusual about him?"

He had a 15-foot wingspan and his talons were overdue for a pedicure?

"He was in my back yard. That's pretty unusual." I turned back to the photos. She scribbled notes between questions while I searched for a commonality among the women.

Ki Wakanabe, PhD from Japan. Disappeared during guest professorship at MIT, Boston. Asian, 32 years old. Black hair. Brown eyes. Missing as of 04/07/11. Note # 4.

Harmony O'Brien, 24 years old, Julliard graduate. Auburn hair, blond streaks. Brown eyes. Disappeared outside LA coffee house where she was performing. Missing as of 08/17/11. Note # 6.

Gracie Evanston, 29. Broadway dancer and instructor. Taken from backstage. Kenyan immigrant. Black Hair. Brown eyes. 03/22/11. Note #1.

"These women have nothing in common. I mean, they're all educated or successful and have brown eyes, but for a human trafficking ring—they are all over the map, literally." I looked at Agent Mendelson. "So why do you think the kidnapping cases of these women are even connected?"

"Well, the notes, for starters. They were all either witnessed being abducted, or there were signs of struggle. In all cases, a note with a number was left behind. Just like the note in your Jeep."

"Oh."

"So once again, there was nothing unusual about this guy you saw? No distinguishing marks?" Agent Mendelson studied the yellow legal pad as she spoke.

"Like tattoos or scars?" I shrugged, glancing back to the photos, focusing on their faces. "He looked like he had some kind of writing tattooed on his ribs. On the left side."

"Could you tell what it said?"

"It was in a different language, sort of squiggly calligraphy, you know?"

"And nothing else about him stood out. Miss Montgomery, this is important. Please think back. Picture it as it happened."

As I sat down in the chair across from Agent Mendelson, a tickling sensation began between my shoulder blades. She looked up at me with a serious expression and I felt *compelled* to tell her about the wings, the talons. My tongue curled into the words, despite the fact my brain screamed, *Don't do it!*

My face contorted as I fought against the urge to speak the words I knew would condemn me as a lunatic. Just as my mother had been condemned.

The air thinned and the room felt claustrophobic. My mouth uttered the words, "Well, there was one thing." The pressure between my shoulders increased. I couldn't breathe.

"Yes?" Agent Mendelson encouraged.

"He had—"

"How's it going in here?" Agent Drake breezed into the room. All at once, I could breathe. The pressure released me, as though from an invisible grip.

I gasped, gulping oxygen and clutching the table as sparks danced in my vision.

"Fable, are you okay?" Agent Drake lunged, gripping the arms of my chair. He rolled me up against the table to keep me in the seat as I tilted.

"She's having a panic attack, Drake. Go get some water and a paper bag." Agent Mendelson nudged him out of the way, taking his place as he fled the room.

I sucked in one lungful after another as she touched her hand to my forehead. "Just breathe, Fable. Breathe. Calm down. You're in good hands here. Safe."

My breathing slowed as she smoothed my hair. The panic attack was replaced by an incongruent rush of wellbeing. I felt fine when Drake bolted back into the room with a bottle of water and a folded grocery sack, a few moments later.

"This is the only paper bag I could find." He saw me sitting at the table and exhaled. "You okay, then?"

"I'm really sorry. Not really sure what just happened, but thanks." I felt detached from my body as I spoke.

That was not grief, or loss or fatigue. That was something else entirely.

Agent Drake sat in the chair closest to the door. "Good. That's good." After a moment, he said, "So you took the news pretty hard, huh?"

"I hadn't gotten to that part yet," Mendelson interjected.

Agent Drake frowned. "Maybe you'd better take these." He pushed the bottle of water and paper sack toward me.

"What news?"

"Fable," he began, leaning forward. "Those prints we lifted are not in the system. Meaning he doesn't have a record. The good news is the prints don't match any of the prints from any of the other scenes. The bad news is the sweep of your home revealed that his prints are everywhere inside your house."

"What? But you guys have been with me for the last four days."

"Think about the timeline. You got here from New York on Monday of last week. I met you at the medical examiner's office on Thursday. Friday, your Jeep was vandalized with a note that put you headlong into this investigation, and we've been parked at your

63

place with security and surveillance since. Which means…" He trailed off.

"He was either in my house last Sunday through Friday—or sometime before," I finished.

The room was too bright.

Was he in the house while I was home alone?

"So what exactly does this mean for me?" I asked.

"We can't tie him to the other abductions. We can't even prove he's the guy from the subway. We can only surmise the man you saw in your back yard was, at some point, in your house."

Agent Mendelson jumped in. "Regardless, you cannot be too careful or too safe at the moment."

"I agree." Drake leaned back in his chair. He'd shaved since we got to FBI headquarters and put on a clean shirt. "We asked you to take a risk by letting us stake out the inside of your house. You were brave to let us use you as bait, but I can't ask you to do that anymore. He was in your yard while we were in the house, and we didn't even see it."

"But what do I do now?" I wondered. My body felt unbearably heavy. "I don't know what to do anymore."

"Miss Montgomery," Drake said softly, "I'd like you to consider being removed to a safe location in protective custody."

"What? Like witness protection? Seriously?"

"It would only be until we can catch this guy or find the girls. You'd be completely safe, off the radar, protected. We can't force you." He leaned forward. "But please, seriously consider it."

The room was too small. Hell, the world felt too small. Celeste would know what to do. She would know how to handle all of this. She was always so strong. I stood up.

"Where are—"

"I need a bathroom," I said.

"Down the main hall." Mendelson stood with me. "Here, I'll walk you."

• • •

We walked down the hall in silence. Mendelson left me at the door to the ladies room that was more like a long closet with black stalls and cold steel sinks.

I'd never felt so alone in my life.

Glancing at the mirror, I took in the way my hair frizzed at the sides. I'd stopped wearing makeup, neglected my skin. I looked awful. Bruised eyes. Chapped lips. Yet it was really the eyes that shocked me. I looked…lost.

I splashed my face with water then patted it dry with a scratchy paper towel. It had never really bothered me that I didn't have friends. I knew I didn't fit in anywhere, so I managed fine with my imagination when I was a child; as I got older, my pursuits were more intellectual and I remained a loner. But as I stared at myself in the mirror, I wished I had friends. Real friends.

I dug through my purse for my cell phone and scrolled through the names until I got to Erik.

"Do you really want to call the man who left you for a woman with stripper pigtails and 13 piercings in her face?" Celeste asked.

I looked up at my reflection. Celeste stood beside me in the mirror. Foolishly, I glanced behind me, but realized I was still alone—and yet, Celeste continued to smile out at me.

Just seeing her, just thinking I smelled her white orchid perfume opened a vacuum inside me. "I really need you right now. I really miss you, and I need you!"

"It will be okay, Fable. Hush now, and listen."

In the reflection, she stroked my cheek with her knuckles. I closed my eyes, leaning into her touch, wishing I could actually feel her, aching that I could not.

"You must listen carefully. Do not trust the FBI! Trust yourself. Trust your instincts that are your blessed right. Trust the NaNas—they will help you beat this."

"The NaNas?" I sniffled. "What do they have to do with this?"

"They will help you remember how to protect yourself." She smiled sadly. "I've missed you." Daylight streamed through the small, frosted window above the stalls. The soft glow illuminated the mirror but didn't highlight Celeste's reflection.

"Pull up your bootstraps," she continued. "Trust me when I tell you that all will be well. Go take a walk outside the building, near the dumpsters in the alley."

"But—"

"Go. Go now!" she shouted as her image faded.

I jumped at her tone and turned around as the door to the ladies room opened. Whether it was the urgency in Celeste's voice or the need for fresh air, I shoved past the brunette walking in to the bathroom and ran out of the building. I slowed to a stroll long enough to pass through the outgoing line on the left of the metal detectors. Once through the double glass doors and onto the sidewalk, I fled at an ungainly hobble.

Autumn air burned my lungs as I ran down the street and turned the corner. The movement and the extra oxygen cleared my mind and I made my way around the next corner at a leisurely pace.

Around the back corner was a small city-owned parking lot full of late-model compact cars with government plates. On the back half of the lot were two green dumpsters with the lids down.

A silver object flashed atop one of the closed lids. I halted, drawn by the glimmer.

A loud *caw*! rang out, ricocheting off the buildings. I jumped, guilty. I was alone but for the crow sitting on a lamppost at the edge of the lot.

It wasn't like I was doing anything wrong. I truly intended to go back inside and finish with Drake, but...silver glinted in the sunlight. A step toward it resulted in another *caw!* but I continued on until I reached the edge of the first dumpster and heard a feminine voice.

"No, I tried but she still has very strong shields."

"*Caw! Caw!*"

Agent Mendelson stepped out from a gap between the buildings next to the dumpsters. "Hang on!" she said to someone on her phone and walked a few feet into the lot, looking around.

I crouched, wedging myself between the dumpster and the wall. The stench was awful. Something smelled like death. I pulled at my sleeve and covered my nose. Even breathing through my mouth threatened to make me retch and give away that I was…well, what was I doing? Spying? Eavesdropping?

"No, it was just the crows," Mendelson continued. "They're everywhere these days. I can barely keep up." She paused. Metal scraped on the second dumpster. "No. No sign of the ravens yet, just crows."

Cawcawcawcawcaw!

A chorus of voices began from across the lot. The lamp post and power lines were covered with a dozen or more black birds with razor-sharp beaks and claws.

"I have to go. I'm sure she's pulled herself together by now. It's amazing she even has shields left at all. Must have been someone pretty powerful to set her up so long-term off the radar. They're probably waiting on me. Yeah. No. I'll check in soon."

Special Agent Mendelson stood in front of the dumpsters long enough for me to see her drop her phone into a jacket pocket and swipe at her hair, checking all was in place. Then she adjusted her shoulder holster and re-buttoned the gun. "Nasty creatures," she hissed, then walked away.

The dumpster stench was nothing but a background annoyance as Mendelson's words turned through my mind.

Surely, she wasn't talking about me.

Shields? Radar?

A thud echoed off the dumpster. I jumped. *Caw! Caw! Caw!*

The ever-crying birds drove me from my hiding place out into the open lot. A lone crow stood atop the dumpster.

Caw! It tapped its beak on the lid.

Caw! Caw! Caw! The other birds waiting across the lot on their perches echoed.

It shuffled its feet with a terrible screeching of claws. Black, beady eyes stared. It tapped the lid with its beak again. *Ping. Ping.*

"You want me to open the lid?" I asked, glancing around, hoping not to get caught talking to a bird. One backward step set off a choir of *Caw! Caw! Caw!*

Ping-ping, insisted the solitary bird on the green metal box.

"Ooookay. So, talking to birds and doing their creepy bidding. That's not crazy." I inched forward toward the dumpster, where once again the stench overwhelmed me. It was unusual that the trash wasn't locked. Most bins downtown were locked to stop illegal dumping, but the silver padlock had clearly been shattered.

The bird hopped over to the second lid but kept beady eyes trained on my every movement. Carefully lifting the top, I gagged and gave in, flinging the lid with a hard thrust. It flew up and back against the building. I covered my nose and mouth with my sleeve and peeked inside.

In the trash amidst bags and refuse were six dead crows. I turned to flee, but my knees hit the car behind me, setting off the alarm.

Then there was an explosion of movement as the blaring horn echoed off the buildings. The solitary crow jumped into the dumpster and flew out again, clutching a stiff, feathery corpse. Five more crows leapt from the wires and dove into the reeking trash, each emerging with a body of one of its brethren until the air was full of black wings.

Caw! Caw! Caw!

I was running again. I couldn't explain why crows were in the dumpster, or what it meant that wild animals would carry off their own dead like claiming the fallen after a battle. Bolting away from the brazen car alarm and skies filled with screaming birds and wings, I didn't run back to Drake or the FBI. I just ran.

• • •

I hadn't intended to go home. I hadn't intended to go anywhere. I ran, walked, hobbled and galloped with my injured foot. Then I wandered until I found a rhythm of "just one more block," "just one more street," and let my mind float off somewhere above as I trekked the streets of Northwest until I found myself on my own doorstep, hungry, thirsty, sore, and pissed.

On top of it all, there were two dead mice on the welcome mat.

I just stepped over them and into the house, where the unexpected aroma of fresh baking bread derailed all my thoughts. A female voice sang out, "Fable!"

Startled beyond reason, I screeched in holy terror, swinging my purse. I screamed and screamed and kept on screaming as though my life depended on it while grabbing at the umbrella handles for a weapon.

"Fable! It's Biddy! Fable! Fable?"

Three faces I recognized peered into the entryway and I fell silent.

"Oh, dear, it seems we may not have gotten here in the nick of time at all, then." Biddy pried the umbrella club from my fingers and led me into the house. I hadn't been expecting them until tomorrow—but finally, I wasn't alone.

She directed me to sit and I burst into tears, shaking with relief.

"I'll get the booze," Biddy said jumping up.

"I'll get the glasses," LeeLee chimed.

"I'll get the cards," Eleanor added.

The NaNas were not related by blood, but I'd begun calling them the "other aunties" or "NaNas" when I was eight. They came over twice a week when I was young and gathered for their writing group with Celeste in the basement till the early hours of morning.

What kind of writing the NaNas did I never knew, but over the years some of their projects would end up on the kitchen table, and I would catch a glimpse of what looked like Latin. Sometimes I saw old pieces of paper, yellowed and cracked, with character lettering like Chinese or Japanese.

When I asked about it once, Celeste said, "You know how paranoid LeeLee is about her writing. She does everything in code."

They sometimes even came over for the tea ceremony on Sundays or popped in for brunch or supper. They never showed up empty handed, and they never left without asking about my life, school, and boyfriends and offering entirely unsolicited advice on all three topics.

When Celeste had to leave for a conference and I couldn't go because of school, the NaNas would take turns staying at the house, looking out for me in their own ways.

For Biddy, with her full four-foot seven-inch frame, white curly hair and lipstick that bled into the cracks around her mouth, her idea of looking after me was to teach me how to swear in every language she knew, most proficiently in Russian, of which she still had a slight accent. It also meant every time Biddy stayed in to take care of me, she'd order pizza, call in my absence to the school, and we'd spend the days in front of the TV watching re-run episodes of *Perry Mason*—wherein she'd lament every hour on the hour how sad it was Perry Mason was probably gay because she would have taken him home to Russia and done "unspeakable things to that beautiful man."

When LeeLee came to watch me, I would endure mornings of being woken up ten minutes before dawn and "tsked" all the way down the stairs to the kitchen where breakfast already waited. LeeLee insisted on driving me to school every morning and asked on several occasions to see my grades. She never raised her voice, but her straight, slender frame and elegant stature—combined with white-blonde hair in a bun, and one green eye, one brown—granted her instant and unquestioned obedience. When she stayed over I felt comfortably snug in her watchful care and entirely free to be myself, even on the nights she required me to empty my backpack and prove I'd done my homework.

Ms. Eleanor Pike remained my secret favorite of the three. She'd sweep into a room like a 1940s lounge singer, black hair in a glossy bob, penciled eyebrows, and vintage frocks. I swore I'd be just like her when I grew up, with her silver and turquoise jewelry and voluptuous figure, even in her late sixties. She turned the heads of men half her age—and she knew it.

It wasn't just my childlike fascination with the enigmatic creature that she was, but also the way she lived her life. Bold.

She even wore hats.

Eleanor took me to get my bellybutton pierced a month before I graduated high school. She was the NaNa I went to when I was having trouble with a matter of the teenage heart; the first person I told when I lost my virginity to Kevin Jenks in the hallway closet at a party. I told her I was in love, and she said, "Wonderful, *Cherie*. Enjoy it while you can. Be safe. Be smart. Find happiness wherever you can! Ah, young love! The very definition of inspiration."

Kevin Jenks and I lasted all of a few months, but Eleanor supplied tissue and comfort one night as I cried about it, and she asked, "But wasn't it splendid while it lasted?"

I didn't have a wealth of friends, but between Celeste and the NaNas, I was rich in a family of eccentric old ladies who filled the role of my guardians admirably.

Biddy was the first to return with two bottles of blueberry-infused vodka from the pantry. "Looky what Celeste had stashed!" She plopped on the couch just as LeeLee joined us with four glasses and Eleanor took off her wide red hat and sat down with a deck of tarot cards.

LeeLee produced a hanky from her purse and passed it to me. "We tried to get here sooner, but we were all the way on the other side of the world when Mr. Grosskopf called with the news."

"Where?" I asked as I struggled to pull myself together, tears of relief and exhaustion threatening to spill over.

"Prague," Biddy said.

"Prague?" LeeLee wondered.

"Right. Prague." Eleanor agreed.

"It's true, but we are here with you now, and there is so much we need to talk about," LeeLee continued as Biddy poured a shot in each glass. "So much indeed."

Chapter Six

So comes the day worlds wilt on the vine
And cosmos dance, drunk on Muses' wine

The NaNas never really pressed me to be one kind of person or another, which was one of the reasons I loved them so deeply. For sure, if I were in danger of ever really hurting myself, they'd voice an opinion about the wisdom of my choice—but they always gave me room to decide for myself what I wanted. So if I wanted to travel, they packed my bags. If I wanted to meet boys, they drove me to a school dance. If I wanted a drink, they poured me a glass.

So it was six (or maybe it was eight) rounds of shots poured and drunk over the next two hours as the NaNas caught me up on what they had heard from Grosskopf, Celeste's lawyer. Then I spilled the news and latest developments since I'd spoken on the phone with Eleanor. When the blueberry vodka ran out, we opened the last bottle of rum Celeste had stashed at the back of the pantry.

I reached the end of my tale and announced, "Icarusessesss wings! I think I'm drunk."

"No need to put it nicely, dear. The truth is, you're trashed," Eleanor said.

"Shit-headed," LeeLee agreed.

"Faced," Biddy amended. "I think we all are."

"And that's not all of it," I rambled on. "I've been having really weird dreams, and things are happening around the house, and I keep seeing things out of the corner of my eye, and that guy I told you about? The one in the back yard before the tree exploded from lightning? Yeah. Him. He was a bird. A *bird*! But also a man. A man-bird. Probably a *mird*. But don't get me wrong…he was one really hot mird!"

"I think you're done," LeeLee said, rescuing my glass.

"She sure is!" agreed Biddy, who chuckled and filled my glass again. I reached for it, but LeeLee passed it back to Biddy, who swallowed the rum without hesitation.

"I *swear it*! I'm not crazy! I saw him, and he was a birdman!"

"No one is disagreeing with you, *Cherie*. I've seen plenty of bird-men in my time," said Eleanor.

"Me, too," said Biddy.

"As have I."

Tears burned my eyes. I pointed at the sliding glass door. "Why don't you believe me?" I said. "He left a hand print! A physical handprint! He was real!"

I tripped around the front of the coffee table, feeling like I was walking across a log floating down a turbulent river. "I'm not crazy."

Eleanor rose from her perch on the loveseat in one graceful motion, as was her way. She took my arm, led me back to her spot, and sat us both on the cushions. "No one is saying you're crazy. In fact, I think we are just teasing you a bit, because most of the 'birdmen' we know prefer to be called 'Avian' or referred to by their clan."

Space. Floating in space.

Every movement, each thought, was executed painfully slow at zero gravity. I frowned at Biddy then LeeLee in succession before gazing back at Eleanor. "What did you just say?"

"We've all seen the Avians. They are very much a part of all our lives."

"What do you think, ladies? Is she softened up enough?" Biddy wondered.

"Any more softening, and I think she'll be sacked out completely," offered LeeLee.

"Agreed," Eleanor said. "I'll start. You ladies jump in if I miss anything."

"Miss any of what?" I asked.

"Fable," Eleanor began, "there is far too much to tell you all at once. Much of what I am about to say has its beginning hundreds of years before your story even starts. Celeste wanted to tell you all this herself. Unfortunately, circumstances dictate your ignorance will harm you more than the truth itself." Eleanor inhaled and let out with, "Fable, you are a Muse."

I don't remember clearly what happened next, as I managed to catch only one sentence of every three or so. My thoughts swam in blueberry-infused rum-ka, swirling around a drain of drunken unreality.

"Her phone is blowing up again," LeeLee worried. "Caller ID, Agent Drake."

"He's trouble with a gun and badge, that's what he is," Biddy said.

I vaguely remember taking the call from Drake and slurring my way through a conversation, something like, "Got home thanks my other aunties are here not interested leave me alone yes I'm drunk why shouldn't I be?" I remembered him saying he would leave an agent watching my house in case I needed help and he would call again tomorrow.

Hanging up, I sagged sideways against Eleanor. "I'm gonna yarf," I groaned and closed my eyes for just a moment, or so I thought.

When I opened them again, I was lying on the floor with a mixing bowl near my head. The coffee table was gone and I was on my side in the center of the living room. Candles flickered from a dozen spots around the room, and the NaNas stood around me humming scales and chords. I thought of the hall outside the choir room in high school where the music kids would stand around and warm up.

Then I was out again.

• • •

"Harder to do while missing Celeste, but possible," LeeLee was saying when I woke up briefly.

"True, but I think she needs to have a choice in this," Biddy added.

"The truth is we're dropping like flies around here. We might not be around much longer, and then who is going to protect her? How will she know which way is up or down or sideways, if she doesn't have all the facts to make a choice?" Eleanor argued.

"I'm not disagreeing with that point," LeeLee began. "But ambushing her while she's drunk…?"

"Do you really think she's going to believe it and stay still long enough for us to work on her if she's sober and awake?"

"No," Biddy admitted.

"Not really," LeeLee conceded.

"Okay, then. What choice do we have? I love her as much as both of you, and I love her enough to let her be all she was born for—*then* let her choose."

"But taking the shields down when we're one voice short…" LeeLee began.

"It can be done," Eleanor said. "Carefully."

"Please, goddess, let her forgive us for all we've been a part of."

"It is the Law of Nine," Biddy added.

The ladies gathered around my body.

"Oh! You're awake!" LeeLee murmured. "Lie still, and this will all be over by morning. Trust me, you'll feel like a new woman." She placed a long knife against my arm. "This will only hurt a little teeny tiny…"

"Ouuch!" I moaned drunkenly as LeeLee cut the inside of my left arm. "Whatjou do that?"

She bent and kissed my forehead. "Sweet dreams."

Fighting against nausea and heavy eyelids, I tried to put into context what I was witnessing. The room was full of smoke, and the women held their arms above their heads and began singing. Shortly thereafter, I vomited into the bowl and passed out.

I woke a final time as my body was lifted, carried like a child up the stairs to my bedroom. My mouth tasted like I'd licked a toilet. My limbs hummed with a strange vibration, my blood felt charged. I was floating, but when I opened my eyes it was too dark to see. My drunken impression was something religious. I relaxed, allowing my limp body to hang in the arms of an angel.

My bed took me in like a stray. The comfort of its embrace overruled the oddity of how I got there. Blindly rolling into the comforter, I snuggled in.

Someone tucked the covers up to my chin and caressed my face.

As sleep claimed me, I imagined I heard a masculine voice murmur, "Dream safe, Fable."

My dreams were wracked with images and feelings I'd never experienced in a dream before; lucid and powerful. I woke repeatedly covered in sweat, heart racing, body throbbing with sexual need. The disorienting weight of sleep always pulled me back toward the pillow, and my pounding heart would steady long enough to drift toward oblivion only to be ushered into dreams so real I actually orgasmed in my sleep and woke to my own scream of climax.

Arching in to him, I ground my hips into his body, my breasts pressing firmly against his chest. Wrapping my arms around his neck, I pulled him down to me, my Samaritan. My winged man. Excitement shivered up my spine and rippled through my lower belly at the throaty growl of pleasure he couldn't contain.

I knew I must be dreaming, but it felt so real. So powerfully, overwhelmingly real.

Enormous wings tickled the back of my thighs with erotic, feathery delight as his hands cupped my breasts, thumbing my nipples, his delicious lips crushing my mouth with desperate force.

He was an angel, or only part man, searing me with the intensity of pre-dawn blue eyes. In dream delirium I knew it would kill me to have him, and I didn't care. I wanted him, every inch of hot skin, every curved muscle and feather. I wanted every breath of his lungs filling my body.

He bent me back, strong arms supporting my weight, sharp teeth grazing the vulnerability of my throat, tousled blond curls sweeping across the tender skin of my shoulders. His guttural moan set me quivering, and just as I opened my mouth to beg, he nudged his left knee between my legs, pressing me against the muscles of his thigh.

I moaned, clutching his shoulders as he rocked my body against him. The erotic movement set my dream mind a cluster of images:

Flying over a snow-capped mountain range of razor peaks.

Wings flapping through smoke.

Water stretching out for miles beneath my body.

A black ink tattoo crawling across pale skin.

An orange funnel of flames stretching from a pyre toward the glowing moon.

The canopy of a forest rushing up to meet me.

A chipped teacup with gold edging.

A glowing blue river.

Then I was diving or falling or swimming toward earth at terminal velocity, the world focusing into a pinpoint of death, and...

I screamed and my eyes flew open to a field of plastic glowing stars on the ceiling of my bedroom. To my amazement, my body still convulsed mid-orgasm, and the fire of my dream washed over all reason. I let go, allowing the tide of pleasure to complete while I clung to my pillow, moaning.

When the after-glow subsided and my breathing returned to normal, I lay awake, staring at the stars, enjoying the hum in my body, and trying to remember if I had ever had such a vivid sex dream. For sure, I'd had silly little dreams about the barista down the street or fantasy dreams of Johnny Depp—but they were dreams barely remembered, such as a flash of images incongruently linked by a ridiculous romantic dinner and corny walk on the beach.

I'd never had such powerful sexual responses in my sleep.

The clock read 6:00 a.m. I wasn't the least bit tired. In fact, as I lay thinking about how amazing the dream was, I suddenly became inspired to write it down—to capture the creature of my dream imagination.

Tossing back the sweat-drenched lavender covers, I climbed out of bed and hit the light. Then I suddenly remembered how drunk I'd been less than eight hours earlier.

Shouldn't I be hung over? Maybe still queasy?

I was surprised to see I looked oddly refreshed in the mirror, like I'd just come back from a vacation spa. Even my hair looked glossier, curlier. My skin glowed, cheeks pink and eyes sparkling. My injured foot felt normal again.

What was in that vodka?

The fact of the matter was I felt like doing jumping jacks or maybe going for an early morning run, but I didn't want to waste my fantastic high on exercise when I was so inspired to capture the dream. My imagination was afire, and I needed to put pen to paper. Celeste always said, "Never waste inspiration. The Muses won't humor you later for squandering the now."

So for the first time in almost five years, I stretched out on the window seat near the Tiffany lamp and began writing fiction. I wasn't writing for an editor who wanted bad news, or a magazine that wanted articles telling women they're fat, or lifeless blurbs to fill a corporate memo.

My fingers flew across the keyboard of my laptop, and a whole different universe opened up. I was able to articulate a character, a scene of high fiction, purely from my imagination.

At 9:00 a.m., I was knee deep in the first Chapter when Biddy shuffled in to the study to put a cup of coffee on a nearby stand. She moaned, clutching her head, muttering. She left without saying a word, and I continued on my spree.

Twelve hours later, as my seventh Chapter staggered to a close, I realized I had to pee so bad I wasn't sure I could make it to the bathroom. Had I really been writing non-stop for 12 hours? I hadn't even drunk my coffee or eaten the lunch LeeLee brought in at some point. The sandwich glared up at me, bread dry, apple slices browned. Though I hadn't gotten up or eaten in hours, I felt great. Tired for sure, and drained, but deliriously happy.

And I wanted more. Lots more. It was like discovering oxygen and wondering how I'd breathed for the last decade without it. Nothing mattered when I was writing. Nothing hurt me or made me feel vulnerable. I could live vicariously through my characters and explore a life filled with challenges not my own and adventures that didn't end with heartbreak.

I wrote a character who brought her crow servants to life from the tattoos on her own body by paying a blood price. I wrote about a city built entirely of rose quartz. I imagined a race of creatures that spoke only in musical notes. The fictional world I immersed myself in was far more intriguing and much less painful than my own reality—it felt like a vacation from unmanageable grief, and I didn't want it to stop.

A quick trip downstairs revealed the NaNas playing poker at the table.

"You've been up there a long time. You working on a project?" LeeLee asked. "There's a plate in the oven for you, if you're hungry."

"Not a project," I replied. "Just inspired. Sorry I've been hiding. I guess I could come be social." I hovered in the kitchen, torn, just wanting some water and a snack I could eat while typing.

"You could be social, but we're in the middle of a game, and Biddy is about to lose her whole pile of chocolate to me. I don't think you could afford the buy-in at the moment," Eleanor said.

"Go finish up, Little Thing. We're not going anywhere," Biddy agreed. "But if you don't want that agent coming by, you should call him back. He's left you three messages."

I didn't wait for them to change their minds but grabbed a box of crackers and a water and bee-lined back up to the study. I knew Biddy was right and called Drake. Luckily I got his voicemail, so I didn't actually have to talk to him. I left a rambling message about being busy, fine, and no need to keep checking in.

Over the next two days, I was vaguely aware of nibbling crackers and drinking the juice one of the NaNas brought by. I rarely got up from my seat for anything but water, coffee, and bathroom breaks. I slept a few hours each night, but the urge to write woke me up before daylight and the cycle started over, and through it all I was blissful, gloriously fulfilled.

On the third day of my bender, I woke up from the floor of Auntie Celeste's study with a splitting migraine. My laptop screensaver played pictures of birds. I wondered how long I'd been asleep on the floor, seeming to have fallen right out of the chair.

What day is it?

I shuffled to the bathroom, flipped the switch, and regretted the harsh light immediately as I fumbled in the medicine cabinet for a bottle of aspirin. After popping a few pills and drinking a handful of water from the tap, I stumbled on wooden legs back to my bedroom to collapse on the bed.

The next time I woke, it was early morning and the soft glow from the window slid across my eyelids, gently kissing my still-waking mind with the welcome promise of a new day.

For the first time in the past week, I opened my eyes without feeling the weighty burden of loss. I tossed back the covers and stepped onto the carpet, rejuvenated. Freer. Lighter.

Pausing at the Juliet window, I peered out at Forest Park. Something was different. I felt…connected. As though I could feel the naked trees of the woods, feel the ivy yearn toward the mossy limbs. I could feel the sky shiver into a new hue as daylight yawned across the city.

It felt like I was finally becoming whole when I hadn't even known I was hollow.

All but floating downstairs, I hummed, practically skipping to the kitchen to start the coffee. My stomach rumbled. The NaNas had left me a note:

Fable, we ran to Biddy's to pick up some things. Call or text if you need anything. LeeLee is at the Eagle's Lodge. Will be back soon. Love, Eleanor.

I frowned as I checked the fridge and cupboards. Everything required effort. I decided to go out for breakfast—in the real world.

The Glade Café was less than a mile away, and I enjoyed the walk, autumn leaves crunching under foot. I had a new manuscript tucked under my arm and couldn't help but wonder if Celeste felt so deliriously satisfied whenever she completed a story.

As I approached the café door, I heard footsteps behind me and opened the door for whoever it was to go in first.

Whoever said chivalry is dead?

A young woman, small framed and petite, met my eyes as she walked by, and a tidal wave of recognition rocked my body. I knew her, but I didn't.

Where've I seen her before?

She could have passed for a boy were it not for her feminine face and hands. Her slender body was covered with a black hoody, sleeves rolled up, revealing arms covered in interlocking tattoos of crows. In skinny jeans and flats and a black cropped ragged hairdo tipped with blue, she looked just like the every-day Portland hipster, complete with lip ring.

I swore she was familiar, but the way she dismissed me as I walked into the café behind her made me think I probably thought I knew her because she looked like every other 20-something kid in the area. Shrugging it off, I followed her inside and let the aroma of fresh-brewed coffee part the curtain of morning.

Oh, god, yes. Waffles and warm syrup.

Food. It seemed like I hadn't eaten in days. I sat at the first table by the window, plopped my manuscript down, and picked up a menu, intent on ordering three of everything.

Chapter Seven

Abra sat at the table outside the Glade Café, smoking a hand-rolled cigarette and watching the woman inside near the window. The Glade Café was a typical Portland coffee shop with a small all-day breakfast menu run by local guys who looked like they dropped out of college and stopped taking showers. Despite Abra's distaste for their typical Portland granola-hippy styling, she grudgingly admitted they made the best coffee in a two mile radius. Whether or not they knew a razor was for shaving, the passel of co-op kids who ran the place managed to make a mean stack of waffles and kept a devoted clientele.

She also conceded they did a decent job of hiding the Gate in plain sight.

Abra picked at her plate of waffles with marionberry compote, and eyed the sky. The dingy light and marbled grey clouds meant rain would not be far off, and trailing her target through a storm didn't sound the least bit entertaining.

Already she'd smoked ten cigarettes and eaten three waffles to maintain her cover outside the café.

Fable Rose Augustine Montgomery had finally started the great wheel turning. Abra trailed the girl to the café and watched from the sidewalk table as Fable ordered enough food to feed a third-world country and ate every bite: eggs, sausage, hash browns and a side of bacon, French toast, and coffee...then, to everyone's astonishment, a stack of waffles and a half order of biscuits and gravy. Abra wondered where it all went, as Fable was not a particularly large woman. Fair to middling in looks and size, Fable wasn't what Abra would call stunning, but she certainly gave off waves of creative power.

Even if the last three days of other-world vibrational energy coming from Forest Park and pulsing from the epicenter of the Augustine Montgomery house hadn't been proof enough that the girl was awakening to the source power, the fact that a girl could sit reading a massive stack of papers, presumably a manuscript of some sort, and not even realize she'd just eaten her weight in food, was the final proof Abra needed to begin her preparations.

She smiled and dragged on her cigarette. After all these years, finally there would be some-much deserved apologies from the higher-ups. Abra had warned the Eventines years ago that the little girl with the mass of curly auburn hair and freckled skin playing at dragons and fairies in Forest Park—Celeste's little brat—was actually the very one they sought. There would be apologies, thanks, and promotions abounding.

But first she needed to get her hands on that manuscript.

When Fable reached for her purse, picking up the tab to walk to the register, Abra left her cash on the table and ducked around the corner of the building. Checking to see she was alone, she rolled the long sleeves of her hoody up to her elbows, revealing intricately woven, interlocking tattoos of crows on her left arm, making the skin almost completely black, and a single raven on her right inner forearm.

She pulled a pocketknife from her jeans and flipped it open. With tender precision she dug the blade into the eye of her raven tattoo.

Blood gushed down her knife, splatting in fat drops on the pavement.

Her tattoo bulged, shifting and stretching. The ink ballooned outward, pulling flesh and peach-fine hair away from Abra's arm as the creature took shape. His feathery body emerged from her arm like a malignant blister, swelling, contorting. She groaned and leaned against the building, reaching her arm up for her indentured raven, Tassos, to be birthed. He took shape in fits and starts: his head, neck, and the ridge of his body. At last his wings burst free of her flesh, spraying a fine, bloody mist back at her as he burst free from her skin.

He lurched skyward with the sound of silken feathers and a ragged caw!

Tassos perched on a nearby phone cable and turned for instructions. Abra panted. Sweat broke out on her forehead. She tasted the copper of her own blood on her lips as she turned the knife blade, cutting into her left arm.

Chapter Eight

Murder of Crows!
Murder of Crows!
Murder of Crows!

I left the Glade Café in the early afternoon. I'd been there for nearly four hours. Even though I'd eaten more food than I would have at two Thanksgiving dinners, I was still hungry. I wondered, as I paid my giant tab, if I'd contracted a stomach worm.

"That was a lot of breakfast," the waiter said as he rang up my check. "How was it?"

"It was delicious." I suddenly couldn't remember what it tasted like. "My Aunt Celeste mentioned this place to me a while back and said I should check it out. She liked coming here to write."

"Earl Grey with cream and sugar?" he asked.

"Yep, that's her," I said. A wave of loss washed over me.

"I'm Gabe." He offered his hand.

"Fable."

"I hope we get to see you around more, Fable."

"Oh, I'll be coming back, and telling my friends about you, too."

"Please do."

For the first time, I noticed his long dirty-blond dreadlocks pulled back in a ponytail emphasized his alabaster skin and angularly beautiful features. Whiskey-colored eyes and slender limbs brought to mind the sudden, hallucinogenic idea he was not a human at all—but, cleverly disguised as a café owner with fluid grace and flawless beauty, he must indeed be a fairy king, or some otherworldly creature of fantastic origin.

"Would you like your card back?" he asked with a smile that seemed to include slightly pointier teeth than before.

I hesitated, my brain somersaulting between fiction and reality, knowing I was a woman in a café in Portland and yet feeling like I was also simultaneously standing on mystical alien turf.

"You okay?" he asked.

I blinked and took the card from his fingers, which seemed too long and slender to be real.

"Yeah. Thanks."

"You have a good day, then. It was nice to meet you."

Had he really been waiting on my table for four hours and I never noticed? I blinked again. He turned away with an odd look over his shoulder, and just as quickly, he seemed perfectly human again. Strangely beautiful, but human anyway.

I shook my head, gathering up my purse and the stack of papers I'd brought to read. I'd printed all the pages created on my laptop in the last three days, and the printout came to a staggering 240 pages. I couldn't believe it. The worst part was I could barely remember it. It was like a fuzzy dream or an opium haze. Maybe that's why the waiter seems so unreal, I thought. I'm sleep deprived. Just to prove it, I glanced at him one more time as I walked out the door. He was already helping another table, his back turned.

Leaving the cafe gave me the strange sensation I was parting with an old friend. Stepping out onto the sidewalk, several drops of rain speckled the pavement. I gripped the loose manuscript to my chest, wishing I'd thought to put it in a backpack before leaving the house. It was only ten blocks home, so I started to speed-walk, determined to get back before the full rain began.

As I was about to round the corner of the building, a voice behind me shouted, "Miss! You forgot your sweater!"

Everything happened at once.

Chaos.

From around the corner of the building, a flock of crows burst outward like black and crimson cannon confetti. They swooped in a mass toward the road, then as if by some practiced carnival trick, they veered in unison like a deadly cloud directly toward me.

My nightmare of the crows flashed through my mind, and Auntie Celeste's voice rang out *"Hold your ground!"* in my head, but human instinct took over. With the weight of black feathers and screaming beaks bearing down upon me, I stumbled sideways and lunged toward safety—a gap between two parked cars, and then the freedom of the road.

In my panic, I darted between the cars and into oncoming traffic.

I had enough time to see the grill of the number 17 bus as it was about to end my life. In slowed time, I registered the panicked horror on the driver's face behind the flat panel window and heard the horn blare, brakes screeching.

A tremendous weight slammed into my body.

Pavement cracked against my elbows, hips, and side. My head seemed miraculously cushioned by something soft and warm. My body flared to life with a sense of bruising all over.

The sound of people yelling was eclipsed by the cacophony of shattering glass, groan of bending metal, and the thunderous crash of vehicles crushing each other. I tasted blood and heard the flutter of dozens of wings, whispering feathers, and a woman's scream.

I opened my eyes and realized I was the one screaming. Hundreds of loose sheets of paper fluttered amidst scrambling people, swerving cars, and crazy crows. It was a scene right out of Hitchcock. In the background, my manuscript drifted on the wind.

Birds screeched in a deadly mass, a chorus of off-key *caws!*, angry beaks, and empty beady eyes.

I was not only alive but wrapped securely in the arms of a stranger. Recalling neither how I got there nor even caring, I turned my face to his chest and clutched him as though my life depended on it. Then I felt the hands of yet more strangers pulling me from behind. Gabe's face loomed before me. The ground was littered with papers, black feathers, and glass.

"Are you okay?" Gabe asked, his face pinched and bloodless, his hands shaking.

I glanced around at the carnage of a wrecked city bus and a green SUV. People in the streets were being bombarded by crows. A man pounded on the door of the bus to be let in as wild birds mauled his face. It was like the *Twilight Zone* or a horrific nightmare and I wanted desperately to wake up.

"*Are you okay?*" Gabe shouted as he grabbed my arm and the strange man with whom I'd found sudden safety took my other arm, and together they lifted me off my feet and dragged me back inside the café. Gabe shoved me into the first booth and ran back outside to help several more people escape the tornado of vicious beaks and claws.

I watched out the window in horror. People curled up on the ground to shield their faces or ran in circles, swatting at dive-bombing talons.

It was too unreal. Too fantastical. I pressed a hand against the café window, and a crazed crow flew into the glass against my palm. I jumped, screaming. Large hands clasped my shoulders, turning me, pulling me toward a strong body. It was a measure of my fear that I didn't resist but went gratefully against him, quaking.

Several had minutes passed when the screaming outside died down and I had enough courage to look. I couldn't believe what I was seeing. It was like an explosion had gone off on 23rd Avenue: wrecked cars, the bus and people on the pavement like a bizarre terrorist attack of glass, black feathers, and blood.

"Are you hurt?" His voice was barely a whisper, as though he feared scaring me further. My body ached from bruises and a burning sensation on my chin and cheek, as well my left elbow and knee. I sniffed again and shook my head.

"No. I think I'm okay. Just bruised. I don't think the bus hit me," I mumbled as I tried desperately to remember what had actually happened. The bus was coming right at me. My face was about to meet the bottom of the driver's side window, but I was struck from the right. Something slammed into me and I landed on my left side, protected by something—someone.

I looked up then; perhaps five or six minutes had passed since I first darted into traffic and the chaos erupted, then subsided with freakish unreality. Even though it was mere minutes, it seemed like hours in hell. In all that time, I had not really looked at him. I had the sense he was big, not just big but possibly huge. I turned my head and tipped my gaze up—and up and up some more, and I wondered who was this man, this stranger, that made me feel so safe.

"You saved me," I said as I finally realized the truth. I recognized him instantly. Blond hair in a mess of curls escaping from a ponytail at the base of his neck. His face was scraped and several cuts along his jaw were bleeding. A rivulet of red seeped from his hairline, running slowly around eyes a haunting, piercing blue.

My Samaritan.

The birdman in my back yard.

The man I'd been thinking about for months. The man whose erotic dream set off an inspired writing spree. The man the FBI believed wanted to hurt me.

"Again," I finished lamely. "You saved me again."

I wanted to look away but couldn't. I couldn't move. Couldn't breathe. I knew it was a war zone of destruction just outside the window, but all I saw was his face.

"You're real." My throat was tight, voice strangled. I nodded then shook my head.

"I meant, are you physically injured?"

I shook my head again, slowly, not wanting to blink or move too fast or lose a second of him. He sighed, shoulders relaxing. "That is good."

"Who are you?" I asked. I was not afraid of him. The FBI would expect me to run, to scream, to get help. Reaching out a finger, I gently poked his chest. He was solid. Earthly.

He smiled then, a devastating boyish grin, hitching into a dimple on the left. "I'm Liam, your Guardian."

"Are you going to kidnap me? Hurt me?"

"Icarus' wings! No. Never."

Letting out a long whoosh of breath, I leaned back. "Okay."

"My only directive is your safety."

Safety?

"Thank you," I said, "for saving my life, and not just once. I'm not sure how you go about repaying someone for that."

Gabe limped back into the café with the arm of an injured man over his shoulder. The commotion ripped our fragile moment apart. Sirens blared to life on the street. Somewhere in the café, someone was crying while another voice offered comfort.

Liam rushed to help Gabe ease the man into chair.

"There are many who need help," Gabe said as he turned to head back outside.

Liam glanced at me, his expression torn as he followed the blond dreadlocks toward the exit.

"No," Gabe said. "Stay with her. *She* is your charge." He motioned to me and disappeared out the front door again.

Liam stood near the door, watching out the window, checking the skies for signs of dark shadows. There were 16 people in the café who'd taken shelter or been enjoying their lunch when it happened. The most recent man rested against a table with a bloody gash across his temple, his shirt torn, and jagged claw marks on his skin.

While Liam kept guard, I made my way to the counter and helped myself to a stack of napkins and a glass of water. I took napkins to the man and set the water in front of him.

"I'm sure help will be here soon," I said.

Keeping Liam in my line of sight, afraid he would somehow disappear again, I placed the napkins against the man's head wound, using his own hand to hold it in place.

Then the skies ripped apart, unleashing torrential rain that hammered against the café windows.

Other people in the café began taking napkins and water, tending to one another. Shortly thereafter, a second café waiter, I remembered someone calling him Zane, lead another man in a suit in out of the rain while carrying a small clump of papers.

Outside the window in the worsening downpour, red and blue lights flashed through the gray. Rescue workers and officers arrived on the scene. Zane approached Liam, bending his head in deference, and handed him the papers, some soggy, others crumpled or folded.

From where I stood filling a glass of water for a woman with a baby, I saw them talking. Liam shook his head. Zane shrugged. Soon Gabe joined them, and the three spoke in hushed tones, arguing. Then all at once three heads turned toward me. Three gazes piercing.

Liam broke away from the group and approached me with the papers Zane had given him. He pulled me toward the empty corner. "We must speak."

Just then a pair of officers entered the café. "Does anyone need emergency medical attention?"

People began moving forward for help. The officers assisted some and called paramedics to tend to others. A triage zone was quickly being constructed, and those injured the worst were funneled toward bandages and warm blankets. The commotion offered us a kind of privacy.

"Do you need medical help?" Liam asked.

"I don't think so. Nothing I can't take care of at home with some peroxide and Band-Aids, thanks to you. You?" I asked, reaching toward the gash on his scalp with a paper towel. "You might need stitches in this one."

Liam clutched my wrist, tenderly, as though conscious of how small it was in his giant grip. "I am fine." He paused, as if what he were about to say next pained him. "Fable, are these papers yours?"

He held the soiled manuscript sheets toward me. Muddy, bloody, and dirty-water stained, the papers were crumpled and stacked askew. "Probably," I said. "I had a project with me when I left earlier. It's likely all over the pavement out there."

"These were the only sheets Zane could find or retrieve from the birds. There are no more pages outside."

"What?" I took the stack and flipped through it quickly. "There's only like 13 pages here. There were 240 when I walked outside before this all started. There's got to be a mess out there."

I looked down at the top pages spattered with blood and rain, and the first words to catch my attention were on page 39.

Interlocking tattoos of crows on her left arm.

A shiver rippled through my body. Somewhere in the recesses of my mind, thoughts clicked into place. Impossibly jagged jigsaw pieces that should never have been allowed to fit snapped together. Frantically I wiped a hand across the smears on the page and scanned the words.

Ink ballooned outward, pulling flesh and peach-fine hair.

Pages 38 through 42 were stuck together with syrup I'd spilled at breakfast. Pulling them apart, I quickly read page 40 and my thoughts raced with the impossibility of what I was seeing.

Burst free of her flesh.

Grill of the number 17 bus… Pavement cracked against my elbows. Off-key caws!

The ground was littered with papers, black feathers, and glass.

And it went on to page 42:

It was like an explosion had gone off on 23rd Avenue: wrecked cars, the bus and people on the pavement like a bizarre terrorist attack of glass, black feathers, and blood.

"Oh. God," I wheezed, sinking into a nearby chair. "I wrote this."

Most of the details were hazy, as I'd written it all so fast—240 pages in three days, a fugue-like state of creative abandon. It was a blur.

Am I psychic?

My mother thought she was psychic. She was just crazy.

Then I remembered walking into the Glade Café earlier and holding the door for a girl I thought I knew.

Abra.

"I saw her."

"Who did you see?" Liam asked.

I held up the papers and my hands shook so hard Liam reached out to steady my wrist. "I saw the girl I wrote about. This morning I saw Abra."

Shaking overtook my body, and I swallowed back the huge breakfast climbing up my throat. Cold crept into my belly and joints. "I wrote about you, too. Wrote about this whole thing, before it even happened. Is that even possible?"

Liam crouched beside my chair, his body giving off waves of heat. Such blessed warmth as he touched my legs and met my gaze. "Yes. It is possible." The intensity of his blue eyes burned. I looked away, down at the stack of incriminating documents. "Fable, please listen to me. This is important. More important than you likely understand now. Do you have the other pages saved somewhere? A second printing? A disk?"

"On my laptop, back at the house." I glanced at an officer only ten feet away. "This is crazy. This can't be happening."

Blinking and visibly exhaling, he said, "I very much need you to hold together. We must get to the second copy *right now*. Lives depend on this. Please trust me."

Officers and paramedics milled around, bobbing blue uniforms in a cluster of bewildered faces. One officer, a young guy in his early twenties with a baby-smooth face, took notes from a witness then spoke into his shoulder radio.

Liam saved my life, twice. That alone was reason to trust him. I closed my eyes, letting out a long breath. I realized it felt right to be near him.

Having him near feels as natural as sunlight on my freckles.

It was insanity. But the rest of the manuscript might offer more of an explanation about what was going on. Maybe my subconscious had leaked information onto the page. Maybe I actually was psychic. Maybe once I saw everything else I'd written, I'd realized the pages describing this horrific scene were just a fluke. A strange coincidence. The only way to find out was to get the full 240 pages.

"Okay," I agreed. "But if we're gonna get out of here, we'd better do it while there's confusion or we'll be here answering police questions all day and then some."

Liam visibly relaxed and took my hand in his. "Let us hurry."

The room was crowded and noisy. It was easy to slip past most of the emergency crews toward the front door.

As I squeezed between a woman holding her child and an EMT wrapping a bandage, a blue-gloved hand fell on my forearm. I jumped.

"Miss? Do you need medical attention?" a young female paramedic asked.

"I…I think I'm okay."

"You have open cuts and abrasions on your face and arms. Were you scratched or bitten by any of the birds?"

"I'm okay. I don't remember if they actually scratched me or bit me. Why?"

"We're compiling a list of people who'll need to be contacted and offered the rabies vaccine. None of the birds were recovered so they could be tested, but their behavior signals a possible rabies epidemic. What's your name, miss?"

"Fable Montgomery."

The paramedic wrote my name on a notepad. I gave her my contact number and address, and she advised me the vaccines should arrive within the next two days, and she suggested I make an appointment to receive my vaccine at Emmanuel Hospital. They'd be expecting me.

"What if I don't go get it?" I asked.

"Rabies is fatal. It would be a shame to die of something so treatable."

"Oh, god! How would I know? What are the symptoms?"

"Headaches, hallucinations, malaise, and so on. Sepsis, coma, death." She stuck her pen in the front pocket of her shirt and looked around the café. "If you don't need help, then I hope the rest of your day is better than it started.

"You, sir, were you scratched or bitten by the birds?" she asked Liam. "What is your name, and I'll add it to the list for the vaccine."

"That is not necessary," he replied. "I am immune."

He walked away, dragging me behind. She watched with a bewildered expression before turning to the next victim.

Headaches and hallucinations? Maybe I caught rabies last week!

Plump raindrops splashed against my face as we hurried out onto the sidewalk. I caught my breath as I saw the devastation. The broken city bus was wedged sideways on the narrow road, each end molded to different vehicles going opposite directions. A tow-truck crew and some firemen attempted to move the crushed SUV to open the road for an ambulance. I realized the SUV had crashed into a black van with government plates. Police and rescuers rushed around, tending to victims and interviewing witnesses.

One crew loaded a body onto a gurney into the back of an ambulance. Another helped an old man who sat in a doorway across the street, holding his chest. Black feathers littered the wet pavement, and as I stepped over the gutter, blood swirled in the water.

"Did I...?"

Is this my fault? Did I cause this somehow?

Even as I thought it, the sheer arrogance of the idea embarrassed me.

"Did you what?"

"Nothing. Never mind."

"We must move faster," he insisted.

The carnage was spread over two city blocks. No matter how hard I tried not to look, I couldn't help but stare as we rushed past.

Liam pulled my shoulder into his side, protecting me from the worst of the view. Yet I craned my neck, taking it all in, and realized I had just been in the epicenter of one of the strangest events in Portland in anyone's living memory. Then it caught up with me, how close I'd come to death, again. How near to being an obituary because of such a confluence of oddities—and how I was still somehow caught up in something unexplainable, surreal, and probably deadly.

Each of his strides equaled two of my own. I gripped my necklace as I rushed to keep up, willing my malachite pendant to offer an anchor through the chaos.

"I want to know what's going on," I insisted. "You owe me the mother of all explanations. Who are you? Why you are on this side of the country? Everything. What does my manuscript have to do with all this?"

We reached a street corner with a leaf-clogged gutter, and Liam lifted me up by my hips as he sloshed through the water. I opened my mouth to protest, but he was already setting me on the opposite side of the pool.

"You should be told," he agreed. "This involves you, and I promise to tell you everything, but we must first get to your laptop." He paused to meet my eyes, rivulets of rain running down both our faces. "Fable, I swear you are safe with me. No harm will ever come to you. You must also believe that your manuscript is a matter of life and death."

God help me, but I believe him.

I nodded. "Okay. I'll take you to it, but you have to promise to answer every question I ask."

"It is a bargain," he said with a smile.

"You're very strange," I mumbled as we rushed down the sidewalk.

I scanned the houses as we passed, watching the trees and side-walks, expecting to see someone, anyone, jump out at any moment with a roll of duct tape and a knife. I clung tighter to Liam's side and noticed that at every corner of our route, a crow sat atop a wire, or a lamp post, or the roof of a nearby house, watching—following our every move with glassy, soulless eyes.

Chapter Nine

How fragile is illusion
The matrix of the mind
To grant such grand confusion
Be it evil, be it kind

Celeste's house was dark. The FBI van that had been parked out front when I left for the café was gone. We made our way up the path to the front door, which stood wide open. A dead crow lay on the doormat like a hideous promise.

Liam pushed me back and stepped into the dark house. "Wait here."

As he disappeared inside, I stood shivering on the porch, staring at the crow corpse. A cat bumped my legs. I jumped, squeaking like a toy.

A black cat with a white face and paws head-butted my calf. I was never a cat person— strange, aloof animals that made my eyes itch—but I made an exception under the circumstances, and bent down, retrieving the animal and crushed it to my chest like a life-preserver.

At length, Liam returned. "It's safe to come in."

I stepped over the crow, whispering to the cat, my face in its soft fur, "You didn't do that, did you?"

The beast purred.

The house was dark. I flipped the nearby switch, revealing the desecration of my home. The destruction of all I had left. Liam shut the front door. The cat yowled, leaping from my arms. It raced through the front room amidst destroyed furniture, overturned lamps, and shattered fairy figurines. Ripped books and scattered loose pages were tangled in the yarn from Celeste's knitting basket, threaded across the room. Crockery shards and porcelain pieces of the heirloom tea set we used every Sunday littered the floor. I brought my hands to my mouth.

Tears burned as I ran through the debris shouting, "Biddy? LeeLee? Eleanor?"

"No one is home. The house is empty."

I scrambled through my pockets for my phone and dialed Eleanor. It went to voicemail. Biddy's phone went to voicemail. LeeLee's phone rang before she answered.

"Hello?"

"Thank god! Are you okay? Where are you? Biddy and Eleanor?"

"Calm down, Fable. Breathe, I am fine. What's the matter?"

I burbled between a wash of tears and rambled incoherently about the ransacked house and the bizarre crow attack. "Are Biddy and Eleanor with you?"

"No. I'm at the Aerie, but they texted me not an hour ago from the market on Burnside. They should be home in a moment. I'm sure they're fine. Lock the door, and whatever you do, don't call the FBI. I'm on my way."

I hung up, taking in the mutilation of my home. The photo albums were ripped apart. Pieces of photos peppered the rubble of dishes. The "Best Auntie Ever" mug I'd given to Celeste lay in shards on the dining room floor amongst the hand-crafted afghans, cut into strips. Slivers of glass, splinters of wood, and stuffing from the sofa littered nearly every inch of the floor.

"Fable, where is your laptop?"

Dazed, I stepped over a broken kitchen chair. The shattered remains of Celeste's fairy collection were spread across the hardwood.

My eye fell on the little fairy with the fuchsia bob that I continuously moved to the mantle. The figurine rested on its side, intact. For whatever reason, I bent down, picked it up, and placed it back on the mantle. Proof at least one thing had survived.

Liam followed me upstairs to Celeste's study where I had last been at my laptop. When I saw the ruined state of her sanctuary—ripped apart, dismembered, made unholy—I clenched my fists to keep from hitting something. "In there. I left my laptop on her desk."

Her books had been pulled down onto piles on the floor, pages ripped out like so many carelessly tossed leaves. The lamp broken, Tiffany glass shattered. The collections of seashells on her desk had been strewn about the floor and ground into the rug. The desk was overturned, pillows from the window seat cut open and the batting pulled out, and draperies ripped off the rod.

Liam picked through the rubble. My phone rang. Eleanor's ID popped up, and I let out a ragged, grateful gasp as I answered. "Are you okay?"

"Fable! What's happened? Biddy and I missed your call. We're on our way home. LeeLee called. Are you hurt? Are you alone?"

"I'm with a man named Liam. I'm not hurt, just really freaked out. How far away are you?"

"Trust Liam. He's one of us. We'll be there in less than ten minutes, coming the other way because 23rd Avenue is blocked for some sort of accident."

"How do you know Liam?" I asked.

"I'll tell you when we get there. Stay with Liam. Don't go outside!"

"My aunts will be here soon," I said as I hung up.

Liam looked up at me with a pained expression. "The laptop is not here. Did you make a backup? Save it somewhere?"

"No. I didn't think I needed to."

He sat heavily on the shredded window seat. "Do you remember what you wrote? Any details?"

"No," I snapped. "It's all fuzzy. I wrote it down so I wouldn't *need* to remember it."

"So all we have are the 13 pages." He tipped his head back against the window.

Rage bubbled up from the depths. In the hallway where pictures lined the walls, untouched in their black frames, I was overcome. I grabbed the nearest one, a photo of myself and Celeste in the backyard by the roses. Snatching it off the wall, I launched it down the hall where it exploded in shards of glass against the wood landing.

"You missed one!" I screamed, reaching for another. "You missed this one, too, asshole!"

"You missed *me*, too!" I threw another picture."You. *Missed!*" Glass chimed into fragments, wooden frames cracked.

"Fable."

My name spoken softly, just a reminder of myself, was all I heard. I turned, chest heaving, out of breath, face flushed. I gazed at Liam as he rested, backlit by the gray light of the window, his T-shirt soaked with rain and blood. His arms were covered in cuts and scrapes and the road-rash he'd probably gotten while saving my life. He bled through a gash in his jeans along the outside of his thigh.

"I'm sorry about your home," he said.

Pull it together, Fable. There he is, bleeding all over the place while you're having a meltdown.

I went for the nearest first-aid kit under my bathroom sink.

"What are you doing?" Liam asked, following.

"Have a seat on the bed."

He frowned, as I collected iodine, peroxide, alcohol, bandages, and cotton balls.

"Sit," I said, motioning to my bed, which appeared to have been trampled on by feet.

Liam had to step over piles of strewn clothing and my dresser drawers that had been poured out and then tossed into a heap in the corner.

Focusing on just one thing made it seem less like I was swirling down an abyss. I dipped the cotton in alcohol. "This will sting," I said, and touched it to the scrapes on his chin. His shoulders flinched, but he didn't move.

I cleaned the blood on the side of his face and checked the cut on his scalp. It appeared to be superficial, but like any scalp wound had bled plenty. A butterfly bandage fit perfectly.

He sat still through my ministering, watching my movements. His arms and hands were next to be cleaned. His right forearm needed to be wrapped. They were large limbs. Muscular. Strong, calloused hands.

"The wound on your leg seems pretty bad," I said, unsure what to do. I could ask him to pull his pants down so I could get a better look, but sudden flashes of my erotic dream turned my mouth to desert.

"It can wait," he said, taking the bottle of alcohol from my fingers and a cotton ball from the bag. He touched the cuts on my face carefully. Because he had not whimpered or squirmed, I very well could not, so I bit my bottom lip. The longer his fingers lingered on my skin, the warmer the room became.

He wrapped my elbow and left wrist, put Band-Aids on the cuts made by tiny talons, then softly touched a bruise on my shoulder. "I have a salve back home that would help this."

"I'm sure Celeste has one in the pantry. She might even have something that will work on that leg."

He glanced down at the bloody hole in his jeans.

"I'll go check while you work on that," I said.

Stepping away from him felt like prying my body off a magnet. A vacuum opened between us, sucking cool air into the space where our bodies had nearly touched.

I hurried down the stairs and tiptoed through the disaster in the living room to the kitchen pantry, where surprisingly nothing had been touched. I pulled the string for light and read the labels of the home remedies Celeste kept handy.

A long feline hiss startled me, and I peeked out of the pantry in time to see the cat I'd brought in, streaking across the counter after a dark shape the size of a coffee cup. Whatever hadn't been destroyed by the burglary was quickly being knocked over or spilled by the cat and a blur of prey. The flour canister launched off the counter to shatter on the floor as the cat dug for whatever it was trying to catch.

"Mice! I knew it!" I shouted. "If you can catch it, I'll give you a can of tuna!"

The salve was easy to find, labeled *Kilmarijn* in Celeste's handwriting. Her pantry was full of infused oils, vinegars, alcohols, and tinctures. She had a shelf of canned fruits, ciders, and pickles, as well as a rack of drying herbs and jars of spices. When I was young and needed lunch articles, the bottom shelf was mine: cereal, bags of chips, sandwich fixings, and so on. Since I'd been gone, she'd turned that shelf into an apothecary nook. I also grabbed a couple of dried comfrey packets from an open wooden box next to a bottle labeled *Blood of Angeline* and a ceramic jar titled *Coulda Woulda*, and made a mental note to come back and investigate all the contents of the pantry when I had time to look up the labels in the recipe book she kept.

Knocking on my bedroom door, I asked, "Is it safe to come in?"

"Yes," came the reply.

Naturally I opened the door, but what I didn't expect to find was Liam with his jeans pulled down. I caught a glimpse of naked thigh and ass before I spun back around. "What the hell? I asked if it was safe to come in!"

"There is no danger here, so it is obviously safe."

"Safe but *naked*!"

"Clearly."

"Here's the salve and a comfrey pack," I said, staring into the hallway, aware there was a naked man in my bedroom in Celeste's house for the first time since high school. "You do know what a comfrey pack is?"

"I am not an idiot."

I didn't respond but made my way down the stairs just as the front door opened and Eleanor shouted my name. Hopping over the last two steps, I said, "I'm so glad you're all right!"

Eleanor and Biddy took in the ruination of the house and my bandages and bruises. Biddy rushed to my side and touched my scraped face. "Did they do this to you?"

Eleanor shuffled through the porcelain shards. "Were you here? Did you see who did it?" She bent to retrieve a sliver of mirror.

"No. I was at a café down the street, where we were attacked by a flock of rabid crows." I waited till I had both their gazes to continue. "And I would have been killed if it weren't for Liam. Just how do you know him anyway, Eleanor?"

"Eleanor has been close with my family for many years," Liam said as he came down the stairs. "Biddy, LeeLee, and Celeste, too."

"Oh, goddess! Agatha!" Biddy yelled. "Agatha!"

"I'm over here!"

On the mantle, the fairy figurine with the fuchsia bob bent and stretched as though trying to work a kink out of her tiny back.

She was alive.

"What the fuck?" I yelled.

Agatha rolled her eyes then lunged off the mantle and zipped toward me. She hovered in the air while I stared, open mouthed.

"You're…" I trailed off. My voice echoed in my mind as though from a great distance down a tunnel.

Agatha looked at Biddy. "You said she was smart."

"I said she wasn't stupid. Give her some time. It's all new again."

"It's not polite to make a lady hover," Agatha said pointedly, in my face.

Hesitantly, I stuck my hand out. She landed in my palm, a living, breathing incarnation of the porcelain figure I'd handled maybe a dozen times in the last week.

"There's a Sniffer in the house," Agatha told Liam. "Vojhane's groupies brought it in. The cat's been trying to catch it, but I wouldn't suggest saying anything you might not want them to hear."

"I'll get it," Liam promised and trudged through the wreckage toward the kitchen.

The fairy glanced at me, crossed her arms, and looked at the ladies. "I think you broke her."

"She'll remember eventually," Eleanor said. She turned and ushered Biddy up the steps, saying, "Go gather her things. She's going to be gone a few days." They left me alone, their footsteps crunching on glass in the stairwell.

I stood in the entry of my ravaged home, holding a delicate creature fashioned from the fabric of legends. It would have seemed impossible, were it not for every event in the last two weeks leading me closer to the point of no return—where either insanity or belief were the only two options. I refused to blink, my hand frozen in a cradle for a creature that could not possibly exist. Then, in that moment, I surrendered to something far beyond myself.

Everything was out of my control. The only real option remaining was to embrace it.

I was part of something I couldn't possibly understand. Something tremendous. Fantastical. My NaNas were part of it. Liam was part of it. Celeste must have been part of it...which meant I was part of it, too. In some incomprehensible way, I knew I was connected to everything strange that had been happening, but I couldn't define it or even give it context in my brain.

Agatha buzzed up to float in my view. "So, what about it, Fable? You broken? Or do you want to at least *try* to be helpful?"

"I'm not broken," I said.

"Yeah? You look broken, like a whiny little pampered goddess gonna cry in her milk."

"I'm not broken!" I said harder.

"Really?" she egged me on, hands on hips. "You sure you aren't gonna cry?"

"Really," I snapped. "Fairy or not, if you don't get out of my face, I swear to god, I'll find a flyswatter and—"

"How is she?" Eleanor asked as she came down the stairs.

Agatha shrugged.

"It can't possibly get weirder than this," I said.

"Aw!" Agatha pouted, flew over, and pinched my cheek with her itty-bitty fingers. "You're just so cute."

Liam returned, followed by Biddy who walked with a slump in her shoulders.

"He got everything. Fable's laptop and the backup we made; he even took Celeste's two computers. It's all gone." Biddy sighed. She suddenly seemed so old. "I just can't figure out how they got in."

"What is going on?" I demanded.

"We shouldn't talk here," Liam interjected. "The Sniffer is loose. Cat lost its trail, and the protection runes are obviously damaged enough to allow anyone to listen or even break in."

"The runes are damaged?" Biddy gasped.

"How else would they have gotten in?" Eleanor murmured.

"The lightning-struck oak shattered the runes in the yard, and the ones around a door or window must have also been compromised. The point is, this is not a safe place to talk until security is re-established," Liam said while rebinding his hair in a knot.

Biddy sighed. "I'll text LeeLee and tell her to meet us at the Gate."

I wasn't expecting to go back to the Glade Café. As Biddy pulled up to the curb, I asked, "What are we doing here?"

Most of the chaos from the crow attack had been cleaned up since we'd left over two hours earlier. Traffic was moving. The sidewalks were clear except a feather or chip of glass here and there.

"This is the Gate," Eleanor said. "It's time for you to have answers."

I could tell there had been an accident of some sort, but I was astonished that little of the actual wreckage remained. All the victims had presumably been taken to the hospital or gone home to their families and the protection of their normal lives.

When did I start thinking other people had normal lives? Two weeks ago, my *life was normal, too.*

The blinds were pulled on the Glade Café. The open sign was turned off and a note hung on the door: "Family emergency. Closed for the day. Sorry for the inconvenience."

Inside, Liam sat at a table while the two waiters from before, Gabe and Zane, wiped down tables and cleaned up. Biddy closed and locked the door behind us.

"Why are we here?" I wondered. Everyone turned to look at me. "Eleanor, what's going on?"

"Fable," she began, opening the shoebox she'd carried Agatha in, "it's time for us to help you remember some things."

Agatha zipped to the glossy wooden bar and sat with her legs crossed, arms over her chest. "This should be interesting."

Reaching behind me to find the nearest chair, I sat heavily. Eleanor was jittery and pale. Scared. I'd never seen her shaken before. It unnerved me more than I thought it would.

Biddy stood behind me, her hands on my shoulders. "Okay, boys. Show her."

Liam unlaced his boots, kicked them off, and strolled barefoot to the center of the café. He stopped in the middle of the room, where the tables had been pushed aside. "Don't be frightened," he said, and pulled his shirt over his head to stand bare-chested in the incandescent light. He grasped the corded metal chain hanging from his neck and unclasped the latch.

With a whoosh like billowing sails, enormous wings opened behind him and his posture altered, adapting to their weight. Giant umber wings tipped with white feathers spanned 15 feet across the room. His chest seemed larger, his eyes a brighter blue, and his feet—talons.

I held my breath, afraid to blink, swallow, or twitch. Afraid if I moved, he'd return to a figment of my imagination.

"Do you want to see?" he asked.

Biddy urged me from behind, nudging me from my seat. "Go touch him. See for yourself."

I didn't feel my legs move me across the room. I didn't remember getting there, only standing awesomely close to him, feeling his radiating warmth. A puff of air moved by me as he contracted a wing, pulling it closer to his body. I flinched.

"I am William Odhyn Gunthorson of the Snow Eagle Clan, Elite Forces of Inter-Realm Relations, and liaison to Avian Affairs. I am a sworn member of Sublime. I am also your Guardian, Fable. My one and only directive is to keep you safe."

What does a girl say to such a declaration?

He was spectacular. Unbelievable. The left side of his chest and shoulder bore three white-ridged scars, much like talon wounds. Another ridge of scar tissue, this one more pink, stretched a hand-width beneath his right ribs and disappeared down across his hip-bone, beneath the waist of his low-rise jeans. Calligraphic lettering in an unrecognizable language was scrawled across his ribs and side.

I drank in all the details of his body and gained confidence, edging behind him to examine the joints of his wings. When I reached up to touch the crest at the back of his neck, he crouched so I could get a better look. The joint of his wings attached at either side of his spine, feathers trailing in a thin line down to the small of his back, disappearing under the lip of his Levis.

I followed the arch of his wing with my hand, running it along the boney top, his silky feathers seducing my skin with their sleek satin. As my fingers slid down to his pinions at the tip of his wing, he flexed, drawing his wings up to his body.

"Do you remember?"

I shook my head.

"Do you at least believe?" he asked.

I nodded, words trapped in my throat. How could I not? I had more questions now than before, but at least I wasn't crazy. Biddy and Eleanor saw him, too. Not that I understood any of it for sure.

"Tell me everything," I said, breathlessly. "You promised."

"These are the Talons." Liam motioned to the waiters. "Zane."

The man with the long black dreadlocks stepped forward and offered a short bow. Then he unclasped the chain around his neck and unfolded hawk-like wings with the rushing swish of feathers. He was startlingly handsome, with light teal eyes, caramel skin, and the red-tipped feathers of his clan.

"And my brother, Gabe."

Gabe stepped out from behind the bar and grinned before unleashing his own eagle wings. Once it was brought to my attention, I saw the family resemblance in their size, coloring, and wings; Gabe had a more youthful air of playful mischief, while Liam seemed far more serious.

A tap sounded on the window. Eleanor rushed to the door to let LeeLee into the café, but for a fraction of a moment, all three Avians crouched, flexing for a fight. Three birds of prey ready to strike. When they saw it was just LeeLee, they visibly relaxed.

"It is no longer safe for you to be on the Earth side of the veil, Fable," Liam said. "I recommend we adjourn to Aria, so we can better hide the signature of power you are releasing until you learn to control it."

"What does that even mean?" I snapped. As of yet I only had more questions. More impossibilities unfolding. No real answers.

"Fable..." LeeLee began.

"No! Don't 'Fable' me." I spun around to face Liam. "You promised to answer any questions I had. *Any*."

He dipped his head, acknowledging the truth. "Ask what you will."

I pointed at the necklace. "What is that?"

"It's a type of framing magic. A *yuerick*. You might call it camouflage."

"Why do you ask if I remember something I've never seen?"

"You have seen it, Fable, 14 years ago," LeeLee jumped in. "We suppressed your memories to hide your power and keep you safe. We did it out of love. You've seen all this before."

"Suppressed my memories? How?"

"With a different kind of magic," Eleanor said. "Layering it into your mind, your power, and your person. We worked on you twice a week during what you thought was our writer's group in the basement. It was really Celeste and the three of us, ensuring your shields stayed strong and you remained hidden from those who would harm you." She eased onto the maroon vinyl of the booth seat.

"The writing group was a witches circle?" I asked, aghast.

"More or less," Biddy added. "But with booze."

LeeLee touched the loose strands of hair escaping her usually perfect bun. "We started lifting the shields a few nights ago. See how fast you're recovering your true self?"

"Obviously not, LeeLee! I don't remember any of this." I pointed at Liam's wings. "I think I would remember *those*!"

"The shields can't be lifted all at once. They are woven into your memories. Ripping off the shields could tear your memories," said Eleanor. "But you are remembering, even if you don't realize it."

"How?" I demanded.

"Do you know what *Kilmarijn* is?" Liam asked patiently.

"No. Of course not."

"It's a plant from Aria Major. My home. A plant used for healing. If you didn't know what it was, how did you know to bring me the jar from the pantry?"

"It must have said what it was for on the label."

"Actually, it only had the word *Kilmarijn* on the label. Nothing else." Liam turned to me, drawing his wings in, blocking the rest of the group. "You recognized what it was good for, even though you didn't consciously remember the language."

He continued. "You are a Muse, Fable. Your aunts only did what they had to do to keep you safe. Did you not wonder why Celeste was so prolific a writer when you were near? How your fiancé could not stop writing once you moved in together? How your friends in high school and college went on to publish poetry, essays, books, and movie scripts, but you—you couldn't finish anything longer than a short article for your magazine?"

His words struck a hard chord after years of bitterness that I'd never been able to achieve my own dream, while those around me found it seemingly effortless.

"You managed to inspire, motivate, and use your power to create Story all around you—even when you were so heavily shielded. There are those who would use you to control the flow of inspiration to whomever they chose, or to starve those they deny, and destroy one of two worlds. It is time for you to awaken from the long sleep, Fable."

"Water," I croaked.

Zane pressed a full glass into my hands as Liam led me to a table. Once seated, it still took both my hands to get the water to my lips. Liam didn't wait for me to recover.

"I believe the attack at the café today was organized by Abra of the Mountain Crows. But more important, she is a known agent of the Eventines, and she has all but 13 pages of the manuscript you have been working on for the last three days. Do you know what that means?"

I shook my head. "I don't know what anything means right now."

"You have the power to see Story, to record epic storytelling as it happens, before it happens—and even possibly control it." Liam grabbed my purse off the table and retrieved the 13 crumpled pages. "It means you wrote a manuscript that may or may not be able to lead us to the other Muse who has been kidnapped. All we have left of that manuscript are these pages."

"You wrote this, Fable." Liam waved vaguely to encompass the café, implying the earlier devastation. "You wrote it three days before it happened," he insisted. "And whatever else you wrote is now in the hands of those who are working against our rescuing the other Muses."

Gabe touched my arm. "Now that you are opening to your power, you are a flashing beacon to any creature that recognizes such energy, even from across the world. And not all of them are friendly."

LeeLee took my hands in hers like a mother dropping off a child on the first day of school. Her lips quivered. "You will be safer with Liam than anyone in the two worlds. He's good at what he does. He's the best. It's why Celeste insisted on him." She brought my shaking hands to her mouth, kissing my knuckles. "We love you very much."

Biddy and Eleanor each approached. They each hugged me, their voices crooning goodbyes.

"Here's a bag of clothes and a few things we thought you might need," Biddy offered. She kept her shoulders square, chin rounded, eyes gleaming. "You know, toothbrush and hairbrush, and some clean panties." She smiled sadly, but even a goodbye could not prevent Biddy from adding, inappropriately, "And I put a couple of the really cute thongs in there, just in case. And a raincoat."

"Oh, lordy, Biddy," LeeLee said, appalled.

Zane took the bag from her hands. "I will carry it for her."

"We'll see you at Celeste's wake," Eleanor said.

"Celeste's wake?"

"The Avians reclaimed her body. She's is a high ranking diplomat, a hero in many ways to them. She gave them permission to return her, put her to rest in Aria."

"And you didn't think it was important for me to know that? How could you keep that from me? How?"

"We couldn't tell you until your ban was lifted," Biddy said defensively.

"But we really, really wanted to tell you!" LeeLee moaned. "It was so hard all these years seeing you not as your true self, seeing you at less than your full radiance. Lying to you. You will never know how hard it was."

It was that admission that set my mind to the task of leaving. My only real friends besides Celeste, and they had all lied to me—and that probably wasn't even the half of it.

I turned from the NaNas to face Liam, cold creeping through my belly.

I snatched the 13 pages off the table and stuffed them in my purse. "Let's go."

LeeLee sobbed softly and Biddy consoled her as I followed Liam toward the stairs leading to the basement. Glancing back one more time, I saw that Biddy held LeeLee, whose shoulders shook. Eleanor watched me with sparkling, watery eyes. She lifted one hand, nodded, and smiled wearily.

I turned, then, not wanting to lay eyes on them ever again, but even that thought hurt low in my belly.

The ones I love the most kept the most secrets from me. Secrets that could have gotten me killed. Enough with all the secrets and lies.

"Families," Gabe grumbled as he followed me into the stairwell, ducking his wings and head. We turned the landing and walked further down to an open space where crates of café supplies and dry ingredients were stored.

"Yup," agreed Zane, who brought up the rear.

Agatha buzzed past us all, flashing around the bend on the landing and disappearing into the room below. "I wouldn't have missed that for the world! Priceless."

The basement of the café was lit by five incandescent lights. Silver racks stacked with sacks of flour, sugar, and bottles; crates of dishes and a slew of linens lined all the walls, save one. The western wall was an oddity, with a large wooden door a foot off the ground.

"This is the Gate," Liam said, pointing to the wide doorway built from aged wood, paneled with dings and dents from years of use. "This is but one of many portals into Aria, a fixed gateway."

Gabe grasped the dark bronze handle hanging like a giant bull ring on the mission-style door. With what seemed like little effort, he swung the wood door out of an otherwise-plain brick basement wall.

Behind the door was a round portal built of older, different stones. Through that entrance was a pathway leading into an ivy-drenched, autumn garden saturated with natural golden light.

"Holy shit! It's like friggin' Narnia!" I said.

"Go quickly," Gabe said. "The longer a gateway is open, the more likely it will draw notice."

Zane went first with Agatha and the backpack, stepping into the garden like he was walking into any old park that just happened to be inside a basement wall.

Liam followed then turned and reached for me.

I hesitated. If I went in, it might mean never coming back.

Would that be so bad? What did I have worth staying for? A job and fiancé that both dumped me the same week? A house that belonged to my dead aunt in which every spoon, notebook, and blanket reminded me of her? A connection to a kidnapping case, insane crows, FBI hovering, and a trio of NaNas who'd been lying to me for years?

There's nothing left for me on Earth. At the end of my life, do I want to be able to say I went to another world, or not?

Taking his offered hand, I relished the calluses of his grip. Liam's fingers wrapped around mine. Closing my eyes, I took one last breath of air from Earth.

Then I stepped into another world.

Aria.

Chapter Ten

Aria, song of my heart
Lullaby of my soul

Immediately, I was overwhelmed by the scent, the deep forest aroma of moist vegetation rich with growth and decay. I knew that smell, I'd recognize it anywhere. It was the fragrance of Auntie Celeste's house, the perfume of my childhood imagination. I breathed deeply, becoming lightheaded, intoxicated.

"Breathe shallow until you adjust," Liam said. "Aria has more oxygen than Earth."

The garden corridor stretched before me in a wonder of wild ivy and autumn leaves fallen from trees so tall I couldn't see the top of the canopy through the lattice of still-shedding, patchy limbs. Despite the density of the branches above, golden light still filtered down, giving the trail a soft hue.

I glanced back. The door was closed. Suddenly I knew what C.S. Lewis's characters must have felt when they stumbled through the wardrobe, cut loose from logic and familiarity.

We waded through fallen leaves four inches thick. The mulched trail was a moldering mixture of bruised shades of scarlet and russet, all of it in contrast to the flourishing still-green ivy and clusters of moss and ferns.

Liam watched me, his blue eyes full of concern. I swiveled, lost in the marvel. It felt like walking into a painting, vivid and rich. I lagged behind, observing the differences between Aria and Earth. For certain the air was clearer. Cleaner, as though it had been scrubbed.

I remembered photos from Oregon history class of old-growth trees brought down by loggers, trees the width of a school bus. The trees of Aria dwarfed the images in those pictures. I'd never seen trees so tall or wide. They were draped in ivy and swaths of what appeared to be Spanish moss. I stopped to touch it and realized it wasn't Spanish moss but a similar-looking kind of lichen hanging from the branches like unbound hair. The velvety texture had small nubs, and I picked at one until a tiny lavender pebble popped free.

"I'yealenides?" I wondered. "Is this a seed?"

"Yes, it is." Liam said. He stretched his wings and flexed his arms. "It is the flower of life and death; an infusion with the petals will heal a lung infection. The roots are bitter, like your Earth anise, and poisonous."

I dropped it and wiped my hands on my jeans. "Oh."

We walked for what felt like a mile through the undergrowth of old forest. I'd begun sweating, my gray shirt stuck to my skin, leaving dark circles under my arms. "It's pretty warm. Where are we, exactly?"

"Another mile and we will be to the Oak Glade. A half day's flight or so beyond that and we will reach Kalloar, where we will rest for the night."

I trudged behind the group, winded by their speed. Zane's back was a wall of hawk feathers moving down the trail. Agatha flitted and zipped beside him in a fuchsia blur.

After a time, I focused solely on keeping up with them; so intent was I to put one foot in front of the other that I crashed into Liam's back when he stopped at the edge of a great clearing.

Wool light filled a vast glade that stretched in open reverence around a gnarled ancient oak tree. Beside the oak, a wide crystal pool fed by a steaming geyser gleamed in the sunlight. White marble pillars surrounded the Oak Glade, giving the sense of an open, outdoor palace—complete with sheer cloth drifting lazily on the breeze around couches, tables, and benches situated along the meandering stream. Through it all, tiled walkways wound between places of rest bordered by tall grasses.

Zane launched into the air with a joyous shout. The gust from his wings bent the nearby grass. Agatha was blown sideways by his blast, bobbing and tumbling through the air until she righted herself.

"Flying monkey!" she yelled, shaking a small fist.

Zane laughed from above as he pounded the air, unbound his dark dreadlocks, and spiraled around, stretching.

"We'll meet you by the oak," he called down before he and Agatha sped off toward the pool in the center of the Glade.

"They are off to rejuvenate in the healing waters," Liam explained. "We must meet the Oak Witch, so she may grant her blessing for you to enter Aria proper. There is no violence in a Glade. No threat of war amongst rivals of clans, no fear of scarcity. In a Glade, all is provided, and the Oak Witch sees to all the needs of those in her care."

"Did you think I would try to hurt someone?" I asked.

"No, of course not, but you must observe something. Do you still have your cell phone on you?"

I dug through my pockets and purse and realized I must have left it back on Earth.

Did I just think that? The "back on Earth" part?

"No. I must have forgotten it," I moaned.

"You did not forget it. It was taken from you at the first Gate. The Glade is the second Gate into Aria."

"What do you mean it was taken?"

"Aria is surrounded by magic. The veil separates us from Earth, and Earth from Aria. The veil is as much a net as it is a curtain. Whatever is banned will be caught in the net and left in the

Midway, the fold between worlds. That is why we could not bring you to Aria until the ladies lifted your ban as well as the shield. You might have been caught in the Midway—which is what happened to your cell phone when you passed through the Gate."

"Damn it. I loved that phone."

"There is a Glade surrounded by forest at each fixed Gate. To pass the forest and Glade to Aria, you must go through it. Other things, the small things that are banned from Aria but not worth troubling the strength of the veil, will be taken by the Guardian of the Glade."

"What are you getting at?"

Liam shrugged, his fine features chagrined. "You must part with the Swiss Army knife toy on your keychain, and the can of mace in your purse. They are not sanctioned weapons."

My mouth fell open. "Seriously? The Swiss Army knife the size of my pinky is a weapon?"

"I know it must seem strange to you. Even stranger is that on the other side of the Glade, inside Aria, you may be able to find a trafficker who has actually smuggled one such toy somehow. But the truth is, the Swiss Army knife has complex parts and may be used as a weapon, and the Oak Witch of the Glade will likely take it from you when we enter. In Aria, all of our weapons are simple. Skill and strength are the truest weapons. You will not find guns or bombs, or any weapon that does not involve meeting your enemy on the field."

"But a Swiss Army knife isn't really that complex; it just looks like it. And I'd have to be near my enemy to use the mace...so I should be able to keep them both," I reasoned.

"You may argue or try to walk them through and see what happens."

"This is worse than airport security. Will she want my nail file? Should I take off my shoes, too?" I asked sarcastically.

Liam cocked his head. "It is not required."

I sighed and followed him into the Glade. "By the way, I noticed the café was called the Glade." As we walked toward the Oak and the warm spring, knee-high grass waved around our legs. A flicker of light burst from the blades of grass and zipped off toward the forest.

"Anyone from my world who happens to be on Earth would recognize the café because of its name and aura, and they would know they'd be welcomed back to the safety of Aria and the neutrality of the Glade through our doors."

"Then why were we attacked by crows right outside the café? It was obviously something from your side of the veil, so why didn't they obey the neutral thing?"

"It is troubling, and I shall ask the Council about it, you can be sure."

The clearing opened wider and longer than several city blocks. A small brook ran through it from one end to the other, passing by the pool of hot water near the Oak along its burbling way. We walked along the water, which seemed to chatter over the rocks and pebbles. I vaguely had the sense that the brook was speaking to me, telling me a story. I shook my head and focused on Liam.

"So what is an Oak Witch, anyway?"

"You ask a lot of questions."

"And you promised to answer anything I asked."

"It is true," he said heavily. "I believed you would remember more and ask less." He frowned, glanced at the sky, then added, "The Oak Witch is an Undjinn. A root soul."

I shrugged, not comprehending.

"You might call them orphans, or changelings."

"Like the sick kids left out on rocks to die in the Dark Ages kind of changeling?"

"Yes, but the practice was long ago abolished in our world. Yet back when it was practiced, the ill children forsaken by families or homeless orphans would be left at the edge of the woods; by dawn they would have been claimed by the Undjinn. Their homeless souls were bonded and seeded by dying lines of the tree ancestors. They grew up sharing a body and mind with a sapling, their life-forces brought into harmony. An Oak Witch rarely outlives the tree. A tree rarely outlives the Witch. They are spirit-bonded and die of grief without each other."

"So there are only Oak Witches?"

"There are many kinds of tree witches."

"How long do they live?"

"Stories claim several thousands of years, but I have never met an Undjinn older than 900."

Several thousand years?

"What happens to the dying line of trees without changeling children to seed?"

Before he could answer my question, we were approached by a creature of staggering beauty. She stood from a crouch where she'd been talking to Zane. My breath caught.

Easily eight feet tall, she bore tree branches much like antlers from her head. She looked like a smaller, human-ish version of the Oak in the center of the clearing. They both bore ochre and crimson leaves in their branches that looked ready to shed at any moment. Though the Oak had ivy hair, the witch had a mane of white that dragged on the ground near the hem of her rust-colored robes.

She walked with the grace of wind in tree limbs, swaying toward us without haste.

"Welcome back to the Oak Glade, Liam. May you find peace and healing." Her voice was not unlike the rustle of leaves.

Liam ducked his head. "My appreciation, Gwendollyn. I present Fable Rose Augustine Montgomery, child of Angelica and Clark, beloved of Celeste."

Gwendollyn approached, surprisingly graceful for her size and composition, with arms like tree limbs and the slender fingers of a woman. She knelt on the grass before me and crouched even further to be eye level.

"Fable, of the Nine. One of the Maior. Beloved of Celeste, who was beloved of I." Gwendollyn's voice took on the sad chord of branches weighed upon by snow. "She is greatly missed, and you are returned just in time." She bent in, her long, chiseled nose brushing my hair. She sniffed me.

Can trees even smell?

But she was as much a beautiful woman as an aged oak. Not knowing what to do, I froze.

Is this like a canine introduction? I hope she isn't expecting me to smell her back.

Finally, she sat back on her heels. "You do not smell like her. Your power has not yet fully risen. Tell me, do you hear the forest speaking to you? Do you hear the babble of the brook?"

A swift, a small bird little larger than a chicken egg, flew into the branches of her hair to perch on a limb and watch me with curious, expectant eyes. In fact, three pairs of eyes sought answers to a question I didn't even understand.

"Um, no. I'm sorry. I don't think so."

Liam's wings drooped.

"Have patience, Liam. She is still bound by the restrictions of shielding that have not shed. But she will still bloom into her spring and summer."

For a moment, I imagined they were disappointed in me. I felt terribly inadequate. And for what? Not hearing the forest talking? Or the water blabbing?

Gwendollyn rose to her feet again and held her hand out for the swift to perch upon. It chirped a set of rapid staccato tones before she released him. He sped away, vanishing into the forest.

"The Gate's opening was sensed. There are those whom you would likely prefer to avoid headed to the new energy of a Maior on Aria's soil. If you are not in need of healing here, I think it best you fly on to safety."

"But I thought they couldn't hurt us here," I said.

Zane and Agatha climbed from the healing pool of water, scrambled for the clothes they'd left on a nearby stone, and began dressing.

"They cannot harm you within the Glade, but they may wait for you to leave and follow you. Perhaps you would like to get a head start." Already she was turning away, fitting herself into a space in the side of the great Oak that was exactly her shape and size. Like interlocking pieces of a puzzle, the Oak Witch and her tree became one entity.

"Come, Fable, we must fly," Liam urged.

"What? Like fly like hurry? Or fly like, you know…" I pointed up.

"There is no time. We must make it to Kalloar before we are confronted, unarmed."

"We will fly ahead and warn the others," Zane said as he adjusted the backpack to ride on his chest. Agatha zipped herself into the front pocket. "We will meet you at Arista Castle."

Zane launched into the air, blasting my face with wind. The flurry of motion and tense faces brought acid bile up my throat.

Reaching into my purse, I clutched my can of mace, grateful Gwendollyn hadn't confiscated it. Liam was already standing behind me. Reaching under my arms, he grasped his own wrists over my breasts. Before I could get a word in edgewise, he squatted then launched us into the air. I shrieked, nearly dropping my purse and mace, and scrambled to grip him with my right arm. My legs dangled in the air.

Air whistled past my ears. Jolts shook my whole body as Liam pounded the sky with his wings, gaining altitude, jarring us like a beginner driver with a stick shift and a clutch. The ground slipped further away. Gravity sucked at my legs, pulling my heart into my shoes.

As we reached the height of the canopy surrounding the clearing, I said, "I guess she let me keep my mace, huh?" I felt a disproportionate sense of pleasure that he was mistaken and that I'd be able to keep something of my world close in a place so utterly foreign. Yet as we passed the edge of the tree line, the slick black can of mace vanished from my fingers. I looked down, thinking I'd dropped it, then understood it wasn't dropped but taken—absorbed into the Midway.

Liam laughed against my back. The sky bloomed above us in hues of blue as the world faded below in patches of autumn, and an unbelievable landscape unfolded in breath-taking majesty. I found myself overwhelmed with gratitude and suffused with awe.

Chapter Eleven

Let starlight guide thee home.

Flying. Actually flying. It was spectacular. Invigorating. Mind-blowing.

At first, I was gripped by fear that Liam would drop me, or I'd be too heavy and we'd plummet to the ground. After we leveled off at a comfortable altitude, he said, "I am going to pull your legs up with mine."

His talons reached down to my hanging legs, gripped my ankles and lifted, leveling my body parallel to the ground. The length of my back pressed intimately against his chest and hips. His muscles contracted, working his body against mine, to keep us both aloft. Soon we had a rhythm, a balance with the sway and lull of his striking wings and the dip of gravity before a longer glide. Once situated, he stroked harder against the sky. Wind blasted my skin as we gained speed.

The view filled me with a combination of wonder and terror, excitement and queasiness.

I'd been on a good many airplanes in my lifetime, both passenger jets and rinky-dink two-seaters that barely got off the ground, while on remote digs with my father in South America. Yet of all the windows I'd marveled from mid-flight, nothing could compare to the land of Aria.

Carpets of fall vegetation, whole forests of gold and ruby patchwork, butted up against evergreen and ivy-covered mountains. Occasionally a dirt highway snaked through the woods, climbing a pass through the hills.

We flew over a river that wound through a canyon of gray shale, and the water was so clear and smooth that I glimpsed our reflection, as though we were flitting high over the surface of a mirror that trailed across the landscape. There were spruce valleys and redwood forests and tawny fields ripe with the promise of a bountiful harvest.

We flew over jewel-blue lakes encrusted with small settlements and villages, but each time we drew near, Liam climbed higher, altering our course to avoid eyes from below.

Eventually, my hands and face froze. Shivering set in, then my eyes dried out and I reluctantly squeezed my eyelids tight and blew on my stiff fingers.

"Do you need rest?" Liam yelled over the wind. "We can stop a short while so you may warm yourself."

"How far do we still need to go?"

"It will be about a half hour more."

"Don't *you* need rest?" I asked, astonished he had the strength to keep us both in the air.

"Not at present."

Moments later we dipped toward the ground, gliding in a long, declining angle. The forest had become plains; we'd been in the air for two hours and the plains were edging toward hills, and in the very far distance there shimmered a vast expanse of ocean.

As we came in for the landing, I instinctively tried to thrust my legs out to catch myself, but Liam managed to keep my legs tangled in his own before swooping at the very last second, then he backbeat his wings so we arched vertically and landed gently in the grass.

Already I was warmer out of the wind, and Liam's heat thrummed the air in waves from the extra exertion of flying for two. He breathed a little heavier, cheeks flushed.

"We are at the edge of the Interioria, about to cross the Hartland Hills into Avian territory," he said as he pulled my shivering body against his bare chest and rubbed my arms. His warmth enveloped me like a summer day. If I stayed in his embrace too long, I thought there wouldn't be much left of me but a puddle.

"Where are we going?"

"We must make it to Kalloar tonight. My childhood home is but a day's flight from there."

"A day's flight?"

"We will gather supplies to make you a harness and clothing to keep you warm in Kalloar. We have allies there, but we must still work to keep you hidden until the Council can determine a course of action."

After 15 minutes, I could feel my fingers. I wasn't looking forward to freezing again and thought about pretending to be cold just a little longer to stay in his embrace.

"Are you warm?"

I bobbed my head. "I am still stunned by all of this," I said. He stepped in front of me, looping my arms around his neck and pulling my hips into his. My mouth went dry. We stood with our chests crushed together.

"Your ride will be warmer if you keep your face in my neck and your hands tucked between us once we are airborne." He drew me tight and locked his arms behind me.

"Okay," I whispered.

Liam launched without warning. I yelped in his ear. The hard powerful strokes of his wings jarred our bodies together repeatedly until he gained enough altitude. I wrapped my legs around him, instinctively clamping my thighs on his hips and locking my ankles behind his knees. I was immediately aware of the thrusting momentum of his wing strokes and the erotic connotations of the position. It felt good. Too good. I quickly let go and my legs dropped back, hanging as dead weight.

"No. Please," he said. "We had good balance. Please wrap your legs around me, if you can. The better our center of gravity, the faster time we will make."

I didn't speak, afraid my voice would say it all, but I again tangled my legs around his waist then clenched my eyes shut and silently practiced long-division math equations.

Wind buffeted us, but he was right: It was significantly warmer facing his body with my nose pressed to his neck, inhaling his odd mixture of musk and autumn leaves. In fact, I was a little too warm.

The sun was setting in carnelian hues when we landed outside Kalloar, touching down in a field outside a large white-washed estate, complete with a columned façade and a stretch of land to the west devoted to what looked like vineyards.

The road leading up to the house was lined with shedding maples which ended at the front entrance, a bright red double door beset by columns. As soon as our feet touched the ground, Liam rushed us toward the side door.

"We need to get out of the open," he explained as he dragged me across the field.

"Whose house is this?" I wondered.

"This cottage is owned by a friend. He rarely visits, so it is maintained by a teacher and her students for half of each year."

"This is a cottage? Holy crap!"

He dragged me so hard my feet came off the ground, and I shouted, "Easy! I'm coming!"

"Quiet. It is not safe. Eyes are everywhere."

I ran to keep up, frantically glancing around the bushes and trees, expecting to see beady eyes staring back.

Liam banged on the wooden side door three times, waited for a count of ten, then banged twice more and walked in, lugging me behind like tiresome baggage.

"There's been far too much of that going on today," I scolded.

The door entered into a kitchen. Three young Avian creatures immediately stopped their stirring of soups, chopping of vegetables, and laying out of dishes, and stared blankly at the two of us.

"Too much of what?" asked an Avian woman in the chair by the fire.

"Too much pulling me through doorways into the unknown," I answered.

She was a delicate creature less than four feet tall. She stood with painfully awkward movements, as she was crippled, her wings broken. Misshapen, bent appendages with white, satin feathers.

I tried not to stare at her wings or the grotesque scar stretching across her neck and face, but as much as I tried to look away, I could not. She limped forward, dragging one twisted leg with the aid of a cane.

She tsked. "Liam, where are your manners?"

"Delia, may I present Fable?"

"Yes, you may," she said.

"Fable, Delia is one of us. A sister of the Sublime."

"There is more to it than that, but Liam is not one for words and explanations, is he?" She smiled. "Come. Sit down. I'm sure you are tired, hungry, and full of questions." She took my hand and led me to the fire, where she urged me to sit.

Built of stone and warm-hued woods, the large kitchen had three fireplaces and a huge center island. The young Avians stood on the far side of the chopping counter, staring openly, mouths still frozen agape.

"Don't mind the children, Fable. They have never seen a Muse before…well, come to think of it, they have probably never seen a human, either." Delia glanced at the young girl. "Myra, the soup is scalding."

The girl jumped and rushed to stir the kettle hanging over a fire.

They were indeed children; their wings were featherless. They were dressed in brown sack-like clothes with holes cut in the back for their naked bent limbs.

"Liam, go help yourself to dinner and bring us ladies something to refresh ourselves," she said. To my surprise, he went without hesitation, leaving me alone with a creature both frightening and lovely.

Enjoying the heat of the flames, I took in Delia's profile as she stirred the logs with a poker. Her face must have been very beautiful, once. The features not ruined by the ragged scar were delicate. She had no other blemishes on her pale skin and wore her hair in a pixie-cut of fine white strands that emphasized her fragile bones. In all, she was a picture of snowy porcelain perfection that had met with a brutal alteration. A broken china doll.

"I see Liam did not warn you of my condition so you might be prepared," she said slyly, poking at the fire before turning to pierce me with eyes like turquoise shards.

"Which condition would that be?" I asked.

She laughed, a genuine chime. "I am a White Crow, one of which is born only every couple hundred years or so. I am not unlike you—rare." Delia took her seat, and I glanced off to the kitchen where Liam spoke to the children as he dished up plates of food.

"They are still fledglings," she said by way of my gaze.

Liam popped a slice of something in his mouth, spoke to a boy chopping vegetables, then rumpled his hair and they laughed.

"Fledglings are precious. Two hundred years ago, I might have had a schoolroom full of 50 children." She sighed as if in physical pain and adjusted her leg. "But that's not why you came to see me."

Settling back in the chair, I held my hands toward the flames. I didn't know why I was where I was. Until eight hours ago, I could have passed my last two weeks off as a horrific nightmare, or gone to a good doctor for some drugs to cope—but this?

Do they even make drugs for this?

My hands ached from the heat, and I realized I'd been quiet for some time. Fearing I was being rude, I blurted the first question on my mind to keep conversation flowing. "Why are Muses and White Crows rare?" I asked.

"I only know what everyone else knows about the order of births for the Muses—or Nine, they are also called. One Muse is born only every 12 generations. The full powers of one Muse ignite widespread social evolution in the thoughts of man and creature alike. The worlds cannot handle more than one Muse at a time. It is said the ripples of that power, of inspiration, travel through 20 generations' worth of creative work, enlightening, inspiring social expansion, deeds, thoughts, and so on and so forth." She idly touched the scar on her neck. "And yet now we live in times when all Nine have been born into the world at once."

I tipped my head back, thinking of my history classes, wondering which periods in time were likely influenced by a Muse. The Renaissance, obviously. But what else?

Liam pulled up a chair and sat. We were served plates of food by the fledglings. A girl no older than 14 offered me a glass of dark burgundy wine. Her eyes were much wider and spaced further apart than a human child's. She didn't blink as she served me dinner and barely looked away.

"Thank you," I said. The girl flushed before scurrying away, her talons scraping the stone floor.

"I see Delia launched right into the lessons." Liam spoke around mouthful of fish.

"You were once my student, too, Liam. Fable is just beginning her education." Delia sipped her wine, glancing back and forth between Liam and myself. A smile touched her lips.

My plate was a colorful serving of salmon, autumn squash, and greens. I didn't realize till that moment how hungry I was.

The fledglings left us to our conversation and went about their duties in the kitchen.

"I have a question," I said. "How do you know which Muses are born, and when?"

"It is said that the Muse born to mankind every 12 generations possess the power most needed by Earth's and Aria's creatures to further their enlightenment." Delia sipped her wine and continued in the sing-song voice of a teacher before a classroom. "If the worlds are struggling with language, mathematics, astronomy, the arts, etcetera, the Muse of that particular inspiration will be given life to bring evolution of thought to those in need of it."

"So why is now so different?" I wondered. "Why are Muses being born all at once? If there is more than one, what will happen to the world? Worlds?"

"No one is certain why now. There are as many theories as there are feathers on Death Cloak. Everyone believes something different. Some believe it is the End of Days, or what is referred to as the 'Convergence'; others believe it is the Great Enlightenment. Ideas are endless. Answers scarce." Delia adjusted her leg again. "Savion, my rest, please."

A young boy rushed forward. His wings were beginning to show a tuft of silver down around the ridge of his shoulders, contrasting beautifully with his ebony skin. He brought a footrest and helped Delia prop up her crippled leg before the fire.

"Thank you," she said with an affectionate smile. He returned to the kitchen, and she whispered conspiratorially to me, "Savion is my star mathematics pupil. One day a proof from him, for sure." She appeared lost in thought. "Where were we?"

"The reason for all the Muses being born in this time," I offered.

Liam went back to the kitchen for thirds.

"Yes, no one is certain of the answer to that question, but one thing is sure." She met my eyes. "Whoever controls the powers of the Muses will determine all our fates. For this reason, the Nine must be protected and allowed to bloom into their full inspirations. Not one but two worlds are at the mercy of that destiny."

It was heavy news. Impossible news.

"What happens if one of the Muses were to, you know…die?" I asked.

Delia shifted her broken wings and gazed at the fire. "Both worlds would see the beginning of a new Dark Age. A future void of enlightenment."

133

The room was quiet for a moment. Only the fire whispered agreement.

No pressure, right?

"Come now, of lighter topics," Delia said with a sigh. "Please, Fable, can you tell me what has happened on the television show *The Island*? I haven't had an update since Celeste was here last, and I am dying to know who got voted off."

Liam followed me up a spiraling marble staircase. The interior of the manor was spacious, obviously built with Avian residents in mind. He held a lantern with a blue glowing bulb. The light revealed the masterful artwork and murals on the plaster walls and ceiling.

"This manor has been in Ronan's family for several hundred years. It has been a school for fledglings during the autumn and winter for nearly as long. His family is responsible for much of the old ways being carried on to new generations."

"It's a beautiful home," I replied.

"I will be in the next room over. If you need me, just call out and I will hear you."

The students slept on the second floor. As I peeked down the corridor, I noted the hallway stretched on for half a dozen doors on either side. Light only escaped from beneath three.

On the top floor, the vaulted ceiling arched nearly 20 feet, allowing for a full wingspan. Liam and I stopped at the first room where light and heat glowed, inviting us to join.

"There you are," Delia said. "Come in, come in. We are just putting on the final touches."

Delia stoked the fireplace, while the fledgling, Myra, tucked in the sheets on the bed and fluffed the pillows. The bed was enormous, built for a wingspan I obviously didn't possess. If I tried to sleep on the mattress, I'd be lost and never found again.

"You didn't need to do all this for me. Really, a sleeping bag on the floor would be fine."

The girl's eyes widened in horror. She flapped her bare wings and the webbing swooshed.

"Are you okay?"

"She's fine, dear. She just cannot imagine stuffing one of the Sacred Nine in a sack and leaving her on the floor. No, no."

The girl shook her head.

"All right, then, the bed is wonderful. Honestly, after the day I've had, I could really use some sleep."

Moments later I was alone in the giant room. The fire cast a soft lullaby of music and the sky blossomed with stars. The huge empty bed was daunting, and I barely made a dent in it as I sat on the corner and gazed out the window to the night sky.

The stars were different, and yet they were not entirely unfamiliar.

When I was 14, my class had gone on a trip to the Portland Observatory one night. It was a strange field trip full of hot chocolate, a gargantuan telescope, and newly-minted teenagers gone a little nutty when it was too long past a normal bedtime.

When it had been my turn to sit in the telescope seat and draw in the close-up of our galaxy, it seemed foreign. The stars I saw when looking up at the heavens from the Juliet balcony of my bedroom were the same stars in the telescope—except they were sharper, closer, more colorful.

But they were not *my* stars.

At the end of the trip, the observatory gave us all a bag of trinkets: astronaut ice cream, a lunar calendar, and a booklet of plastic, stick-on, glow-in-the-dark stars.

When I got home, I told Celeste about the two boys who clogged the observatory toilet with a shoe and got sent back to their parents. She and I shared the astronaut ice cream, which was powdery and dissolved like a cotton candy. Then I told her, "The

Portland Observatory is missing constellations. I don't think their telescope is big enough to see them…or maybe they can't see them because they are on our side during the day. They are missing whole sets of stars."

"Missing whole sets of stars?" Celeste asked, aghast. "Perhaps we should write our own astronomy books, then." She smiled in the way she always did when she kept a secret or made a joke.

"Fine, then," I said. "I'll make my own sky."

So I'd taken my booklet of plastic stars up to my room, stood on my bed, and stuck them to the ceiling to form the constellations missing from the observatory. I slept peacefully beneath the neon glow of shapes I called, Icarus' Folly, Apollo's Chariot, and the Weaving Fates.

Alone in a bedroom with grand furniture built to scale for much larger creatures, I wondered what possible place I might have in all this. What could anyone possibly want with a Muse who struggled to make deadlines at a third-rate fashion magazine? I wasn't the next great American novelist. I wasn't out there winning Pulitzers or making social waves. I could barely pay my rent each month.

What kind of Muse struggles to pay rent?

The brass latch on the oversized Avian window unhooked with ease, and I pushed the two wide panels into the night. A gust of autumn air lifted loose curls off my shoulders. The black sky unfolded before me, a dark theatre curtain opening to reveal what I somehow already knew. Glancing up at the sky, I gasped.

These are my stars.

Emotion welled with such ferocity I clutched my stomach in pain. It was real. It was all real, and somehow, someway, even when I was shielded, I knew my home but just couldn't remember it.

"I'm home."

The weeping that overcame me was pure relief. Powerful, bone-aching relief.

For years, I hadn't consciously been aware of *not* being home.

My stars. My home. How is this possible?

The constellation of Apollo's Chariot charged across the sky, drawn by the horses of dawn. When he reached the horizon, the sky would awaken with sunrise as the trail of stars behind him were harnessed to the sun. Icarus' Folly would ascend in a couple of hours, and the Weaving Fates were just reaching their zenith.

I raced into the hall, dashed to Liam's room, and burst in with an excited shout. He lunged to his feet from the seat near the fire. Dark wings snapped open as he crouched for a fight.

"What is it?" he asked, relaxing.

"I was born here, wasn't I? I am from Aria."

"You are remembering?" he asked hopefully.

I rushed past him to the window and pushed open the glass panel. "My stars. Not the stars of earth. Mine. I mean, they're the same stars, they're just a different angle. I mean…ah! I'm not saying this right."

Tossing my hands in the air, I sighed and frowned. "They are and they aren't. But they *are* mine, the way they are on my bedroom ceiling at Celeste's."

Liam joined me at the window, "Yes. You were born here. You were conceived here as well, I understand."

"How do you know?"

Liam gripped my shoulders, turning me back toward the sky. He stood behind me, wrapping his wings around us both, cocooning us from the cold night air. "Icarus' wings, how I want you to remember. You have no idea how badly I want to tell you everything—but these recollections must come from you. If I tell you all I know, I may damage the shape of your memories with my influence, and you may never be able to trust your recall completely.

"I can tell you this much," he continued. "I know about your birth and conception here, because your mother and father were often guests in my family home. When you come to recover more of your own memories, my mother and father will be able to fill in any missing pieces for you."

His wings were blissfully soft, like silk-lined comforters stuffed with down. The strength of his arms and the encompassing shelter of his feathers, though slightly ticklish on my neck, were so relaxing I closed my eyes and leaned back against his body. Safe.

Liam's heartbeat was a metronome against my back, and with his body so close, I thought about our flight earlier and found myself breathing a little heavier. I wanted to turn to him, put my arms around his neck and pull his mouth to mine. He felt real and solid, safe when everything about the last two weeks had been anything but.

Moments ticked by, and each time he exhaled, his breath tickled the back of my neck. My belly clenched.

Do it. Kiss him. Do it before you lose your courage.

But I couldn't move, could barely breathe.

It felt like an hour passed. His arms tightened around me, drawing me closer. He pressed his nose into my hair, breathing me in.

Desire, like an electrical storm, raced beneath my skin. I twisted in his embrace, ready to throw myself on him.

"Liam…" I began, but whatever else I was going to say was halted as I met his eyes.

How quickly I'd forgotten he was not exactly human. He had a man's body but he was also distinctly Avian, and the look in his eyes, almost wild, scared me like nothing ever had before. Even more terrifying, something in my belly coiled with pleasure at the thought, and I shoved it away in fear. The heat that had been rising in my body, the wanting ache, froze. Blinking rapidly, I tried not to reveal my surprise at the animal lust I'd seen in his gaze. The near-feral creature that terrified me.

"Fable…" he husked.

"I'm… sorry," I said. "I should go back to my room."

The hungry light in his eyes dimmed as he straightened his shoulders.

"That is probably best." He watched as I backed away, his blond hair capturing glints of firelight. Then he turned to the window, lifting his wings as a barricade.

I jerked open the door to escape. Escape him and my strangely deep desire for him, a creature as much animal as man.

As the heavy door swung inward, I came face to face with a monster in the corridor.

An Avian with a bald head, gold hoop earring, and a hulking bodybuilder frame stood in the door with one hand raised, as though he were about to test the knob. His black wings were stretched out, and he looked as startled as I felt.

It was one too many surprises for the day, and I screamed loud enough to wake the house.

The Avian recovered quickly and charged. he bowled me into the room, lashing out with a left hook that caught me in the jaw. I flew backward but Liam caught me as I fell and spun my weight toward the plush bed, where I disappeared into a puff of down comforters, my face splitting with pain.

I heard the fighting and met my own battle in the sinking mattress and blankets. My arms and legs grappled awkwardly with the shifty bedding. The pain in my face was so acute I thought my cheekbone might be broken.

Sounds of furniture tipping, glass breaking, and wood snapping filled the room, followed by grunts and the flat snap of fists hitting flesh. I managed to pull myself up enough to see the attacker pick up a chair. He hurled it at Liam, who ducked.

The chair clipped his wing, and he flinched even as he kicked out with a taloned foot, goring the vulture-winged Avian in the chest.

Blood sprayed the plaster. The Avian roared. Then he pulled his hands together, inhaled, and thrust his palms outward. A pale blue ball of light exploded from his hands and slammed into Liam's shoulder, flinging him across the room.

I screamed, slid to the edge of the bed, and hopped to the floor.

The vulture raced toward me, reaching out. Liam recovered, running to intercept in three desperate strides. They crashed together in a fierce grapple. Furniture overturned. Wings knocked over paintings and dishes. The bald Avian punched Liam in the side as they wrestled. Liam's lower back turned red and swollen as it took the brunt of the hits.

From the hall, a screech of fury preceded a blur of white, and two young fledglings followed Delia and a mob of limbs and wings descended onto the Avian attacker.

"Go! Go! Go!" Delia shouted.

Liam stepped away as the vulture disappeared under a pile of children.

I picked up a broken chair leg for a club and barreled forward for some payback. The children couldn't possibly hold him down for long.

"Go! Damn you! Get her *out*!" Delia screamed.

An electric blue light shimmered around the horde of children holding down the larger creature. The blue light took form and shape, lines crisscrossing into a net. One by one, the children stepped off. The Avian remained trapped under the blue mesh. The vulture yelled, twisting under the energy shield.

Liam didn't speak but grabbed a quilt off the pile of blankets by the fire. He ungraciously snagged my arm. Before I could protest, he wrapped me in the blanket, picked me up, and ran for the window.

"No!" I shrieked as he dove for the night sky. "We can't leave them! Go back!"

When he jumped, I flinched. We plummeted toward the ground, only to pull up in a glide across the field. Grass whipped the back of my head as Liam grunted with the effort to keep us airborne. My stomach lunged into my throat as his wings hammered against the darkness.

"They will buy us time."

"They could be killed!" I screamed. "They're just kids!"

"No Avian will ever harm a fledgling. They are protected, and Delia is very powerful. They will be fine. They will buy us time."

I didn't know what to say as we flew through the darkness, guided only by the stars. My stars. I wasn't sure that I even wanted them anymore.

Chapter Twelve

If fish had wings, and birds breathed water
Then chaos be order for Mnemosyne's daughter

Dawn broke over a great cluster of towers looming in the distance at the edge of a rock face, far above the ocean. I could make out orchards within the high walls of a small city. We flew over pasture land full of oversized horses moving as though harvesting golden rows of crops. Liam's strokes slowed to glide, and as we dipped ever closer to the ground I realized they were not horses at all.

"Centaurs!"

"Yes."

"They're real! Not myth!" I exclaimed happily. "Next you're going to tell me there are mermaids, too, right?"

"Yes, Aria is home to many Merfolk," he replied, voice heavy with exasperation.

"And dragons?"

"Yes."

"And Santa?"

"Do not be foolish."

"It was worth a try."

We landed just inside the walls on a stretch of verdant grass near trees laden with apples and a path leading to the gate of a castle. The inner-gate portcullis was up, and the tunnel through the stone led to a bastion of medieval defensive construction six stories high. Battlements and ramparts were soldiered by a handful of Avian centuries in silver plated armor and crimson fabric.

Liam waved to the guard on the portcullis ledge, who lifted his spear in acknowledgement as we walked through.

"Seriously? You live in a castle?"

"Welcome to Arista Castle. Does it look familiar? Do you remember anything?"

I took in the gray granite stones the size of city buses, the ramparts, the spires. I noted the sound of surf in the distance and the taste of salty air. With extensive gardens between the outer and inner walls, a small forest of apple trees, and fields for planting, it was picturesque and yet functional. It spoke of age and generations, with worn stone pathways and gnarled roots along the orchard rows. It was well lived in and yet made for the purpose of protection.

"I'm sorry. Nothing looks familiar."

Liam's wings drooped, and he smiled courageously. "It will come to you."

I was following Liam toward the main building when he tilted and grabbed for the wall to steady himself.

"What's the matter? Are you hurt?" I gently touched his back, where a red fist-sized welt glared near a kidney. "Liam, I had no idea you got hit so hard. That's going to turn into a nasty bruise."

"You were also hit hard. I am sorry. It is already starting to show color."

I touched my own face where it still ached from the fight the night before, and I joked, "Yeah, I always meant to work on keeping my right up."

"Right up to what?"

"Nothing. Never mind." I reached to put one of his arms over my shoulder. "You can clearly fly, but can you walk?"

He sighed. "I am not hurt so much as weak. I must eat soon."

I hadn't even thought of that. He had been working to keep us both in the air, doubling the already-tremendous amount of energy it must take to fly…especially since we'd flown straight through the night. I was starving, so he must be famished.

"Are we going to meet your parents?" I asked. "I haven't been to meet a man's parents in years," I joked, trying to keep the mood light as we hobbled together over the lawn. "Are they nice?"

"Of course," Liam said. "They have always liked you, Fable. You were much a part of the family."

So much that I can't actually remember it.

We stopped at the front door. Liam hammered the bronze knocker in the shape of an eagle holding a heavy ring in its beak. Then he pushed the door and entered.

An Avian crone, her back bent with age and wings stiff, shuffled into the entry with a happy shrill. She moved as though her joints pained her, and her pale, cloudy eyes looked us up and down.

"Children, your father is waiting upstairs in the Red dining room."

"Noel, it is good to see you! Next time you tell my father to get the door. He shouldn't be making you take the stairs."

"Hush, child, I was already down here waiting for you." The old woman grinned, revealing an absence of teeth. "Fable? Is that you?"

I stepped toward her and she took me into her arms. "It does my heart good to see you well." Her *S* whistled without teeth, and she rocked me from side to side, downy gray hair tickling my neck. "When you get done with all your important business, you come back down here and catch up with an old Kestrel."

I nodded, praying to god I could remember her when the moment came.

Liam was already climbing the stairs. He paused on the landing to wait for me. The steps were slick with wear, the brown stones polished and glossy where hundreds of talons had tread. My boots slipped, forcing me to grip the railing as I climbed to catch up.

• • •

I noticed the overwhelming color palette upon walking in, highlighted by a gold gilt ceiling and fixtures. The Red dining room was so named, I assumed, because all the tapestries and furniture were upholstered in monochromatic scarlet hues.

The Avian man standing before the open cathedral windows had to be Liam's father, Gunthor. As he turned to greet us, I noticed the resemblance in his nose and deep-set eyes. His long white hair had probably once been like Liam's, and his dark brown wings were tipped with more white. He was the very image of a majestic bald eagle and man.

Gunthor left his spot at the window. I fought the urge to step backward and locked my knees to keep from moving under the intimidating gaze of a bird of prey.

"Fable," he said, his voice like the surf far below. "It is our honor to have you once again in our home."

"Is she here yet?" a feminine voice called out from the hallway. The door opened behind us, and a woman's squeal interrupted what Gunthor was about to say. "Fable! You are home!"

"Sybil?" The name came to my lips from the shadows of my mind without effort.

She ran at me, a tornado of billowing green satin, brown feathers, and a red tower of hair.

I knew her. But I had only ever met her in a dream.

A strong sense of recognition without context, love without knowledge of why or whom, and joy of reunion without the awareness of separation, flooded me as we threw our arms around one another. I giggled happily, hugging her with tremendous, powerful relief.

"How long can you stay? What has happened since last I saw you?" Sybil burbled questions faster than I could understand, her accented vowels thick, her voice clogged with emotion.

"Let the girl talk, Sybil. By Styx, she hasn't even had a chance to sit down," Gunthor said.

There was much commotion and surreal reunioning. It was surreal because for them it was as though I'd just come home to my dearest loved ones, and for me—well, I didn't know who the hell they were.

River, Liam's mother, entered and pried Sybil off me long enough to squeeze in her own hug. Between the two of them shooting questions at me faster than I could answer, I didn't see Noel arrive along with another Avian who reminded me of a finch, and together they served breakfast.

"Let her eat, Sybil," Gunthor commanded as he took his place at the head of the table.

Sybil didn't give me a chance to protest as she dragged me to a chair beside her and started dishing food onto my plate. Glancing around, I noted Liam was gone and a sudden panic erupted.

I don't know these people. How could he leave me alone with them?

Just then he returned. He'd changed out of his jeans and into a dark red skirt-like wrap. It was a piece of clothing I would have expected to see on a samurai, all drapes and folds down to the floor, leaving his chest bare, wings free.

"Thank the goddess you changed out of those vulgar pants," said River with a delicate shudder. Her hair had long gone white, and her ivory skin and dark wings gave her an austere yet exotic presence.

As they ate, I pushed my food around on my plate, not really sure what it was, a paste of seeds with spices and chunks of gray chewy bits. I nibbled, but the gritty texture and odd bitterness put me off. I was starving but not hungry enough to eat whatever it was.

When Noel put a plate of muffins in the center of the table, I gratefully helped myself to something I recognized while I listened to them talk. The muffins were delicious, sweet, and warm, with a strange grainy quality.

"The Ryders are gathering strength along their boarders. A strike into Valkyrie territory is imminent," Gunthor told Liam.

Liam swallowed. "They wouldn't dare before the Ice Cap Treaty is fulfilled." He glanced at me before looking at his plate.

Sybil rubbed my shoulder as though comforting me, and I noticed River and Gunthor gazing at me as well.

"These muffins are delicious," I offered weakly.

They looked away.

Did I miss something?

"You've been gone for several months and the Northern negotiations have intensified. The Minotaur are contemplating treaty at last," River said to Liam.

"The Norns are threatening still to join with Xabien and take Ice Cap," said Sybil as she slathered bright orange jelly on an open biscuit. "Although I believe they are waiting to make their final decision until after the Council lays down the terms of new Northern borders—much of which will be determined by the treaty."

"We will have full war. My son, you have returned at a delicate time," Gunthor said with a beleaguered sigh. "How is Gabriel?"

"Gabe is well, Father." Liam nodded. "He and the Talons have proved invaluable to the Earth movement. He has done much you would be proud of."

Gunthor grunted.

Liam swallowed and dished a second plate, eating as they talked. "Father, you must call a meeting for the Sublime. There's much Fable and I must tell them. It could change the course of our involvement in these events."

"A meeting was called the moment I heard you'd entered the Gate. They arrive this afternoon."

Sybil fingered the fabric of my sleeve. "What is this?"

"It's a T-shirt."

"Yes, a shirt, but what is this material? It is so soft."

"You've barely touched your plate." River said. "Do you not prefer Avian food? Is there something from Earth we can prepare for you to help you feel more at home? Perhaps some coffee?"

"Coffee would be a lifesaver." I barely had a chance to answer before River ordered the finch to bring me some coffee.

"Anything else? You have but to name it. Would you like more of the eel?"

My stomach turned when I realized what I'd just been picking at.

"Some pit-zza?" River asked. "Celeste showed us the recipe and said it is a great favorite on your side of the veil. Please just ask, and you shall have it." She smiled, and I was struck by how much she looked like Sybil.

Protein sounded palatable. "I'm fine, really. Or, well, maybe just a couple of scrambled eggs, if—"

Sybil's fork clattered to the china. Noel gasped.

"If it's no trouble…" I trailed off.

The room was silent. Paralyzed. I glanced at Liam, who looked pale, shaking his head ever so slightly. Expressions ranged from disgust to horror, embarrassment to fear. I froze.

Eggs, jackass. You asked bird people for eggs. Might as well have asked for a plate of scrambled children on sourdough.

"I'm sorry." I stalled. "I mean an egg of…butter. You know, a butter egg?"

Really? A butter egg?

Gunthor spoke tight, politically. "We are unfamiliar with butter eggs. Please explain precisely what you mean."

Yes, Fable, do explain.

"Well, it's the new rage on my side of the veil, to, um, to have a pat of butter shaped like a small egg. They put it on a slab of toast and smear it. Do you have toast on Aria?"

Everyone glanced at Liam, who presumably had spent the most time on my side of the two worlds. "It's true," he said, "the butter-shaped egg on toast is the new thing. It was thought up by those they call *veg-e-tarians*. Yes, Fable, we do have toast on Aria."

A collective sigh of relief and "oohs" filled the room.

"What an odd and vulgar culinary custom," Sybil said, perplexed. "I'm sure Earth has many harmlessly barbaric traditions. I cannot wait to hear about them all!"

Liam sighed and dished himself another plate, but he met my eyes with a look that seemed to plead for breakfast to be over soon.

"I didn't mean to be a difficult guest," I said. "I'm fine, really, the eel's delicious."

"For tomorrow's breakfast, then, we shall all try this new way of eating buttered toast!" River proclaimed.

The rest of breakfast passed uneventful. I ate every bite of the revolting eel, hoping to draw suspicion away from my blunder, and when the finch brought me a steaming cup of black coffee, I could have kissed him.

Mostly I simply answered questions about Oregon, school, college, working in New York, and a surprising number of questions about "the cinema."

"Oh! New York!" Sybil sighed. "Did you ride the subway train? Were there a great many taxied cabs? How romantic."

"Yes there are many cabs, and I did ride the subway."

I opened my mouth to tell them all about the day Liam had saved my life in the subway, but his head shook a subtle warning, and I finished with, "Yes, New York is very romantic."

When the dishes were cleared away, Gunthor stood and walked to the window with a mug of dark liquid. It smelled hoppy, like a kind of warm beer. The finch gave mugs to Liam and Sybil, but River passed, and she shook her head, warning him away before he could ask me.

"*Uroosh* is too heavy for human blood. It is a drink to keep up strength for flying," River whispered. "Would you like more coffee?"

"The time for catching up and pleasantries must be put aside," Gunthor said, "as we are expecting company for affairs of state. Fable, when they arrive, I must ask you to recount for us all that has happened since Celeste's brutal murder and your arrival here.

All you know of the Muses and the threats. Liam, you as well." Gunthor exhaled, curling the steam from his mug outward. "I never believed it could happen in my lifetime."

"Who are they?" I wondered.

"A few select members of our order hail from the Council Minor. Others are allies from tribes and clans around Aria. The Sublime are mostly heads of state, warlords, and leaders who support, unequivocally, the Law of Nine."

He stood behind River, absently stroking her wing. "I am sad to say we are not the majority in that conviction."

I wasn't sure exactly what that meant or what it had to do with me, but I knew it was important.

"I can tell you everything I know," I agreed, "but I have a lot of questions."

"With the many of us present, perhaps one or all of us will have the answers you seek."

Later that afternoon, the delegation began arriving. Liam was catching up on sleep from our all-night flight, but I was too anxious and overwhelmed by details to close my eyes. Sybil showed me around her home while River fluttered around the house, issuing orders to staff and preparing for company.

"I wasn't certain you would return to us." Sybil leaned over the balcony of the fifth floor suite which Noel had prepared for my arrival with fresh autumn flowers and a plate of cookies.

"I'm not entirely sure I have," I mumbled, sniffing the flat round confection. "Ginger cookies are my favorite," I said.

"Don't sound so surprised," Sybil laughed, returning to my side. We stood in front of the mirror vanity. I looked so insignificant beside her otherworldly beauty and grace. "We all know your favorite things."

"But what if…? I mean—" I looked away. "What if the shielding altered *me*, my likes, my favorites, what I would have been."

"I'm quite sure it has," she agreed. "You are very different in how you speak, and even how you carry your body. We knew at the time that it might happen this way, but Celeste has kept us apprised of your life, your evolution. She brought us photographs and clippings of your work."

Sybil sat on the edge of the bed and her wings wilted to the sides of her feet. "It was very hard to let you go. Even though we were children and you knew it meant forgetting, and I knew it meant not being able to grow up with you—we were still young. I don't believe either of us comprehended *exactly* what that meant."

I picked a small violet crystal off the vanity. It was a familiar weight and size. I glanced around at the Avian furniture, at a bed too high for an average human with bedposts carved in a floral motif, a chaise lounge with no sides, so an Avian could relax without crushing her wings.

"You mean I agreed to it?" I wondered, setting the crystal back beside a silver-handled hairbrush.

"Yes, as much as you were able to understand."

"But why would I agree to give all this up?" I asked.

"You never told me exactly," Sybil said carefully. "But I believe you saw something, a vision of the future that you needed to forget. In truth, I'm not sure you really knew you would be gone so long. I sure didn't. You were my only friend."

She paused, and a feather drifted off her wing to settle on the black coverlet. Picking it up with slender fingers, she glanced in the mirror and tucked it in the hive of red curls atop her head. "You were my only confidant. I prayed you would return before I fledged so we could go flying together, but my feathers came in and I cried that you weren't here to see it."

She shrugged and smiled. "Although you probably would have laughed. My first set of down made me look like a fluff-dried turkey."

I smiled, able to visualize it.

"If it makes you feel any better," I sat on the bed beside her, "I didn't have friends my own age. I had the NaNas and Celeste. In college I tried to have boyfriends, but I always ended up being the girl that gay guys tried to go straight on. So until I moved to New York, I was pretty much alone in my own head, until I met Erik. I got engaged and started planning a sad future with him, but I realize now I never actually loved him—I just didn't want to die alone. So you see, you were never replaced."

Sybil cried out, "Icarus' wings! I would never have wanted that for you! I would never wish not to be replaced, if I knew you were all alone." She crushed me in a hug, wrapping silken wings around my body. "I was only able to let you go because I believed you would be safe, happy, and well loved!"

She shuddered against me and moaned in my neck. "I can feel all your years of not having a flock. It was awful. I'm so sorry."

As she cried, I awkwardly patted her shoulder, the shoulder of a stranger who was actually a long-lost best friend I couldn't remember.

Are they all this emotional?

"What do you mean when you say you can feel all my years?"

Sybil sat up; her wings shuffled and she wiped her nose. "I can feel your *sawyang*. The emotions of your spirit."

I shook my head. "What does that mean?"

"It is a kind of empathic gift. My *sawyin* is to influence another's *sawyang*, or experience their feelings." Shrugging, she touched my hand and I felt an overwhelming sense of peace and happiness for my own safety.

"What the…?"

"You can feel how happy I am that you are returned to us. Whole and well." She sniffed, and I felt an incongruent sense of loss. "I am sad that I lost so much time with you, and sadder still you had no friends to confide in, or loves to find joy with, while you were away."

Warm contentment spread through my body, and she continued. "But then, you are still safe, untouched by the Eventines, or the Sylphans, or the others who would harm you. So I guess, despite the memory loss, the shields did what they were designed to do—"

"So you're an Empath or something?" I pulled my hand away.

"I do not intentionally use my *sawyin* in a negative way, Fable. There are those who use *sawyawn* practices to alter the truth of an outcome or do damage to others by controlling them. I am not such a practitioner, and neither is my mother."

"River, too?"

"You knew all of this at one time, and you will remember again. But we are ever, as always, your friends."

"I will remember all of this?" I wondered in amazement. "It seems so impossible to forget."

Stoically, she adjusted her wings and sat taller. "Your memories will return, your powers will emerge, and everything will be as it was." She exhaled a cheerful sigh, wiped her eyes, and smiled. "Now, I have some paste that will hide your bruise."

Chapter Thirteen

Thirteen Pages

The entertainment hall on the ground floor of the castle was easily over 100 feet long, 50 wide, and had windows floor to ceiling, 40 feet up. The vast room featured six marble fireplaces and hundreds of bronze sconces on the wall every other stride. The hall was filled with nearly two dozen creatures I only knew from myths and fairy-tales. I blinked. Sybil pushed me into the room. I held my breath, wide-eyed.

A centaur's bulk: the scent of sunlit plains, horseflesh, and leather overwhelmed me. I flung my hands out to stop Sybil from pushing me into the side of a bay horse, but my hands were caught by those of a man—the man half of the horse—and I babbled, "Ohmigod. I'm so sorry. Wow! Ohmigod, that's so cool."

His hands steadied me. Huge hands. Hulking hands, that could have crushed my skull like a peanut. "Greetings, Maior. I am Anderon of the Silver Plains Clan. I welcome you home." His voice, a deep rumbling bass, reverberated in my chest like a diesel engine.

"Thank you," I said. "I'm Fable. So cool to meet you!"

Craning my neck as far back as it would go, I took in his dark skin, the same shade as his bay coat. He wore his black mane in thick braids, woven with flax. Anderon's face was angular and broad, with deep black eyes and a wide grinning mouth. Sword straps crossed his chest, their hilts sticking up above his shoulders, and he was chorded in muscle from head to flank. He even wore steel shod shoes, tipped with spikes.

Thank god he's on our side.

Liam joined me, having pushed his way forward. "I see you've met Anderon, our centaur representative."

The men nodded to each other before Liam led me away. I glanced back and gave a little wave. Anderon waved back awkwardly.

We passed Delia, who I was grateful to see. She looked well, no worse the wear for the Avian attacker the night before, and I was comforted to see a familiar face, but wondered how she'd arrived so quickly, since she couldn't fly. Liam led me to a chair by his father on a dais. My purse, which I'd left at Delia's in our mad dash escape, sat on the floor beside my seat. I smiled at the White Crow Avian and mouthed a quiet, "Thank you."

She smiled and nodded.

I sat before the congregation. Dozens of eyes bored into me: large watery eyes, small dark eyes, wolf-like eyes, oversized and glittering. Avians, centaurs, creatures of two species, a tree-lady, an elk-man, and a woman with the body of a snake. There were fairies, nymphs, and a man with two faces.

An iridescent blur and high-pitched buzz streaked to the front of the room. Agatha flew in at the last moment, zipping to a perch on the table near the front of the gathering. I smiled, happy to see another familiar face. She rolled her eyes.

Silence settled over the hall as Sybil closed the giant double doors. The electricity in the air made the hair on my arms stand up. Clothing rustled and a few clips of hoof on stone echoed as they all took their seats. Everyone except for Anderon, who stood near the back of the group.

Gunthor stood at the front of the dais. "As you all know, the Convergence is upon us. We are in the last years of the Great Cycle, and time has blessed us with the return of one of our lost daughters of Mnemosyne." Gunthor's voice carried over the group. "Fable has come home."

There was a resounding, deafening…silence.

My senses swam in a room of feathers, silk, hooves, and antlers, heady with the scent of deep woods and musky beasts. Like a bouquet of flowers in profusion of summer bloom, beautiful but overwhelming, I saw it all and felt only detached amazement, as though I were sitting in a theater watching an elaborate play.

I tried to take it in, but the magnitude of all I had seen and all that stood before me was too immense. All I could focus on were snippets, small details. My mind rejected the sensory overload. So I noted wings, all shapes and sizes of wings: blue feathers, grey feathers, long willowy white feathers, short hard black feathers. I noted iridescent blue-green butterfly wings on a Sprite, lucid opaque wings on a Dryad, and the leathery bat wings of a small gargoyle-like creature.

I thought of my tattoo: a pair of wings from my first summer in college. Each wing was the size of my hand, placed along my spine between my shoulder blades. They were just black stylized ink outlines of feathery limbs, but I'd felt so much more complete after the ink filled in a hollow part of myself. Even when they were still tender and red, I'd smiled, finally centered in my body for just a few artistic etchings on my skin. The artist had asked if there was any symbolism in my tattoo choice, and I'd said, "No. I just like them. I see them in my dreams and draw them on all my notebooks." I hypothesized they meant escape, or freedom, or maybe release.

I dreamt in feathers and wings. I dreamt of home and didn't know it.

"Half of our brethren are unable to be here, so we must get word of what we learn tonight to our sources," Gunthor continued. "Liam and Fable bring news."

Liam stood and reached for me to step before the assembly. I took his outstretched hand, finding anchorage in his warm, calloused touch. My free hand sought my lucky pendant, and I clutched it for all it was worth.

"I present to you Fable Rose Augustine Montgomery, daughter of Angelica and Clark, ward of Celeste Augustine, and Maior of the art of Epic Story."

A murmur of voices followed his announcement. Liam's fingers curled around my own, his silky wing braced my back.

"Ordinarily our customs would dictate that each one of us receive you in a line and pay respects as well as welcome, but we are not in ordinary times, and sadly we are pressed to quickly deliver the news," Liam said, for my benefit.

"I disagree, Maior," a voice from the end of the second bench called out. A six-foot man with a full rack of antlers stood. He was dressed in clothing made of buckskin, and his gray hair was woven around horns sprouting from his temples. He made his way in front of the group. His features were graceful and thin, made for speed and stealth.

Liam clenched his jaw and flexed his wings but made no move to stop him.

"Taereath, of the Heartland Northern Herds, Fable of Montgomery," Taereath said as he curtsied in front of me, taking pains to protect my eyes from his sharp antlers. "In times of war, I believe it is more necessary than ever to protect the customs of the lands for which we fight."

Reaching into a buckskin satchel, he retrieved a small, delicately wrought wooden carving of a doe. He held it out for me. "Please accept our welcome, and a token of friendship from our herds."

His warm, brown eyes and earnest demeanor prompted me to reach out and accept the beautiful figurine. It settled into my palm.

Immediately I sensed the thundering earthquake of thousands of hooves across the tundra. My heartbeat quickened and air burned my lungs with winter breath. The ground shook.

Then I stood before the gathering of Sublime, heart racing, the ecstasy and freedom of endless tundra and forever-skies lingered in my veins like a glorious promise.

Liam watched me quizzically, brows furrowed.

"Taereath," I said breathlessly, still feeling the distant jarring of a stampeding herd.

"You hear the story she speaks." He smiled knowingly. "This is good. Our gift to you, Maior, is a touchstone of the Northern Wilds in appreciation of your sacrifice."

Sacrifice?

"Thank you," I said. "That's amazing. Thank you."

Taereath curtsied again, antlers swinging dangerously close to my face before he returned to his seat—but not before all the others had formed a line before me.

"It seems a welcoming will happen," Gunthor said. I hadn't even noticed his approach. "Taereath, you speak true. In times of war, it is more important than ever we preserve our customs."

One by one, the members of Sublime came forward to offer gifts and welcome me home. At first I was embarrassed by the attention, even intimidated by some of the creatures. Varia was a woman with the body of a snake. Her torso was an emerald stretch of scales, and her shoulders and breasts were clothed in liquid golden fabric. She slithered upright toward me, and I thought of the story of Medusa and was afraid at first to look at her; but once I did, I saw she was actually quite beautiful. Exotic and graceful.

"Please accept the welcome of my people and our token of your homecoming." Varia's voice lingered on her *S* and she blinked at me, the lids of her eyes closing sideways.

I took the bracelet she offered, a weighty piece of gold jewelry that jingled. She insisted on clasping it around my wrist. At once I was baked by desert heat. I felt sand against my skin and radiant light all around. I gasped.

"We are pleased you like it," she said, her long tail coiling around my leg.

"Thank you, Varia," I said and meant it, soaking in the eternal sigh of wind against dunes and the shrilling voices of belly dancers in a faraway land. She bobbed her head once and turned away, her tail caressing my thighs before she returned to her seat.

Amazement quickly overturned fear, and I desperately wished I had my camera. Why had I been so worried? I stared. Gaped. Fought the urge to reach out and touch them, caress wings, touch the point of a horn, or stroke a furry pelt. What I wouldn't have given to take pictures of the man who walked to the front of the room with a huge gray wolf that stood to his shoulder.

"Maior, I, Jespin, and my brother Warren welcome you home." The man wore tight leather clothing and carried a broad staff. He offered a threaded bone fishing hook on a twisted cord of leather.

I took it carefully, eyeing the monstrous wolf. It lolled its tongue and appeared to smile before dropping to its haunches and tilting its head. I closed my eyes and felt along the smooth edges of the bone hook. My fingers slipped into the groove and in that moment I heard the howling cries of a winter pack.

I opened my eyes to the great hall. The wolf whimpered and threw back its head with a long rumbling yowl. Then he stepped forward, sniffed me with a snort that lifted the hair off my shoulders, and I heard him speak in my mind, *Well received, little sister.*

My mouth fell open as they turned to leave, and I stammered, "Thanks."

Within an hour I'd met dignitaries of herds, flocks, packs, and prides. I'd become acquainted with fairies and nymphs, and even a gargoyle. The menagerie of creatures suddenly had names. The 20 races and cultures present were more like potential neighbors than hordes of mysterious threats.

The last in the receiving line was a nymph. She was everything I'd ever imagined the mythical race to be: small and willowy, wreathed in cascades of black satin hair, olive skin, and clothed in diaphanous teal robes.

"I am Lucina. Welcome home, Maior. Please accept this token of favor."

I had to lean in to hear her clearly as I reached to take the crystal chalice she offered. I took the strange cup with thanks, examining the craftsmanship of the chalice that appeared to be carved from one piece of clear quartz.

Suddenly I was being held under water. I thrashed and kicked, but I was pinned down. Clouds of blood drifted through the water as I fought to free myself from the weight holding me under.

Panic. Terror. Pain.

Then familiar faces in the hall peered back. Air flooded my lungs and I choked, gasping. The crystal chalice slipped from my fingers, tumbling toward the stone. Liam caught it as I clutched my throat, wheezing.

I stared at Lucina in horror. Her dark eyes widened. She curtsied and rushed back to her seat.

Gunthor was already approaching the front of the room to speak. "Brothers and sisters, thank you all for observing the homecoming customs. Taereath, we thank you for insisting." He raised his hands. "Now we must talk of more unpleasant topics."

While Liam placed the chalice on the table of gifts, I scanned the faces of the crowd. How could they not have seen that? But the exchange appeared to have gone largely unnoticed, as folks had been in whispered conversations with one another.

The only indication that I'd been gifted an object of some terrible fate came from the astute eyes of Jespin and Warren, who watched me closely. Liam came to stand behind me again. He placed a hand on my shoulder, squeezing softly.

Light spilled through the windows, burnishing the room with late afternoon glow. The size of the space made the gathering seem smaller than it had before. It was just a chalice, I told myself—not a bloody sword or a weapon of mass destruction.

I tried to focus on the room, chiding myself for being so shaken. A scattering of statues decorated the hall, marble effigies of Avians in aerial combat. The one directly across the hall from where I stood sported a broken wing tip.

"Liam, my son, has been stationed on Earth as Fable's Guardian, and what he has seen must be discussed." Gunthor left Liam and I standing at the front and returned to his chair.

Liam waited for the resulting murmurs to die down and quiet to return to the room. Then he said evenly, "The Glade Armistice has been compromised."

Five heartbeats of spectacular silence passed, then dozens of voices rose in angry disbelief.

"Silence. Hold for news!" Gunthor shouted. "He speaks the truth! Hear them out."

Disgruntled stillness filled the space, and Liam continued. "The Glade Café, where all living things are welcomed in peace, fell under attack yesterday morning by a murder of crows."

Gasps and shocked whispers erupted.

"The Glade is also the entrance for the Interioria Gate. While no one was mortally wounded, many humans were injured, and Fable herself was nearly killed."

"Outrage!" Anderon shouted. "Who is to blame?"

"Listen, and I believe we will have answers," Liam continued. "Fable has written a manuscript. I believe this collection of writings was the actual target. All that remains of the 240 pages are these 13 sheets of paper." He pulled the rumpled documents from the folds of fabric binding around his waist, revealing the loose pages of the manuscript covered with blood and dirt and syrup. "These last pages are what remain of our hope of finding the other Muses."

He held them out to me. "Fable, will you please?"

What? Me?

"Uh…" Skimming over the crowd of expectant eyes, I took the pile of papers of out Liam's hand, shuffling the loose pages, stalling.

"I guess I could just read to you what they say." Suddenly insecure, I felt the need to explain. "But you know, keep in mind I haven't edited anything. These are only random parts out of context; I wasn't really focused on character development or structure, I was just trying to get it out while I could so, you know, it's…well, it's a rough draft."

"Just read it," Liam begged.

"Um, well, okay."

I frowned, took a deep breath, and read.

"Page number 38. *Abra sat at the table outside the Glade Café, smoking a hand-rolled cigarette…*"

I continued reading aloud and found it strange that I knew the words on the page not because I remembered writing them but because I'd lived them: *"From around the corner of the building, a flock of crows burst outward like black and crimson cannon confetti. They swooped in a mass toward the road, then as if by some practiced carnival trick, they veered in unison like a deadly cloud directly toward me."*

I was both in the story and outside of it, watching. Like a dream. After a couple of pages, my confidence grew and I found myself projecting my voice and adding a cadence to my tone.

Standing before a crowd, speaking, felt right. Maybe it was the years of drama in high school, but for just a moment, as I recited out loud before a congregation, I imagined myself as a storyteller of old, dressed in Hellenic robes in a circular amphitheater, regaling the masses with an epic tale.

It was so vivid, like a memory, as if at one time in my life I had actually been a bardic storyteller of yore. My voice stammered, and I trailed to a stop, confused.

I was not in an amphitheater beneath the vibrant skybowl. I was not dressed in swaged white folds or speaking to thousands, but reading before a group of 20 in what was once an opulent gathering hall that showed signs of wear. Not a sky above, but a gold-painted ceiling, flaking and chipped. Not an open hillside, but walls lined with portraits and windows. Not robes, but jeans and a T-shirt.

"Are you well?" Liam asked.

It had seemed so real. Nodding, I tucked the page I was reading behind the stack and continued. *"I glanced around at the carnage of a wrecked city bus and a green SUV. People in the streets were being bombarded by crows. A man pounded on the door of the bus to be let in as wild birds mauled his face."*

I peeked up from reading from time to time and saw the rapt faces of those present. Anderon leaned forward. Varia swayed from side to side, listening intently. When I read, the feeling returned that I was not in the hall. I could feel sun on my hair, a breeze lifting the hem of my dress. I felt as though I'd done this all before, perhaps a thousand times.

"...like a bizarre terrorist attack of glass, black feathers and blood." I finished the last sentence of the first five pages and blinked. I stood again in the great hall.

The room erupted in a cacophony of heated conversations.

"The Glade Armistice has been broken!" Taereath hissed.

"Is Abra working for Xabien?" Varia wondered.

"Is Abra the creature responsible for Celeste's murder?" Carilynda asked.

"If Abra and Xabien are in alliance, this attack on the Glade Armistice would nullify the Ice Cap Treaty with Xabien as well!" Jespin shouted.

Questions, curses, and the clip of hooves on stone echoed through the hall.

"Silence!" Gunthor yelled, coming to his taloned feet. "Silence! Let her speak!"

The room rumbled to a murmur then to quiet.

"Fable," called Taereath, his antlers bobbing with each movement of his head, "is this a work of prophecy you have written?"

My mouth dropped open. "Prophecy? Me? No."

The murmur started up again.

"But you wrote these pages prior to the events, is that not so?" Anderon shouted from the rear of the group.

"Well, yes, that's true," I said.

"Then it is prophecy," Varia agreed. "*The Prophecy of Crows*."

"Wait, no," I countered. "I don't actually believe in prophecies."

It was like I'd fired a live gunshot over the crowd. They froze and stared at me, wide-eyed.

"Fable," Liam began gently.

"No, seriously," I said, "I believe the future can be altered."

Silence.

"Think about it: If there's such thing as prophecy—and it's going to be accurate—then there would have to be thousands of versions of the prophecy to account for the thousands of variables of choice, human error, folly, and all the unforeseen probabilities or interpretations. Right?"

Silence. Followed by more awkward silence.

I glanced at Liam for support, but he furrowed his eyebrows at me and tilted his head.

"Okay," I continued, "I admit it was spooky and weird that I wrote this and then it happened. But think of it this way: I wrote it maybe two days before the events; that's not a lot of time for a significant amount of variables to take place. Let's pretend for just a tiny minute these five pages are some kind of outline, and I could, you know, psychically predict anything—and I'm not saying I can. But a two-day head start doesn't give much time to make a difference to anything."

Even as I spoke I realized I actually believed what I was saying. I paced in front of the crowd, explaining, "If I were writing a fiction novel and I knew my characters, I'd be able to estimate, based on their character, where they might go and what they might do—but this is real life, and people aren't characters, and they don't always do what you think they are going to do…"

"Yet you did write it?" Jespin asked.

I exhaled with a whoosh. "Yes."

The crowd began talking over one another. A buzz of conversation made the hall seem smaller than it actually was. Pillars around the room supported sculpted busts. The evergreen velvet curtains pooled on the floors near the windows. Looking closer, I realized many of the drapes were moth-eaten and worn.

"Perhaps the remaining pages will have answers," Gunthor suggested, and the idea swept through the room, drawing down the quiet so I might continue.

"Please, read us more," Varia hissed, her tail coiling around her body.

Exhaling, I tucked the front page at the back of the stack and continued.

"Okay," I said, clearing my throat. "Page 87. *The moon rose, luminous and full, shining a silver path over the still ocean toward the mourners. The Canto Mors Mortis, loosely translated to Song of Death or Singing the Dead, began first when two dozen Avians circled around the pyre quickly engulfed in flames.*

"*Fire licked upward toward the stars, reaching for the skybowl as the Avians turned their backs to the pyre.*

"*Kal crooned the first note, deep and soulful, holding the resonant tone for a beat of 20 before moving his black wings in slow undulation. The Avian to his right harmonized with his tone, carrying the song. Each Avian in the circle took up a turn and began the slow flap of their wings against the flames. When the motion went around the circle once, the note changed and the beat of wings increased from an undulation to a regular tempo. Two dozen Avian wings moved in a wave, spiraling the air current counter-clockwise. Gently, rhythmically, until the harmony changed and a drum beat echoed from behind the gathering, resonant and deep.*

"*As the drums began, so too did the song of the gathered mourners, carried on the drafts of minor chords, longingly, reverently. Sung with breaths and feathers, wings and soul. The counter spiral of the air around the pyre teased the flames into a funnel of fire, each revolution driving the conflagration higher, spinning the orange-gold filaments toward sky and illuminating the Weaving Fates as they worked their loom of starry destinies.*

"Canto Mors Mortis echoed across the black ocean. A song of passing sung by all gathered to put a soul to rest, free of regrets, beloved of family, and with gratitude expressed. All who raised voice to the Canto sang their forgiveness of all transgressions, their hopes for the blessed afterlife of the soul, and the last goodbyes to one they held dear."

I finished the page and gazed over the crowd. Grief hung in the air like the scent of earth before a storm.

"Who have we lost?" Delia asked softly, her pale white wings were draped across the floor near her chair. "The Canto Mors Mortis is reserved for Avians. Who has been lost…or will be lost to us?"

I wished I knew.

Please god, not Liam.

"I don't know," I said. "I really, truly wish I could say, but I have no idea if this page is like the others. I just don't know."

"Perhaps this Canto Mors Mortis is being sung for Celeste," offered Gunthor carefully. "I can only hope it is for she; after all, Kal was the singer mentioned on the page, and he would preside over her rites."

"Why?" I wondered. "Who's Kal?"

All eyes were on me as Gunthor replied, "Kal is Celeste's mate these 30 years. He, by law, is the first to sing her to the other world."

I could not have been more astonished. "Celeste is *married*?" It was like finding out I had a lost sibling, or that I was born in Canada.

"Fable, I know you are surprised, but you know Kal and you know of their life together. Please just trust that you will remember." Gunthor spread a wing behind me.

Shocked, I tried to remember Auntie Celeste with a man. Ever. I couldn't. I couldn't recall her ever having had a boyfriend, a lover, an interest of any kind. A vast sadness opened up as I realized, she had a lover, someone from Aria she couldn't be with…because she'd been busy watching out for me on Earth.

My heart broke for her. For them.

"There is still no certainty that this funeral rite is for Celeste," Anderon was saying.

"It is the easiest answer, but also unsettling," Carilynda, of the Low Plain Swamps, added. Her slick grey skin and large wide eyes made her appear partly amphibious and partly human. "The troubling part of that answer lies in the timeline. If it is Celeste's funeral on the page 87, and the crow attack happened on 38 to 42, then, chronologically, tomorrow is page 87—for Celeste's rites are to be performed tomorrow. Therefore, all pages after are yet to happen."

The room bubbled up in chatter and commentary, arguments, and theories.

Liam rubbed his eyes. "Maybe the other pages will reveal more clues."

The rectangles of light from the tall windows began to slant, turning the afternoon toward evening as shadows darkened the corners.

Varia hissed, her snake torso swiveling back and forth. "Which page comes next in the order? Please read more to us from the *Prophecy of Crows*."

"Page 120 and 121 half," I replied. "Page 121 is a half-page, probably for a Chapter break."

"Please continue, Fable." Taereath adjusted his bulk in his chair and tipped his head to listen.

I cleared my throat and continued. "*Maya stepped up to the door of the house at the end of Thurman Street. Crinkling her nose at the dead mice on the mat, she poked at the doorbell button and stepped back.*

"*From outside, she could hear the brassy chorus ringing through the home. A long delay followed while she shuffled. It was the address Celeste had given her. This had to be the place. Safety. Celeste had promised.*

"*It was risky, coming to a stranger, but what choice did she have? A few weeks ago, her life had completely fallen apart. Her boyfriend had turned up dead in Seattle's harbor, and her little sister vanished from* school. The cops thought Maya was responsible. No one was even looking for her sister because they had already made up their minds about who was guilty. Gutter punk. Homeless. Orphan junkie. She'd heard it all before.

"She'd met Celeste in a little French patisserie near Pike's Market a few days before Maya's whole life came crumbling down. It was the last normal conversation in a coffee shop Maya could remember.

"Celeste approached her while she was jotting down some notes at the table. She'd complimented Maya's knee-high leather boots, and Maya thought the old woman was going to try and sell her a bible, but instead she started talking about the book Maya left sitting in the chair—Emily Dickenson. Then they started talking about rhyme and poetry, and soon the two were chatting up a storm. For an old lady, they'd just clicked.

"Before she left, Celeste had given Maya her phone number and address in Portland, and said, 'If you ever need a safe place to work on your chapbook or poetry, come stay with me for a while. I would love to have you, and you really must meet my niece. You're peas in a pod.'

"Maya glanced around as she stood on the porch of the house in Portland. It had taken all her courage and the last five bucks to her name to hitchhike from Seattle.

"She thumbed the doorbell again. 'Please be home, Celeste.'

"Maya didn't know why she trusted the old woman, or why she'd risk running to a stranger she'd only met once in a coffee shop and hope she wouldn't turn her over to the cops. She didn't understand any of it, but she knew that if she couldn't find someone to help her, and soon, she couldn't run anymore—and then there wouldn't be anyone left to find her sister. Maya was out of ideas.

"She heard footsteps coming from inside the house toward the door. Hope surged in a desperate wave, up the back of her spine as the knob turned.

"But the person who answered the door was not Celeste. Not Celeste at all.

"'Holy shit!'" Maya screeched.

I finished reading. Puzzled expressions and worry creased the lines of half a dozen faces.

"Maya?" the name was whispered over and over. "Maya?"

"Is Maya a Muse?" Delia wondered.

"What does it mean?" Jespin asked.

I shrugged. "I don't know, but by the description of the house, it's most definitely Celeste's home."

"I agree," Agatha said. She flitted up, bobbing around restlessly before returning to her seat.

"You do not remember who she sees when she opens the door?" Gunthor wondered. "You wrote it. Do you not remember?"

Shaking my head, I felt like a failure. "I wrote this all in a fog. I can recall some images here and there. A setting, but no context." I shrugged and mumbled, "It was like a trance or something. I went in and wrote and came out and had only the pages to remind me."

A murmur of voices buzzed around my declaration. I sighed and glanced off at the windows while they spoke to each other in hushed tones, discussing Maya and the possible reasons she'd shown up in my story.

Outside, the flourishing lawns beneath the trees beckoned, powerfully inviting. I hadn't slept in the last 24 hours. The second I realized it had been that long, I began to feel gravity and developed a hyper-awareness of my joints. A little nap on the grass as the sun was going down would work wonders.

"Fable, please read the next page, and perhaps it will give us context as to who Maya is and whether or not she holds any importance for our cause," Delia suggested. She resituated herself in her seat, which was far too large for her small frame, and her wings hung to either side like akimbo umbrella spokes at broken, awkward angles.

"The next set of pages are 140 and 141."

"Please continue," Gunthor agreed. "We can piece together what we may, when we have heard all you have to tell us."

"Okay," I took a breath. "Page 140.

"*Special Agent Drake walked through the hospital halls. People moved away from his hard stride and dark expression. The elevator was empty, and Drake took the opportunity to check the strap on his holster. Adjusting his gun under his jacket gave him a new sense of control. He took a deep breath before the doors opened and found himself in a hall with a dusty rose wallpaper border. He made his way down the corridor to the room under guard by two armed officers.*

"*The first, Officer Bradley, a baby-faced young man with a cleft chin and round gray eyes, checked Special Agent Drake's badge then stepped aside to let him in the room.*

"*'Anyone in or out?' Drake asked.*

"*'Just the old ladies,' Officer Bradley replied.*

"*Drake stepped inside and closed the door behind him, his heart in his throat.*

"*She lay in bed, wired to a saline drip and heart monitor cables. The steady beep of machinery gave the illusion of stability, but her sleeping form was a testament to his failure to protect her. Pulling up a chair, he sat by the bed and took her hand in his.*

"*'Fable, what happened?'*

"*He should have been there. She'd collapsed in her cell. The cell he thought would scare her into talking, giving up something useful, or at the very least keep her locked away from whoever was snatching up women. Hiding her away for a day was supposed to buy him some time and keep her protected.*

"*'You were supposed to be safe. What happened?' He held her hand. Her fingers were soft and pale. 'You are safe for now' he murmured.*

"*The doctors were saying it was some kind of poison that mimicked arsenic. Possibly ingested. It might have been something she ate. Since she'd been searched before she was put in holding, and she was fine the day before, it must have been something she ate in the cell—something she got a hold of, or something someone gave her. He'd find out one way or another.*

"*Until the blood tests came back, they wouldn't know for sure.*

"'I…' Drake whispered.

"Fable's fingers moved, sluggishly uncoordinated. Her green eyes fluttered open and for a moment she struggled to focus her gaze. Drake squeezed her fingers gently.

"But the effort of waking was too much, and Fable drifted back to sleep."

"This is an outrage!" Anderon shouted. "A Muse has been poisoned? I declare a tribunal!"

"It hasn't happened yet," Delia said forcefully. "Be quite and listen."

"But I too am concerned. The ramifications of these last two pages…" Carilynda's words were long and drawn out, stretched whisper-fine.

"Be calm! This has not happened and may yet be prevented! Let us hear more before we discuss each page," Taereath interjected.

Between grumbles and glares, all eyes turned expectantly to me.

Knowing what happened at the café, and considering what would potentially happen in the future, my stomach felt like a batch of night crawlers before a fishing trip. Was it even possible the last couple of pages could happen? Could it actually be prevented?

You don't believe in prophecy, huh?

I shivered.

"Fable."

"Right." I took a deep breath. "This one is also only half a page. Anyway, page 191.

"*Clark gently brushed the dirt off his latest find with worshipful reverence. At last. He wanted to scream. Shout. Jump up and down. But it was too soon to celebrate—the bowl would need to be cleaned and the runes examined before a positive identification could be made.*

"*But this could be it. Finally.*

"*Carefully, as though handling the most fragile and precious object in the world—because that's what it was—he used a fine detailing brush to dust the sides where clay-based soil still clung stubbornly to the ceramic.*

"As flakes of earth fell away, a design emerged.

"Nine girls holding hands, dancing as they circled the outside of the bowl. And on the inside, a panoramic scene of planets and suns in their tethered sky dance. In the center of the bowl, on the bottom, two worlds inside one another.

"The Lieat.

"Proof positive. The Lieat Sacramentum at last.

"Finally. There was hope."

"Who is this Clark?" Jespin wondered. "Who is this man who claims to have found the *Lieat*?"

"He does not claim it," Anderon replied. "It is Fable's prophecy."

"It's not my prophecy, and Clark is my father." I frowned as something tugged at my memory. "He's an archeologist in Siberia."

What does Dad have to do with all this?

"Why does he have the *Lieat*?" Jespin persisted. Warren lilted his large wolf head, one ear flicking forward.

I shrugged. Things were getting stranger by the page. What did my father have to do with Aria? Last I'd heard, his answering service was claiming he was in the deep tundra of Siberia, unreachable.

Every page I read confused me even more. There was no context to the events, no order or reason for anything to be happening as it was.

Gunthor held up his hands, wings flaring out to either side. "Please! Let us hold all our questions to the end. We are nearly finished; then we may be able to put the pieces together."

"Page 207," I read. "*Darkness. It even sounds dark, Harmony thought, pulling the sleeves of her hoody over her hands. It was the sound of darkness that bothered her the most. No scuffles or drags. No drips or echoes. Only the occasional sound of Handel's Hallelujah chorus, as though coming through the ground, resonated from the stone of the cavern from the other side of the planet through the earth then disappeared at random intervals. Then she realized she must be going crazy. Or maybe she was humming it to herself to fill in the darkness.*

"The air smelled like copper and tasted like moldering damp earth and metallic tanginess. It felt like months. Maybe it had only been days. Then again, a whole year could have passed. The only measurement of time she knew in the cold, dark caverns were the regular meals. Strangely, they were meals fit for royalty. While she rotted underground in some kind of abandoned mine with tattered blankets and a bucket in which to relieve herself, a creature brought her meals, served her fine wine, tender meats, and roasted vegetables. Well-seasoned foods, rich in flavor and texture that she would have expected to be eating at a fine restaurant with a six-month reservation wait.

"She'd asked the creature once, 'Are you planning to make me *into dinner? Am I some organically fed delicacy or entrée?'*

"The creature, four feet tall with slick scales and webbed fingers, answered with a bobbing nod, then a shake of its scaly blue head. Its eyes blinked sideways. Its forked tongue flicked its flat nose and it nodded again.

"'Do. You. Speak. English?'"

"The creature lifted its lamp. It shook its head then nodded.

"'Espanol? No?' Harmony chewed her lip, then said, 'Er…sprechen Sie…French?'

"Tilting its head, it leaned in and inhaled a long whistling breath. Then, to her horror, it licked her arm."

"Harmony, the name of a Muse," Taereath said. "She is one of the Nine?"

"Is she Maior, Fable?" Gunthor asked.

I held up my hands. "I don't know. But Celeste was helping the FBI track down a missing girl named Harmony."

"Another Muse stolen?" Delia whispered. "This does not bode well for any of us. We know of only one other."

173

"If you know about another, why haven't you rescued her yet?" I asked.

"She is beyond the reach of our magic, perhaps on Earth or else shielded. We do not know." Delia rubbed her crippled leg, grimacing.

The sun was setting outside the windows. Gunthor walked to the main doors and called out into the hallway.

Shortly, the finch followed him in and began lighting the lamps on the walls. It was an onerous task, for the more than 50 sconces around the large room. He appeared to be trying not to listen but still kept his ear toward the voices. He strained on the tips of his talons to reach the candles, as Gunthor continued, "We only know she has gone missing because the Guardian set to watch her was murdered. A good Avian, killed. His charge is unaccounted for."

"So Harmony is a Muse?" I wondered.

"It is likely," Delia agreed. "Why else would she have appeared in your prophecy? It is reasonable. Reasonable also that the other girl, Maya, is potentially one of the Nine."

Hearing the word *Nine* again triggered the memory of the note in my vandalized Jeep, and I blurted, "She is! She's a Muse. Harmony is a Muse. Agents Drake and Mendelson told me that the kidnapper had left the other abducted women notes with a number on them, just like I got. They were marked somehow."

"You also had a note?" Liam asked. "Why did you not mention this?"

"I've had a lot on my mind, Liam. The number on my note was *Nine*. But the other women…" I frowned and tried to think back to my afternoon at the FBI offices. "Three others on the missing persons board had notes."

"Three?" Gunthor gasped.

"Three? Are you certain?" Anderon wondered.

"There was Harmony. A Japanese woman from MIT, and a Broadway dancer from Africa."

"What were their names?" Delia sat forward and a white feather drifted from her pale wings. "Can you recall any details to lead us to them?"

"Uh." I glanced off toward the finch lighting the sconces. He was on the other side of the room, but I felt him straining to hear my words. I didn't know what to say so, I burbled all the details I could remember. "Um, they all had brown eyes. The Japanese lady was taken from MIT. Harmony was taken from a coffee shop in Los Angeles. The dancer was from Kenya."

Shaking my head, I sighed. "That's all I can remember."

"Three," Liam said as he took his seat again. "The MIT student was not on our list, nor was Harmony."

"She wasn't a student. I think her name was Ki, and she was a professor." I paused. "So you knew about the dancer?"

"We knew the dancer, Grace, was abducted," Gunthor confirmed.

Oh, no! If all the abducted women on the FBI list are Muses, Drake is looking in all the wrong places. He'll never be able to find them if they're on Aria.

"So that makes how many out there that you know of?" I asked as I counted on my fingers how many Muses I'd heard mentioned thus far.

"Four, including yourself. Five if Maya is yet another. And six when the Tuatha DeDannon reveal their generational gift." Delia said.

"What does that mean?" I asked.

Carilynda blinked watery eyes. "The followers of the ancient god, Lugh, were granted a source line of Mnemosyne's gifts as a debt of gratitude from the goddess herself. A Muse of significant power comes from the Tuathan line every so many generations of the Nine. It is assumed that, because all the Muses have been born within the same generation, at least one of the sacred Nine will emerge from the coven shields of the Tuatha DeDannon."

I didn't comprehend half of what she said, so I shrugged. "Oh, right. Okay. So when is that supposed to happen?"

"We have sent multiple emissaries but have not yet received a response from the delegates who answer to the Council seats representing the Tuathan Coven."

The finch appeared to be finishing up the last two sconces. Large bronze filigree fixtures spaced every five feet held a handful of candles each. The light from the windows waned in copper tones, clashing with the golden light of the candles and the half-dozen fire pits blazing around the room. The faces of all gathered appeared deep in thought, contemplating all we'd discussed and the ramifications of such heavy revelations.

Chapter Fourteen

Trust the story, Rose
Till the end of the line

Throughout the afternoon, I'd watched Lucina, easily picking out her dark hair near the back of the crowd. Each time she noticed me looking at her, she'd turn away or engage in conversation with her neighbors. I'd been hoping for a break in the discussions long enough that I could ask her about the chalice.

At last Gunthor called a pause to the meeting to eat and refresh.

Noel and the finch, along with several Avian servants, set up a table at the back of the room, loading it with food and drink.

The congregation began to feast while continuing to discuss all the possible meanings of what they'd learned thus far.

I was starving so I lingered near the food table, but not much looked appetizing or recognizable. Yellow soup with floating chunks of gray. A platter of fish fillets. Breads. Pastries. And a salad made of what looked like cashews and green slime. There was a platter of bright fruits—at least, I thought they were fruits: round purple bulbs with red flowers on the ends. Hard oblong yellow curds. A bowl of silver pods. Dishes of seeds and breads that smelled savory and spicy.

God, I'd give anything for a bagel from Aleph's. With a cup of too-hot coffee and a dish of blueberry cream cheese and a morning copy of the Times *to read on the subway. Is it too late to get my old life back?*

Even as I thought it, I knew I could never go back. But some edible food in this new life would make things a little easier to cope with.

The finch approached as I stood near Carilynda. He held out a bowl of what looked like tapioca pudding for Carilynda. "Mistress said it is your favorite."

Carilynda's face lit up as she took the pudding. "Please give her my thanks!"

Tapioca, that's not so bad. Maybe I'll ask if there's extra.

Then her long tongue flicked out, streaked into the pudding, dug around, and surfaced with a sugared dragonfly. She sucked it in her wide mouth and bit down with an echoing crunch.

"Delicious," she declared.

"Will you please excuse me?" I asked as I covered my mouth and fled.

Note to self: no tapioca pudding.

I hoped to find Lucina, but every time I thought I saw her someone intercepted me for conversation. Anderon wished to discuss the other Muses. Varia wished to know what I ate on Earth. Delia scolded me for looking so tired. Finally my stomach's growling and the wear on my nerves were too much. I snatched a piece of honey bread off the table and made my way to the windows, where I waited for the night to end so I could finally get some sleep.

Lucina was nowhere to be found.

Gunthor called over the crowd, holding a mug of *Uroosh* as he spoke. "Brothers and sisters, we must continue our discussions. Many of us must be back to our posts by the first light of day and have far to travel in the night."

The gathered creatures found their seats. I watched carefully, but Lucina remained absent, her chair empty.

"Please continue, Fable," Gunthor said, offering me the spotlight. "We have but one last page, by my count."

Setting my cup of tea on the table, I took the last page to the front of the room and picked up where we left off. Liam glanced off toward the nearest fireplace. Outside the windows dusk had fallen and the stars were aglow.

"One more?" Jespin asked.

I cleared my throat. "Okay. Last page. Page 239. *I always thought it would be easy to kill in self-defense, believing the line between right and wrong straddled a sea of black and white, and that self-preservation was the obvious, easy truth.*

"*Kill or be killed.*

"*Yet in that moment when someone has their hands around your neck and your windpipe is failing, your hands slapping helplessly at their face, kill or be killed doesn't even cross your mind. Instead, you want only to live. It's not about killing. It's about seeing the face of the man you love. It's about listening to Vivaldi, or tasting honey, or feeling your family in your arms.*

"*It's about one last chance to say "I love you."*

"*Groping to the right, my hand slid along the ground to where the gun landed. My fingernail scraped the grip. I choked on a sob as my pinky slipped helplessly over the cool metal. So close, but it may as well have been the moon.*

"*My lungs burned. The knife wound in my side ached. My entire body was swamped with pain, and I didn't want it to stop. As long as there was pain, I was alive.*

"*In one last surge of adrenaline, I gave up on the gun and wriggled my fingers around the throat of my attacker. I fought for my life. I fought for all that would be destroyed if I died and the world lost the power of Story.*

"How the hell did my life come to this?

"*Darkness swallowed my vision. My muscles buckled and my arms dropped to the grass.*

"I should have told him.

"How much of my life have I wasted not knowing the truth?
"Then I felt the gunshot."

My hands shook. The room was hot, and cloying scents of animal and forest stuck to my tongue. I thought I might be sick and shuddered as though someone had just walked over my grave.

"What happens next?" asked Delia "Do you win the fight for your life? What's on the next page?"

Page 240 was missing.

The last page of the manuscript had been taken by Abra and her birds. I scrambled through my thoughts, back to the day I'd written the last few pages, but I couldn't actually recall how it ended. I remembered waking up on the floor of Celeste's study. I remembered leaving the file to print while I took a shower and got dressed. Then I'd grabbed the stack of paper off the printer and walked out the door to the café without actually reading the end. I figured I'd see what I'd done when I read the full manuscript later. But later never happened.

Am I gonna die? Ohmigod, I'm gonna die.

"I...I don't know how it ends," I whispered.

The silence was terrifying. Profound, hanging-by-a-thread-over-a-bottomless-cavern kind of silence.

Then all at once the arguing erupted. Voices clamored over each other. "We have the power to prevent this! The pages are our guide."

"What if we change anything from the pages and upset a balance, which creates an even larger complexity of events?" Jespin asked.

"We must try to avoid this outcome at all costs," Delia argued.

Wave after wave of emotion rocked my body like so much driftwood against a shore. I was hearing them. I knew I should be listening, but I couldn't focus. I was caught in the lull of knowledge that I would die soon.

"I'm going to die."

"It will not happen," Liam murmured. His large wings flared behind my body protectively. "I will not allow it."

I drank in the certainty of his features, the calm surety…and yet. I couldn't feel it. Couldn't buy his declaration as truth. Page 239 was the end of my line.

Chapter Fifteen

Thoughts of love from moonlight shine
Banishing cobwebs from memory's shrine

Delia insisted that, with Celeste's funeral of state in less than 18 hours, we would soon know whether or not the outcome of any one page could be altered if we were to change the events of the funeral from how they'd been written in the Prophecy of Crows.

Gunthor argued that Celeste was owed the honor of a proper funeral, which was what I'd written, and we had no right to alter anything.

Liam suggested we didn't even truly know if the funeral in the manuscript was Celeste's.

Jespin claimed Celeste's funeral should be forgone altogether, because the manuscript outcome could be entirely changed if the upcoming scene were never to take place.

Carilynda, her amphibious head bobbing up and down, agreed with Jespin…until Anderon pointed out that if all the scenes were altered, we'd have no real direction as to the outcome of events at all, much less control over the major events themselves—such as a real significant chance to find at least two other Muses.

Then the debating began all over again.

Ultimately, they were going nowhere in making a decision, and I needed a break, some fresh air and quiet.

"Liam, I need to get out of here," I whispered.

As I stood, heads swiveled in my direction. I announced, "I just need some air."

They returned quickly to their conversations.

"I'm going to die," I whispered, leaning against the rocks of the cave.

Liam had flown us to the low-tide caverns at daybreak. Many of the Sublime were still deep in deliberations.

At the low-tide caverns, the scent of ocean and sea vegetation hung in the air, dampening my skin and coating the back of my throat.

"You will not die, Fable. Not the way you wrote it, and not any time soon." Liam stood at the edge of the ocean, foam rolling in on the surf, clinging to the hem of his skirt-like wrap. "I will not allow it to happen."

"I don't think you can stop it."

"Of course it can be stopped. If you know how it will happen, you can alter the events." He threw a rock out into the waves. "Besides, did you not say earlier you do not believe in prophecy?"

"I currently reserve the right to be freaked out by a confluence of events and weird supporting evidence," I said. "I'm not being fatalistic; maybe I'm just buying into the mumbo-jumbo."

"Do you believe you are *supposed* to die?" Liam faced the sunrise. Amber light turned droplets of water to diamonds cascading from the pinions of his wings.

Blinking rapidly, I took a deep breath and tried not to admit it out loud—but, yeah, I was supposed to die. It should have been me and not Celeste. Maybe my death would be the universe's way of righting that somehow. She'd given up her last 20 years to raising and keeping me safe—ignorant, but safe anyway—and she'd been murdered for it. For me.

I was a helium balloon drifting toward the sun without Celeste as my anchor.

Celeste clearly had a connection to this world. It was important to her to keep me safe and to find those girls. It was the very least I could do: to finish where she left off.

Either I'll die or I won't. Fine. But not until I finish Celeste's work. Everybody's gotta die sometime, right? But until then...I want to live.

I admired Liam's back, the strength of his spine and the graceful arch of his wings. I soaked in the fantastical juxtaposition of bird and man. Then I walked toward him and rested my cold hands on either side of his deliciously warm hips.

I trailed cool fingers along the ridge of his wrap, then up his sides along the muscles of his ribcage. I said, "I don't know how long I've got, but until page 239, I want to live—really live, Liam. Feel something. Be a part of something." I reached up and stretched my arms around his neck as he bent toward me. "To mean something."

His lips were scalding hot against mine, and I liked it. I pressed against his chest. The scent of his sun-warmed skin mixed with musk and sea salt drove me a little crazy. I wanted him. I didn't care anymore that he wasn't completely human. It didn't matter that the noises he made when he pulled me in were throaty, creature sounds that human men didn't make.

The surf rushed against my feet. I gasped and Liam slipped his tongue inside my mouth. A sharp bolt of desire ripped through my insides. I moaned, leaning into him, letting him take my weight as his fingers threaded through my hair and drew me closer.

I wanted his breath in my lungs, his skin inside mine.

His wings wrapped us in a silk cocoon as my heart exploded against my ribcage again and again.

Finally, reluctantly, I nudged against his shoulders. "Can't... breathe."

He nuzzled my lips with his nose and placed a soft kiss on my eyelid as I panted, resting dizzily against him. Waves thrummed against my ankles as the tide washed in.

Liam lifted a wing and the breeze from the motion freed a curl from my mass of tangled auburn hair. It fell over my face, bouncing with the wind.

"A curl wisp has come loose again, Whispina."

Blinding white light seared the inside of my head. I arched and cried out in pain.

"What? What is it?" His frantic voice sounded from a growing distance.

"What did you call me?" I gasped raggedly.

"Whispina."

Light split my vision like shattering glass. Pain burst through my skull. I shrieked, clutching my head. Light tumbled everywhere and my pulse rang in my ears as my knees hit the wet sand.

"Fable!"

Everything went dark.

The maze hedges were trimmed at neck level for an adult Avian.

I'd been in Capitol City for three days, waiting for the verdict on my schooling. It wasn't fair that I couldn't go to normal school with the other children—but then, the other children made fun of me because I had no wings. Stupid useless flaps, anyway…it's not like any of them could even fly yet. I'd be 11 at the beginning of the month, and my humanness was more apparent than ever, as the summer brought the first coat of down feathers for most of my friends.

I jumped, trying see over the juniper hedges. The last several turns consisted of three lefts, two rights, and a left. Or was it three rights?

This trip to the maze was special; I was going to meet Sybil. She'd come to Capitol City with her father on business for the Council.

The note had come by courier, in the special code we used, to meet in the Alder Quarter maze center at noon to tell stories and picnic on the pilfered chocolate I'd brought from Earth.

"Sybil? Are you here?"

I rounded the bend with my backpack, but the center of the maze was empty. I went about setting up our picnic, laying out a red and white checkered bandana, the can of soda, and the chocolate bar.

Noon came and went.

Several hours passed, and I began to wonder if I'd read the message wrong. The Adler Quarter maze was the closest to her father's Council residence, so it made sense…but maybe I'd gotten confused.

The moon was high and full by the time I'd screamed myself hoarse begging for help, for someone, anyone, to find me. The soda and chocolate were long gone, eaten for dinner and comfort. I'd been lost for hours, backtracking and trying new routes in a frantic effort to be free.

Finally I curled up under a hedge, hoping to wait out the night and find my way in the morning. Then an Avian landed heavily on the next row over.

"Fable? Are you in here?"

I thought about staying hidden. After all, I didn't recognize the voice; but then, it was getting cold and it was too dark to remain alone.

"I'm here," I croaked, voice raw and painful.

"Stay where you are."

I heard the swoosh of wings, then a set of talons crashed gracelessly into the dirt in front of my face.

"Fable?"

A young man's face appeared in the moonlight. His wings were likely only on their second molting but sturdy enough to fly. "Hello. What are you doing under the hedge?"

"Sleeping," I lied.

"Everyone is out looking for you. They're all worried. Sybil has been crying all afternoon."

"I got lost," I admitted, then sniffed. "Are they really mad?"

He settled on the ground and peered under the bush. "Well, Celeste is angry." He paused then stretched out a hand. "I'm Liam, Sybil's older brother."

I reached out from under the shrubs and shook his hand. "I'm Fable. I thought you were at the Academy. I was told you'd be coming home next spring."

"I have come home for my father's induction." He tilted his head. "I have heard about you, too, but we will have to talk later. We should go back to the others, before they worry too much."

I wriggled out from my hiding spot. "Celeste is going to kill me. She's probably really pissed."

"Celeste would never harm you," he corrected. "But if it will make you feel better, I give you my pledge: I will never let anyone hurt you."

I finally got to my feet, and he looked me over. The moonlight emphasized his high cheekbones, and his hair shone golden. "Your hair is wild and sticking out," he stated.

"It gets wispy when it's going to rain," I said, self-consciously re-binding my hair into a ponytail and trying to smooth out the curls.

"What does *wispy* mean?" Liam asked.

"It's kind of like *floaty*." I thought about it. "I guess it's kind of like a description for fuzzy and fluttery at the same time."

He smiled, and his boyish grin caught in a dimple on the left. We stood in silence for a moment before Liam picked up my backpack. "I cannot fly us both for long, but I will get us out of the maze with a few hops."

I nodded and let him put his thin arms around me. He wasn't much taller than I was, but since he had molted enough to fly, he must have been about 15. Before he launched us for the first jump, he said, "Hold on tight, Whispina."

Liam leaned over me as I opened my eyes. "Fable? Are you ill?" he asked. "What happened?"

The deep lines of worry between his eyebrows made me smile. I reached up, touching the perfect curve of his lips. He was obviously older, with a scruff of blond beard and a much larger, more muscular body.

"I remember you," I said.

Liam rested on his talons with a sigh that sounded both relieved and resigned. "Do you remember everything?"

"I remember the day you found me in the maze." I sat up, slowly. The world tilted slightly.

"Do you remember Aria? The castle? Sybil?" He reached out and steadied my shoulder. My legs and butt were soaked with seawater.

I shook my head; even that small movement hurt and sent sparkles dancing in my vision. "No," I groaned, "but I glimpsed pieces of story, fragments of images of other memories, so I believe now they will come back to me eventually." Moaning and clutching my head, I tried to stand. "I need some aspirin or something."

"Let me help you," he said, taking my hand.

At his touch, light bloomed through my head again. The pressure seemed to crush my skull. Then I was falling back toward the surf.

"I'll only be gone a year or two. It can't stop us from being sisters," I said. "When they're done with the spells, I won't remember you for a while…but that doesn't mean you won't still be my best friend."

Sybil sat across from me on her bed. She'd been crying, her large eyes swollen and red. "But you are coming back? For sure? Promise?"

"Nothing will be able to keep me away."

"Will the shield keep you hidden from the Eventines?"

"It's supposed to keep me hidden from everyone, including Xabien and the Sylphans. When it's safe, they'll lift the shield and the ban…and it'll be just like waking up from a long nap."

Sybil threw her arms around me, and we clung to one another. "Please come back in a year. I will have fledged my first down, and then soon we can go flying. I will make you a special harness while you're gone."

"I'll be back. I promise."

"I know."

Pulling away, I fought to keep a brave face. "And I'll bring books, and makeup, and magazines." I slipped a letter from my pocket. "Will you give this to Liam when I'm gone?"

Sybil took the folded paper. "He feels really bad about what happened, you know."

"Me, too," I said.

"Does Xabien know you're leaving?" Her featherless wings flapped in distress.

"I don't know. I don't really want to talk about Xabien."

She shuddered. "I don't either."

"Will you give it to him?" I begged.

"Of course," she agreed, tucking the letter into her pocket.

A knock at the door startled us both, and Liam poked his head in the room. "Sybil, Mother needs you to size Fable's harness."

Sybil climbed off the bed, her awkward wings tangled in her legs. She tripped before she turned and rushed back to swamp me in one last hug.

Then she hurried out the door, leaving Liam and I alone. I'd met him a few years earlier. He and Sybil were all I could think about during my trips to Earth…well, I thought of Liam all of the time, actually.

"I heard," was all he said.

"I'll come back when the danger's gone." I slipped off the bed and joined him at the window overlooking the ocean. "I'll be back, Liam."

He gazed down at the surf. He was growing his first tawny beard. "It is better that you go," he said. "I can't protect you."

Clutching his arm, I hissed, "That was not your fault; it was Xabien's, and we all know it."

He wouldn't look at me. I tugged on his arm and tried to turn him toward me, but he was a solid trunk since his growth spurt last summer, when he'd taken the shape of a man. His final molting had come in, and the dark ridge of his wings walled me off as he broke free of my touch, turning away.

My eyes stung. I nodded and walked to the bed to finish packing my clothes. I zipped the backpack and turned. He stood behind me, his once-skinny arms now corded limbs from aerial combat training. He pulled me in, crushing my body in his embrace, then wrapped his wings around us both and nearly squeezed the air out of my lungs.

I never wanted to forget this moment: the surf outside my window, the scent of sunlight and salt on Liam's skin. The fierceness with which we clung to one another.

I hugged him back with everything I had, wanting to hurt him for all the pain of being forced to leave. After a time, I felt his grip loosen, his breath coming in ragged gasps at my ear. "I have something for you."

He released me and drew a black velvet pouch from his pocket.

With shaking hands, he poured the contents into his palm and lifted it up for me to see: a thin silver chain with an oblong malachite pendant. "I picked it up at the market in Capitol City when you were in the Reaches." He lifted it over my head and worked the clasp until it clicked and the stone came to rest in the hollow of my neck. "It reminds me of your eyes."

Peeking in the mirror, I smiled at how it brought my eyes to life—or maybe it was Liam in the reflection that gave me such color. "I love it."

"As long as you wear it, I will always be able to find you, even through the shields, and I will know you are safe."

"You had it *charmed*? That must have been a fortune, Liam. I can't."

He stroked the necklace around my throat. "When you return, I will challenge Xabien for the right to your betrothal contract." He pulled me in. "If you don't come back soon, I will come for you."

"Liam…"

"Fable?" Celeste's voice echoed up the stairs.

Liam bent to kiss me, his soft lips unschooled, hands clumsy on my face. I kissed him back awkwardly. My first kiss, timid and strange, a tentative meeting of mouths.

"And not a moment too soon, it seems," Celeste remarked from the doorway with a put-upon voice, her heart-shaped face a mask of exasperation. "Lord almighty, how does anyone survive teenage girls?"

Liam flushed.

I stammered, "Okay. Okay. I'm ready."

Celeste had picked up my backpack, and Liam jumped to take it. "Here, let me help you."

Early afternoon light cast gold rectangles across the wall. I opened my eyes to a ceiling mural of a black centaur rearing up on hind legs and throwing a massive barb-tipped spear at a giant horned Minotaur, who in turn raised a wicked axe toward his opponent. Other scenes of battle were painted in fleshy layers on the ceiling mural: a green dragon and her Ryder bedecked in chrome armor and shield dove toward the battlement of a castle lined with elk-horned archers and flaming arrows.

I stared at the painting, trying to remember where I was.

Was I drinking last night?

It came back to me all at once as the scent of ocean air wafted through the room. I sat up. Sybil slept in the window-seat, her long satin skirts draped down to the floor.

I am a Muse. I was born in Aria. I was supposed to be gone for a year…14 years ago.

The room was like most other Avian chambers I'd seen, which was to say, disproportionately large for a human woman. I was in a bed that was more like a lake of feather comforters and down pillows, but I didn't remember how I got to it.

My nightgown, luxuriously soft, white satin hanging in drapes from one shoulder, looked like a gown I'd have paid a fortune for at Barney's.

I threw my feet over the edge and dropped down to the floor where my toes met lush carpets. A nearby chair held a set of black Avian-style clothes tailored to my size.

"You're awake," Sybil said, rubbing her eyes.

She was beautiful, sleepy and lit by the soft window light.

"How long have I been asleep?" I wondered.

"A few hours. Liam brought you in this morning and said you blacked out." She sat up. "He wanted me to tell you not to let anyone else know you are recovering your memories."

"Well, I don't remember much, just a couple of things."

"Oh." She frowned. "But even that…" She slid off the window seat, straightened her burgundy skirts, and patted her hair. "Everyone on Aria knows you have lost your memory."

She reached for a blue bag she'd been using as a back-pillow. It was the bag the NaNas packed for me.

"Here," she said. "I had to sleep on it to keep it safe from Mother." With an apologetic frown, she sighed. "While you were asleep, Mother burned the clothes you were wearing."

I took the bag and unzipped it.

"Zane dropped it by and said Eleanor and Biddy packed it for you."

Inside were two fresh changes of clothes, jeans and T-shirts, toothbrush, paste, and other toiletries, along with several clean pairs of panties. "Oh, thank god," I murmured. "Wait. She burned my clothes? What? Does she think I brought the plague or something?"

"No, of course not," Sybil said. "But you might remember Mother has an aversion to the vulgarity of jeans and other clothes from Earth."

"Damn. I loved those jeans."

"I'm sorry. I hid the backpack as soon as Zane delivered it, because I figured it might have Earth clothing inside."

"And granola bars," I added, digging through the loot. "And chocolate."

"Chocolate?" she asked, trying unsuccessfully to hide the excitement in her voice.

Laughing, I held it out to her. "I remember you liked this once." I crinkled the wrapper suggestively.

"Oh, no. I couldn't," she demurred with hungry eyes.

"Go on. It's okay. Are you afraid it will spoil your lunch?"

I thought she would argue but she agreed. "Okay, but only if you share it with me."

While she carefully took it from my fingers and began unwrapping, I picked out a change of clothes and turned my back to her while I dressed.

"So why am I not supposed to tell anyone else about my memories?"

She swallowed a piece of chocolate then said, "We believe some of our enemies will brave themselves out in the open if they think you might not remember who they are. Not all who welcome you home are supporters of the Law of Nine."

"You mean I've met some of them?"

"How much do you remember?" she asked.

"I remember Liam finding me in the maze."

Sybil shuddered. "What a horrible day that was. I was never so frightened in my life." She paused. "Well, except for when you were actually kidnapped."

"Kidnapped? You mean, when I was taken to Earth?" I picked up the chocolate, and her eyes followed it.

"No, when you were kidnapped by W'ryick. Don't you remember?"

"What? I know that name…" It tickled my mind but didn't spark a memory.

"Of course you do."

When I saw her eyes return to the half-eaten bar, I paused. "You know, it's far too early in the day for chocolate for me. Would you mind eating this, so your mom doesn't decide to burn it with all the other Earth paraphernalia?"

Sheepishly, she took it. "I suppose I could do that. Are you sure you don't want any?"

I shook my head. "I remember knowing I was taken hostage, but I don't remember the circumstances. I only remember Liam felt guilty for it for some reason. And the only other memory I have is when we were all saying goodbye."

"He wasn't watching you," she said with her mouth full.

"Did you just put that whole thing in your mouth?"

She shrugged abashed, shook her head in denial, then nodded reluctantly with wide eyes. "I'm sorry."

"Don't be sorry!" I burst out laughing. "Don't ever be sorry for chocolate. Chocolate will never be sorry for you!"

She smiled, lopsided, and I couldn't help thinking she seemed so young, so innocent, even though we were nearly the same age.

Fourteen years have passed? Really?

"You were saying Liam wasn't watching me?"

"I think he still feels like your being kidnapped by W'ryick was his fault. We know now it was only possible because Xabien encouraged it. Liam was fishing and left you alone to read, and they snatched you right off the island."

"Xabien…" I murmured. The name was familiar. More familiar than just being mentioned in the last day of conversations. Familiar and unsettling. "I gather he's somehow related to the Dragon Ryders. At least that's what I heard over breakfast yesterday. And I understand he has something to do with a treaty and a territory to the North. But who *is* he?"

Sybil's eyes widened. "Liam was supposed to have reminded you." She reached for my hands and cupped them gently. "He's your future husband, Fable. Your betrothed."

Chapter Sixteen

The wilt of summer bloom
And autumn's last leaf
Goodbyes come to all

"'Betrothed'?" I couldn't connect with the word. "As in, the Middle-Ages kind of betrothal?" I shook my head.

Sybil nodded, her tower of red hair bobbing. "As in, Xabien is your soon-to-be *husband*."

"Wait. What? No. I don't think so." I held up my hand, shaking my head. "Is this some kind of bad joke on Aria? Celeste would never have let that happen!"

"Celeste opposed it," Liam said from the doorway. He was dressed in Avian clothing: soft, ultra-thin black fabric in drapes and swags, with a layer of black banding wrapped around his torso several times and knotted in the front like a kimono.

"It's not going to happen," I said. "It must be a mistake. If Celeste was opposed to it, then why are we discussing it?"

"Because *you* insisted on it." Liam swept into the room. "You, Fable," he hissed, pointing at me with emphasis as he jabbed the words, "you insisted on the betrothal to bind the Ice Cap Treaty."

"To spare our country war," Sybil added.

They were serious. Both deadly serious.

He stepped forward, expression softening. "To save your mother's legacy, you offered yourself up as a compromise to invasion from the Northern Reaches." He took my hand and cupped it to his chest. "I wanted just a few days with you, without his shadow hanging over us. Your sacrifice bought us 14 years of tentative peace and an armistice that saved countless lives."

How can I not remember something like a betrothal? Why didn't Celeste prepare me for this? Any of it?

Sybil's large eyes searched my face. Liam's jaw worked, chewing silently on whatever he couldn't say. I pulled away, stalked across the room to where my backpack lay on the floor, and snatched it up as I stormed toward the door.

"Wait! Where are you going?" Sybil rushed to catch up, her skirt rustling.

"I need some space."

"But…" Her wings shivered frantically.

"You chose *him*," he hissed, finally spilling whatever he'd been struggling not to say. "You chose to be married to Xabien on the first red moon of your return to Aria. No one forced you to choose him." His wings snapped open, slamming the air with a violent draft.

"How long have you been saving that argument? Huh?" I shouted. "Then spring it on me when I don't even know what the fuck is going on!"

His wings drove the air as he bellowed, "Too long!"

"Please, stop it, you two!" Sybil whimpered. "Your anger is sharp and it hurts."

I took a deep breath, my whole body shaking. "This is bullshit. I'm out."

"Wait. Please just wait," Sybil begged. "Please listen."

Glancing at the door, I measured the distance.

What? Outrun Avians?

Walking slowly with her hands out, she pleaded, "I know you feel like a lot is happening. Everything has been out of your control.

You feel swept up. Overcome. Small in a world where the machinery has gone on long without you, and you have lost your memory and the knowledge of how that machinery works."

"Stop," I warned. "Don't you be using your Shawshank whatchma-powers to read me. I'm pissed, and I have every right to be pissed—everyone's fucking holding back secrets on me!"

"We are sisters," Sybil said softly. "Trust me, please, when I tell you that I have spent the last 14 years studying the legal contract of your betrothal." She stepped between me and the door. "I have a plan," she finished.

Gently, as though calming a spooked horse, she rested her hand on my fingers, clutched tightly around the backpack. "Please. I cannot help you if you break the truce, but I can help you legally negate it."

At her touch, warmth spread like loosed steam through my limbs. The backpack tumbled to the floor. The room turned soft. "What are you doing to me?"

"Liam," Sybil said from far away, "I think I've used too much. Catch her!"

My legs folded and he sprinted to catch me as I crumpled against him.

"Icarus' wings!" he said. "How much did you use?"

"Enough to have stopped *you*!" she yelled back. "She's just smaller, and I wasn't calculating!"

My body thrummed to life. The slightest touch became a sensual caress. I writhed in Liam's arms, every inch of my skin suddenly pulsing with need. Wave after wave of pleasure suffused me as his curls tickled my neck. "What did you…?" I panted.

"It will wear off soon, Fable. Sybil's *sawyin* is short lived. Don't fight it."

I didn't want to fight it—it felt great. Like sinking into a hot tub with a glass of champagne. Deliriously sexual. Languid. And beneath all the dreamy heat…

"I'm really horny."

"Hell's pretty tinkling bells." Sybil frowned. "I should not have eaten that chocolate!"

"Go get some coffee, or some of the whiskey Father keeps in the closet," Liam ordered.

"I don't know about the whiskey. That might make it worse."

"Celeste's funeral is in five hours, Sybil! Go get something to shock her system, or she'll be a mess."

"Don't tell Mother," she begged.

"And brush your teeth," he added. "I can smell the chocolate from here."

"It's just chocolate, Liam." I defended her. "Chocolate is so… mmm…like silk bed sheets, and…sexy." I caressed his face. "You're so beautiful…"

"I'm going!" Sybil shouted, darting from the room. The door slammed behind her.

Liam caught my fingers. "Don't struggle against her power, Fable. It will pass."

"It feels so…so…"

A deep, insistent pressure built between my thighs. Humming. Needing.

"This is why," he said, "you don't give chocolate to an Empath."

I moaned as his fingers touched mine and an orgasmic wave crashed into my body. I arched, gasping.

The room became an echo chamber for my heart. Each sensation—clothes against my skin, Liam's hair tickling my cheek, air in my lungs, feathers against my flesh—rocketed pleasure through my body.

"Oh, god," I moaned, panting. "This feels amazing."

"Shhh. I'm here."

"Yes, you are," I agreed and pulled him down to my pulsing, throbbing body.

My mouth took his in a feverish haze of lush, wanton passion. The taste of his breath and the heat of his flesh excited my already rabid desire. I wrapped my legs around him. Caught in the tide of my heat, he responded in kind, pulling my hips against him, threading his hands in my hair.

"I cannot," he murmured. "You are not mine to claim," he said, even as his tongue lit up my flesh and his wings fanned the air.

"But I want you!" I begged.

Any argument he may have had was engulfed by the blaze of our two bodies. My suppressed passion and pent-up grief back-drafted into a sensual firestorm.

"Liam…"

He growled and stood, lifting my body, twined with his, and carried me to the wall, where he crushed me against the stone and ground his body between my legs. I bucked my hips as we fought for control. Arms tangling, mouths fumbling. His wings worked like bellows to our flame. His feathers shivered as they beat the air, driving his body, adding force to his thrust.

"My jeans," I groaned. "Get my jeans off." My fingers scrabbled against the ties of his wrap. I gasped ragged, gulping breaths. "I need you. I need you in me, Liam."

"I cannot!" he nearly howled. He rested his forehead on mine as he groaned and pressed the ridge of his cock against the seam of my Levi's, which drove all thoughts from my grasp. I clutched at his clothing, trying to rip it away, but he fought my hands, gripping my wrists, lifting them overhead, and pinning them to the wall.

"Fable." His passion-filled voice breathed in my ear, trembling through my blood to the center of my belly.

I fought against him, desperate to tear our clothes off. I wanted the real deal, not a high-school dry-fucking grind.

"Please, Liam."

But even as I begged for him, all dignity lost, bucking against the restraint of his grasp, he felt too good. His heat, the musky scent of his skin. The seductive caress of feathers combined with the weight of his body against the juncture of my jeans.

Orgasm shimmered deep in my core as he ground his body against me. Every sensation was amplified by the empathic power in my system, and I moaned, "Yes! Right there! Liam!"

"Dear gods, I'm going to Hades," he groaned.

It hit me hard, throwing my whole body into spastic lurching. I cried out. Liam's mouth covered mine as I screamed into his lungs, orgasm shredding through me. Spasms rocked my body against him while flashes of visions tangled with the gossamer ripples woven through my climax.

A constellation of stars on my ceiling.

The swooping dive of a black dragon in gold-plate armor.

Doves flocking through a cloud of smoke.

An oak tree collapsing in a Glade.

The sound of a gun in the quiet of morning.

Black feathers drifting, drifting, drifting.

I sagged against his chest, breaths sharp and sore. My mouth was so parched from panting I couldn't speak.

Liam rested his cheek against the top of my head. His own jagged gulps of air and the furious beating of his heart against mine filled the small space between us. We held each other as the afterglow burned through my limbs. I felt dipped in molten silver, still radiating, pulsing.

I wrapped my arms around his neck and held on as he staggered to the window seat and collapsed with my body straddling his lap.

Breathing as though I'd just sprinted a mile, I stared at him in the amber light of the window. His blue eyes, rich as lapis, gazed back at me, and he smiled, his boyish dimple catching on the left.

Sybil burst back in to the room and stopped short, gaping. "Oh, gods. Tell me you did not, Liam."

He couldn't catch his breath, but he shook his head and croaked, "We were caught up, but did not."

Her wings relaxed and she closed the door behind her, a bottle of dark liquid and a glass in one hand. "Thank the gods you are not so foolish."

With each lungful of air, my thoughts shed fuzz and my senses returned to normal. "What the hell just happened?"

Sybil tilted her head. "You don't need whiskey after all?"

"Hell, yes, I need some whiskey," I countered.

Sybil poured a drink as I shimmied off Liam's lap, suddenly self-conscious. Awkward.

"I'm sorry, Fable," Sybil said. "I didn't mean to use so much *sawyin*. I was still feeling the pleasure of the chocolate, and I used too much force. I was just trying to stop you from leaving, and I panicked."

"Breathe, Sybil," I said. "I'm okay. Feeling…better…"

Liam shuffled behind me but I didn't dare turn to look. Instead I took the glass from Sybil and threw back the shot of whiskey. It scorched and I coughed, but the trail of heat down my throat centered me in my own skin.

"Are you okay?" Sybil wondered. "I've never seen anyone ground such a high dose so quickly."

My face flamed. "Liam, um…" I shrugged. "Liam helped work it out. Uh, sweat it off."

Truthfully, I still felt the lingering song of something delicious in my blood. Maybe the pearlescent post-glow or just heightened sensual responses, though it was lower, more on the fading side of awareness.

"Interesting," she said, leveling a glare at Liam. "I'm relieved my error was not more serious."

"I must go prepare for the arrivals." Liam cleared his throat and headed for the door. "Mother and Father understand you will want time alone with Celeste before the funeral. They will meet us at the mausoleum."

Suddenly I couldn't meet his eyes in front of Sybil. And he looked anywhere but at my face.

The door clicked shut behind him, and Sybil put her hands on her hips and sighed. "That was all my fault and I know it. I'm very sorry."

An uncomfortable silence hung in the air. I looked toward the window seat. A white pinion feather had drifted on to the cushion. I picked it up. Liam's feather.

"Are you sure you are well?" Sybil asked.

It was the same kind of feather I'd found in my room, or in the yard, or on my way to school, for years. I had a box under my bed where I'd collected these feathers until it seemed silly to keep picking them up and saving them when they were so obviously abundant. I'd used them as bookmarks and decorations, even hung them in dream catchers.

I knew it in that moment, as I held his feather in my hand that Liam had always been around—even when I wasn't aware of him.

I murmured, "Wonderful, really." I touched the malachite pendant at my throat, the same pendant I'd worn for as long as I could remember. The necklace Liam had given me. And I realized that I'd never truly fallen in love, because no matter how good Celeste was at casting her shields, I'd never completely forgotten him.

Tucking the loose feather in my hair, as I'd seen Sybil do earlier, I turned around. Her face was a mask of displeasure.

"What?"

She raised an eyebrow at the feather. "It might not be wise to flaunt any promises you and Liam have made to one another before your contract is legally annulled."

"We've made no promises."

Sybil plucked the feather from my hair. "This time around, maybe not, but if you go wearing his feathers in public, you might as well just announce your intentions to free-fall."

"Why are you the one getting pissy? I'm the one you just doped with *E,* and I practically mauled your brother—through no fault of his own...or mine, either, for that matter." I glared. "If anyone should be cranky, it's me."

Sybil ducked her head. "You are right." She frowned.

With a sigh, I crossed the room to the pile of black silk clothes set out by the bed. Stripping off my shirt and pants, I asked, "How do I get out of this betrothal thing?"

The sun lingered near the horizon, casting a dusky pallor over the doors of the towering granite mausoleum with a spherical domed roof and garden of statues on the surrounding green acreage. Sheer cliffs fell away from the eastern border of the graveyard and dropped hundreds of feet below to the surf, which battered eternally against the last resting place of the Avians.

As we approached, I could see the graveyard was not really the landscape of headstones I'd been expecting. Instead, the verdant lawns were webbed with walking paths through great marble statues, monuments, and smaller family mausoleums. From above, it was easy to see what appeared to be a mourner's trail, where those who came to pay their respects were already moving down the winding paths, one by one, toward the field outside the Primus Aerie.

We landed near the steps of a massive building. Liam walked beside me, up the wide path between behemoth marble creatures 30 feet tall. We passed below the arch of two sculpted women touching their palms together over the walkway, their ivory-veined skin reflecting the dying daylight, their colossal wings spread wide. To those passing below, they looked more angelic than Avian.

It seemed fitting, then, that they watched over the mausoleum.

I tried to meet Liam's eyes but could do little more than glance at his lips before looking away. Our flight to the mausoleum had been quiet. Tense. My funeral attire, a gift of Avian-style clothing from Sybil, included long black satin skirts, boned corset, and matching black satin jacket, all of which made me feel at once drowned in fabric and completely vulnerable. I ached to speak with him but couldn't find any words that didn't feel desperate, so I hadn't said a word during the whole two-hour flight.

Liam stood near the open door. "I will wait for you here."

"You're not coming in?"

God, Fable. Can you at least try *not to sound needy?*

"I have made promises to her already," he whispered.

"You mean you made your peace?" I asked.

"It is the same, is it not?"

I slipped through the doors to enter a spacious hallway lit by candles, thick with incense. The sharp scent of frankincense and sandalwood mixed with the pungent reek of burning sage.

I followed smoke and candlelight down the corridor to an archway that opened into a dome. The ceiling soared ten stories up to the dome constructed of stained glass panels. From floor to ceiling, the circular room housed thousands upon thousands of nooks holding every shape, color, style, and size of urn. My skirts rustled along the stone.

In the center of the round room a stone table bore Celeste's body. Her white shroud draped to the floor.

A gathering of creatures loitered in the space; a cluster of Avians held bowls of smoking incense, and a centaur wafted a large wooden fan. They saw me and whispered to the others I had arrived. River and Gunthor sat on stone benches before the altar. River was first to greet me.

She embraced me warmly, kissing my cheeks. Then she stepped back and looked at me from head to toe with an odd expression.

Still feeling the lingering effects of being drenched in Sybil's *sawyin*, my face flushed as I imagined she knew exactly what I'd been up to with her son. I cleared my throat, and she seemed to remember where we were.

"We will all step out," she said, "so you may have time with her. If you need anything, you have but to call and someone will come."

I didn't even notice everyone leave the room as I stepped up to the shrouded figure on the stone table. The sheer white fabric whispered in the cavernous space as I drew back her veil.

Celeste lay porcelain fair. Lifeless.

Her still form had been dressed, stitched, and made lovely once more—a fact for which I was grateful, as Agent Drake had tried to warn me of her gruesome state. What skill or magic had made her so now, I wasn't sure, but it didn't matter. She looked perfect, as though she were simply sleeping in a white gossamer gown with autumn roses tucked around her body.

I don't know what I'd been expecting. Maybe I thought she'd open her eyes and say, "It's time to get up for school, Fable," and I would realize this had all been a terrible dream.

But the ashen hue of her skin, the vacancy of tone, and the sickening reality she was dead hit me harder than I'd expected, and a garbled sob burst from my throat and echoed through the room, followed by uncontrollable, gut-cramping weeping.

Even as I wept, I smoothed her auburn hair, wrapping my fingers through the streaks of silver. She used to let me brush her hair when I was anxious or sad. It was still soft, even though she didn't live in it anymore.

"I'm so lost without you."

The autumn Celeste drove me to Seattle to begin my freshman year of college, I'd been both excited and terrified. She helped me carry my boxes into a little dorm room and set up my space before we went out to dinner one last time.

"I'm only three hours away," she said. "You can come home anytime you want."

"I know," I mumbled, stabbing a French fry in ranch.

I should have been happy, delirious. I was a grownup, off to make my own life, have adventures, meet boys, and maybe fit in somewhere. But I wasn't happy. I was depressed, feeling weightless and disconnected. I was terrified I'd fail at even the simplest part of the human journey—letting go of home. What if I decided I didn't want to go into journalism? What if I flunked my classes or couldn't make friends?

As if reading my mind, she said, "You're your own woman now. Go make as many mistakes as you think you can survive—then you'll really have something to write about."

Over the years, I'd phone her about some idea or plan, taking a new job, moving across country to New York, meeting a new guy. She'd ask, "What do you think? Is it a mistake?"

I'd reply, "Maybe only a little one." And we'd laugh.

I could survive any mistake because I knew she wouldn't let me really fail. I had infinite security in her support. It tricked me into having confidence that nothing was really ever as big a mistake as I thought it would be.

But what about this? What about Aria? Liam? A Muse? A betrothal?

None of these were "maybe only a little one" kinds of mistakes. If I fucked up, other people might die, go to war, or destroy a world. Going off to college and starting an apocalypse were not even in the same category of "oops, my bad."

"Auntie Celeste, I can't do this without you. I really need you right now." I cupped her hand, cold and stiff. "I miss you so much." I kissed her temple. "I love you."

"She loved you very much, too," a deep voice answered.

I spun around, hands flying to my chest.

An Avian sat on the bench behind me. I hadn't heard him enter the room. He wore a black wrap, and his black wings folded behind him like a cloud. His black hair was knotted at the nape of his neck, and black tattoos scrawled up both muscular arms. The only colors he wore were large turquoise and silver bracelets on each wrist. His bronze skin and dark brown eyes triggered my memory, but I couldn't pull up an image, only a sense of familiarity.

"I know you, I think."

"We have spent much time together, Fable." He rose and joined me at the stone table, where he kissed Celeste's pale lips.

We stood beside one another in silence, and I took comfort in his proximity.

"It will be some time before you recover all your memories. Celeste was very good at her craft. I am Kal, Celeste's husband."

My jaw dropped.

"You are surprised now, but when your memories return, you will remember that you knew this." He studied my expression. "I suspect you are tired of hearing that."

"You have no idea."

He sighed and gazed at his wife. "She was my song. The only notes worth singing."

Several minutes passed as we stood together. I took a great deal of comfort in the knowledge that Celeste had a lover, a companion. It must have been a tremendous sacrifice, and I felt guilt mixed with gratitude.

"I don't mean to be rude…but you look half her age. How long were you married?"

Kal smiled. "We met 40 years ago, when she trespassed on my family land while on a diplomatic mission. I arrested her. I am five years older than she, but Avians age slower on Aria than Earth. We spent 35 years as husband and wife."

Aging slower on Aria? 35 years?

"Did you have any kids?"

Kal shook his head sadly. "We lost both children in the womb."

My heart squeezed. She'd had miscarriages. Heartbreak I never even knew.

"Celeste was studying the blight these last few years, trying to discover the cause of the low success of birth rates on Aria, but I guess we will never learn her results."

We passed a few more moments in silence. Kal trailed a loving finger down Celeste's cheek. I looked away from the intimate gesture.

Out in the room, along the base of the walls, were large sarcophagi with sculpted marble figurines resting in poses of death.

One particular sarcophagus lid was sculpted with a pair of lovers intertwined. Because the boxy stone coffin beneath was larger than the others, I surmised it contained two bodies rather than one. The male lover was an Avian, his marbled wings spread out like a blanket over the bottom half of his sleeping lady. They lounged atop the sarcophagus as though they casually lazed away a Sunday morning.

"It was her favorite story," Kal said, following my gaze. "'The Lovers of Lost Rook.'"

"How does it go?"

"He was an Avian warlord of the Ice Raven clan, and she was a mermaid."

I smiled, despite the circumstances. "Well, every relationship has its problems."

Kal smiled, a soft tilt of his lips. "She was also a Muse."

I gasped and looked up. "A non-human Muse?"

Kal snorted. "Frequently, yes."

"What happened?"

He brushed a hand over Celeste's hair. "It is said they loved one another so much that they both made dark deals to be together. In secret, they separately sought out the same Rhue Weaver of tremendous power. Ereatith gave his kingdom away for fins, while at the same time Olyia traded her father's priceless book of underwater magicks for wings."

"That sucks," I said. "What happened?"

"They met at the place of their lovers trysts on the rocks near Lost Rook—he swimming, and she flying. They realized they'd been tricked. What the Rhue Weaver was truly after was Olyia's power of Inspiration, as she was the Muse of Music."

I looked closer at the sarcophagus. I couldn't tell if she had a mermaid tail because Ereatith's wings covered her lower half, but as I studied the sculpture I saw Olyia had what appeared to be partial wing nubs, as though the sculptor had run out of stone.

"The Rhue Weaver claimed he had only enough strength to return Ereatith's form to his natural state—and would do so only in exchange for Olyia's power."

"That's awful!"

"It is, because she tried." Kal turned to me, dark eyes drilling into mine. "Because a Muse cannot give away her power, nor can it be removed without the death and the destruction of worlds—so Olyia lived in captivity of the Weaver as he tried desperately to force her inspiration to his will."

"Why didn't she just fly away?"

"The Weaver thought of that and had her wings shorn off."

My hands flew to my mouth. "God!"

"Ereatith spent ten years and countless attempts to rescue her. The world suffered during her captivity and grief. Music began to disappear, chords were lost, tunes forgotten. At last the Weaver released her, broken and depleted. Her power fading from her broken heart, as she'd believed Ereatith had forsaken her to her fate."

I listened, wide-eyed, breathless.

"When Ereatith found her, she was near death. He flew her to Lost Rook where he nursed her back to the living, but she was changed. Darker."

"What happened to music?"

"It eventually recovered—but it did not burst forth in a powerful cycle, as it would have otherwise. They say that is when dissonant chords were first created and minor keys flourished. The two lived out their days near Lost Rook, dying only moments apart in old age."

The marble coffin across the room, suddenly took on an even more somber cast. "That was Celeste's favorite story? It's very morbid and depressing."

Kal smiled. "She always liked the fatalistic ones, I suppose."

I couldn't help but smile, remembering her stash of weeping, heart-breaking movies and books of poetry both terrible and tragic. "She did, didn't she?"

"She once made me read this book…" he began.

And together we finished, "…*Wuthering Heights*."

He chuckled. I grinned.

"Yeah," I added. "She read it every winter."

A moment of remembrance. A casual sharing of her beautiful life with someone who treasured it as much as only I could, brought a tremendous sense of relief. They'd been married for longer than I was alive, and yet I'd had her longer.

How unfair is that?

It was no wonder Celeste loved tragic stories—her life had been one long sacrifice.

Kal turned to me then, lifting his black wings high. "I must take her soon to the pyre." He tilted his head, dark eyes searching my face. "I must speak with you about things she told me you will need to know. But first we will put her to rest."

I nodded, sniffing and wiping my nose with the back of my hand.

"I wish a few moments with my wife."

I looked at Celeste once more, memorizing her deathly visage and storing it with my memories of her smiling, radiant face. I touched the silk edge of Kal's wing and walked from the room as the light from the dome ceiling began to wane.

I slipped out the door and came up short to a congregation of hundreds of mourners with torches spread out over the green acreage.

"Many heads of state have begun to arrive for the procession," Liam whispered in my ear as he joined me on the steps. "Those who are not yet here are waiting at the pyre for the procession to arrive at sunset."

"Are we going with the group?"

"Yes. My father will carry two torches, so I can carry you with the bearers."

A terrible whirring of air like ripping burlap made me clap my hands over my ears. A gust of wind kicked dirt and a vortex of loose grass up between the congregation and the steps. I squinted up to see what caused the small tornado. My startled scream was choked off by Liam's large hand.

Panic warred with amazement as a dragon's scarlet belly dipped over the crowd, banked a wide circle, and flew to a spot between myself and the mourners, where it landed, back-beating wings the size of a sailboat canvas. Hundreds of torch flames wavered as its great bulk came to rest on the grass.

"Do not be afraid. It is just a dragon and her Ryder. Xabien."

My body stiffened, heart thundering in my chest.

"Do not scream," Liam warned. I nodded and he lifted his hand.

The beast was enormous, easily four times the size of an elephant, with a long tail spiked with a gold-plated spade. The Ryder remained seated in a saddle on the creature's back. His golden armor matched the dragon's, reflecting the setting sun. The beast shook its head, jangling its metal harness.

I knew the Ryder watched me through his visor.

"Do not worry. This is a ceremony he will not dare interrupt," Liam said.

But even before the words were out of Liam's mouth, Xabien patted the animal's neck and the creature dropped to its belly. The Ryder threw his reins over the saddle horn, swung his leg over the side, and dropped to the ground gracefully.

I sucked in air as I realized he intended to come up the steps. Liam moved forward, blocking me with his wings. Peeking around the wall of feathers, I briefly considered running back into the safety of the mausoleum.

Xabien removed his helmet.

He was frighteningly, beautifully, cold. Long dark dreadlocks and sharp muscular features emphasized the brittle gaze of his black eyes. He took the steps two at a time and stood before Liam.

"You'd do well to come out, Fable." His voice was deep, hoarse.

"Not if—" Liam began.

"Silence, bird." Xabien spat. "Fable, why do you hide from your husband-to-be?"

I could barely hear him over the blood pounding in my ears, but I stepped out from behind Liam's back.

"Hello, Xabien."

He appraised me. Just taller than Liam, he appeared to be mostly human, with the exception of pointed ears and bone spikes protruding from his elbows.

"You've grown into a woman," he stated. His voice was like churning gravel.

I swallowed.

"Come. I will fly you to the pyre." He turned away and stalked back toward his beast.

I didn't move. Couldn't. If I went with him, I'd end up on a milk carton, or whatever passed for one on Aria.

Xabien soon realized I wasn't following him. I stood rooted to the stone, staring at the dragon in a daze. My thoughts were like buckshot. I couldn't remember what Sybil had told me about the betrothal contract.

"Fable. Come."

His tone jarred me from the stupor, and I snapped, "I'm not a dog, Xabien."

"But you are *mine*," he declared.

"Not for another two months." I straightened my skirt. "Until the Red Moon rises, I am my own."

He lifted his head, watching me, studying my body. Then he smiled. His posture changed, and he seemed to notice for the first time that the entirety of the gathering, heads of state and lords and ladies were watching.

"Very well. But two months will go by quickly in the frenzy of planning our nuptials. I will see you after the funeral." He paused, calculating. Xabien sized up Liam then gazed at me with something akin to a hungry dog, and finished, "To make arrangements, of course."

He turned and his dreadlocks snapped around his broad shoulders. Then he replaced his helmet and climbed up in the saddle. The dragon shook its head, jingling the metal chains of its bit.

Acid washed the back of my tongue, and I realized my knees were locked so hard that when I tried to step, I lurched and grabbed the wall to steady myself. Liam braced the small of my back with his large hand. Xabien watched us through his visor.

This just gets more fucked up by the minute. A dragon? Seriously?

The sun disk finally dipped all but a thumbs-width below the horizon, spilling rosy hues across the skybowl. Stars blinked to life.

All at once, the crowd let up a collective wail. A grief-filled, keening melody.

Kal emerged from the mausoleum doors carrying Celeste's shrouded figure. He lifted his wings, and the wailing stilled. He bore the body of his wife with stoic strength, the drapes of her white veil a dramatic contrast to his black clothes and wings.

His voice carried steadily over the crowd: "Celeste Augustine Duraith, we are gathered here to ferry you across the eternal waters."

Liam sidled close to me, fanning a wing around my back and surreptitiously resting a hand on my forearm. I didn't care who saw; I took his hand in my own, lacing his fingers through mine.

"Celeste has been sister, daughter, aunt, and mother. She was wife and lover. Celeste was a light bearer and a beacon of hope to many." Kal lifted his voice. "Those who saw by the torch she carried, lift your flame and guide her to the Silver Moon Path."

A strange song, alien and discordant, began to take melody in the gathering. First one voice, then ten, then hundreds. Long lilting words built of vowels and thirds. One by one, the crowd lifted to the heavens. Bodies disappeared in the gloaming darkness, but their lights filled the air like a cloud of stars.

When the sky was lit by song and torches, Kal launched, carrying Celeste. He flew into the midst of the wavering lights. They grouped around him as they made off toward the island where the pyre had been built and the rites would be performed.

Xabien remained on his mount, waiting.

"Are you ready?" Liam asked.

Wrapping my arms around his neck, I nodded, and my memory flashed to the moment just hours before, when I'd tangled my legs around him and screamed in agonizing pleasure.

Liam lifted off, and I was surprised by how accustomed I'd become to the jarring beginnings of launch. I gazed out at the sea of floating lights reflecting off the ocean as the funeral procession flew toward Celeste's final rest.

I couldn't help but tally the day's total shockers.

I'm burning the body of my dearest aunt, falling for a birdman, marrying a Dragon Ryder or negating a treaty that will start a world war...and if all goes according to schedule, I'll be dead in 152 pages. Jesus Christ, Fable! Just how many mistakes do you think you can survive, anyway?

Chapter Seventeen

Canto Mors Mortis
Along the Silver Moon Path
Come home, my sister
Come home

We flew among the torches, bathed in songs of lament. It was impossible to make out any details of the landscape, but the drifting lights and the moon reflecting off the water gave the impression of mountainous islands and a treacherous strait. The Isle of Crossing rose like a giant stump from the ocean, a wide, flat plateau stretching 300 feet above the water at the end of Willows Waning Fjord.

Sybil had explained to me earlier that the isle had been used for all things ceremonial in Avian culture since before recorded history.

The procession drifted ahead of us, lighting the way. The whirring beat of dragon wings in the darkness served as a menacing reminder that Xabien was close behind, keeping us in sight. I kept glancing back, assuring myself he wasn't actually trying to close the distance. In all, it was less than a 20-minute flight from the mausoleum to the isle.

As we neared, I estimated the length of the plateau to be half a mile and another quarter–mile wide. The blaze of two dozen bonfires illuminated the gathered masses. All those who could not fly had gathered on the plateau to await the arrival of the procession. I couldn't make out faces, but I was shocked by the sheer number of mourners. Thousands. Enough people filled the island's flat top to pack a college football stadium twice over.

There were no trees or outcroppings, yet there were constructed pillars—nine of them—around a ceremonial amphitheater of what looked to be white coral buffed to a glossy sheen by the relentless ocean winds. However, we did not fly to the amphitheater on the south end of the isle but to a smaller, more intimate stone structure on the north side.

The torch bearers swooped in like so many falling stars, leaving tracers of light in the night sky.

Kal hovered above the crowd, waiting for everyone to land. Liam brought us in near the stacked wood pyre and touched down gently. As soon as my feet were safely on solid land, I glanced at the sky, anxiously looking for Xabien. He circled his dragon once around the plateau before landing near the back, far from the pyre.

The song picked up again, a wordless lullaby this time, as Kal sank from the heavens to lay Celeste's shrouded corpse atop the pyre. The cords of wood were interlaced in rows of ash and cherry, soaked in a musky sweet resin, and stacked eight feet high.

As her body came to rest, four Avian women, including River, launched into the air, flying in a clockwise circle around Celeste and singing as they pulled back the shroud from her face, sprinkled oils atop her body, and tucked bundles of herbs and flowers around her still form. The aroma of myrrh and sandalwood mixed with cedar and pitch smoke from the torches.

When the caretaking was finished and the Avian women returned to the throng, River flew to my side and stood with me, taking my hand as Liam took the other. Mourners came forward through the crowd to place gifts and offerings near the pyre. A centaur with the body of a bay horse hung a copper medallion on the pyre. Agatha flitted behind him and offered a small sparkling stone. Once she'd placed the scarlet gem, she zipped back to where Liam and I stood and settled wordlessly on Liam's shoulder.

Avians poured pitchers of oils and wine on the tinder around the stone circle, while others brought bundles of flowers, reeds, and feathers.

"She was loved," River whispered. "Celeste was responsible for much of the return to our old ways."

Kal carried a torch toward the tower of wood bearing the remains of his wife. He began singing, a tortured sound in a language of long vowels and minor chords.

Leaning in to Liam, I whispered, "What is he saying?"

He listened then replied softly, "It is difficult to translate into English. Our language is meant to be understood only in song." He paused, listening again. "But his melody means 'We ferry you, Celeste, to the underworld, where all worlds hold court at the end of days. Sail the Silver Moon Path across the water to eternal music, and I will join you soon.'"

That Kal had plainly loved her, and that she had loved him for so long, gave me a sense of peace. She'd had some happiness in her life, despite all the grief and trauma my being with her entailed; at least she'd been loved as a woman.

He lifted the flame to the trail of oil. The fire caught, running across the circle and up the pyre where the resin-soaked wood and oils flashed and erupted into a golden-orange pillar.

The burst of heat lifted the hair off my shoulders and stung my eyes.

The intensity of the blaze and the hungry roar of flames mixing with burning oils and flesh filled the night, and I let myself feel it. Just feel the pyre flame bring light to a dark place inside that I'd been hiding from since I'd gotten the news of her death. The hollow knowledge that nothing would ever be the same.

The moon rose, luminous and full, shining a silver path over the still ocean toward the mourners. The *Canto Mors Mortis*, loosely translated to *Song of Death* or *Singing the Dead*, began first when two dozen Avians circled around the pyre quickly engulfed in flames.

Fire licked upward toward the stars, reaching for the skybowl as the Avians turned their backs to the pyre.

Kal crooned the first note, deep and soulful, holding the resonant tone for a beat of 20 before moving his black wings in slow undulation. The Avian to his right harmonized with his tone, carrying the song. Each Avian in the circle took up a turn and began the slow flap of their wings against the flames. When the motion went around the circle once, the note changed and the beat of wings increased from an undulation to a regular tempo. Two dozen Avian wings moved in a wave, spiraling the air current counter-clockwise. Gently, rhythmically, until the harmony changed and a drum beat echoed from behind the gathering, resonant and deep.

As the drums began, so too did the song of the gathered mourners, carried on the drafts of minor chords, longingly, reverently. Sung with breaths and feathers, wings and soul. The counter spiral of the air around the pyre teased the flames into a funnel of fire, each revolution driving the conflagration higher, spinning the orange-gold filaments toward sky and illuminating the Weaving Fates as they worked their loom of starry destinies.

Canto Mors Mortis echoed across the black ocean. A song of passing sung by all gathered to put a soul to rest, free of regrets, beloved of family, and with gratitude expressed. All who raised voice to the *Canto* sang their forgiveness of all transgressions, their hopes for the blessed afterlife of the soul, and the last goodbyes to one they held dear.

When the spiral of fire took on a blue tint, the Avians finally began the decrescendo of music and the bellows of their wings slowed. They stepped back to the gathering to hold their loved ones and watch the flames die to ash, humming in chorus until the pyre burned to coals and crimson dawn broke the horizon.

Sometime in the night, I'd wound my arms around Liam's body and been cocooned. When red dawn leaked over the ocean, he whispered, "We should go. Kal must be alone to gather the cremains into her urn."

Smoking coals were all that remained. Kal stood at the edge of the plateau, black hair drifting around his shoulders, face upturned to the sky. I wanted to tell him goodbye but could see by his faraway gaze he was someplace else, with his memories. I didn't want to rob him of his last moments with her.

I sighed, feeling as though I'd been drained by heat and tears. I tried to hook my arms around Liam's neck but they flopped back; weakness and exhaustion made my limbs too heavy even for me. Even my eyelids seemed too weighty and gritty to blink.

Without comment, Liam bent, scooped me up, and launched. I murmured, "It was just the way page 87 said it would be."

Neither Liam nor I had had a full night's sleep in the last three days. At best we'd managed naps in stretches of three or four hours here and there. As we landed on the third-story balcony of his family home, I could see exhaustion in the shadows of his face, bruised under-eyes, and heavy brows.

I likely didn't look much better. We both trudged toward the door, his talons dragging while I stumbled over the hem of my skirts. We staggered in, beat and silent. I realized he'd landed on the balcony of his own room.

Like all the other rooms of the castle, it was spacious, well lit, and sparsely furnished with oversized pieces; but the difference was in the collection of weapons and armor hanging on the walls and statues.

Liam went straight for the bed and collapsed in a heap of down and fabric, legs dangling over the edge. He sighed. "Just a few hours."

Despite exhaustion, I couldn't look away from the weaponry. I crossed the room, stretching fingers out to test the edge of a wicked-looking samurai-like sword. I jerked my hand back before I drew blood. They were defiantly not for show. They were sharp, deadly, and ready for use.

Perhaps ten different kinds of blades, a handful of staffs, and a dozen lancing weapons with long spear shafts and barbed points lined the wall. There were three sets of armor with lacings, buckles, and straps, mostly silver and black with scarlet under-dressage.

Then I thought of the scars I'd seen on his body and knew he must not have been wearing his armor when he'd taken the point of something near his left hip, or when a set of talons gored his shoulder.

I was only alive thanks to luck and Liam's fast thinking. But that thought sank in in a completely different way when I saw his stash of arms: Not only was I alive because of him, I was unharmed, unscratched, and unmolested in any way because he was protecting me with all the skills at his disposal—and not once had I seen him need to draw a blade.

Something about the knowledge that he probably knew full well how to use any weapon in his collection with deadly force, and yet he had only ever held me tenderly, made me warm. I wandered back to the bed where he was still and silent.

One eye cracked open, but he didn't speak.

Climbing up on the bed, negotiating the swath of black satin skirts, I shuffled on my knees to his side. "Here let's get you settled better." I slipped my hands around his body and tried to drag him up further on the bed, but he was a solid trunk of muscle.

"Ouch, you're on my wing."

"Oh, sorry!" I scrambled, falling sideways across his body.

He let out an "oof" as his arms banded around my waist. "What are you doing?"

"I was trying to pull you up, so you can get some decent sleep, but you're really heavy," I whispered against his chest.

His breathing changed as I lay atop him. His eyes darkened and broad hands slipped across the slick fabric of my waist. The electric response in my body was immediate and startling. I pushed against his shoulders and sat up.

"Are you hungry?" I asked.

He nodded, setting my insides to simmer with his gaze.

"Me, too," I said, voice wavering. "I'll go get us something to eat."

Slinking down his body, I couldn't help but notice the fine sculpture of his limbs beneath my fingers before I slithered off the bed, my breath coming short. "You get some rest, and I'll go gather up some food and that stinky beer you drink."

He didn't argue as my feet landed on the rug. I turned back to see him watching me. He groaned, flopping back into the covers. I hurried from the room, my lower belly in knots, heart fluttering.

Stalking down the corridor, I mumbled to myself, knowing that if I took food back in to Liam I'd better have made up my mind about what I intended to do with all the sexual tension crackling like the beginning of monsoon skies. "Why not, Fable?" "Because he's a bird and you're a human, and what kind of life would that be?" "Icarus' wings, you're already thinking like 'settle down and have kids' and he might only be thinking, you know, a good quickie lay." "Friends with benefits?" "That might not be so bad, but…I don't think I could, not with him. He's different."

I turned the corner into the kitchen and found the whole place was empty. Then I remembered one crucial part of my own argument. "Oh, and I'll be dead soon. Or married to a dragon creep and *then* dead soon—so what difference does it make?"

The kitchen was only one of many. Three hearths and a large stove faced opposite ends of the room with cupboards and butcher blocks for preparation in between.

Since I was alone, I set to gathering supplies on a tray. A loaf of bread sitting on a wooden block and a ceramic jar of butter were added to a pile of items to take upstairs. Some fruit that looked like oranges but smelled like apricots and a dish of black seeds I'd seen the Avians sprinkle on their buttered bread. A pitcher of water and a jar of honey. I found a wooden keg of the smelly beer, poured a mug, and added it to the tray. It was a substantial amount of food, but then, I'd seen Liam put away twice as much in one sitting.

Carefully, I lifted the platter, balancing it with my chest, and ambled out the door to the hallway.

Heart hammering, belly fluttering, I'd made up my mind. The knowledge that I intended to take him breakfast, then make a meal out of him, made my feet move a little faster.

Don't overthink it. Just go with it.

"There you are!" Sybil's voice cracked through the corridor. I nearly dropped everything as I flinched, face flaming with guilty intentions.

She caught up to me, babbling faster than I could understand her words: "Here, let me take that. They're up in the Tide Chamber waiting for you. He's really angry, so you'd better go. Remember what I told you." She caught the tray, practically jerking it out of my arms. "Xabien can't force you into a marriage if you're not in your right mind. And you're not, remember?" She looked at the tray. "What's this for, anyway? You must be really hungry."

"For Liam," I mumbled through the shock of her words.

"I'll take it to him. You just go."

Sybil turned with the tray and left me alone in the hall. I sagged against the wall, my mind racing with my few options.

And they were indeed few: Run or walk.

Resting my head against the stone, I looked up at the window. The stained-glass mural depicted a nymph brushing her hair near a pond. In the water, breaching the surface just beyond her gaze, a dark-eyed creature watched her, lurking.

It resonated. How could it not? A girl going about her business, doing her own thing—and just out of sight, cloaked in secrets and mysteries, were those bastards of dubious intent. Everyone had an agenda. Everyone had plans for her. But no one asked her what she wanted.

The more I thought about it, the angrier I became. I shoved off the wall and stormed down the corridor.

The Tide Chamber was an antechamber built off the fourth floor. All the floor-to-ceiling windows were cast open, filling the space with the distant sound of surf and the scent of sea. As I entered, Gunthor rose and Xabien slowly followed. River and Delia remained in their chairs by the hearth.

"Fable," Gunthor greeted. He was so well put together, with his white hair pulled tight and his red and silver drapes perfectly pressed, you'd never know he'd been up all night grieving an old friend. "I introduce you to Xabien, your future husband."

Xabien was even more intimidating in daylight. He'd tied back his dreadlocks with a leather band. His olive skin looked freshly shaved, though the grit of travel clung to his clothing, and the pinched corners of his eyes exposed his true exhaustion.

"We've met," I stated.

Xabien flashed a puzzled expression before recovering. "My condolences on your loss, future *wife*."

"How thoughtful to bring your condolences in person. But I'm not your wife yet." Affecting a smile of ice turned out to be effortless.

"But that is not the reason for my visit," he continued.

I interrupted. "What reason could you have for intruding on my time of mourning?"

"It is also the time of planning your *wedding*," he said through his teeth.

"Luckily, I'm not a big-white-wedding kind of girl. No planning required."

"Planning *is* required. You have a pilgrimage to make, and traditions to adhere to, because you will be *my wife*!"

All the logical arguments I'd planned while walking up the stairs vanished as his anger mounted. Each word he emphasized changed his face. Small spikes bloomed from the edges of his eyes, and the horns on his elbows lengthened.

"If you do not intend to take the traditions of my people to heart in this arrangement," he shouted, "I can only conclude you have no intention of keeping with our contract." His face darkened as a small trickle of blood trailed down his forehead, followed by an emerging horn. Blue veins throbbed at his temples.

Xabien's show of fury brought out my own rage. All the violent anger of my circumstances, loss, and the blatant manipulation of my life narrowed to a pinpoint. At last, I had a target.

"How dare you question my intentions!" I hissed. "How dare you try to intimidate me in my time of mourning or press me to your own agenda!"

"How dare you negate your promise!" he bellowed.

"I've done no such thing, you jerk!"

River jumped to her feet, throwing her arms wide. A sheet of fog fell across my emotions, dampening my fury. The sounds of the ocean lessened and the air in the room thickened.

Xabien's sudden sway and confused expression hinted he felt the same muted response. "Don't use your witchery on me!" he snapped at River, but his horns retracted. The bone spikes on his body slid back under his skin.

"Everyone please calm," Gunthor said. "Diplomatic agreements are rarely reached with screaming."

"She belongs to me, and I am here to claim her," Xabien stated.

I glared. "I don't belong to anyone for two months, am I right?"

"Technically, yes," Delia offered. "The betrothal states the first red moon rising, which is two months hence." She sipped at her tea then settled the cup and saucer on the burgundy napkin in her lap.

"Then there's nothing to talk about," I said, turning on my heel and storming for the door.

"You will not walk out on me, Fable," Xabien warned.

I turned back. "Really? I've had just about enough of anyone telling me what I will or will not do, or what's expected of me, or what their plans are for me. So how about this?" I took a deep breath. "I am clear in understanding that political marriage to exemplify peace mandates the two proposed candidates be of sound mind and body, and not under duress or fear of bodily harm."

The silence in the room answered my question, so I continued: "I am within my rights to insist on time to recover my memories."

The room went still. Gunthor frowned. Xabien narrowed his eyes.

"You were all of the above when you agreed to the contract," Xabien said dangerously.

"Because my memories are incomplete, I have no way of knowing that, now, do I? I have two more months to mourn my aunt and try to recover my memories…and I swear to fucking god, if you push me before then, I will do everything in my power to legally negate this contract—due to my unsound mind."

"Perhaps we should seek the Council's advice on the subject sooner rather than later," River said casually. "We could put it to rest now, rather than wait the two months."

Xabien sighed and cracked his neck. With a short glance at Gunthor, Xabien said, "With certain members of the Council present, I would speculate putting the choice to them would mean the end of our treaty." He flexed his jaw as he snatched the leather gloves from his belt. "You will make your vows to me and bring prosperity and fertility to my nation, or I will come for you with all the wrath of my hordes."

He didn't so much as blink as he marched by me on his way out, but then he paused and spat. "And when you are my wife, you will not be permitted to keep company with that filthy bird." The door slammed behind him, cracking the wooden frame.

My knees wobbled. I staggered to a chair and collapsed.

"That was fast thinking," Delia said, hiding her smile with her teacup.

"It is perhaps not wise to antagonize him," Gunthor warned.

"Fable is well within her rights, Gunthor, and you know it." River poured a cup of tea from a pot on the table. The sea breeze from the open window lifted the edge of the burgundy tablecloth.

Gunthor appraised me differently than he had before.

At length, my body stopped shaking. "We all know I have to get back to Earth."

"The manuscript page of Celeste's funeral did indeed mark page 87," Gunthor interjected.

My throat tightened. "I noticed that, too."

"It can no longer be denied," Delia agreed.

"I need to get back to Earth, before the next manuscript page happens," I said. "I need to intercept Maya before anyone else does."

I thought there would be an argument, that they'd try to make me stay or convince me of my foolishness. But to my surprise, they didn't disagree. In fact, they didn't say anything at all.

"Liam needs rest and food; if he wants to go, we'll leave at sunset. But if he doesn't, I'm going to have to ask one of you to fly me back to the gateway." I smoothed my hair and stood.

Gunthor sighed. "You would not be able to keep Liam from going with you even if you could harness the full force of the tide."

I was beginning to understand that what Gunthor said was probably true, and the knowledge made my heart beat a little stronger. "Thank you for everything," I murmured. "I hope we will see each other again soon."

River and Gunthor each hugged me goodbye.

Delia hobbled to the door, her white wings trailing as she ducked into the hallway and we stood alone. "No one will blame you, Fable, if you choose not to come back."

"What do you mean?"

"I mean much has been taken from you. You have been robbed of a great deal, and you have a right to some happiness." Her ruined face looked up at me and she smiled. "To be a Muse, to inspire— you deserve joy. You must have happiness to be able to spread it.

If you make it to Earth and can do more good there, then there is where you should stay."

She leaned in close and whispered, "And, Fable, do not dismiss what part your feelings for Liam may play in the shape of this story. Trust your story."

I couldn't even fathom what she might mean, but I hugged her gently, and then made my way to Liam's room.

My mind looped through arguments: "Will you please put your life on the line for me *again*? Would you mind being a target while I spend my last weeks trying to find answers to the questions that got Celeste killed?"

No biggie, right?

The door to his room was still closed. The tray of food sat on the floor in the hall. I opened the door, bent to retrieve the food, and made my way into the chamber lit by morning light. Closing the door with my hip, I crossed the room and put the tray on the bedside table.

He was so painfully beautiful. Dark wings spread across the bed, tousled blond curls against the russet silk coverlet. I didn't have the heart to wake him. I shrugged out of my jacket and climbed up onto the bed. Then I slipped across the covers to the nook against his chest where I snuggled in under his arm and it flexed around me, but he didn't fully wake as I relaxed against the protection of his body.

Despite the warmth and comfort mixed with exhaustion, I couldn't sleep. I could only lie awake in his arms, breathing in his scent, counting his heartbeats, and wishing I hadn't lost so many years with him.

Why did I agree to go under the shield all those years ago? If I could only remember.

The slow realization of what I needed to do had been growing, stretching in the back of my mind like a hibernating bear. I knew it was dangerous, possibly even deadly, and god knows the last thing I wanted to do was poke at it.

The 13 pages laid out the path, and Liam wasn't in any of the remaining cues. If the *Prophecy of Crows* actually was prophetic—and I hated to admit it, but it did have some eerie similarities—then the only thing I could do, should do, was find the other Muses in the pages. That's what Celeste would have wanted.

As I lay pressed against his side, I knew I would do whatever needed to be done, for Celeste, the Muses, and most of all, Liam.

I also knew he'd never let me do what clearly needed to be done.

Celeste's voice drifted unbidden into my thoughts. "Sometimes, Rosebud, the only way to put your feet on the right path is to close your eyes and step one foot in front of the other. Trust your story to give you the proper journey—then the path will do its part to find its way under your toes."

Trust your story? Delia had said it, too. What does that even mean?

Finally, after an hour of agonizing, I carefully climbed out of bed.

"Where are you going?" he whispered groggily.

"To the bathroom," I lied. "Keep the bed warm for me. I'll be right back."

He sighed and shifted, closing his eyes.

I stared at him, at the marvel of the creature-man, memorizing what he looked like spread across the sheets.

I snuck out the door into the hall and carefully clicking it shut behind me.

"What took you so long?"

"*Gah*!" I flinched at Sybil's voice. "Why do you always seem to catch me when I'm guilty of something?"

"I hear it's a human thing. So much guilt," she teased.

She was dressed in a pair of my jeans with a sky blue Avian top. Her red hair was pulled into a tight bun and wrapped in a sheer scarf. In one hand she held a flight harness, in the other my back-pack. "If you want a head start, we should leave right now."

"How did you know?"

She shrugged and turned to the stairs. "You're not very good at shielding your waves of energy. It's a good thing my brother doesn't have an empathic bone in his body, or he'd have caught on to your determination before you did."

I followed her down the stairs. "Then you know why he can't go. So why would I put you in that danger?"

On the landing she tossed me the backpack. "You wanna fly in a dress or in pants?" She rubbed the denim with obvious enjoyment. "I hope you don't mind I borrowed these."

I dug in the bag as I responded, "Sybil, I'm serious. Why?"

"I can't tell what you're going to do. It doesn't work that way. I can only feel your resolve because it's so powerful, and I'm going because you're not leaving without me again, and that's that!"

She crossed her arms, raised an eyebrow, and fixed her stance for a fight.

"Yeah, okay, you can take me to the gateway—but that's as far as you can go."

"What was it Celeste used to call you?" Sybil tapped a finger against her chin. "Oh, right, *bossy.*"

I grinned at the memory. "That's funny; she always said that when I was trying to direct the plays in the courtyard."

Sybil smiled. "You remember."

I slipped a pair of jeans on under my skirt. Glancing at Sybil, I smiled. "Yeah, I remember that!" I quickly changed out of the skirt and left it folded on the window seat of the landing.

"Wonderful, "Sybil exclaimed.

"I know, right?" I took her hand. "Let's go."

Peeking down the stairwell, she checked to see that the path to the second floor balcony was clear. "He's going to be upset, you know."

"Yeah…but he'll be alive," I said.

"Okay, it's clear."

Sybil sprinted ahead, running out onto the balcony. She held the harness out so I could step into my half while she buckled the straps around her body. It was a two-part piece. The Avian side looked like a backpacker's harness with three D-rings on the front.

My side had a sleeve for my lower body like a hang-glider pouch and three clips which hooked to the D-rings on the Avian harness.

"Did you make this?" I wondered, fingering the soft green sleeve. It had been embroidered with gold feather designs.

"I told you I'd make a special harness while you were gone." She spun me around so we faced one another as she clipped my harness to hers. "You ready?"

I nodded, reached out, and grabbed her as she squatted and lunged over the wall of the balcony, plummeting toward the ocean.

She yelped with delight as I clung for dear life, not certain she had Liam's strength to pull us both out of the dive. But her wings banked and tilted, and we caught the updraft that shot us skyward, catapulting us both above the cliffs and back over the castle. I thought I might be ill and gulped air to keep from being sick.

Sybil squealed, pounding the air with her wings. "Wasn't that fun?"

"No," I said, swallowing several times.

"Are you still worried about Liam?"

"I just hope he doesn't hold it against me too long."

She laughed as the valley passed beneath and the autumn tree line of the forest approached in a wall of yellow and ruby leaves. "You do realize he will catch up, right? He's only going to be a few hours behind, and he will be able to shorten that between his anger and fear for you, and my slower speed. So whatever it is you need to do alone, you must do it quickly."

"I know." I paused. "Sybil?"

"Yes?"

"Thanks."

"Anytime." She laughed. "So are you going to tell me what it is we're doing that my brother can't be a part of?"

"Trusting the story."

Chapter Eighteen

Rock
Feather
Talon

We stopped several times on our way to the Gate. At sunset, as Sybil's strength waned, we landed to have a light snack on a peak overlooking a lush valley bright with the bronze and copper shades of fall.

She'd stuffed my backpack with dried fruits, smoked salmon, and breads.

"We cannot linger for long. I imagine he is already on his way."

I washed a chunk of bread down with water. "It's really beautiful up here."

Perched on cold stone, we gazed over the valley as the sun dipped between two mountains in the distance. We ate, watching the sunset and waiting for the stars, so we'd have light to fly by.

"Did you…?"

Sybil tilted her head. "Yes?"

"Didn't we used to talk about boys?"

She beamed. "You remember?"

"Well, no, but as best friends, it seems like we would have talked about boys a lot." I bit into a dried fig.

She nodded and turned to the view, her sharp features highlighted by fading light. "We used to talk about boys. Then you started talking only about Liam."

"Oh."

I felt an odd sense of loss, like I'd given something away that meant a great deal but I didn't know what it was. I chewed the fig, peering down into the valley. A clear river reflected the sunset, and trees all hues of gold and rust lent the landscape a magical painted quality.

"Do you…do you have a boyfriend?" I wondered at last.

She licked her lips, fingering a bread crumb off her chin. "There is someone I love, yes."

"That's cool! What's he like?"

Sybil smiled, her face changing as she ducked her head. "He's of the Snow Owl clan."

"What's his name?"

"Quinndrian."

"Well? What's he like?"

She gazed off toward the valley. The light was nearly gone, the stars beginning to wake. "He's very bold." Grinning, she said, "He kissed me once. We were on the landing sand of the East Court. I hadn't seen him for almost a year, as he is stationed in the Reaches, along the border. We both touched down at the same time, and he didn't even wait for me to fold my wings or say hello. He strode across the sand, took me in his arms, dipped me back, and kissed me hard."

"Wow! That's so romantic! How long had you been together?"

"We weren't. I'd only met him a couple of times before. I was translating Fairnish messages he brought back to the Capitol City command."

"So you had only met him a couple of times, and he kissed you like that? What did you do?"

"What do you mean? I am a proper Avian lady—I slapped him. Then said, 'Meet me in the sky at sunset and we will fly together.' Then I left him standing on the sand." She chuckled.

"'Fly together'? Is that what you kids call it these days?"

"We went on many long flights and danced with one another in the clouds." Her brows furrowed.

I sighed and looked up at the skybowl of winking stars. "So what happened then? Why aren't you together?"

"It is not so simple." She picked up the remains of dinner and tucked it in the bag. "He is a captain of the Elite Guard and must remain on the Reaches patrol until his service is complete. I am a diplomatic translator and liaison to the Council, of which my father is a member. We cannot, either of us, give up our posts until this unrest is settled and the world is put back to harmony."

I frowned. "I'm sorry."

She smiled sadly, her red brows pinching together. "I wish more than anything, sometimes, that I'd taken him in free-fall when I had the chance. If I'd mated with him when I saw him last, I would have been within my rights to visit him as often as I choose. Then perhaps I would know the joy of motherhood, and he would have a home to return to."

The valley was dark, lit only by the stars and the rising moon which reflected off the river like a ribbon of heaven cutting a path through the trees. It was peaceful, tranquil. How could so much dysfunction in a world on the brink of war for 14 years also contain such spectacular beauty?

"I am refreshed. We must go," she said as she stood and adjusted the harness.

I couldn't help but notice the weighted tilt of her wings and the way she refused to meet my eyes. I had no idea what it was like to love a man so much or to truly feel empty without him.

Quietly buckling my harness, I slipped my legs into the sleeve, shimmied the fabric up around my back, and then shrugged into the backpack.

We took to the air, passing over a sleeping landscape. We didn't speak. There wasn't much to say. Too many years had passed; too much changed. We'd become different people, and neither of us had a frame of reference for the other. A cultural chasm and two separate worlds lay between us.

I'd never felt so alone.

Two more stops in wooded areas throughout the night for short naps brought us to dawn and the promise of safety. As we set out in the morning, Sybil checked the straps on my harness before buckling me in. "We should make it to the Glade in less than five hours."

"How are you holding up?"

"The reprieve of the Glade will be a welcome break."

We'd been flying west for four hours when Sybil glanced back at the eastern horizon near the edge of the early morning sun glare. "Avians," she said.

Craning my neck, I could only just make out three specks in the distance. Without something for comparison, I couldn't judge their size or speed.

"Is that bad?" I wondered.

"There is no way to tell if they are friends or enemies. It is best we hurry."

Sybil struck the air with her wings and picked up speed. Air whistled past my ears and I shouted, "What if it's Liam?"

"Then he will catch up to us eventually, and I will leave the explaining to you."

What if it isn't Liam?

She clenched her jaw, pulled me up tighter to her body to cut the drag between us, and bent her head into the wind, hammering her strokes. I felt the tension in her muscles as I clung to her neck.

Maybe they won't even notice us.

But even as I hoped we would pass them in the distance, I realized they were catching up.

"I will not be able to outfly them," Sybil panted. "We are too heavy and I am spent."

They were closing in. We had a head start, but over the next half hour they steadily gained.

When I heard her labored breathing, I began to worry. "Sybil, it's okay. We can land and fight them off on the ground."

She was too out of breath to speak but squeezed her eyes shut and doubled her efforts, grunting with each stroke as she sliced the air with her wings. I fought the idiotic urge to paddle my hands.

At last they were close enough that I could make out faces and dark wings. I knew her instantly.

Abra.

She was smaller and less bulky than the other two Avian men, but she kept up with them stroke for stroke. Her bare arms were covered in black tattoos.

The Avian men were dressed in grey armor. Their crow wings fueled memories of the attack at the café. Screams. Black feathers. Blood. Breaking glass and papers drifting. Panic boiled my stomach in acid at the glint of their long, silver swords.

Then a screeching cry, a monstrous bellow sounded from behind us. I looked back but couldn't make out anything in the glare of the sun. Whatever caused the noise was coming in fast and nearly invisible with the camouflage of white solar brilliance.

"What was *that*?" I screamed.

"A dragon!" Sybil shouted. "Hold on!"

There was nothing else to do but hang from the harness and pray to the Weaving Fates. I was helpless to do anything hundreds of feet above the ground. I could only watch the scene unfold as wind snapped my hair against my face, and Sybil's frantic flight drove us ever closer to the Glade.

The raging bellow echoed once more and the great red-bellied, gold-plated beast plummeted from the sun's glare. Diving directly at us.

Xabien.

237

We were in the lead with three Crow Avians close behind. One Avian lifted his sword to strike. But Xabien was closer to him than to me, and with a great screaming roar, his dragon attacked. Billowing out its leathery wings, it stretched down with long muscled legs ending in deadly claws. They appeared silhouetted against the sun, a picturesque beast of prey striking the enemy.

Wings spread wide, the dragon caught the Crow Avian by the back of the neck with his right talon then gorged the Crow's wing with his other claw. The Avian screamed as black feathers exploded and blood turned to mist in the air.

The Crow blindly thrust his sword over his shoulder at the animal's armored belly. Before he could bring his weapon around for another strike, the dragon ripped its prey in half, twisting one powerful leg as it squeezed, breaking the Crow's neck and severing his wings in the grip of its giant claws.

I screamed.

The dragon released the Avian corpse and it tumbled end over end, a black mass of feathers, drifting, drifting…drifting. The scene flickered through my memories, like déjà vu, until the body vanished into the canopy below.

Then Xabien arrowed toward us, but Abra was half the distance. She was close enough I could make out the raven tattoo on her forearm. She drew up her sword, metal flashing, wings driving the air to intercept us.

Xabien's war cry rent the air as Abra's blade swung toward Sybil's wing. In the second before the wicked metal made contact, Sybil banked out of reach and Abra was bowled sideways by the dragon's bulk.

With a gasping sob, Sybil battered the air with her remaining strength while Xabien chased after Abra. She ducked, dove, and maneuvered out of reach. The last Avian Crow veered toward them, attempting to strike at the dragon's flank as it pursued Abra.

I strained around in the harness to see what was happening. Xabien continued to give chase. Abra was good at evading, acrobatic and graceful, with her mid-air rolls and sudden direction shifts, almost as if she were anticipating each move the dragon and Ryder would make.

"I'm sorry, Fable!" Sybil shouted. "I can't make it!"

The oak line of the Glade loomed ahead. Beyond the tree line, we would be safe. The protection of the Glade would instantly neutralize any weapons.

We were heartbreakingly close when Sybil's wing-beats faltered and we dropped.

Shrieking, I clung to Sybil as exhaustion finally took its toll. She was only able to slow our plummet by snapping her wings open to catch the current and sliding us into a long glide toward the Glade.

Her body shook with strain, muscles flexed and quivering. I knew she didn't have enough strength left for a landing. Her whole body vibrated with effort. The dive was too steep, the speed too fast.

Until my legs snagged a tree top.

In an instant we went from falling to crashing.

Flipping end over end, our limbs whipped out of control. Branches stabbed my back and legs as we were flung akimbo. Sybil wrapped her wings around us, shielding the worst of the blows. The thunderous snapping of trees, rustling of leaves, and my screams filled the air.

We slammed the ground so hard air whooshed from my lungs. Dust and leaves exploded in an impact-cloud around our bodies.

For a moment I forgot how to breathe, or even move. Sybil lay utterly still. Her limp wing draped over my body scared me more than anything, and I took a painful, halting breath.

"Sybil?" I croaked. "Sybil, are you okay?"

Red and gold flashed above the canopy. Xabien circled the crash. I didn't believe he just happened to be in the area, or that he was just looking out for his future wife. He'd come for me. Thankfully the canopy was too thick for him to get down through the trees to our crash site.

My body hurt everywhere. My ribs were surely bruised, but nothing felt broken. Sybil had taken the worst of the impact. I inched out from under her wing and rolled her onto her back. Dry leaves crunched as I pushed her over.

Blood poured from a long gash at her temple. Her wings bled in dozens of places showing broken feathers and splinters of bone. "Oh, god."

Red wings blocked the sunlight. Xabien yelled down through the tunnel of wrecked tree branches: "Come with me willingly, and I will spare your bird companion!"

I hissed, "Sybil? Sybil, you've gotta get up."

She didn't move. I gripped the straps of the harness and hauled her toward the tree line marking the edge of the Glade and the beginning of sanctuary. She was heavy. Her wings splayed out, snagging on roots. "You're gonna be okay."

As I worked my way closer to the clearing, Xabien shouted down a string of guttural oaths in a language I gratefully didn't understand. The dragon clawed at the treetops, raining leaves and debris down on us.

I knew that if I could just get us there, even if Xabien landed in the Glade, his weapons would be nullified and he wouldn't be able to abduct me against my will.

Dragging Sybil took all my focus, all of my strength. I had to stop every few feet and tuck her wing over her body to squeeze between trees or through underbrush. The ominous sound of snapping branches behind us served as an urgent warning—Xabien decided not to wait. He fought his way down through the broken limbs.

The Glade was only ten feet away. I could make out the shape of the outdoor columns through the trees. Autumn light beaconed safety.

"Stay where you are!" Xabien shouted.

"Not a fucking chance!" I screamed back.

I put every last thing I had into dragging Sybil, lurching her body through the trees and over rocks. One last cluster of tangled roots was all that stood between us and the Glade. I stopped to fold her wings over her chest and continued dragging her by the webbed straps of the harness.

As I put my full body weight into it, one of the straps broke. I fell on my back into the safety of the Glade.

By the time I regained my feet, Xabien was clutching Sybil's leg. She was half in and half out of the protective marker. Just in that heartbeat when I thought we'd made it, he began pulling her back toward the shadow of the trees.

"You need not lose anyone else you love, Fable." His gravelly voice rippled along my spine. "Come with me willingly, and I will let this one go." His black eyes were framed by the bone spikes jutting from his skull.

"No."

"How many people need to die for you to honor your agreement? First your aunt, then your friend?" He looked demonic, terrifying. It only pissed me off.

"Let. Her. Go. You. Fugly-ass. Freak!" I screamed.

"You belong to me!" he howled. "Fourteen years I waited! You are mine by law!"

Xabien reeled us back toward the trees. Blood dripped from Sybil's forehead, mixing with her red hair.

From behind, a female voice boomed over the Glade: "*What is this?*" Gwendollyn's angry shout filled the air and a concussive blast of wind knocked me off my feet.

Xabien was the first to recover, clambering to stand. He was an arm's length from me, too close to pass up. He lunged into the Glade, grabbed me by the neck, and dragged me over Sybil's body toward the trees.

I tried to scream, but his hand around my windpipe cut me off.

Just that fast, we were both sucked up in the air by a funnel of wind. My boots lifted off the ground. Xabien wrapped his other hand around my neck for balance as his legs were ripped out from beneath him.

We spun in airborne circles. Gwendollyn walked toward us. With a casual flick of her right hand, Xabien's grip slipped free and I tumbled out of the whirlwind and collapsed on the grass.

Xabien roared, his dreadlocks flying. He struck out at the wind, screaming incoherently.

"You made an error, committing violence in my Glade, Ryder." Gwendollyn held up her hand; the wind died away but Xabien remained aloft, back arched unnaturally in levitation. "Hear me, Xabien of the Icy Reaches. You have been warned before. You are banished forthwith from this Glade. Forever."

He sneered and opened his mouth to reply.

But Gwendollyn dismissed him with a wave. He flew up into the sky until he disappeared, a speck on the horizon.

"Thank you," I choked, rubbing my bruised throat.

"We must get her to the healing waters," Gwendollyn replied.

I bent to drag her again, but the Oak Witch laughed. "I will move her, Fable."

Sybil's body lifted on a gentle breeze and hovered just above the blades of grass. Then she drifted across the clearing to the warm waters in the center of the Glade, where she sank slowly, submerging to her neck.

"Come," Gwendollyn said. "Some refreshment."

We walked to the healing pool. All the while, I was aware of a faint buzz, like a hive of bees. I swatted around my ears, but the sound persisted.

"I'd love to," I said, "but I just need to see Sybil is safe, and then I have to go."

"I understand."

Sybil floated in the water, her wings spread wide over the surface, her body sunk below. Her hair drifted like fiery seaweed. The bleeding already slowed, and the crack in her head appeared to be stitching together.

Fierce, hot relief stung my eyes to tears. I'd only just found her again, after 14 years of being without my best friend. After having her back in my life for a couple of days, I already couldn't imagine my life without her.

"Thank god," I murmured. "Sybil, you're going to be okay."

The Oak Witch looked down at me. "Do you yet hear the brook?"

She'd asked me the same question several days earlier. I hadn't known what she meant then, either.

Gwendollyn knelt to meet my eye. "You have not the time to spare, Fable. This day proves events are far more advanced than even Celeste knew." Her crown of branches seemed suddenly too heavy for such a slender neck.

"Were you and Celeste friends?"

"It is true." A long finger caressed my chin. "Here then, close your eyes and I will show you something of your nature."

I closed my eyes and heard her voice like rustling leaves.

"Fable, you are the goddess, the servant of Story. You are both bearer and midwife." She gestured to the water. "Hear the brook."

I strained my ears for the sound of water bubbling over the rocks.

"Everything has a story. A beginning, a journey, and an end. You must know each story in order to facilitate its purpose."

"Why are you telling me all this?" I opened my eyes.

"Because our sisterhood has run out of time for you to remember it on your own. I can but tell you where to look—the rest is up to you." She smiled sadly. "Celeste's mission for the rescue of our world lies with you. Now, close your eyes."

I closed my eyes.

"Listen to the water. It will speak to you."

Somewhere in the distance, a lark sang. I did hear the water, but it just sounded like a stream.

"I don't hear anything…"

"You are not listening."

"I just got chased by a dragon and Crows and a maniac, and fell out of the sky, and my best friend is broken, and I'm a little distracted," I snapped. "It just sounds like water, and I don't speak wet, or drip, or gurgle."

"Fable. You are a woman, a goddess, who has run out of time."

I opened my eyes. She was gazing at me sadly. "What do you mean?" I asked.

"You will no longer flourish cloaked in ignorance. It is time you claim your power—or die." When she stood, I craned my neck. "And with your death, so die our two worlds."

"Great. Fine print…" I mumbled.

"Separate yourself from the worry of your friend, from the worry of safety. Let go of all outcomes, all personal expectations, and serve only the story."

With a deep breath, I closed my eyes and listened.

At first there was only a trickle, the tinkling burble of water over rocks. But then it sounded suspiciously like laughter. A watery chuckle.

"It's laughing!" I said.

"Yessss. It is," Gwendollyn agreed. Her shoulders sagged and her head dipped forward. "At last." The Oak Witch sighed and smiled. "Welcome home."

Sybil opened her eyes. "Fable?" she whispered.

"Oh, thank god, you're awake!" I said. I crouched beside her, touching her wing.

She tried to sit up and water swished around her body, which appeared to be mostly healed. "You must go, Fable. Run for the Gate!"

"I can't leave you like this."

"You do not have much time," the Oak Witch said. She motioned to the ground. A small pebble drifted up to her palms.

"This stone will take you to the Gate. Even now, Xabien will be flying toward another gateway or even devising a way to rip through the veil. You must go."

"Go. I will be alright. I am safe here." Sybil's soaked clothes were torn, but the blood was gone and the bruises fading.

I nodded. "Okay. Tell Liam I'm sorry. I have to do this for things to make sense."

"You can tell him yourself; it is possible he will catch up to you," Gwendollyn said. "I feel him approaching." The pebble in her hands glowed as she spoke, taking on a blue, opalescent light. Then it flew from her fingers toward the trees.

I glanced back once at them both before darting after the zipping tracer of light, into the depths of the forest toward the Gate back to Earth.

Racing through the woods, I tripped over roots, flailed into brambles, and swiped my face on branches. I swatted at limbs, panting, trying to keep up with the light as it wound around trunks and over rocks. It wasn't following the trail we'd traveled just days earlier. The beacon took the most direct route to the portal—whether a human could keep up or not.

With my lungs burning and body bleeding from a hundred scrapes and bruises, I climbed over a fallen log crusted with moss and rot and nearly fell into a ravine on the other side. There at the bottom of the bank was the trail leading out of the garden path, to the Gate.

Clinging to roots and small shrubs, I slid down the dirt and leaves to the bottom. I stared at the opening in the hillside. Surrounded by wild ivy and golden light, the only thing between me and my life back on Earth was a simple wood door in the hillside. Suddenly, all I wanted more than anything at the moment were the NaNas.

Footsteps crashed through the forest behind me, breaking twigs, snapping branches. Liam's familiar voice shouted my name.

He would never understand what I had to do.

I turned the knob and shoved against the door with all my weight, expecting it to be a difficult budge. To my surprise, the door flew open and I launched into the basement supply room of the Glade Café.

"Damn it!" I swore as I careened into a silver rack storing restaurant supplies.

The shelf tilted, dumping pots, pans, and vegetables in a clatter onto the concrete floor. I yelped as my momentum carried me into another rack then sent me crashing to the ground. Stacks of ceramic plates shattered in a heap around my legs.

The Gate slammed behind me and disappeared into the stone as though it never were.

I lay on the concrete, surrounded by cookware and tubers, panting and bleeding. "Holy shit."

"Who's down there?" a masculine voice echoed down the stairs.

"It's just me!" I said between gulps.

"Fable?"

The barrel of a gun came around the corner, followed by Special Agent Drake.

He stood in the middle of the mess I'd made, staring at me, covered in dirt and blood—a ragged mess. "Fable?"

He glanced around the room, holstered his weapon, and rushed to my side. "How did you get down here? I was just here! Where'd you come from?" He had the pallor of someone who saw a long-dead relative help themselves to a slice of pie.

"Julius?"

He hunkered beside me, hazel eyes searching my face. "I thought you were…"

I didn't realize until that moment how much I'd missed him. How much his solid, earthly anchorage was part of my reality.

He was a man. A musky, hard, warm man, and he seemed for all the moment more like a life preserver thrown into a vast ocean where I'd been drifting haplessly with the tide.

"Thank god you're here," I murmured and threw my arms around his neck. "How did you know?"

"This was the last place you were seen." Drake pulled away, gently touching the bruises on my arms and shoulders. "Who did this to you?"

"I crash-landed."

"What?" he demanded.

"*Shhh*. Listen!"

"What happened? Who did this?"

"Drake?" Agent Mendelson's voice carried into the basement. "Where are you?"

"Down here! I found Fable Montgomery."

Agent Mendelson stepped around the corner. She looked as surprised to see me as I was to see both of them, but she recovered and quickly holstered her gun. I was strangely happy to see her as well, with her familiar slick black bun and tailored gray suit.

"Thank god! We were so worried. We thought he had you." She hurried to join us, kicking a pot out of the way. She squatted beside me. "Are you okay?"

As she rested her hand on my shoulder, I was flooded with the desperate need for sleep. My eyes fluttered, fighting the force of her strength. I couldn't believe it.

Mendelson? An Empath? What the fuck?

I muttered "*Sawyin*!" then leveled my best glare at her...which probably looked more like I crossed my eyes, before I flopped back into Agent Drake's lap, sound asleep.

I woke staring up at the ceiling of a white room, resting comfortably in a hospital bed.

"You're awake," said a nurse as she pulled apart a Velcro blood pressure gauge and wrapped it around my arm. "There's a man outside who's very anxious for some words with you."

"Is he blond?" I rasped.

She chuckled. "Nope. He's with the FBI, and he's been waiting on the lobby for eight hours—so you'd be doing us all a favor if you just let him tell you what he clearly needs to be sayin'."

"What do you mean?" I wondered, trying to remember how I got to the hospital.

She finished checking my blood pressure and shook her head, wobbling the extra skin around her neck. She tucked the instrument in the pocket of her sea-foam green scrubs and sighed but didn't answer.

Drake entered as she made her way to the door. "She's fine."

"Thank you, Nurse Becks," Drake said.

She smiled and left, throwing a pointed glance over her shoulder in my direction.

"I'm okay, Julius. Really, I feel alright."

"What happened? You were talking, and then your eyes just rolled back and you passed out." He leaned against my bed.

The sheets were stiff, hard. The room had a dull industrial feel that they'd tried to spruce up with a rose wallpaper border and off-white curtains.

What would I tell him? His partner had super-empathic powers, and she'd used them on me before I knew what they were? Even in the FBI office, right under his nose? Even if he believed me, he probably wouldn't ever forgive me.

"I…I can't tell you."

God, I can't tell him anything. How would his brain not explode?

"What do you mean you can't tell me?" His eyes flashed hurt, angry.

"I can't tell you for your own good."

"Don't you worry about my own good. You watch out for *your* own good! You could have been killed! Kidnapped! Sold off, where I'd never find you!" His neck flushed with color, and his voice climbed pitch. "Tell me what happened, or I swear to god, I'll arrest you for obstruction if for no other reason than to keep you safe for 15 minutes!"

"I can't tell you." I frowned. "You won't believe me, and once you know, you can never un-know, and it would always put you in danger."

"Fable…" he warned.

"Julius…" I countered.

With a hefty sigh, Drake clenched his jaw. "You are making a mistake. I'm one of the good guys. If you don't help me get this bastard, it's likely he'll come after you again—and we may never find the other women."

I shook my head.

Defeated, he reached behind his belt and drew out a pair of shiny silver handcuffs. "Fable Rose Montgomery, you are under arrest for obstruction of justice." He took my wrist and clamped on the cold metal bracelet. He refused my eyes. "You have the right to remain silent…"

Chapter Nineteen

Neither here nor there is nowhere at all
But a fable makes a fine bridge indeed

Drake and Mendelson transported me straight from the hospital
to an interrogation room at FBI headquarters, where I stayed for
several hours. There was no real way to tell time without clocks or
windows, only the shadows under Drake's eyes to measure that he
hadn't slept. The constant lack of answers appeared to be wearing
him down.

"Where were you?" he pressed, leaning back in the chair, scrubbing the dark scruff on his jaw.

"I can't explain it," I answered.

"How did you get there?" Mendelson wondered. She tilted her
head, and the reflection of florescent lights shone on her sleek bun.
She'd been pacing, and each time her heel clicked against the floor
I clenched my teeth.

"You wouldn't believe me," I muttered.

"Who were you with?" Drake asked, running a hand through
his dark locks.

"A friend."

"If he's a friend, why can't you tell us who he is?" Mendelson
asked with a sly smile.

"He's very shy."

"Fable," Drake snapped. "You owe us answers. The missing women deserve answers—Harmony, Ki, and Grace. You owe them."

I crossed my arms over my chest.

"Do you know this man?" Drake asked.

He slid a picture of my exterminator across the table. The craggy old face of the man I called Deloy stared up at me.

"Yeah, he's my exterminator."

Deloy? What does he have to do with anything?

A long pause filled the room. Drake and Mendelson glanced at one another before Mendelson silently took a chair next to her partner and rested her hands on the table. She'd recently had a manicure.

"Fable, there were a few developments while you were gone." She exhaled. "This man"—she tapped the photo—"was taken into custody after attempting to break into your home."

"What?" I gasped.

"He claimed he was there at the appointed time to check some traps but decided that since you weren't home, he'd let himself in. He claims the door was unlocked." Mendelson smoothed her forehead.

"He was picked up by the surveillance team, and his prints show that his was the hand on the back window—and his prints matched those all around the house." Drake's voice was dark, raw. He stared at me across the table, hazel eyes cutting.

My mind spun. I clutched at my necklace, chewing my bottom lip to shreds.

Deloy's hand on the back window? He went on the back deck to pick up the dead crow.

"He couldn't be dangerous," I reasoned. "I was alone with him for over an hour while he went through my house, cupboard by floorboard." I scrambled through my memory, trying desperately to remember if Deloy had touched the window when he'd picked up the crow.

"There's something else you need to know," Mendelson added softly. "When we arrested him, he quickly confessed to Celeste's murder. Apparently, he thought that was why he was being picked up."

The room tilted. Florescent lights blistered my eyes as tears welled. "What? Deloy killed Celeste?"

"He knew things about the crime scene that were never released to the public." Drake reached across the table, gently touching my hands. Mendelson watched her partner thumb my knuckles, offering comfort as he said, "But Deloy also claims he was not working alone. We need you to tell us where you were and who you were with."

Tears spilled down my cheeks. Deloy had come into my home and been artificially kind to me—after he murdered my aunt.

But I couldn't reveal Liam or Aria. I shook my head. "I'm sorry. I can't tell you."

Drake grabbed both my hands, clutching them in his grip. "I can't protect you if you don't talk!"

Mendelson blew out a put-upon sigh. "Drake, out in the hall." She straightened her shirt and led him from the room.

The door shut behind them and I sat staring at myself in the mirror.

Multiple lacerations. Death by exsanguination.

I looked like I'd been made over with electric shock therapy. I wondered if there was anyone on the other side, or if they were just recording my interrogation. My curly hair was a mess of frizz, and my clothes were wrinkled, stained, and torn. I could see the shock, the disbelief in my eyes.

He was nice to me. Grandfatherly.

I'd committed myself to coming back to Earth. To face the truth of the story as it would unfold. But I'd been unprepared for the revelation that Celeste's murderer would confess, and that he wasn't working alone. If the 13 pages were right, the next events were fast approaching.

Mendelson walked in, heels clicking. She shook her head and reached out, grasping my upper arm. "Okay, Ms. Montgomery. You don't want to help us, but we're going to help you, anyway. We'll keep you safe in a holding cell for the next 24 hours, and then you're on your own, bad guys and all."

I stood watching Drake as he leaned against the doorframe. Mendelson snapped the cuffs around my wrists and turned me toward the door.

"Please," Drake begged, "let us help."

He looked so tired, so close to giving up. I wanted to reach for him, but even as I thought about it, Mendelson shoved me from behind and I lurched forward into the hall. Drake stepped sideways out of my way as she led me toward the elevator.

I glanced back once to see him resting against the wall, head dropped forward onto his chest, looking defeated. Washed sickly by the lights.

Something clicked. It was as though he were a puzzle-piece sliding into place. He was tied to all of this somehow; I felt his place in this crazy story I was living, like the support cable of a suspension bridge.

I could not get from one side of the gap to the other without him.

"Julius!" I shouted, stopping in the middle of the hall.

He lifted his head and turned his gaze to me.

"Let me think about it for a couple of hours and I'll come up with a way to tell you what you want to know, safely."

He shoved off the wall, ignoring me, then disappeared around the corner.

"You had your chance," Mendelson said, nudging me toward the elevator.

I frowned, unsure why I'd even said what I had. Confused that words spun out of my mouth without anything to back them up. I had no intention of telling him anything at all. Why had I said so?

The elevator door closed and Mendelson looked over at me in the too-bright light of the small space. I inched as far away from her as I could. It was the first time we had been alone together since I'd returned to Earth, and I blurted out the first thing to come to mind.

"Does Drake known you're an Empath?" The question left my lips and I braced myself against the far elevator wall as she turned to me with a surprised expression.

"So your shields are coming down, huh?" she asked.

"You're from Aria?" I asked.

She shook her head. "From Orange County."

I cocked my head, not really sure what to make of her reply.

The elevator stopped and the doors opened, and Mendelson reached over and closed them again. "I have a few unusual talents that serve my position in law enforcement. I'm not sure where they come from, but if they help me catch bad guys, I'm going to use them…within the law, of course."

Then she reached past me to open the elevator doors again. "You want something to eat or drink?" She checked her watch and added, "Guard shift ends in an hour, and they'll put the lights out for the evening crew. Hungry?"

"Actually, I'm starving." But as I walked beside her down the hall, I couldn't shake the feeling something wasn't right.

We checked in at the desk and walked through the gate after it beeped and unlocked. The basement of the building housed five temporary cells.

A female officer patted me down, but I didn't even have my wallet on me. I'd escaped from Aria with only my clothes. She was in her mid-thirties with cropped brown hair and wore an expression as bland as her uniform.

"Remove your boots," she mumbled then glanced inside them before handing them to Agent Mendelson with a nod. Then she walked back to a room full of monitors and sat at her desk behind a thick glass window.

"I'll grab something from the vending machines. The kitchen service is closed," Mendelson offered.

"Thanks," I said.

Special Agent Mendelson walked me to the narrow room with a cot on the wall and a toilet. The dingy lights overhead gave the gray interior a greenish tint, and the metal toilet reflected back at me as if taunting "this is what your life has come to." She handed me my boots, and I dropped them on the floor by the cot and stood on the cold, painted concrete in my socks.

Closing the heavy metal door, Mendelson yelled, "Clear!" and a buzzer sounded before the electric deadbolt clanged. Her face appeared in the window on the door and she sighed.

"He feels something for you."

"What?" I asked confused.

"Drake. Don't act like you can't tell."

I thought of Julius. His smile, his hazel eyes.

"He treats you like I've never seen him treat anyone. But he's too professional to do anything about it. Believe me. Too professional to compromise his work." She frowned, eyebrows drawn together.

Then she left me alone. Sitting gingerly on the edge of the cot, I wondered if it would actually take my weight.

I wasn't sure what I expected from a holding cell. The reality was so much less climactic than the movies I'd seen of community cells full of loitering delinquents. Knowing what was about to happen, I suddenly wished I wasn't alone. I'd rather have been in a crowded cell with deadly criminals than waiting in a closet for one terrible end or another.

Liam.

I rested my head back against the cold wall and looked up at the tiny frosted window crisscrossed with bars. It must have been dark outside, as the window offered not even the typical Portland gray.

Back on Earth.

What a strange thought. The sound of cars outside. The electric hum of lights. A busy, almost frantic energy around everyone and everything.

After spending three days on Aria, the difference in how people rushed around to do even the simplest of tasks was almost dizzying. It wasn't that the creatures of Aria were slow, I realized; they were just more mindful and deliberate with their actions. Less anxious to get the mundane, everyday functions out of the way.

Fifteen minutes after the door closed, the metal slider opened and a tray was pushed through the slot.

"Thanks," I said and the metal slot ground shut again, leaving me with a bag of chips, a candy bar, and a carton of milk. Vending machine supper of champions.

Sitting back on the cot, I looked over the food. My hands shook. I needed to eat.

I don't know if I can do this.

I set the tray of food on the floor, watching it as thought it would coil up and strike me.

Pages 140 and 141 were very clear that I had been or would be poisoned while in custody of the FBI. That knowledge had pulsed in my mind through all the hours of interrogation.

Everyone was suspect. Mendelson. Drake. The female guard. The vending machine stocker. Even the janitor. It could be any of them.

For the last two weeks, everything had been out of my control. If I had any chance of making it through the end of the *Prophecy of Crows*, a choice needed to be made.

A choice to trust the story—or not.

A sudden vivid memory flashed through my mind. I sat with Celeste on a low rock wall near the cliffs of an ocean. The sky was too blue to be Earth's, the grass too green. A charming white cottage, bedecked in climbing roses, nestled behind us against a verdant hillside. I knew the place as a kind of summer home.

Celeste wore all black, her face younger, hair longer. She held my small hand in her lap as we watched the surf crashing against the rocks below.

"Didn't she love me?" I asked.

"Of course she loved you, Rosebud. She loved you more than anything in the world." She kissed my head. "As do I."

"But why did she do it?"

"We might never know the truth."

"It hurts a lot," I cried, climbing into her lap, where I fit comfortably.

"I know," Celeste crooned, rocking us back and forth.

"I don't like this part of the story," I wailed. "I want her back!"

"I know, dearest…but what must we do when we don't like the part of the story we're in?"

I cried a long while then sniffed and wiped the back of my hand across my nose. "We must get through it to the other side."

Celeste squeezed me hard. "Yes, my dear girl. We get through to the other side, but we never forget." She continued to sway until drops splashed onto my forehead. Celeste wept, her face contorted in grief. "We must never forget her."

The sea breeze lifted Celeste's long, auburn hair, tangling it around us. "Don't cry, Auntie Celeste. We will not forget." My small hand cupped her face. "The story will always get us through to the other side, if we believe, right?"

Her eyebrows pinched together and a strangled sob escaped as she clutched me tight, nodding wordlessly.

"Then I believe," I whispered.

I sat in the desolate holding cell at the FBI, completely floored by the memory. I had not been able to recall more than one single image of my mother's death, for as long as I could recollect.

I remembered looking into her casket. The waxy, alabaster doll I swore was not my mother had given me nightmares for years.

Therapists believed it was simply too traumatic and I'd blocked out all other memories of her death, a suicide.

But the memory of sitting on Celeste's lap at the edge of the ocean was so vivid I could practically taste the salty air, feel her tears.

My memories were coming back. Bits and pieces. I wondered how far back it would go, and how much of my life I'd simply misplaced, set aside to pick up again at some other time.

I used to believe in the story. The child in me used to, anyway.

I thought back to all the books I'd read, the hours in the window seat while Celeste was working. The days spent curled up in the stacks at the library, the blissful joy of being lost in a good story. It never occurred to me, back then, to doubt. I had total child's faith in the outcome of every adventure I plucked off the shelf, believing it to the last letter. All happenings inside the framework of those epic adventures supported each other, creating a bridge that allowed readers to walk across from one side to the other.

Did all children have such faith in the story? Or is it only the Muse of Story who sees all tales begin, then journey, then end?

Maybe faith used to be effortless because the stakes were lower. No one really died from reading a book. But what about living a story?

I stared at the chips, milk, and candy. I picked up the chips, the least likely item of the three to be poisoned. They were salty and crunchy, satisfying the worst of the hunger. But as I chewed, I knew—Celeste never took the easy way. She'd given up her life with the man she loved for my safety. She'd taken care of me when my mother died. She'd nurtured me to become an independent woman, a Muse.

I ripped into the candy bar and ate every bite of too-sweet chocolate, then drank every drop of milk. The lights went out and I turned onto my side, pulled my feet up onto the cot, and rolled over, belly satisfied…and waited.

"This is probably going to suck," I whined.

No one ever said you had to go to your fate with grace.

The night wore on and sleep, despite how badly I needed it, eluded me. The cell grew colder, and after a few hours I slipped beneath the scratchy wool blanket, but it was too flimsy to actually keep me warm. I sat up and fumbled around in the dark for my boots.

My fingers skimmed the leather and I pulled the left one on first. As I slipped my right foot into the other, a sharp jab of pain nicked my big toe. I yelped, dropping my shoe and clutched my foot. It was gone quickly and I wondered if I'd been bit by a spider.

Feeling tenderly around my foot in the dark, I couldn't find anything, so I shook my boot out and slipped it on again, slower.

Whatever it was had fallen out. Probably a sliver. I curled up with my shoes on, and I felt ten degrees warmer already.

As I finally drifted off to sleep, I thought, *It's been a few hours for sure. If the food were poisoned, I'd be feeling it by now.* Then I felt foolish about how much I'd agonized over the decision to follow the story.

See? That wasn't so bad. All that stressing for nothing.

I closed my eyes and slept.

I woke to the sound of sirens. Convulsing. Pain. Burning from the inside, freezing on the outside. The staccato rage of my heart hammered inside my head and the clammy slime of my own skin were distant confusions next to the full abdominal contraction.

"Roll her!" yelled a masculine voice.

Strong hands rolled me on to my side as my stomach heaved and vomit erupted out my nose and mouth, splashing onto the metal floor of the ambulance.

"Can't…breathe…" I gasped.

My throat was seared by the burn of acid. Not enough air.

"IV is in."

Too much light.

Too much sound. I was burning to death of cold, muscles cramping. I heaved again, spewing up fire. Burning coals. Brimstone. My leg muscles cramped into bricks. Pain lanced up my veins, stabbing my joints.

Sirens ricocheted in my skull and my body jerked wildly as I tried to steady myself, tried to tuck into a ball. Blue gloved hands pushed me back. A face swam into my vision, a young man with a scruffy copper beard.

"Hold her down."

"Nope. Roll her!"

"What's hap—" I heaved again, mostly bile, stinking volcanic bile.

"Five minutes," The masculine voice said.

"Ten CCs of…"

And there was darkness.

I woke again on my back, rectangles of light flying by.

"Choking!"

"Room three!"

"Stomach suction."

The floor turned and the lights dipped. Darkness.

Beep.

Beep.

Beep.

"Vitals steady."

"Stable."

"Wait, roll her."

• • •

Caw!
Caw!
Caw!
Neon lights seared my eyes. An incessant beeping *Caw!* stabbed my ears.

Caw!
Beep.
Beep.
"Swallow. Come on, Fable. Swallow it," a high-pitched voice commanded.

Rancid powder coated my tongue. A cold burst of water. Blinding lights. A blur of fuchsia and iridescent movement. I swallowed. It stung all the way down my raw pipes.

Caw!
Caw!

"Fable." Auntie Celeste's voice came from across the table. "You've barely touched your tea."

She sat across from me at the table in the back yard. The sky was overcast, likely to rain at any moment. I looked around, disoriented. "I thought I was in the ER."

"Yes, darling girl, you are." Celeste adjusted her wide-brimmed lavender hat. The blood stains from my last dream with her had turned brown and flakey.

"Was I poisoned?"

"You already know the answer to that," she said as she poured more Earl Grey into her cup. It was a fine china teacup with chipped gold edging. It looked familiar. "Would you like a warm up?"

"But…"

"There's no sense in being in your body for such unpleasantness."

• • •

Beep.
Caw!
Beep.
"Roll her!"
My body was a firestorm trapped in a glass jar.

"I stood at your pyre, Auntie Celeste. I felt the heat of the flames. How are you here?"

She sighed. "Never the small talk with you, is it?" Her cup tinked into the saucer and she tilted her head. "Very well then."

Caw!
Caw!
"*Clear!*"
Lightning scorched my eyes.

"Do you remember the imagine game?" Her lavender dress fluttered lightly in the breeze, and I glanced at the garden, which shocked me for its disarray. Gone were the walls of flourishing green ivy, replaced by crumbling piles of stone and blackened vines. The rows of roses were all cracked and dead, the once-vibrant lawn a stretch of mud pocked by footprints.

"Do you?" she asked again.

"Do I what?" I gasped when I looked back at her. Her once lovely face was sallow and gaunt. Paper skin stretched over sharp bones. Her dress hung in loose swags, slipping off a decomposing shoulder.

"Do you remember the imagine game?" She sipped her tea. Earl Grey dripped down her chin.

"Yeees. Yes. I remember."

• • •

Beep.

Beep.

"Fable. You need to swallow more."

Rancid powder. Burst of water. Burning. Fuchsia blur. Rancid powder. Burst of water. Burning. Iridescent wings.

Fuzzy lights.

Beep.

Beep.

"Do you remember the hiding place under Mr. Lincoln? We used to play the imagine game, and sometimes we'd put gifts in the safe."

"I don't remember what you're talking about."

Clouds scuttled overhead and a soft mist began to fall. Rain drizzled into my tea and spattered Celeste's dress.

"Auntie Celeste? Did the old man, Deloy…did he…?" Suddenly I choked. Fierce coughing overtook my body until I coughed so hard I retched. The taste of a rancid, dry powder filled my mouth.

"You must use the imagine game to see what is right in front of you. Reality is obscured. It is not what it seems to be."

A flurry of black feathers drifted down with the rain.

I glanced up but saw only roiling clouds.

She was skeletal, bones clinging to a chipped tea cup.

"My days in the Midway are now gone." She squinted up at the sky as it opened, and a torrent of water pelted us. "I was able to leave a part of myself in the Midway—the place neither here nor there—just long enough to offer some small guidance."

She placed her cup on the table, stood, and pushed her chair back with a scrape. She came around to my side and her skeletal fingers caressed my cheek, slick with tears and rain. Then she kissed my forehead with parchment lips and whispered, "I stayed in the Midway only long enough to tell you I love you more than life, my dearest Fable, and I saved all your memories and entrusted them with Mr. Lincoln. All the years, the truth, and my love for you, are stored with him. I'm so proud of you, Rosebud."

Drinking me in with eyes turned opaque, she added, "And a time will come, not too distant from now, when you will wish for my blessing in love." She smiled, lips cracking, and cupped my cheek. "You have it, dearest. You have my blessing with much relief and joy. It gives me peace that you have love."

"But…"

Beep.
Beep.
Beep.

"Celeste, I miss you! I love you so much!" I wailed as thunder rattled the crumbling walls.

"I know, dearest. I know."

She kissed the top of my head once more and turned toward the broken walls.

"Wait!" I grabbed for her hands, but she slipped through my fingers. My chair tipped sideways. One leg gave out and I toppled onto the porch in a heap.

Lightning shredded the sky. I turned toward the horizon as the flash rippled through the clouds.

When I looked back, she was gone.

Her lavender hat rolled across the muddy landscape. I stood to retrieve it, but wind blasted through the wrecked back yard and snatched the hat up, carrying it toward the storm.

"Trust the story," the wind seemed to say. "It will get you from here to there."

I stood in the downpour, and knew this time she was really gone.

Caw!

Caw!
Caw!

Beep.
Beep.
Beep.

Chapter Twenty

A favor for an eye
A gift from your mother
Who loves you

"…stabilized for now," a man's voice was saying.

"…guard outside the door at all times," said another.

My throat burned, my body ached.

"Sleep."

"Vitals are strong," a woman stated.

"… lab says substance unknown."

Footsteps shuffled around me. I opened my eyes to machines, blinding overhead lights. Then I went gratefully to the sheltering arms of sleep.

I woke screaming. Muscles cramped and burning. Lights flashed on. Bodies filled the room. Fire raged under my skin.

"Hold her down."

• • •

Then I stood in the Midway, that place neither here nor there, and purple clouds scuttled over a barren, wind-blasted, shale landscape as far as the horizon.

"Celeste?" I called out.

But I knew she was gone.

I skidded on shale that cut my bare toes and screamed into the wind, "I want to go home! How do I get home?"

"Stable," a woman said.

"Do we know what it is yet?" asked a man with a deep voice.

"Toxicology can't identify it," replied another.

I slept.

Shoes scuffed across the floor, followed by a screech as a chair was dragged closer. I tried to open my eyes, but they were too heavy.

My hand was folded in a warm grip. Agent Drake murmured. "Fable, what happened?"

I tried to squeeze his hand, let him know I heard him, but my fingers were so incredibly tired.

I'm made of lead, even my eyes. Why am I lead?

"You were supposed to be safe," he said. "What happened?"

His voice was rough, dry. His forehead against the back of my hand radiated gentle heat.

I'm here, but I can't come up from the deep. Must sleep.

"You are safe for now," Drake said.

I wanted to respond, but tar-like darkness pulled me back under, and I slept.

Narcotic dreams. Incoherent, jumbles of images. Scenes from childhood cartoons. Snippets of books come to life, *Alice in Wonderland* and *Twenty-Thousand Leagues under the Sea*. A woman who looked like Mendelson with white hair and whited-out eyes screamed at Godzilla. A massive red planet rose over the mountains. Liam nuzzled my neck. A tuxedo cat hissed at a tree full of black birds. Biddy played poker with the table of dogs from the painting. Then I swam underwater, and the water was clear, electric blue, and alive. I was a mermaid, elated by my new tail, breathing the ocean. I swam to a sunken coalmining cart still on the tracks, and I settled into the cart, dangling my tail over the edge as it began moving, rolling along the seabed then climbing as though on a rollercoaster, up, up, up toward the surface where there was light.

I opened my eyes. The TV in the hospital room played *The Little Mermaid*. Morning light blazed through a gap between the drapes. Actual sunlight.

The interior of the small room came into focus, filled with machines, a light green curtain, blinking lights on monitors, and a vase of pink roses.

My throat burned like I'd swallowed ground glass with a vodka chaser. I was parched, tongue swollen. A water bottle with a straw beckoned from the tray beside my bed, but even leaning as far as I could, I still only managed to stretch my hand half way before dropping my whole arm and panting.

"Here you go, honey," a familiar voice murmured.

LeeLee stood from a chair at the edge of the curtain. Her disheveled blond-white bun stuck out around her temples and her skin looked thin, shadowed with blue.

"LeeLee?" I croaked.

"Of course it's me." She leaned across my bed, grasped the water bottle, and gently placed the straw to my lips. I managed a few sips before gasping and closing my eyes to catch my breath.

Being awake exerted a tremendous amount of effort, and the weight of drug-induced sleep was too heavy to fight.

When I woke again, Biddy sat in the chair reading a paperback book with the front cover ripped off.

"Biddy?"

She glanced up from her book. "Well, good morning to you, kiddo! You really had us worried this time."

"Whatchya"—I swallowed—"reading?"

Biddy sighed. "Well, you know, one of my favorite kinds of stories…"

"Porn?" I rasped, reaching for the water bottle. "In a hospital?"

She stood to help me with the water. Her white curls and wrinkled round face bobbed over me. "I prefer to call it *smut*."

I gulped down water before flopping back. "Thanks."

She gazed at me. "I missed you, little thing."

"I missed you, too, Bids." It hurt to speak.

She stared a moment longer before waddling back to her chair.

"It's just getting to the good stuff," she said and cleared her throat before reading aloud: "'*Miss Elyssa Masterson gasped and drank in the sight of Mr. Humphries standing in nothing but his bronze skin beneath the coursing white water of the falls. As if he'd heard her, he turned, glancing toward the brush where she crouched. She held her breath, but it was to no avail as he strode across the rocky sand to stand naked before her bush.*'" Biddy laughed, a low grumbling chuckle. "'Before her bush…' It's so terrible, it's wonderful."

I smiled, splitting open my bottom lip. Despite everything that had changed, Biddy would always be blessedly the same.

"'*Mr. Humphries reached into the shrubs, grasping Elyssa by the elbow and dragging her to her feet. The waterfall roared, but Elyssa couldn't hear it over her own beating heart. His eyes raked her up and down, and she felt suddenly as though her bodice were too tight.*'"

I drifted off to Biddy's voice.

"'*His lips descended…*'" Biddy sighed. "You'd better cover your ears; it's about to get juicy," she warned with a chortle.

I fell asleep, half-smiling.

When I woke again, Liam sat in the chair by the window. He wore the thick silver chain that disguised his Avian nature, and normal human clothes. He read from the same book with the torn-off cover.

He looked up then jumped to his feet. "How do you feel?"

"Cottonmouth."

"What is that?"

"Water..."

He helped me sit up so I could drink heartily. Finally strong enough to hold the water bottle, I desperately sucked the straw.

When my hands shook, he removed the water and took my fingers in his. I couldn't help but notice the IV and tape, and how frail my pale digits looked, compared to his tanned, muscled hands.

"Why did you not wait for me?"

I could tell by the thin line of his lips, he was angry. Furrowed eyebrows, clenched jaw.

"You could have been killed."

My raw throat ached to speak, but there were no words. He would have tried to stop me from doing what needed to be done—and we both knew it. Instead, I squeezed his fingers.

"What..." I coughed, drank more water, and finished, "are you reading?"

Liam sighed. "Never do that again." He met my gaze with eyes like hard blue nuggets of worry.

Then with a frustrated shake of his head, he dropped my fingers and retrieved the book. "Biddy gave it to me at shift change." He looked bewildered. "She said I might be able to learn a thing or two, but..."

I laughed out loud then coughed violently. I couldn't say why it struck me so funny. But despite the pain and coughing, I laughed and coughed more as I pictured Biddy's wrinkled mischievous face, passing off a smut novel to poor innocent Liam.

An alarm sounded on the machine near my bed, and Liam held water toward me, coaxing me to drink. As a nurse pushed open the door, I glimpsed the navy-uniformed legs of an officer sitting in a chair in the hallway. He leaned forward, peering into the room.

He was young, perhaps in his early twenties, with short brown, buzzed hair.

The nurse moved past him and closed the door on his gaze. She was pretty, in her scrubs and a loose blond ponytail. "Uh, oh," she said. "What's going on, sweetie?"

I shook my head then nodded. "Laugh," I choked. "Then cough."

She was a proficient flurry of motions and calming vocal tones. "I'm gonna need you to take a couple of slow, deep breaths."

I tried. My throat was raw and constricted, cauterized from vomiting, a stomach pump and breathing tube, then cottonmouth.

"There. Better?" she asked casually. "Things get back to normal faster with some oxygen, right?"

I grimaced, rubbing my throat. "Thanks."

"You want a lozenge? Or maybe you wanna try and eat something? Jell-O?"

The idea of food made me queasy. I shook my head.

She continued to bustle as she talked. She checked the saline bag attached to an IV in my hand. The hanging bag of fluid was nearly empty, so she retrieved a full bag from a drawer and swapped out the drip.

"Aside from the coughing, how are you feeling?" she asked.

"I actually feel okay." Even as I said it I was surprised. "Lethargic and sore, like I just got done working out, but okay."

"That's good," she said. She checked the machine then pulled a sliding keyboard from the stand-up computer and typed in some notes. "Yesterday when I asked you, you said your muscles hurt and you were having trouble swallowing."

"Really? I don't remember talking to you yesterday."

She smiled sadly. "You needed some strong drugs to stop the muscle cramps."

"Really?" I asked, astonished.

"Three days has been a great improvement. We weren't sure you'd pull through, and I think it was nothing short of miraculous."

She pushed the keyboard back in the slot and looked at me. She seemed nice. Efficient. "If you're feeling up to it, you should really try some juice or maybe some Saltines. Nothing heavy."

"Juice," I agreed, to satisfy her. "Thanks."

She looked at Liam before leaving and said in a serious tone, "And no more jokes. Laughing is currently off-limits."

He bobbed his head, all wide-eyed seriousness.

As the door opened, the officer on duty leaned in again and scanned the room before the door closed.

Is he here to protect me? Or keep me in custody?

A chill passed over my body, and I felt a sense of time slipping, as if I were supposed to be somewhere but couldn't remember where; like I was late for a flight or missing my train.

"What time is it?" I wondered.

Liam checked the time on the monitor. "Four-thirty."

I sat up. "I need to be somewhere."

"Where?"

"I don't know." The room looked strange, distorted somehow. "But it's important."

"Fable?"

I blinked, and the room looked normal again. "I'm okay. I'm just disoriented."

"Should I call the nurse?"

Then the feeling of urgency faded, leaving me confused.

"That was weird," I said.

"Are you well?" Liam asked, hovering nearby.

"I don't know," I said, looking around the room. "It was like that panic you get when you're running down the terminal to your gate, and they're calling final boarding."

Liam shook his head. "I do not know such a feeling."

"Right." I sighed. "You never have to worry about missing a flight. Never mind, it's probably nothing." I took another deep breath. "There are a couple of things you should probably know."

"Okay," Liam said, pulling a chair up to the bed.

In short order, I laid out the details of my escape from Aria and Xabien's threats. I told him about Mendelson's use of *sawyin*, and the man named Deloy—Celeste's murderer who also had an accomplice. And then there was the poison.

Liam exhaled and sat with his elbows on his knees. He stuffed both hands through his hair. "Nothing is going the way it is expected."

"How do you mean?"

His expression was tortured. "You are a Muse! Your safety should be assumed, your rightful place in Aria a given. It is not supposed to be so complicated or dangerous to return you to your seat of power."

Something Celeste always said sprang to mind, and I blurted, "The easy way rarely makes an interesting story."

He sat back, shaking his head.

"Liam, we should be getting out of here," I said.

"You are not well enough to leave."

"But Maya will be arriving at the house."

"She arrived safely while you were sick."

"But..."

"All is being taken care of," Liam said. "We took guidance from the 13 pages you left behind. That is how I knew to intercept Maya at the house, and to send Agatha to get a poison antidote to the hospital."

I stared at him. He was truly a marvel.

"You followed the pages? You knew which poison?"

He shrugged. "Well, no, not exactly. But from clues in the pages, I knew it could only be Earth arsenic or Aria devil's flute."

"It wasn't arsenic." Grasping his hand, I reveled in the solid warmth of his touch. "I overheard them talking; they don't know what it is."

"I brought antidotes back for both, and Agatha administered the powder, as she was able to slip in unseen."

Looking around, I wondered, "Where's she now?"

"She went back to Aria to report to the Sublime that you will live."

"If you keep saving me like this, I'm gonna develop that pathetic Lois Lane complex."

"Is that like a disease?"

"Sort of." I smiled. "Thank you." I paused. "Again."

The nurse pushed open the door. The guard was not at his post in the hall. She dragged a rolling table to the bed, where she helped prop me up then placed a bottle of apple juice and two packages of Saltines on the tray.

"I know you said you aren't up for it, but just in case." She smiled. Before she left, she glanced at Liam and said, "Visiting hours are over in about half an hour."

When she left the room, a different officer sat down in the chair outside the room. He had a bald head with an earring in his right ear and looked strangely familiar. His tailored trousers were several inches too short.

The door shut, and I shook off the odd feeling of familiarity. The room was all bright artificial light and hard surfaces. Jagged lines on a machine going up and down. Red and green blips.

Again a pressing sense of time nibbled at me. Maybe I'd forgotten to pay an important bill? Or missed a scheduled appointment? I tried to remember if I was supposed to be somewhere. That feeling of missing an important due date caused a spike on the monitor.

Then the room wavered, shimmered. I groaned and leaned against the bedrail as vertigo struck.

"Oh, god," I gasped.

Tremendous pressure filled my ears, then the sound of sucking and a feeling of being pulled backward through a vacuum eclipsed the dizziness, and I was lifted off my feet.

All the noise stopped. I was freezing.

I was no longer in a hospital bed in Portland but standing on a colossal stone terrace stretching over a vast glacier, ridged and split with deep cobalt crevasses. I gulped air that froze my lungs even as I coughed and tipped forward, nearly falling off the edge of the ridge.

"What the fuck?" I shrieked, wind-milling my arms.

I threw my weight back, stumbling then collapsing onto the cold stones. My hospital gown did little to actually cover or keep me warm. It was ice and snow as far as I could see. Breath left my body in a cloud.

"Stand up." Xabien grabbed my arm. Blood poured freely from the back of my hand where the IV stint was ripped out as I'd been rifted through the veil.

Xabien.

My husband-to-be lifted my wrist, but I was still too weak to fight him. "Convenient," he said. Then he snapped his fingers at a woman standing nearby. "The bowl."

The woman, a tall, hunched brunette with burn scars covering much of her face, placed a pewter bowl beneath my bleeding hand. She watched me with one good eye; the other had been eaten by a molten burn and replaced with an etched piece of aquamarine glass. Her fur coat was well kept and each of her fingers bore intricate gold rings.

Splats of blood plunked into the bowl as my heart beat a wild staccato against my ribs. I tried desperately to comprehend what the hell was going on. The woman squeezed my hand for more blood and I flinched. Two burnished nubs at her temples appeared to have been horns but were either shorn off or filed down and polished.

"Hurry," Xabien said to her. He watched me with eyes full of hatred. "Welcome to the Icy Reaches, little Muse. Soon to be your home."

The stone platform on which we stood was actually attached to a spiraling, multi-tiered city of turrets and buildings erupting from the side of a black cliff. It was ringed by frozen rivers and drifts of snow. It wasn't a castle so much as a city of mismatched architecture that appeared to defy gravity or intuitive design, growing sporadi-cally in a fractal-like pattern, right from the rock of the mountain.

I've seen this somewhere before.

Arctic air buffeted my naked backside.

"Quickly, the stream narrows." Xabien growled.

"She must be willing," said the woman. A gust of brittle wind ruffled the fur on her hood.

Xabien jerked me against his body, propping me up. "She is willing. She signed a contract."

"She must be willing now, or a marriage ceremony will not be bound by law." She turned her face to me, a terrifying spectacle of twisted flesh. "Do you willingly marry this Ryder?"

"Hell, no."

Xabien lifted me by my shoulders and shook me hard. "Consent, or I will—"

"Kiss. My. Ass!" The blood from my stint wound had dripped down my leg, soaked part of my hospital gown, and froze into a dark red crystallized smear. My naked legs burned with cold, and my feet ached from standing on the frosty stone.

He screamed with wordless fury in my face, rattling me so hard my teeth snapped together.

"You cannot force a wedding," the woman said, "but perhaps, since she is here, we can put a *terilik-tu* on her."

A terilik-tu? I know that word…a bind? A seal.

She studied me with her good eye as I hung weakly in his grip, "Blood-bind her."

"What good is that to me?" he hissed. "If she is slain, I will be slain. Foolish woman!"

A deep, rumbling scrape drew my gaze upward. Xabien's great red dragon curled itself around the spire above us. It watched us with mirrored black eyes, flicking its tongue.

The nearest stairs wound up the side of the mountain, zig-zagging back and forth around outcroppings and slate structures before dropping hundreds of feet to the glacier below. There was no escape.

As if it knew what I was thinking, the dragon let out a warbling bellow that ricocheted off the surrounding ice. I flinched, unconsciously pushing myself against Xabien.

"You will always know where to find her, my lord," the witch was saying. "She will never again be able to hide behind a shield." They both looked up to the dragon. "Like giving a scent to a hound," she finished.

I followed their gaze, taking in the ominous wingspan and deadly claws, jagged teeth and glistening red scales.

"Do it," Xabien hissed. "But this does not free you from your debt to me."

I wasn't sure what they were planning, but it couldn't be good.

"No! I don't consent! I don't consent!" I wriggled lamely in his grip.

"Hold her steady," she said.

Xabien crushed me against his body. He reeked of sweat and amber as I bucked and fought, kicking at his shins, biting his fingers. He roared, wrapped an arm around my throat, and held a deadly spike under my chin. I froze.

The witch grabbed my hand. She held it above the bowl and sliced open my palm.

I screamed.

"I cut deep into your spirit, Fable, and I bind your blood to this beast."

This isn't happening!

Xabien whistled, sharp and clear in the cold air. The massive beast unwrapped its girth from the stone and launched for one brief moment into the air before dropping to the terrace with the snap of wings, shaking the ground as it landed.

It lifted a sinuous neck over us, dipping down to peek between my body and the witch's.

It sniffed the air and blew out a wet, phlegmy gust.

My hand throbbed, and blood dripped onto the stone.

Again, the sense of missing an important date struck me with urgency.

The witch patted the beast's shoulder then wedged the knife under a scale. She cut the animal, letting free a stream of dark fluid that filled the bowl with ichor. The dragon didn't flinch but turned and sniffed the wound, flicking its tongue across its scales.

The witch swayed and chanted, shivered and convulsed, then appeared to be deep in trance.

Xabien lifted me off my feet, holding my ear to his mouth.

"Run, little Maior. Run if you must, but Scorn will hunt you." He whipped me around, forcing my face to his with one meaty hand. "Just as Celeste could not outrun me…you cannot outrun me." He swiped his warm, soggy tongue across my cheek. "I will have what is mine."

Celeste. Ohmigod. Celeste.

Then he kissed me, crushed his mouth hard against mine as I fought to keep my lips in a tight line. He smiled against my mouth and licked the corner of my lips, whispering, "One day, Fable, you will kiss me and revel in it. You will bear me sons and daughters to fill our nation."

I shuddered.

"One day soon," he said.

"It is done," the witch said as she tucked her knife into the folds of her fur robe.

Xabien shoved me away. I tumbled across the cold stones, bare legs splayed.

"Run, little wife. Run as far as you can," he said with a sharp-toothed smile. "I will take great pleasure in hunting you."

Then the vertigo hit, followed by the sound of rushing water, and I was stretched backward. My feet came off the ground and I was sucked back through the veil.

• • •

I sat up on the hospital floor, panting, heart hammering.

But the worst wasn't over. I'd reappeared in the middle of a frantic scuffle. Liam was locked arm in arm with the police officer from the hall.

Shouts and screams filled the hall. Hospital machinery blared alarms, and a high-pitched buzz rang over the intercom. A voice called, "Security to room 307. Security to room 307!"

I'd been gone less than five minutes, but long enough for the machines to alert people that I'd been unplugged. The officer kicked at Liam's shin as I scrambled to get out of the way of their feet.

I dragged myself up with the bars on the bed and shouted, "I'm here, see? I'm fine! It's all good!"

The nurse burst into the room with a hospital security guard and pointed at Liam.

"He attacked the officer!" she yelled over the beeping machines.

I suddenly realized why the cop in question seemed familiar. Half of his left ear was missing. He was the Avian from the attack at Delia's house, and I'd also seen him at the coroner's office.

"Vojhane." The name came to my lips easily.

His eyes flicked to me. I saw a silver chain like Liam's dangling around his neck. His shiny bald head and meaty fists reminded me, I owed him one.

The real security guard launched himself into the fray. He was smaller and no match for the two larger Avians in disguise. The three men grappled and crashed around the room, knocking over the chair and cracking the computer monitor. I jumped out of the way as they careened into the bed.

The nurse tugged me toward the hall. I had to help, to stop them somehow.

Vojhane landed a solid punch in Liam's stomach.

"*Hey!*" I screamed, throwing myself into the tangle of bodies.

I didn't think about it, just lunged onto Vojhane's back. I wrapped an arm around his neck and my legs around his waist, and pummeled his head with my bloody fist. He bucked and twisted, careening around the room, trying to scrape me off with the wall. But I clung to his back like a bare-assed monkey, distracting him while Liam tried to subdue the security guard.

Then I grabbed the chain around Vojhane's neck. As he spun around trying to throw me off, I managed to unclasp the silver *yuerick*.

Vojhane's massive black wings bloomed into the room, whooshing out with such force that their unfurling threw me across the room and into the wall. I crashed hard enough to crack the plaster and slid to the floor. The security guard froze wide-eyed for all of a second before throwing himself into the fight again.

Even in the heightened danger of the moment, I had to admire the security guard's ability to take it in and keep on fighting.

Liam's fist cracked across Vojhane's jaw.

The Avian's head snapped back, tatters of his shirt hanging from the arches of his wings. He clasped his hands together, and an electric blue ball of light grew between his palms. Vojhane launched his Rhue sphere.

Liam ducked. The guard did not.

The burst of light slammed into the guard's chest, picking him off his feet and lobbing him into the computer stand with a thunderous crash. Electronic equipment exploded in a rain of sparks. The nurse crouched in the corner, shrieked hysterically.

The rank stench of burned flesh filled the room.

It was the break Liam needed. He lifted the chair over his head and brought it down atop Vojhane's bald skull with a metallic clang. The Vulture Avian staggered and fell to his knees.

Liam was already moving. He snatched me off the floor and ran for the hallway. Even as we moved out of the room in a blur, Vojhane was trying to get his talons under himself. The nurse huddled, weeping in the corner.

• • •

The hall was full of hospital gowns and paper slippers, all come to check on the commotion. Nurses and assistants came toward us in a wall of sea-foam green.

"Where are you going? Put her down!" one woman shouted. "Security!"

No one actually tried to grab him. He held me tight to his body and pushed through with a fierce, purposeful stride and a glare that could stop a herd of charging bulls. People quickly cleared a path.

Liam spoke as we charged through the door to a stairwell with roof access. "What happened? Where did you go?"

"Xabien pulled me through the veil," I said. My head bobbled on my neck so I rested my cheek against his shoulder. "He tried to force a marriage but I wouldn't consent, so he blood-bound me to his dragon…I think."

"Gods, he goes too far!"

Three flights up was the roof access door. He shoved us through. The helipad glowed, ringed by red lights. The sun was setting, nearly below the horizon. Sirens sounded in the distance.

Liam set me on my feet long enough to rip his T-shirt over his head and kick off his boots. Then he unclasped the silver *yuerick*. Dark wings unfolded with the snapping sound of silk tearing through the air.

I marveled at him as something deep within me blazed to life.

The door to the helipad elevator opened. Three guards burst onto the roof, stopping short when they saw an Avian in full-winged splendor. Their faces went slack. The youngest of the three crossed himself and fell to his knees.

There's no hiding it anymore.

"Hold on," Liam said and lifted me into his arms. With his hands behind my back and another under my legs, his scent flooded over me like a homecoming. Before I had time to wonder exactly what he meant, he launched.

Crushing me to his chest, my face in the hollow of his neck, he beat his wings, driving us upward. The hospital fell away and the city shrank as he climbed above the city glow and turned west toward Forest Park. We soared far above the lights of the towers. If anyone were to look up, they'd likely only see the shadowy figure of a very large bird.

The lights along the MAX line guided our path over downtown. I drank in the beauty of the lit bridges spanning over the Willamette River, reflecting the city on a glassy surface. The bouquet of lights and sounds reminded me there were thousands of people out there, the people of my city, who had no idea their town was built on a gateway to another world.

Liam didn't speak, just held me tight. I wrapped my arms around his neck, relishing the tickle of his scruffy beard against my cheek as I snuggled against him. He bent his head, pressing his face into my neck. Inhaling deeply, he nuzzled my skin before glancing back up again to steer us home.

Such a simple gesture, yet so intimate, left me throbbing and warm.

The view of Thurman Street from above was of a quiet little road leading to the darkened trails of Forest Park. This time of evening, everyone in the whole neighborhood was tucked up in front of their fireplaces.

He glided into the back yard. I was worried to see that the only lights on in the house were the kitchen and the front porch. I noticed, as we touched down, that the charred chunks of the lightening-struck oak had been removed. The wall was still broken, revealing an opening to the neighbor's yard, but the whole scene was significantly less traumatic than I remembered. The NaNas had apparently been very busy while I was away.

The back sliding door was locked, so we went around to the front of the house where I dug the key out from under the planter and slipped it into the lock. For once, it went in without the stiff scrape, and the lock turned without the usual fidgeting required.

"That's weird," I murmured. "The NaNas must have fixed the lock."

Liam tilted his head. From the nearby bushes, a cat hissed then yowled.

I pushed the door open and caught a blur of movement and glimpsed a small woman with dark makeup.

"Bloody freak!" she screamed.

Then something hard cracked against the side of my head.

Chapter Twenty-One

Rise up, Rose
Shake off the winter sleep
Your world is in need of making

I tottered sideways under the blow, ears ringing, as Liam lunged into the entryway. He snatched the umbrella out of her hands.

"Maya! It's me, and this is Fable." He turned, gripping my shoulders. "Are you alright?"

I crouched, holding my skull. "God *damn* it! Can I catch just one fucking break? *Please*!"

"I'm sorry…I thought you were someone else," Maya said.

"What's going on?" LeeLee asked as she and Biddy rushed down the stairs to lead me into the living room to sit.

There were no lights on when we approached, but inside the house, nearly every bulb was lit, and a fire glowed in the hearth.

"All the lights were off," I accused.

"Well, it looks that way from the outside," Biddy said. "We've been cloaking the house since Maya arrived."

"She's got some unfriendly followers," LeeLee explained.

I glared. "Probably because she's so good at making friends."

"I said I was sorry. Cripes."

Maya was just barely five feet tall, and only because she wore a pair of black platform, knee-high boots. "You're not like I pictured," she said in a British accent as she flopped onto a nearby sofa, crossing her arms over her chest.

She had black clothes, long black hair, and dark eyeliner. A lip ring highlighted her scarlet lipstick.

"Ditto," I murmured.

She's a Muse?

"How's your head?" Biddy asked.

"Throbbing," I retorted. "Like my hand."

Glancing down, I was surprised by the amount of smeared, dried blood from the knife wielded by Xabien's witch and the ripped-out stint.

LeeLee was already pulling the first-aid kit out of the front closet.

"We must not linger," Liam warned. "They will surely come to the house in search of Fable and me."

"Who?" Eleanor asked as she opened the door from the basement. She walked in to the kitchen and closed the door behind her. "What's happened?" She looked directly at me.

"Where to begin," I said.

Liam pulled his hair back, rebinding it as he explained, "We escaped an attack from Vojhane at the hospital, but his wings were loosed. It is probable the FBI and even Vojhane are headed toward us as we speak."

All at once the NaNas were a flurry of motion.

"I'll take Fable to Skye," Eleanor said, grabbing her coat.

"Maya, now's as good a time as any to get you to that safe house we talked about," LeeLee said. She dragged my hand into her lap and quickly wrapped a bandage around my wounds.

"I'll just get you some clothes," Biddy said. She patted my shoulder and disappeared up the stairs. It was a measure of how desperate the situation was, that Biddy passed up an opportunity to make a joke about my missing pants.

"What? Wait!" I said. "I just got home! I'm tired and starving, and I just want to take a bath and get my bearings!"

"We can't keep you safe here, yet," Eleanor reasoned. "We have not yet fixed all the runes and wards, and two Muses in one location is just too tempting a target."

Liam paced near the front door, wings contracted, tense.

LeeLee finished the quick wrap on my hand while Maya watched. When LeeLee stood and walked to get her purse, Maya switched couches to sit next to me.

Holding out her hand, she said, "Hi. I'm Maya."

"Fable."

We shook hands.

The house lights flickered and the room shook. Porcelain figurines on the shelves clinked together, and the chandelier swayed as we touched. For a brief moment, everything was exactly as it should be. The world turned on perfect axis, the seasons rolled with precision timing. It felt as though something long lost had been rediscovered, and a puzzle piece clicked into place.

We jerked our hands free of one another, each of us staring.

"Did you feel—" she began.

"Yeah," I finished.

"Cool," she said.

Biddy dumped a pile of clothes in my lap. "Hurry, hurry, we need to get moving—I feel a storm on top of unwanted guests coming."

"I feel it, too," Eleanor remarked.

"A big one," LeeLee confirmed.

In the bathroom, I slipped on jeans and a black T-shirt, thankful that Biddy's taste was simple and she knew what I liked to wear. After a glance in the mirror, I was surprised at how different I looked. My eyes were brighter than I'd ever remembered them being, and they matched the malachite pendant around my neck. Curly dark hair framed my thinned-out face, and there was something about me that seemed…well, resolved.

Am I taller?

I walked out and found they were all waiting by the front door, and I was struck by what a ridiculous group we made: three old ladies, a Goth punk, and an Eagle Avian in jeans and all his winged glory, looking impatient as hell.

"Let us go!" Liam said.

We rushed outside. The rain had started, punching down hard, punishing. A typical Portland late-autumn deluge that promised to bruise the city.

"I'll take Biddy and Maya," LeeLee said as she held her umbrella high and scurried to her white Volvo wagon.

"Fable, you're with me," Eleanor shouted over the downpour as I trailed behind Maya.

I knew it then—I would not see Maya for a while. It made sense. For now, our stories were branching in different directions, but they would merge again in the future. Threads woven in different directions would tie back together one day to complete a pattern.

"Wait!" I shouted to LeeLee. "Where are you taking her?"

"We can't be around each other until we're stronger," Maya said.

I paused, knowing she was right.

"Sorry I brained you with your own umbrella."

"It happens." I shrugged awkwardly, unsure of what to say to a sister Muse upon parting. "Take care of yourself."

"You, too." Maya suddenly looked up, rain splashing against her pale features, running her makeup. "Something is up there."

I turned and sprinted toward Eleanor's sports car. Maya, LeeLee, and Biddy all scrambled into the Volvo, slamming doors. The headlights blinked on, and the engine revved.

I ran across the slick pavement and threw myself in the Alfa Romeo Spider as Eleanor turned the key. It was a two-seater roadster. "How's Liam gonna…?"

The car was already pulling away from the curb.

Liam ran alongside the car for a dozen heavy strides, wings arched back, rain pelting his bare skin. Then he launched into the sky as a screeching raptor's cry ricocheted off the surrounding houses, muffled only slightly by the torrent of water.

We sped behind LeeLee along Thurman Street, the wipers beating a furious tempo. I glanced at Eleanor. Both her hands gripped the leather-wrapped wheel, her white knuckles glaring at ten and two. We were going way too fast for the quiet Portland street, yet we kept pace with the rear of the Volvo even as it blew through two stop signs.

"Eleanor! Slow down!" I shrieked. "You just ran a stop sign!"

"No one is coming, Fable. LeeLee would make sure of that." She didn't blink. Her makeup was smeared, mascara running.

"What's up there?" I pressed my face against the passenger side glass, trying to look up, but all I could see was the blur of water and buildings and street lights as we blazed toward 23rd Avenue, a densely trafficked area even on a stormy night.

Eleanor suddenly veered left, down a side street, and quickly turned left again on Vaughn. I was surprised by her deft handling of the small sports car on slick roads.

Vaughn Street, a back entry to the industrial district, eventually merged with Highway 30 which cut though a strip of sparsely populated land running along the Willamette River, past docks, trains, and warehouses, up to the St. Johns Bridge.

I scanned the sky for signs of Liam. But as we sped along Highway 30, there were few lights and even fewer cars.

"Eleanor, where are we going?"

"Hold on!" Eleanor screamed.

From the corner of my eye, a shadow streaked across one of the few streetlights along the highway. In the distance, the lights of St. Johns, the northern-most neighborhood of Portland, gleamed across the river. Without warning, the shadow blotted them out.

Vojhane slammed onto the roof of the roadster. Deadly talon spikes ripped down through the convertible's canvas top. The sound of rending fabric was followed by a deluge of cold water, then a terrible popping rip, and the whole roof of the car was wrenched off.

A barrage of rain flooded the interior. I craned my neck, watching the shredded roof spiral off into the night.

"Put your seatbelt on!" Eleanor screamed over the rain and wind as she buckled herself with one hand. Her black hair was matted to her face and water streamed in runnels off her chin.

I clicked my seatbelt into place, cinched the strap, and shielded my eyes from the worst blasts of storm water hammering against us as we raced down the darkened highway.

Vojhane crashed onto the hood, talon claws goring through the metal panel. Screeching, bending steel mixed with wind. The back wheels of the small car lifted off the ground, and then smashed back onto the asphalt.

Eleanor screamed and slammed the brakes.

The car veered side to side then fishtailed wildly before Eleanor lost control altogether. We spun in circles down the center of the highway.

Vojhane gripped the top of the windshield, leaning into the cab. He seized my arm with a brutal grip and jerked, but the strap of my seatbelt kept me safely inside.

Oncoming lights blinked though the gap between his legs where his claws gouged through the hood. The lights drew near, and the long, warning blast of a trucker's horn blared through the night.

Liam arrowed toward us as we spun. He clutched a wooden pike as he flew full-speed into Vojhane's body. They collided with a sickening wet slap and a flurry of wings as his momentum knocked them both off the hood. They tumbled through the air toward the darkness along the river near the tracks.

He cleared the hood in time for us to see the semi bearing down on us as we slid to a stop, stalled sideways in the road—the grill of the 18-wheeler aimed right for my door.

The truck honked again and hit the brakes, but the slick road and the sudden attempt to stop brought the tanker trailer skidding out from behind the truck's body with a deafening screech.

Eleanor gunned the engine, kicking us into gear. We shot forward, off the road and into a tree with a hard jolt. The semi-truck jackknifed, rolling over the spot we'd just been sitting.

I flung my door open and lunged out of the car in time to see the truck on its side, sparks shooting into the rain as it skidded along the asphalt with the shriek of bending metal, shattering glass, and a deep, resonant groan.

The truck finally ground to a halt, its weight rocking back and forth. The reek of rotten eggs filled the air.

"Eleanor?" I glanced back in the car. "Eleanor? Are you okay?"

Eleanor looked up from the steering wheel with a bloody nose and a cut on her forehead.

I splashed around to the driver side, grateful for the headlights illuminating the tree she'd hit. It was directly in the center of the grill. Beyond the tree was an embankment where we would have rolled down into a ditch.

I pulled open her door and checked her quickly. She seemed mostly dazed. "Are you okay? Does anything hurt or feel broken?"

She patted my hand as I unbuckled her seatbelt. "What about you?" she wondered.

"Better than you."

Eleanor climbed out of the car and rested against the side panel. "Where's Liam?"

"I was just going to go look for him." I touched her face. "You sure you're okay?"

She nodded slowly, brushing my hand away, and started toward the wrecked truck. "Is anyone hurt?" she asked. She picked up speed as she went, and I had to jog to keep up with her.

We made it to the truck. The stench of rotten eggs lingered in the air. "I think we're near a sewer line or something," I said as we walked around the front.

Chapter Twenty-Two

Sometimes saving yourself
Means free-falling right out of the Skye

My whole body burned with cold. We clung together in the mud. I couldn't move, so I stayed in Liam's arms, shaking.

"Shall I fix your room?" asked a deep, proper voice.

Rolling my head slightly, I squinted through the rain at a man on the stones of a nearby porch. He held two robes toward us from the shelter of an umbrella.

"Excuse me?" I blinked and swiped at my face.

"We've been expecting you for supper, but it seems you will also need a room and baths."

"Yes, thank you, Franko." Liam climbed awkwardly to his feet, pulling me with him. "We will also need some bandages."

I stared dumbly at them both. It was like we'd just crash landed at a British mansion, complete with a butler. I tried not to stare at him as we walked closer, slipping on the grass and holding on to one another for support.

Franko met us on the stone patio and offered plush white robes. He was seven feet tall, with an eerily skinny frame and long, thin limbs. His white hair was combed in the immaculate fashion of early 1930s pomade with a swirl; yet despite the strange disproportion of his figure, he could not have been more than 40 years old.

"Please follow me," he said and led us through a back door of the building. The well-lit hallway was lined with expensive carpets and walls of paintings, and it looked like a house out of an interior design magazine.

"I don't want to track mud through your house…"

"It is quite all right, Ms. Fable. I will clean up behind you."

The back of Franko's neck had a vertical ridge the width of a thumb that bulged from the base of his skull all the way down his neck to disappear in the collar of his navy blue suit. He turned and nodded that we should follow him.

Liam nudged me from behind and I stepped forward onto the lavish rug. I looked down in horror, sure I'd just stamped mud all over the carpet—but upon lifting my boot, not a spot of mud had transferred. I stepped again, and after half a dozen feet, I realized something magical kept the mud from being trailed through the house.

"Oh, that's cool," I mumbled. "The perfect trick for Portland."

Tucking the robe tighter around my body, I hurried to catch up, passing half a dozen doors of fine cherry wood.

"Skye Manor was moved, stone by stone, from Scotland, and reassembled here in 1889," Franko was saying. "However, she does update herself, depending on the latest trends and amenities."

"How old is the house?" I asked, noting the lights, brilliantly glossy hardwoods, and light sage walls. "She looks pretty modern inside." Shivering overtook me again and I clenched my jaw to keep from chattering.

Franko paused, frowning. Tapping a long finger against his pointed chin, he said, "Beyond the remodeling to keep up with the niceties of plumbing, the electricity, and the self-cleaning rugs, I believe my mistress is roughly 800 or so. Although it is impolite to speculate on a lady's age."

"Eight hundred?" I gasped, looking around. "But that would make this place a medieval castle, not a 19th-century mansion."

"Quite," Franko said and continued down the hallway.

I glanced at Liam. He shrugged his wings.

Franko led us up the stairs to a landing where the décor of the house became markedly more luxurious. The thicker rugs, crystal chandelier-draped ceilings, and glossy redwood banisters and rails highlighted the eggshell-white walls lined with portraits of the sort of quality I'd expect to see in a museum behind glass and guards.

Is that an actual Rembrandt?

"She would have you together in the Dove suite," Franko explained. "At the top of the next flight of stairs and to the right. The first room is yours."

I stood on the landing, unwilling to walk up alone, as Franko turned and headed past us back the way we came. "My apologies. Please excuse me; I am being summoned to the perimeter for a breech. Please see yourselves to the room, and I will return shortly."

"I'll come with you," Liam offered, stepping forward.

"No need," he insisted. "The perimeter is well protected with ley lines and runes, levees, and our own personal guard. The Seeley are quite prepared to handle anything while you catch up on your rest."

Liam's tense shoulders and drenched wings appeared ready to spring to action.

"Please, sir," Franko said, "your people came to us, and we have accepted responsibility for your safety. It is what we do, is it not?"

After a moment, Liam said, "Thank you."

Franko disappeared down the steps. Liam turned, passed me on the landing, and made his way up the stairs, leaving me to follow his wide dark wings.

"What was that all about?" I asked.

"This house belongs to the Tuatha DeDannon. One of their many strongholds around the world."

"Okay…"

"And by stronghold, I mean anything that attempts entry without invitation will die, in potentially thousands of different ways."

"Wow. Okay." I gazed around at the surrounding luxury. "Why didn't we come here sooner?"

"Because nothing Seeley or Unseeley comes without a price." He glanced back, his tousled wet curls gleaming in the light. "I cannot imagine what Eleanor relinquished to grant us all refuge here."

A hard pit in my stomach made me wonder what the NaNas had done.

"Are these people our allies?"

"For as long as it suits them, yes."

At the top of the stairs stretched a corridor decorated with glass bookshelves and loaded with hundreds of antique books. We turned right and entered the first door, as Franko had instructed.

When I was a child, I dreamed of what it must be like to be a princess in an opulent palace. The Dove suite came as close as any childhood fantasy.

The room's exterior wall was rounded outward like a bay window overlooking the estate. The high ceilings were painted gold and hung with crystal fixtures, reflecting light in brilliant, brassy hues. The walls were not painted but covered in rich, green cloth. Mahogany furniture and an oversized, four-poster canopy bed finished the décor with a countryside-manor house appeal.

Liam rested his hand on mine. "You're freezing."

"Actually, I can't feel anything at all, at the moment."

"Come," he said and towed me toward the bathroom, just as my jaw loosened enough to start clacking my teeth together.

He flipped the switch, illuminating the interior of a bathroom built like a spa. The giant vanilla marble bathtub could fit 15 people, with room to spare. Steps led down into water that curled with steam. Live orchids lined the back wall and recessed lights cast a pleasant ambiance.

"Did someone just turn the heat down?" My shivering returned in force.

"You must get out of those clothes."

"Riiight," I teased. "The old must-get-out-of-those-wet-clothes ploy."

If you insist.

I shrugged out of the robe then tried to slip off my muddy boots, but I couldn't stand on one leg without trembling sideways. I focused on my jeans but my fingers were too stiff to work the button.

"I'm worried about Eleanor," I said, all joking aside.

"Here," Liam offered, reaching to slide my muddied shirt over my head.

His touch was like a firebrand on my frozen skin. I flinched.

"Sorry," I said through chattering teeth, "your hands are really hot."

Everything about you is really hot.

Liam gazed at me with dark blue eyes. A muddy streak blurred across his face, disappearing into matted blond curls.

He finished shimming my T-shirt over my head, careful not to actually touch my skin. I lifted my arms, but as soon as my shirt was off, I covered myself with my own pale muddy limbs, wishing I'd worn a sexier bra.

Liam tossed my shirt to the tile floor with a splat.

Under the furnace of his gaze, I shook harder—whether from cold, shock, or desire, I couldn't be sure.

"Icarus' wings!" Liam swore and squatted down to help me with my boots. "Lean on me and help me get you out of these, before you become hypothermic."

I held the arch of his wings as he knelt before me. He shuffled off one boot then the other. Then he expertly unbuttoned my jeans and squeegeed the wet denim down my legs. When I stood in just my bra and panties, he pulled me into the glass alcove, where three showerheads aimed streams of water.

"It's cold!" I yelped, shrinking away.

"Yes," he said, holding me tighter. "We will warm you up slowly, so it does not burn."

Icy water stung my body as I retreated into Liam's embrace, pushing myself into his body. The wet denim of his jeans felt abrasive against my cold skin. Gradually, the water began to warm. Every minute or so, Liam turned the knob just a fraction, until my shaking subsided.

After a time, blessedly hot water loosened my muscles and I began to relax. I became hyperaware of Liam's naked torso against my chest as the showers washed all the mud and chill from our skin.

The squeak of the knob brought my head up. Liam looked down and moved a wet curl off my face.

"Better?" his voice was heavy, smooth.

I nodded.

He led me from the glass alcove to the main part of the room.

The bathtub steamed with fresh, hot water and a sweet fragrance I couldn't place. A small table covered with bandaging supplies stood near the entrance.

"Where the hell did that come from?" I asked.

"Skye is a living home," Liam said. "She anticipates need."

Slipping my fingers into his palm, I let him lead me down the steps of the deep tub. The water was perfect, sinking into my bones and joints, filling my head with the aroma of something floral and mildly musky…with a faint hint of copper.

"You mean the house is a smart house? Artificial intelligence?"

"There is nothing artificial about her intelligence. She is alive."

"How's your leg? Does it hurt bad?"

"Not as much."

There were not many steps, but the tub was deep. Warm water reached the top of my breasts as I stood on the marble bottom. The orchid forest between the tub and wall lent the room an exotic, tropical air.

Liam sank into the water near the back, his wings stretching across the surface of the water. He pulled me to him, turning my body and urging me to sit between his legs. I hoped he didn't notice the rapid shift in my heartbeat as my backside slid down his belly to rest between muscular thighs.

Jesus Christ, Fable! Breathe!

Liam's right hand wrapped around my hipbone, holding on as he situated us both. We sank a little deeper into the water until all but my head was submerged. Then he tucked his wings into the tub. Feathers tickled my legs. It felt for all the world as though I'd fallen into heaven.

"You should let me wrap your leg," I murmured. The delicious warmth and luxury added a languid tone to my voice.

"Can you smell the flower? *Illytrium*?"

I sniffed the air. "Is that what's in the water? Sort of a coppery orchid scent?"

He scooped water in his palm and poured it down my neck. "It has many of the same sterilizing properties of iodine." With his other hand, he took my left wrist and lifted my bandaged palm. He carefully unwrapped the white fabric and rested my hand back in the water. "Even now, that tingle you feel is your wound being cleansed."

He brought my palm to his lips. I turned my head to follow his action, and the second my gaze met his, I knew it was too late—too late by far. His lips were so close, his chest at my back, his thighs pressed on either side of my hips.

Liam's gaze said everything I wanted to hear.

Before I could think, or speak, or reason, I tipped my head back as he leaned forward, and we came together in a wet, smoldering kiss.

His hands slipped across my body, sliding down my skin to cup my breasts. I stretched my arms back over my head to pull him forward as I tried to turn my body.

His tongue was warm and firm, urging. It drove me wild with wanting. I broke away, panting as I spun around, sloshing water over the edges of the tub. I wove my arms around his neck and straddled his lap. His jeans rubbed against my inner thighs as I took his mouth again.

Liam groaned, wrapping muscled arms around my body, crushing me tight as he threaded fingers through my wet hair. His wings sloshed the water.

"Gods," he moaned, pulling back on the kiss. "I must stop. We must stop."

It was too late for me to comprehend "must" as I trailed my lips down his neck to the crest of his collar bone. "Do you *want* me to stop?"

"No. Gods, no." He breathed heavily, hands skimming down my back to grasp my hips. "We have obligations."

"And…?" I teased, kissing him softly on the lips, his succulent, delicious lips. I murmured, "Who doesn't?"

He paused, meeting my eye, his lungs working for air.

In that moment, I was sure he would say no. I sat back and my weight came to rest on his lap. The noticeable ridge of his cock through his blue jeans stunned me.

"I'm going to burn in Hades for this," Liam said. He stood up and grabbed me fiercely to him. Water sluiced off his wings, spilling over the edge of the tub. He walked up the steps, through the bathroom door, and into the main bedroom.

He strode purposefully past the fine antique furniture and crystal fixtures, carrying me to the bed, where he dropped me on the feather comforter with little ceremony.

Just as I opened my mouth to complain about the apparent lack of romance in his sudden change of heart, Liam popped the buttons on his fly and pushed his wet jeans down muscled legs. His wound looked much better than before but still in need of bandaging.

"Your leg…" I began.

"Can wait," he finished.

At the commanding tone of his voice, the intense heat of his eyes loosed something in my lower belly and I was suddenly weak, breathless. My blood hummed.

He stood naked before me, sculpted like a Michelangelo daydream. I couldn't speak. Gold curls, blue eyes, and the wings of an eagle. Ribs of muscle and black scrawled ink along his chest. He was a marvel.

But I couldn't look away from the nest of blond curls and a very human cock, hard and ready. I relaxed, realizing only then that I wasn't exactly sure what I should've been expecting.

He knelt on the floor between my knees. His large hands rested on my bare thighs, and he said, "I can only give my full self to you in free-fall, but there are other ways to find release."

His fingers trailed up my legs, slick with bathwater, and hooked the edge of my black panties, tugging them down. A tremor of excitement set my legs twitching. Soon I was gasping heavily, dizzy with the need for air.

"Normally, I'm all for the foreplay," I panted. "But I need you in me."

My hands reached for him, grazing his ribs, sliding up his chest.

"Fable," he whispered.

"Mm hm."

He stood, wings stretched to either side of his body as he struggled with my bra. His fumbling was followed by a low growl and a sharp tug. Before I could interrupt and unhook the damn thing myself, he jerked it up and slipped the still-clasped bra over my head.

Well, that's one way to do it.

With one knee up on the bed, he used a hand to push me back and lay to the side as he took his time kissing my body, suckling my breasts, nudging his strong thigh between my legs, and finally slipping a finger inside my body.

The next half hour I arched, moaned, gasped, and begged. Each time I tried to draw him down into me, he doubled his efforts until I wriggled mindlessly, bucking and pleading. He kissed and teased, and tormented me to climax again and again. But despite the deliciousness of the orgasms, they still left me wanting, aching—needing something more.

Even with the spectacular release, satisfaction was stubbornly elusive. A frustrating hollow ache could not be quenched with his ministrations.

"Stop teasing me!" I grabbed his hips and pulled him toward me. "I want you right now!"

Liam groaned, collapsing next to me on the bed. "Fable, I should not take you without your memories." He ran his hands through his hair. "And there's Xabien."

"What do memories have to do with any of this?" I panted.

Liam left the bed in a rush of feathers and heat, stalking to the window, where he opened the balcony door and stood, letting the cool night air tousle his drying curls. "You left me, Fable." He exhaled. "For almost 15 years. That's a long time to wait."

I sat up, drew a red blanket around my shoulders, and walked to stand beside him. He looked at me, long-buried pain surfacing in the depths of his gaze. "I'd pledged myself to free-fall for you when we were but children—and I have held to that promise since." Liam fingered a strand of my hair. It had begun to dry and turn springy. "If I take you to mate, and later you remember why you left—it will be too late. It will already be done. And perhaps you will remember…" He broke off and turned, staring out the window with a hard twist of his lips. "You are not mine to have."

I pressed my body against his, letting the warmth of our two forms heat the cold air. "I am my own to give. Don't I have a say in it?"

He kissed the top of my head.

I peered up. "If we live through this, and I am sent to Xabien—what will I have that's mine, for me, except my time with you now?"

Tension suddenly turned his body ridged against mine. "Do you want me, Fable?"

"Yes."

"Do you want me in free-fall?"

"Yes."

A fated sense of importance filled the small space between us. I felt for a moment that I agreed to a legal contract with my words, and even though it was strange…it felt right. Perfect.

"And you want me?" I asked.

"As always."

Something clicked in me—a sense of finally being in the right place at the right time. An overwhelming sense of rhythm, of belonging.

Tucking the blanket tighter around my torso, my legs naked and free, Liam kissed my lips gently. "Wrap your thighs around me," he commanded, lifting me up.

I snaked my legs around his waist and locked my ankles at his lower back, just as he charged across the balcony, leaped over the ledge, and dove toward the ground. I held my breath, pressing my cheek to his chest where his heart drummed against his sternum.

He arched, swooping up toward the night sky. The rain had stopped, but the clouds remained. Intense, powerful strokes lifted us skyward, past the city's glow and into the shelter of the dark heavens. Although it was cold, Liam's exertion gave off a flood of heat.

I glanced down at the bubble of light around the city. We were somewhere over Forest Park in the midnight hours.

"I will not relinquish you to Xabien," Liam said into my ear as he dipped into a glide.

Closing my eyes, I smiled. Relieved.

He climbed again. With each stroke of his wings, I jarred against him. The swell of warmth from his body made me forget the chilly night air and the ambient glow of the city as it shrank.

I thought only of his arms, the taste of myself still on my tongue from his kissing, and the ache inside he would fill.

He nuzzled my cheek with his nose. "Hold tight to me now, as I let go with one hand."

I shifted my hips so he could reach a hand between us. He adjusted himself to fit me. His wings struck air with a mildly frantic edge as his focus split. When he slipped into me, my body sighed with relief. "Yes, yes," I encouraged.

"Gods, Fable!" he gasped and thrust all the way to his hipbones. I cried out in pain, glorious pain.

Liam's wing beats faltered. We dropped before he regained control. The blanket slipped off my shoulders and drifted down toward the tree line of Forest Park. My body throbbed as I clung to him and he fought to keep us in the air.

My fear of falling warred with the need for rough, hot-blooded sex, and I found I couldn't keep still but wanted only to ride him—wherever he would take us.

"Are you okay?" he asked frantically.

"Yes."

"Did I hurt you?" He moved his hips slightly, tenderly.

"Don't stop."

He resumed his upward climb and the rhythm of his wing beats added momentum to his thrusts. I tried to wriggle into a position to better angle my hips to arch into him.

"Please. Be still," Liam begged. "Must get us higher."

He pumped me again and I turned to jelly in his grip, the pressure inside me building to dangerous levels. I panted. "Liam. I can't… hold it back."

With my words came the desperate and breathless plea of pending orgasm. "Gods, Liam, *now*!"

Liam pushed deep. I locked my ankles tight around his back, my muscles flexing as I was rocked by the severity, the raw awesome power, of an orgasm that ripped the air from my lungs with a throaty scream.

Images and scenes laved over me, clips and snippets of the grander story, of which we were only a small part. But I didn't want to see it. I wanted only to feel Liam inside me, scream his name, and…

Caught by animal lust, his musky scent and burning skin, I closed my eyes and bit into the flesh of his shoulder. Liam threw back his head and moaned, a feral tone that terrified me in a deeply sexual and erotic way. His dark eyes were predatory.

Then he tucked his wings around us like a cocoon and we plummeted, spinning toward the earth.

Terror and orgasm conflicted with one another as Liam continued to drive into my body, pumping his hips into me with desperate, frantic need.

The earth grew larger. Wind burned my ears.

He shouted wordlessly and plunged fully, once more, with a sound that fluttered the chords of my belly. An eagle's scream. The wild bird of prey mingled with the guttural notes of a man. His body flexed and clutched me tighter as he came inside me, convulsing, shuddering, and finally inhaling a great gasp of air.

The earth sped toward us with deadly intent.

"Hold on!" he yelled, spreading his wings like a parachute. We slowed, and Liam drove his wings against the rush of doom, angling his descent into a controlled glide with a concentrated grunt of sheer exertion. He pulled us up from disaster to skim the tree tops, his talons raking an oak and scattering brown leaves in our wake.

Gulping air, he flew toward the house. My heart beat faster than I thought possible. We didn't speak but landed on the balcony to the bedroom of Skye. He carried me inside, collapsing on the bed.

But even as we both fought for air, his hands found my naked backside, fringed with chill, and pulled me into position. "Now that the free-fall is out of the way," he said, "we have all night to take it slow."

I grinned, unable to speak or even catch my breath; but I smiled as my body thrummed and the heat of his touch drove me mad with yet more wanting.

Chapter Twenty-Three

Till death

As morning light glowed through the windows, I collapsed against Liam's side. His wing spread out beneath us, and I curled into him, my body still throbbing with the liquid-silver afterglow of cosmic sex.

As sleep enveloped me, I was blessedly aware of Liam's warmth and the pulse of my many orgasms still flexing through my lower belly, rippling. And after years of emptiness—I finally felt complete.

Hours later, a knock on the door rustled Liam's head from the pillow.

"There are refreshments outside your door." Franko's muffled voice came through the wood. "Skye mentioned you may be needing food."

My face flushed with heat and I murmured, "The *house* knows?"

A smile, slow and mischievous, lit his lips. His lopsided grin melted my insides, and I laughed, wrapping my arms around his body and whispering into his neck, "I'm sure most of North Portland knows." He kissed my forehead and eyelids, and said in his husky tone, "I'm pretty sure they heard you in Aria."

"Heard *me?*" Slipping my hands beneath the covers, I marveled at his ridges of muscle as my fingers skimmed ever downward. "I'm pretty sure I was not the loudest of the two of us."

He chuckled. "I believe you are wrong. Perhaps we should ask someone."

A more insistent knock at the door pulled us apart, just as I started panting from his touch.

I sighed. "I'll get it. Breakfast is a good idea anyway." I rolled off the edge of the bed, dragging a sheet around my body. "God, I hope there's coffee." My body ached pleasantly in all the right places. I smiled.

Liam slipped off his side of the bed. His glorious backside disappeared into the bathroom and the door shut. I sighed.

I could stare at those buns all day long.

I heard the water turn on as I tripped over the edge of the sheet to get to the door. A knock, more urgent than before, set my nerves on edge.

"Okay! I'm coming!"

I jerked the door wide open and gasped.

Eleanor stood in the hallway, fuming.

"Eleanor! Thank god you're okay!"

"They've been stalling me for hours down there! I had no idea if you were all right!" She stormed past me then turned back and pulled the cart of food into the room. "Are you well? I've been mad with worry!" Dishes rattled and clanked together as she rolled the service across the carpet.

"I..."

She was like a bottled hurricane rushing into the room, dark black hair askew, makeup smeared and clothes torn. "*Well?*"

She stopped short and took in the state of the room: the scattered bedding, the bloody wet jeans on the floor by the bed. Then she looked at me. I must have looked a mess, with bedhead curls haloing my shoulders and what I hoped was a gloriously satisfied glow.

"What?" I wondered.

Just then the bathroom door opened and Liam strode into the room. "Was there coffee?"

He froze, wings stiff. His magnificent naked body stood like an angelic messenger.

"Eleanor," he stated.

Her face went pale, more so than her usual alabaster complexion. "Oh, goddess, have mercy," she said, then walked to a chair near the fireplace, and dropped heavily into the seat. "Oh, Fable. What have you done?"

I was totally unprepared for her reaction.

"Liam, please cover yourself." Eleanor clutched her head in her hands and sank forward as though utterly defeated.

Wordlessly, Liam picked a blanket up off the floor and wrapped it around his waist.

The room was well lit by morning light, and my body pulsed with the most exquisite warmth I could remember—I was happy, feeling good. Eleanor's behavior almost made me feel ashamed of myself. And by the hard set of Liam's jaw and stiff shoulders…she was doing a fair job of rattling him, too.

"Liam? Coffee?" I asked.

He shook his head.

I went about fixing two cups of coffee. "Eleanor? Do you want cream and sugar?"

The hospitality cart was an old-fashioned dark wood frame on wheels with a silver pot of coffee and three silver lidded plates. A delicate cream pitcher and sugar bowl sat beside a glass carafe of orange juice and a plate of toasted English muffins. The second level of the cart held two piles of neatly folded laundry.

I handed Eleanor a mug of steaming brew and turned to Liam. "There appear to be clothes on the bottom of the cart."

He took the hint and retreated to the bathroom with a pair of clean Levi's and a slice of toast.

As soon as the door shut, I turned to my favorite NaNa. "Eleanor, you know I love you—but there is no call for you trying to make me feel ashamed for what is my business."

Eleanor nodded, far away.

"I'm a grown woman, almost 30."

Eleanor looked up, eyes sparkling. "*Cherie*, I am the last person in this world who would ever begrudge you your choice of lovers. Truly. You should know that by now." She shook her head. "I'm just afraid for you."

"Don't be afraid for me for this." I snorted. "I should think you'd be afraid of me getting kidnapped by crazies, or murdered by factions or—"

"But your heart is the mechanism of all your power." Eleanor reached out, touching my cheek as I squatted before her. "If you break your heart—truly break it—the whole world will feel it. Story itself will suffer, if your heart is wounded."

"Do you really think Liam, of all people, would break my heart?" I sighed. "I'm happy around him…as happy as I can be with everything going on."

"That's wonderful." She smiled weakly. "But you are betrothed to Xabien, and the lives of thousands depend on you. Nations will be at war without your alliance." She leaned forward, grasping my wrist, finally meeting my eye. "How can you perform that duty if you let yourself love Liam—only to be apart from him?" She paused then sighed. "Will that not hurt your heart? Deeply?"

I sat on the floor and leaned against her chair. None of what she said had even occurred to me.

After a few moments, I felt her hand on my hair, smoothing my curls. I remembered back when I always went to Eleanor for advice about boys. She was the first person I told when I'd lost my virginity. The only NaNa who listened to my escapades and offered advice without judgment.

"Why is this time different?" I asked. "Why, of all the times I've come to you over the years…"

"Because"—she kissed my forehead— "any fool with eyes can see you are falling in love with him again, and this is no school-yard romance. There are worlds at stake now."

"'Again'?" I asked. "What do you mean, again?"

"You are right, *Cherie*," she amended. "You're a grown woman, a powerful goddess, and you have the right to some happiness. The right to take a lover."

Eleanor sipped her coffee and leaned back in her chair. "Besides," she continued, "it's not as though you'd commit to a free-fall ceremony. You're too mindful for that. I'm an old woman, overreacting to my worry for you."

My heart banged inside my chest. I tried nonchalantly to sip my coffee, but scalded my tongue. "What do you mean about free-fall?"

She exhaled. "It's the Eagle custom of choosing a mate. Eagles mate for life, you know."

"For life?" I echoed as the bottom fell out of my stomach.

"Yes, free-fall is a marriage custom." She smiled. "At least we don't have that complication to deal with. It's going to be difficult enough to keep *this* from Xabien."

"Right," I murmured.

"Liam!" Eleanor yelled. "You can come out now. I promise not to change you into anything… biologically unpleasant."

The bathroom door opened, and Liam made his way into the room, looking a strange mixture of guilty, ready for punishment, and oddly full of pride. He wore a clean pair of Levi's.

"Eleanor, I…" He opened his mouth to speak, but when words fell short, he straightened his back, fixed his wings, and stood firm.

"Come now, Liam, I was just surprised." She exhaled, stood, and set her mug on the tray. "I shouldn't have been. It was foolish to think you two wouldn't find a way of being together at some point." Smiling ruefully, she said, "Likely Celeste knew it as much as any of us."

She adjusted her dirtied clothes and reached for the doorknob. "I'm off to get a bath and some rest—but I'm happy for you both.

Truly." As she turned to leave, she said over her shoulder, "With what lies ahead, it's only right you find some joy where you can. Just be careful."

The door closed behind her. I sat on the floor against the chair, coffee clutched in my hands.

"She took that a lot better than I thought she would." Liam lifted the lid of one of the plates. "I'm ravished."

"Famished," I whispered.

I got up, fetched a bundle of clothes off the cart, and walked toward the bathroom.

"Are you well?" Liam asked around a mouthful of bacon.

"I just need a minute alone." I locked the bathroom door and sat on the bench near the vanity mirror and a counter laid out with perfumes and cosmetics. Holding the clothes to my chest, I stared at my own reflection.

My face said it all: I'd just had the best night of sex in my life. Glowing skin, riotous curls, vibrant eyes, swollen lips. But shadowing it all was a hue of doubt. Disbelief.

Married? It isn't possible. How archaic is that?

The more I thought about it, the more furious I became. Why would he lie about something like that? Omit the most important detail like…free-fall meant forever in his world.

But wasn't I the one practically begging? Would I have listened?

I groaned and ducked my head, remembering how undignified, horny, and insatiable I'd been. But the question remained—Why hadn't he mentioned that *mating* meant "till death do us part" not just "crazy monkey sex followed by a walk of shame"?

Furious, I dumped the clothes on the floor, sifted through them, and was surprised to find a pair of jeans tailored like a second skin. A pair of dark brown riding boots and a black sweater all fit perfectly.

"Thanks, Skye," I said to the bathroom.

Did I just talk to the bathroom?

313

I grabbed a few hairclips from the counter of supplies, washed my face, and cleaned up. Once I was sure I could handle the truth, I walked into the bedroom.

Franko stood with Liam. The two men stopped talking when I entered.

"Ah! Mistress, how do you find the clothes?" Franko asked.

"They're wonderful. Thank you so much."

"Very good." Franko beamed. "I have just come to inform you we have taken capture of prisoners. Would you like the honor of questioning them?"

"A prisoner?"

"Yes, mistress. Two Avians were taken into custody last night as they attempted to cross the security barrier. The woman claims to have information only for you—so we have not punished them yet."

"Yet?"

"Fable, it is not wise to put you in the same room as a threat…" Liam said.

"Yes, Franko," I said, "I'll hear her." I glanced at Liam. "Could you give us a moment first, please?"

"Certainly," he agreed. "I will wait for you in the downstairs library."

Liam walked toward me as the door clicked shut.

I held up my hand and took a deep breath. "I need some space, Liam." The wounded pinch of his brows almost made me change my mind. Almost. "I'm gonna go see this prisoner—and then we need to talk."

He made to follow me as I walked away. "Alone," I added.

"Absolutely not," he said flatly. "My directive is your protection."

"But—"

"That is one thing we never have to talk about—it simply is." The hard tone of his voice and the firm stance of his body made it clear pushing him would result in a full-on fight, for which I didn't have the energy.

"Fine," I snapped.

"Agreed."

We made our way downstairs to the lavish main floor. I was still amazed, in the daylight, that this house which was actually a castle looked so modern. It made sense that over the years it had been upgraded, remodeled, and retrofitted for each new era. It was practically a smart house, or something like it.

The library was in the south wing, with large picture windows looking out onto lawns and rose gardens, with the forest beyond. There wasn't another house in sight.

The walls were lined with books of every shape and color, some of them oversized, leather-bound, and sitting in glass cases. Couches full of pillows and end tables with brass fixture lamps encouraged a homey feeling, seducing me with the lure of curling up with a good story. It would be easy to lose myself in such a room with rolling ladders and a spiral staircase that led to a second-floor balcony with a fireplace and reading nook.

Franko stood near a door. "Welcome to the library of Skye." Motioning around the room, he said, "Skye has collected her favorite tomes from the last eight centuries." Turning, he said casually, "The library continues another six floors belowground."

I gasped. "Six floors?"

"And the prison," Franko added. "Please follow me."

Together we passed through the door on the side of the library and into a hidden elevator. It was a snug fit with Liam's wings. Franko pressed a button engraved with a symbol like a sarcophagus.

Conversationally, I wondered, "So, Franko, you have an unusual name. Is it from your family?"

"No, it is in fact my stage name, the name of an actor I heard and adopted…which suits me, as one day I will tread the boards."

"You're a thespian?" I asked carefully.

I didn't see that one coming.

"This is only my day job," he said. "It pays the bills."

In the last two weeks, I thought I'd seen everything that could surprise me, but a creature right out of the *Adam's Family* harboring closet dreams of a Broadway nature was almost too much. I looked at the floor. "Well, break a leg, Franko!"

He beamed. "Thank you, Mistress Fable. That means a great deal, coming from you, Maior."

The elevator lurched and the doors opened. Right away I knew we were in the prison below the library. All I could see by the light of the one hanging bare bulb was concrete: cement walls, ceiling, and floor in each direction. Embedded in the floor was an uneven, winding luminescent vein of blue light.

"To the right, please."

Liam and I both followed Franko's directions and turned down the corridor. The blue vein in the floor offered enough light to navigate, although I found myself hesitant to step on it, adopting an uneven gait. it was the same hue I'd seen in many forms since I went to Aria: lamps, energy nets, and spheres. All the same shade of bright electric blue.

"What is it?" I asked.

"A natural ley line, charged with current from the Rhue."

"Oh," I murmured, although I had no idea what he meant.

"Rhue is a source power. An energy." Liam walked along the hallway with none of my apprehension to step on the ley line. "Rhue can be transported or fused into a natural power structure such as these energy lines, and it creates strength in bonding—like what you might call a kind of energetic super-glue. There are thousands of uses for Rhue."

A metal door at the end of the hall was guarded by a creature as tall as my hip with a wide girth. His grizzled black beard and square physique made it difficult not to be wary of his hard glare. The blue light illuminated his pointy teeth and ears, and layers of leather straps crossing his hips and chest were filled with knives.

He acknowledged Franko with a grunt as we approached. The two exchanged rapid-fire dialog in a language I didn't understand, and the little guy *harrumphed* and drew a key from his pocket. He unlocked the door.

"What did he say?" I wondered.

"He is uncommonly hungry," Franko offered. "He asked when he will be allowed to eat the prisoners."

"Ohmigod!" I gasped, stepping away from the guard, noting his grizzly dark scruff and stubby fingers. He looked like a demonic Hobbit.

A cannibal?

Liam led the way through the door, but I refused to be left last in the hallway with the ravenous creature and rushed into the cell.

Abra stood behind glowing blue bars, her Crow wings spread wide, and her smile something between amusement and disgust.

"Hello again, Fable," she said darkly.

Chapter Twenty-Four

Follow the story to the other side
Beginning, journey, and end

The bars were charged with the same Rhue as the ley lines. The floor of her cell was veined with the same powerful glow. The effect was a prison cell you might expect to find at the back of a black-lighted, kinky club.

She leaned against the back of the cell, against a concrete wall spattered with blood. Two crows strutted around the floor. Their talons left small red claw stamps. Abra's hoody sleeves were rolled back, revealing the gap in her interlocking tattoos where her birds had escaped her flesh.

"It's safe?" I asked Franko.

"Quite."

I edged closer, wanting to get a good look at the Avian that had caused me so much trouble. From when we first met at the café to the harrowing flight home to the Gate, I sensed Abra had much to do with events I hadn't even seen yet.

"What are you doing here?" I asked.

"You wouldn't believe me if I told you."

I approached the bars. "Probably not—but here you are."

She was petite with ragged black hair that looked all too much like a crest of feathers.

Abra gazed at me, her dark eyes lined with even darker make-up—calculating. She stepped away from the wall and walked toward the bars as though she were wading through hip-deep clay. Each step through the cell full of interlacing blue lines appeared to cost a great deal of determination.

When she stood close enough to touch the bars between us, she said, "I came to warn you, actually."

"…says the chick who tried to kill me—twice!" I hissed.

She gritted her jaw, and narrowed her eyes. "Anyone knows I would not have killed you. I have never intended your death—ever."

"Right," I said dryly.

The crows hopped around, flapping wings, unable to get lift inside the Rhue-charged cell.

Caw! Caw!

"Talk," I said.

"Only the Earth factions would ever dare kill a Muse," Abra began. "Any faction of Aria wants only to control the power—we know what will happen if a Muse dies. I would not have killed you." She paused. "On purpose."

"What will happen in Aria if a Muse dies?" I asked.

"The same thing that happens on Earth when a Muse dies before her time—the Dark Ages were a slow recovery on Earth, is that not true?"

"Get to the point."

Abra's lips thinned. "What do you think would happen, Fable, if our two worlds lost Story? What do you imagine would be affected?" She rubbed the bare spot on her arm. "All entertainment is Story. Paintings, dance, performance—all Story. Books, literature, history—all Story." Her voice grew louder as she listed off all the variables I hadn't actually taken the time to think about.

Since I'd been running for my life, searching for a killer, trying to find clues to rescue my sisters, I hadn't sat down and thought about what effect the Muse of Story might actually have on the world.

"Everything about your culture here on Earth is related to story, conversation, retelling, information, and blah, blah, blah." She laughed then, a dry bored chuckle. "I don't give a fuck about Earth. But I would not ever purposefully harm Aria."

"She would have captured you, if she were able, and taken you back to the Eventines," Liam filled in. He glared at her.

Abra was silent.

"But she wasn't expecting the house to be so well guarded," Franko said from the door. "She and her companion were easily caught."

"He's not my companion," Abra said and spat at Franko, who curled his lip. "I knew this was a Tuathan landmark. I came willingly."

"Why?" I shook my head.

Abra inhaled long and deep and looked up at Liam, then me. "Because I have read your pages. I believe you are in danger."

"Why would you even care?"

"Don't you listen? If you die, Aria is harmed…and your murder is written in your own pages. You are no good to me dead."

Caw! Caw!

"Where are the pages?" Liam asked.

"Aria," she replied. "But I got a name off the last page. Page number 240."

Liam exhaled heavily. "Are you certain?"

"The pages claim it to be so." She sneered. "How accurate are the pages?"

"So who the fuck is it?" I demanded.

"Promise to let me go, and I will tell you."

"Tell me who it is, and I'll promise to *think* about it."

It was as good as she would get, because my next offer would be my fingernails in her eyes.

Caw! Caw!

Abra continued to watch me, her gaze measuring. At length she said, "Page 240 calls her *Mendelson*."

Caw!

Chapter Twenty-Five

All is not lost, which has been mislaid
But set aside for another day

I sat with my hands in my lap, chin on my chest. The bed had been made up while we were gone and the room returned to its luxurious shine. I'd come back up to the room while Liam insisted on interrogating the second intruder captured by the Seeley.

My time was short, limited. The walls of a life I couldn't remember were closing in on a life I'd barely lived…and page 240 sat on the line between. I rocked back and forth on the bed.

Didn't I know on some level it would all come to this? Isn't there something in my blocked memory that would have prepared me?

Thinking back to my time with Celeste, I worked through memory after memory, event after event, looking for a clue, a hint—a thread of anything that would make it all make sense. Nothing.

Time after time, I thought of Celeste at her writing table as I sat in the window seat reading or writing in my own books. I remembered working with her in the garden, playing the imagine game, baking cookies for tea, and shopping around town. We traveled. We laughed. We spent days at the library then picnicked in the Rose Garden.

Celeste.

I wanted so much to be like her. I wanted to tell stories and reach the world beyond myself. I wanted to entertain and educate and inspire. What a demented irony, then, that I had all those abilities—but through a trick of birth and power I wasn't aware of it and could only watch her live the life of a famous writer and wish to imitate that life for myself.

Was it because she made me so happy? Or was it because it was impossible for me to be anything other than what I am?

The bed creaked as I rocked.

Even the memories I had of my father at the dig sites he'd taken me to in faraway countries around the world reminded me of how close I was to the power of Story; yet I'd been too young to comprehend what it would eventually mean. I understood now that he must have been aware of Aria, and that I was probably with him on those digs to keep me out of reach of the otherworld. He would sit at his table in the tent at night, lighted by the lantern, writing in his journal about whatever he'd unearthed earlier in the day.

"What do you think of this one?" he'd ask, his hair dusty, clothes stained.

He'd hand me an artifact, a bowl, a shard of pottery or a piece of carving. His blue-green eyes always sparkled, as though he knew a private joke.

I sat on my cot where I'd been writing in my own journal, playing at being an archeologist, and I'd take what he offered and close my eyes.

In the shelter of our tent, I'd let my fingers slide over the texture of the object, and after a time, I'd say, "This was the cup of a servant who had babies with the king." Or, "This piece of pottery is from a bowl used to collect rainwater." Or, "This is part of a carving of the constellations."

Each piece of history, each artifact and shard, revealed to me its story. Sometimes I would be lost in living the story for hours before opening my eyes.

"Good!" my father would say. "Very good, Fable!" His rough hands would take the object, and he'd return to his work. He'd say over his shoulder, "You should write that in your journal. A good archeologist writes everything down, because one day all the pieces will add up. Then you'll be able to see the whole big picture."

It was midday, but I couldn't tell by the light outside. In typical Portland fashion, October hung heavy with clouds. I ambled toward the balcony and gazed out at the molted leaves of the distant forest. Ochre, bronze, and burnt orange mixed with scarlet and gold. The line of trees made an imposing wall of autumn oak, cottonwood, and maple.

What page am I on? If I have only till 240 before Mendelson....

Sadness swept over me.

Liam. Celeste. I'm sorry.

I hung my head with the grief of knowing I only had so long to live, and there was still so much I needed to do. The other Muses were unaccounted for and the answers to the blight remained a mystery.

And Celeste's murderer must be brought to justice.

Mendelson? Really? Abra might be lying.

I thought of my night with Liam, such an amazing, beautiful experience. And I wasn't surprised to realize that I felt something for him. Something deep, urgent. Powerful.

How unfair is that? I finally find a guy I can really...care about. No, not care about. Love. Then I get offed in a few Chapters.

A frustrated sob exploded from my throat and I covered my mouth as I thought of not being with him.

In the distance, all the leaves of Forest Park shed at once.

The tree line shuddered and the 90 acre park dumped its patchwork autumn clothes, leaving a vast stretch of bare limbs, naked too soon for winter.

I sighed and leaned against the doorframe.

Celeste, what should I do?

There was a knock at the door before it opened. Liam entered, followed by another Avian with black wings and black wraps.

"Kal!" I gushed and ran to him. The second before I threw myself into his arms, my memory filled with images of my child self, riding his shoulders. I'd twisted his long black hair into two braids and used them as reins. Celeste shook her head, smiling, as she sat on a blanket under the trees, watching us run around the field.

I pushed myself into his arms and he hugged me close, cocooning us in his raven wings.

"You are back," he whispered. "This is good."

"Bits and pieces," I agreed.

"In time you will be whole again." He squeezed me. "Be patient."

"Easy for you to say."

"Kal was the second intruder," Liam said as he sat on the bed. "He was in pursuit of Abra and was trying to capture her and retrieve the pages when they crossed Tuathan lines."

Kal exhaled. "I failed to retrieve the pages."

"We searched her," Liam added. "She doesn't have them."

I frowned. "What do we do now? We have no way of knowing if she's telling the truth until it's too late."

Kal paced the floor. I went to Liam, leaning against the bed, and rested my hand on his thigh. It felt good just to touch his solid presence.

"I have news about Celeste," I said softly, unsure if I should tell Kal but knowing he deserved to hear the truth.

He turned, visibly steeling himself.

I rattled out the details about Deloy. How he was my exterminator, how he'd left fingerprints in the house, tried to break in, and then confessed.

"But…" I finished, "something doesn't feel right." Something didn't click into place with Deloy's confession and revelation he hadn't been working alone. "I know this sounds crazy, but hear me out. Xabien had the most to gain with Celeste out of the way: There would be no one openly opposing the consummation of the betrothal contract. He said as much last time I saw him. Then Vojhane implied it was easy to murder humans…and I saw him the first time at the morgue. And then there's Abra. I don't trust her. *At. All.* For all we know, she murdered Celeste to set this whole story in motion."

I sucked in a deep breath and exhaled with, "All I'm saying is Deloy's confession doesn't make sense to me. And we don't know Mendelson is actually going to try and kill me, because we could be interpreting the page wrong—or Abra could be lying."

Pausing, I held my breath, staring at both the Avians.

Kal adjusted his wing. "I must ask a favor of you, Fable. Something I would never ask of anyone else, and it will be difficult. But it may provide the answers you seek."

The gravity of his tone warned me I wasn't going to like what he was about to ask.

"Okay…" I said carefully.

Kal stepped toward me, pulling a silver ring from his pinky. I recognized it immediately. It was Celeste's; she never took it off unless she was cooking or gardening. It had Celtic braiding and a stylized seal with at calligraphic letter *S*.

"Oh, god," I said, backing away. "Was she wearing it when…?"

Kal hung his head. "If you do not wish…I will understand."

Understand if I picked up that ring, I might witness Celeste's brutal end? Understand it would be etched permanently in my mind's eye, blazed into my heart? Forever unforgettable?

Multiple lacerations. Exsanguination.

But Celeste had loved me, sacrificed for me, given up a life with the man she loved to keep me safe. She'd been there for me when my mother died and when my father could no longer cart me around. She'd been my best friend, my mentor, my confidant and sister. She'd been my guardian and protector, my own Muse and my greatest champion.

No one on either world had loved me so deeply.

"Give me the ring," I said.

Kal met my eyes, hopeful, wary—and desperate for answers. "Thank you," he whispered. "Thank you."

As the ring dropped into my palm, I flinched, remembering the flood of emotions and sensory images I'd felt upon touching the gifts in the receiving line back on Aria.

Nothing happened. I touched only smooth silver, warmed by Kal's hands.

For years I'd seen Celeste's ring on the dish next to the kitchen sink where she left her jewelry while she made bread or cooked dinner, or in the crystal bowl in the center of the table where she'd leave her rings before working in the yard. But I'd never held it, much less worn it on the middle finger of my right hand as she had.

I sucked in a deep breath and slipped the ring onto my center finger.

At once a stabbing, lancing pain exploded in my stomach.

I collapsed under the overpass in downtown Seattle. The ferry terminal across the street teemed with boats coming and going. A long, resounding ship's horn echoed off the buildings.

A curved bronze knife ripped free of my belly, spraying crimson droplets over the dry leaves trapped in the gutter. I couldn't see the face, darkened by shadows from the overpass.

The knife came down again, slicing. Cutting through fabric, flesh, and the ligaments in my shoulder.

I screamed and tried vainly to shield myself with my hands.

Her face loomed out of the shadows. Special Agent Mendelson cut my scream off with her left hand, her face contorted with disgust. I kicked, but already half a dozen wounds bled my strength and unimaginable agony robbed logic. I tried to call a spell, but the fingers around my throat cut off my voice.

I sucked air through my nose, and the scent of nearby ocean reminded me of my home near the sea with Kal.

Oh, goddess. Kal, my love.

I fought futilely, but the whole attack was over in minutes. Blood ran down the sidewalk. Agent Mendelson's face was splattered with my life. She stuck the ancient knife in a plastic bag and tucked it in her purse.

As I lay bleeding, gasping, gurgling on blood, she leaned over, wiping her face with a rag. She hissed, "Nothing personal, old witch." She dried her hands then added the rag to her purse. "You know how it is. Gotta get the ball rolling." Then she was running away, back toward Pike Place market.

Torturous pain. Blood pooling, soaking into my hair. Heart beating slower…slower…slow.

As darkness crept into my vision, I whispered, "Fable, my Rosebud, I hope you never see this, but if you do—remember Mr. Lincoln. I've left something there for you. I'll wait for you in the Midway." I sputtered on phlegmy blood. "Give my deepest love to Kal, who gave so much to me."

Scarlet runnels filled the gutter, pushing leaves toward the drain. I had strength for one last spell and whispered the words to sunder my consciousness from my body.

Then there was no more pain.

As the Midway drew my spirit to safety, I saw the grisly scene of death. The ferry terminal horn blared again, and I found peace in the scent of the sea.

"Pull it off!" Liam yelled.

"Hold her still!" Kal snapped.

The Dove suite of Skye came in to focus. I was caught in Liam's arms, pressed against the floor as he worked to hold onto my thrashing body. Tears soaked my face and neck. My throat burned from screaming.

I went limp. Drained by what I'd witnessed.

"Fable?" Liam asked, dragging me up from the floor where I was pinned. "Are you well?"

"Are you okay?" Kal asked, face pale, eyes full of worry.

"I'm not hurt," I said, wriggling the ring off my finger. I let it drop to the carpet. "Let me up."

Liam scrambled back, freeing my hips from his weight. "You were screaming." He took a deep breath. "I thought it was hurting you."

I climbed to my feet, unable to find the words for what I'd seen. I said, "I need a minute," and walked into the bathroom, shutting the door on both of their concerned faces.

I sat on the bench in front of the mirror and stared into space as my mind replayed the scene of Celeste's murder. I knew I should feel something.

Water gushed from the three faucets of the massive tub.

"Thanks, Skye, but I don't need a bath."

The water to the tub stopped, then burst forth from the shower heads.

"I don't need a shower, either."

The shower shut off and the lights around the vanity flicked on as soft music played.

"I don't need makeup, either."

The vanity lights dimmed.

"I don't actually know what I need."

But I did know. I needed to make Mendelson pay. I needed to make her pay for Celeste, for her betrayal, for her cruel brutality.

I needed her to admit she'd manipulated Deloy with her *sawyin* to force a false confession. Much like she'd forced me to speak, on more than one occasion. I needed Drake to know what she'd done. I needed to know what other crimes she'd been party to. I needed to know if she had a role in the kidnapping of my sister Muses. But most of all—I needed to know why.

"Skye," I said aloud to the empty room. "I need a cell phone."

• • •

Liam paced the lawn in front of Skye Manor. It was strange to see him outside in the gray daylight of Portland with his wings out. It was one thing to be flying in the dark or above the city where people rarely looked up—but to see him right there in the open… gave me an exotic chill. I glanced around at the forest in every direction, hoping no one was spying on our goodbye.

"Promise me you will stay at the house, until I return with Gabe and Zane," Liam insisted.

A black Lincoln town car with dark tinted windows pulled up the curved asphalt driveway.

"I'll be with Eleanor, and the FBI will likely be parked right out front. I'm sure I'll be safe." I rubbed my eye.

"I'm not sure the house is safe enough yet. Even if Vojhane is gone for now."

"What has been safe up to this point, Liam?" I couldn't keep the edge of bitterness from my voice. "It will be nice to sleep in my own bed, and process some of this." I waved vaguely, encompassing the world and all the chaos and heartbreak of the last two weeks.

The chauffeur got out and walked around to my side. He opened the door, then waited nearby in his black suit and gloves. He reminded me of a wrecking ball; nothing on him was soft or fat, only muscle. He wore sunglasses despite the clouds.

Liam stepped forward, taking my arms and crouching to meet my eyes. He fanned his wings as he turned us away from the driver and whispered, "There is more here at stake than you imagine. Stay at the house. The Talons and I handle things with Mendelson from here out."

I slipped my arms from his grasp and stared at him as he straightened. He took a deep breath, his dark blue eyes searching my face. He opened his mouth to speak then glanced behind me and his lips sealed.

"She hurried down the walkway with a bag, and without so much as a glance at Liam, she brushed past us on the way to the car where she climbed in the back seat and scooted into the dark interior.

"Liam," I whispered. "I…"

With a snap of wings and a blast of air, Liam surged forward, cupping my face, kissing me hard. Despite my mixed feelings about the night before and the looming finale of the *Prophecy of Crows*, I threw my arms around him and kissed him in return.

"You stay safe until I get back." He pulled away.

My knees were weak, and I wasn't sure if it was his kiss, the heady scent of warm skin and musk, or the knowledge that I didn't have any intention of doing as he asked.

"Be safe," I said.

Like ripping off a Band-Aid. Go quickly.

Breaking away, I drank him in one last time before rushing toward the car and throwing myself in beside Eleanor. The door shut behind me and I gazed out the window as Liam watched us drive away. His wings spread to either side of his body and he launched.

I knew he'd follow us far above, watching to make sure we got safely to the house.

I faced forward, trying not to look at Eleanor. As we turned down the road, trees passing by the windows, the weight of my life descended upon me and I couldn't stop the pain in my stomach from the worry.

Eleanor took my hand and squeezed my fingers. "Have faith, *Cherie.*"

Chapter Twenty-Six

Frantic wing beats caged in ribs
Love will set you free

I knew it would be no simple task to break away from Eleanor's watchful gaze.

Once we reached the house, I was relieved to note that Biddy and LeeLee weren't home. I would only have to trick Eleanor…and the surveillance team I knew would be stationed across the street. I'd been thinking of a plan during the ride back from Skye, knowing that if I wanted to confront Mendelson myself, it had to be before Liam and the Talons arrived.

I felt bad for making Liam believe I'd stay in the safety of the house, but there was one more page of the *Prophecy of Crows* that needed to be fulfilled—and the only two people on that page were me and Mendelson.

I'd have to come up with an excuse to get past Eleanor then meet Mendelson somewhere mostly private…then what? How do I get through the confrontation with Celeste's murderer–without getting killed?

The only difference between the girl in the prophecy and myself was that I was armed with information and the desperation to bring Special Agent Mendelson down for her crime.

I never bought into prophecy, anyway. Right?

Celeste always said the future isn't written until you're standing on it.
I would prove that pages 239 and 240 were wrong.

I came down the stairs. Eleanor sat at the kitchen table with Celeste's ring. She'd been holding it since we told her what had happened. She rested it in the dish at the center of the table where Celeste used to put her jewelry while she was gardening.

"When are the boys supposed to be here?" Eleanor asked.

"He said they'd be here just after sunset."

I poured a glass of wine and put it in front of Eleanor. She smiled. She'd never seemed so old to me before. Mascara was caked in the crow's feet around her eyes. Her skin was papery, and her usually shiny black hair was dry and wiry.

"Eleanor, are you okay?"

"I'm feeling my age today, *Cherie*." She sipped her wine then picked up the ring again. "She was the strongest of us, you know."

I poured myself a glass of merlot and sat beside her.

"Well, your mother was the strongest, actually, but then it was Celeste." She drank deeper, gazing out the sliding glass door. "We were supposed to grow old together." She laughed wryly and held out her hands, examining the raised veins and age spots. "Now, I realize, we did."

She held the ring out to me. "Who do you suppose she meant by *Mr. Lincoln*? Did she keep a lover?"

I took the ring carefully, purposefully blocking myself from sensing any of the story contained within. Mr. Lincoln? She'd said it to me in both my dreams of the Midway, and in her death memory. She left something with Mr. Lincoln.

"Mr. Lincoln is a rose bush," I replied. "She named all her roses, but that hybrid tea rose she ordered came with a name she liked."

The memory of Celeste walking in from the rose garden, a fist full of blood-red blooms in hand, came to mind.

She pressed her nose to the blossoms and said, "Mr. Lincoln sends his regards."

I shoved back from the table and ran into the back yard. The damage from the lightning-struck oak looked much less severe. The chunks and debris had been removed while I was away, but the remains of Celeste's beloved roses were still crushed into the muddy earth.

Mr. Lincoln was pruned down for the winter. I knew him because he was planted next to the large garden stone, the one we'd made ourselves one summer when I was eight. We poured concrete into a mold, pressed our hands into it, then decorated the cement with pieces of broken jewelry, buttons, and seas shells. The imprints of her big hand and my little hand were both full of rainwater and green with moss.

Beside the garden stone, Mr. Lincoln was dead. His stalk split right down the center.

I knelt in the mud. "I left something for you with Mr. Lincoln."

With a shrug, I pulled my sweater down over my hand and grabbed the broken stalk, uprooting it from the mud. It ripped free with a crackling pop as his roots lifted from the earth. I dropped the lifeless plant and knelt to dig in the mud with my hands.

"Try this," Eleanor suggested. She held a shovel in one hand and the bottle of merlot in the other.

I took the tool, and she drank right out of the bottle.

I dug for 15 minutes. There wasn't anything under the rosebush. I sagged against the shovel, staring at the garden stone. The memory of the afternoon was so clear: the silly game we played, running around the house looking for tidbits to affix in stone...

After we'd pressed our hands in the slimy gray cement, I held my palm up to hers to see how much larger her hand was. I was right handed, and she was left handed.

"Auntie Celeste, you put your wrong hand in the mud-pudding," I'd told her. "You put my hand in there, but not the hand you use."

She'd smiled and kissed my forehead. "Of course, Rosebud. I put your hand in the mud-pudding, so you can open the door someday." Her eyes sparkled with that gleam she got whenever she told a joke.

The day was almost over, and I stood in my dead aunt's back yard, digging up her favorite roses. I stared at the garden stone. Celeste's *right* handprint. On a hunch, I knelt and swiped the mossy water away. I paused then pressed my right hand into Celeste's imprint. They were the same size.

I'd grown into her hands.

I scrubbed at the garden stone, washing the mud and filth and grime. Her handprint became more vivid—and on her middle finger was the impression of the ring she always wore. The ring she'd worn the day she was murdered.

In a rush of excitement, I bolted back into the house, trailing muck, and grabbed the ring off the table. I ran back outside, leaped off the last two steps, sprinted into the yard, and fell to my knees at the stone.

It took five deep breaths to calm my racing heart and still my fingers. Then, carefully, forced myself not to feel her memories as I slipped the ring on my middle finger. When I was certain I could open my eyes without seeing Celeste's death, I exhaled and reached for the stone.

My hand slipped into the grooves, and the ring locked into place.

The sound of a crank from deep beneath the earth ricocheted up through the soil. A long yawning groan rumbled the ground.

I stood up, stepping backward until I bumped into Eleanor, who gripped my arm and tugged me toward the deck.

The cranking stilled and was replaced by a hiss of steam that preceded a cloud of white smoke billowing out from under the garden stone. There was a sharp *pop,* and the garden stone shot up into the air as though tossed by a geyser.

"Look out!" Eleanor said and pushed me sideways.

Loose dirt and mud rained down on the spot where we'd been standing. A heavy chunk of cement landed with a dull *thud* where I'd been kneeling next to Mr. Lincoln.

A minute passed, and when the smoke finally dissipated, Eleanor and I crept back to the rose garden to see what it was.

An odd safe-like structure was tucked down in a pit the size of a spare tire. The metal door was flung open, revealing a stack of tied-together notebooks, a shoebox of CDs, and assorted odds and ends. On the very top of the pile was an envelope with my name in Celeste's handwriting.

I picked it up. Eleanor bent to examine the contents of the safe.

My fingers shook as I broke the glue seal and pulled out the letter therein. It was dated the month after my accident in New York.

It was short, so short and so shocking that I read it twice.

For good measure, I read it again.

Trust the story, huh? It can't possibly take more trust than this.

"Eleanor, can you do me a favor?" I asked.

She barely glanced up from digging through the notebooks. "Sure, *Cherie.*"

"I have to run to the corner store before they close. Would you mind bringing all this stuff in so we can go through it when I get back?"

"I don't think it's safe for you to—" she began.

"It's like, a block away. I'll be safe for a block. I can't drink coffee without creamer."

Eleanor sighed. "I'll go with you."

"No, that's okay. Really, it's a block away and I'll be back before you're done. I can't wait to dig through all this, but I'm gonna need some coffee to do it, right?"

Eleanor appeared to be considering it when I popped up and made for the door before she could really insist. "I'll be right back," I said over my shoulder.

I grabbed my purse and the cell phone from Skye and bolted out the front door. I knew the surveillance team would be watching me, but it didn't matter. If I followed the instructions, I'd lose them in about 20 minutes. As I jogged down Thurman, I couldn't stop thinking about the letter in my pocket.

How is any of this possible?

I caught the street car on 23rd Avenue toward the MAX station downtown. Once I was on the MAX light rail train, gripping the cool metal bar and watching downtown fly by, I knew I had a chance. The surveillance team struggled to keep up as I hopped from stop to stop until I reached the Hollywood transit center. There I jumped on a bus headed for the Belmont district.

As the bus left the transit center, I saw two men in suits standing near the curb, reading the charts. I slinked down into my seat and hoped they didn't look up before my bus had pulled into traffic.

Once I was safely in the arms of public transportation, I fished the letter out and read it again. The letter that came in a sealed safe under the rose garden and dated five months earlier read:

Rosebud,

As you read this make sure Eleanor is busy digging in the safe. Don't arouse her suspicions. Just read. Think this through quickly, and trust the story.

If you follow these instructions, the men in the van outside won't be able to follow you.

In 27 minutes, you must be on the streetcar toward downtown. Get off at the Glisan stop. Send this message to the one you hate most: "Meet me at Laurelhurst Park at sunset."

Catch next streetcar to SW Morrison. Get off. Walk to Pioneer Square. Catch the Red Line MAX to end of fare-less square. Get off. Walk into Lloyd Center, buy coffee.

Send this message to your only friend in law enforcement: "Meet me at Laurelhurst Park. I'll talk."

Walk back to the MAX line. Catch Red Line to the Hollywood transit Center. Get off.

Run to catch bus pulling away from curb. It should be headed past the Belmont district.

Get off at 39th and Burnside.

Walk to Laurelhurst Park.

Record every word spoken.

I know your mind is spinning, Fable, but you wrote these instructions for me to deliver to you, at the time of your waking. You wrote these instructions before the MAX line was complete. Before texting was even available. You wrote these 14 years ago.

This event in Laurelhurst Park was designed by you, to facilitate the beginning of a new future. If you have any doubts, rest assured that meeting whomever you saw in your vision at Laurelhurst Park, is an absolute imperative for saving your life and the future of two worlds.

Now read this again. Make sure you understand it.

Then figure out a way to give Eleanor the slip!

Go.

Love,
Auntie Celeste

P.S. By the way, 39th was recently renamed "Cesar Chavez Blvd." There's no way even you could have seen that one.

I sat on the bench in Laurelhurst Park, looking out over the duck pond as dusk settled over the trees and autumn leaves drifted onto the surface of the water. My mind still spun around the implications of the letter. It was staggering on its own, but once I coupled it with the knowledge that I had already, just earlier that morning, been trying to figure out a way to attempt exactly what the letter instructed me to do…it just toasted my brainpower.

Only as I'd gotten off the bus at 39th and Burnside, when I saw the sign indicating the name change to Cesar Chavez Blvd, did it actually occur to me how convoluted this had all gotten. It was so far beyond comprehension.

How was it possible that I was participating in an evolution of reality that I'd seen more than a decade ago, when I was a child? Could I have prevented Celeste's murder? What happened on Aria that made me leave? What did I see back then that led to the level of extreme brain-warping—when I'm helping my future self plot out the revenge of my aunt's murder by leaving secret, reality-altering notes?

God, Liam's gonna be so pissed at me.

"Life rarely works out the way you imagine," Celeste would say. "It plots when you're not looking."

I thought I knew what she meant by that back when the colleges of my choice rejected my applications, but Washington State University accepted me even though I didn't remember applying. I thought I knew what she meant when I got the internship for the magazine in New York, even though I'd wanted to be a novelist or travel the world and write stories about other cultures.

I didn't realize it at the time, but she knew my life here on Earth was sort of a part-time gig until my real life returned to claim me. Everything I'd done for the last 14 years was intended to be temporary.

I thought I knew what she meant by "life making plans"—I didn't think she meant my past life is writing plans for my present and possibly altering my future. Next time, Celeste, be more specific.

338

Then again, how could I not feel just the tiniest bit relieved there had been a reason I was so lonely, so cut off from the rest of my peers? How could I not be a little relieved that I hadn't ever fallen in love because my affections were stranded in another world with an otherworldly creature I couldn't remember?

In some ways it was a relief to know that there was a reason I'd never really fit anywhere. It was a relief to understand I belonged to something, not in the way I'd ever imagined, but to something much bigger than myself.

And I saw all of this in a prophecy 14 years ago?

As difficult as it was for my mind to accept it, my heart was a different story. It knew. My mind couldn't recall the truth, but I felt for once that everything that had happened, everything that contradicted reality as I knew it during the last few weeks, was real.

It was true and right and amazing. Weird, but amazing.

But the most interesting discovery, I realized as I sat in the park, was that I *wanted* to be a part of it all. As the bench lulled my butt to sleep and cold sank into my thighs, I gazed out as the lamp-posts blinked on along the trail, and I knew—I didn't want this to be the end. I wanted to live through this. I wanted to see more of Aria, spend time with Liam, and annul the treaty with Xabien. I wanted to recover more of my memories and find out why I'd left Aria to begin with. And not least of all I wanted to find the missing Muses—my sisters. I wanted to be a part of whatever the next future would be.

For the first time since all this started, I was not a hapless, dragged-along weight. I was a woman in control of her odd and unbelievable destiny. Aided in part by her younger self.

Okay, maybe not in control…but in cahoots.

That's it—I'm in cahoots with my own future. At least ready and willing to give it a try and see where it all ends up.

I couldn't go back to working at a magazine after all of this. There was no way I could wait tables, or work an office job, after I'd flown across the emerald mountain ranges of another world, spoken with creatures right out of mythology, and passed through a quantum veil.

How would I ever be able to have normal sex again, after a terminal-velocity orgasm?

I'm ruined for normalcy now. I can never go back to mundane.

The park turned to night as I waited alone. Few people passed as the time of evening approached when Laurelhurst Park was considered unsafe. Closing my eyes for a moment, I said a quiet prayer for the plan to work. The plan devised by a younger me.

I trust our story, Fable.

"I got your text. This is an odd place for a talk," Agent Mendelson's voice pulled me from my thoughts.

She wasn't dressed in her usual professional clothes but in dark jeans, knee-high boots, and a sweater. Her hair hung long and loose, and she wore makeup.

"Did I interrupt a date?" I asked. I swallowed hard to keep the fury in, clenching my teeth.

She shook her head and sat on the bench beside me, her purse in her lap. "Not exactly."

Mendelson looked around the park, quiet and empty. Our area was shrouded in trees, the darkened paths lit by bubbles of light around the lampposts. "It's pretty dead around here."

The hair on the back of my neck stood on end. "Yeah," I agreed. "I was hoping for a little privacy."

"I hear a lot of vagabond-types hang out in this park after dark." She turned to me and stretched a hand toward my shoulder.

I stood before she could touch me. "Yeah, I hear that, too, but it's Portland, so it's not as bad as people think."

Her brown eyes appraised me. Calculating.

This was it. I could feel it. I reached into my pocket, hit the recorder on my phone, and edged closer, heart pounding.

You're so going down, bitch.

"What's this all about, then, Fable?" she asked with a smile that begged me to tell her what she already knew.

"Well, I just wanted to have a little talk."

"Is this about Drake?"

Of course not, but since you went there first…

She continued, "Because I think it's fair to let you know, he could never be interested in you that way—not a case."

"A case?"

"Obviously he could never allow himself to get involved with someone in an open investigation."

Suddenly I knew where this was all headed. Why hadn't I noticed it before? "But he can get involved with a work partner?"

Her shoulders stiffened. With visible effort she relaxed, stretched an arm over the back of the bench, and turned her gaze to the pond. "This isn't what you wanted to talk about." It wasn't a question. "What's on your mind?"

It's time. Right or wrong, stupid or genius, it's time.

"Actually, I wanted you to meet me here so I could ask you why you murdered my aunt Celeste."

It was a gamble. A question meant to stir the pot and see what floated to the surface. What would be revealed by her reaction?

But she didn't huff indignantly or appear wounded by my accusation. She didn't try to feign shock or surprise, or wax demure.

She smiled. A languid tilt of pale rose lipstick.

That simple expression of pleasure bathed my body first in icy shock then burning, scalding hatred. I linked all the parts: the dead crows in the dumpster, the moment in the conference room when I'd been caught in her empathic trance, and again when she ate dinner at my house while I was under her so-called protection. She was the last person I saw before I'd been poisoned.

"Are you working alone?" I demanded, hands shaking.

She turned to me, and it was clear she wasn't the least bit threatened. She causally lounged against the bench, looking at me like I was a puppy that had performed an unimpressive trick.

"Who I work *with* shouldn't worry you, little Maior," Mendelson said. "It's who I work *for* that should keep you awake at night."

My whole body shook with rage. The muscles of my neck spasmed. My head twitched as I struggled to look at her and not leap across the five feet of grass and grab her fucking throat.

"Who?" I demanded.

She took her eyes off me and nonchalantly dug in her purse. "My true employers gave me strict orders: If you prove useless in the recovery of the other Muses, I should have you retrieved immediately."

She pulled out her phone and rose to her feet, watching me as she lifted the device high in the air. "But, barring my ability to capture you upon that eventuality—say, in a struggle…" With a jerk, Mendelson smashed her phone on the cement near the bench and kicked the black plastic shards into the pond. "If I lost my chance to call for backup…"

My heart raced and sweat popped out as the sense of danger eclipsed my rage.

She drew a short curved blade from the recesses of her purse. It gleamed bronze in the lamplight. Her purse fell to the ground as she stepped forward. "And I can't sense a soul in this park besides the two of us—so there'd be no way for you to call for help…"

I began to understand I might have made a stupid mistake. She was, after all, a trained fighter, an officer. She had supernatural empathic powers and an agenda I couldn't even guess at. And she'd easily killed Celeste, a powerful witch in her own right.

Just remembering it again brought my fury boiling back to the surface. Stronger or better at fighting didn't matter—I just had to stay alive until page 241.

"So if I defend myself from your poorly planned attack, no one could blame me if we come up one Muse short."

"You and I both know a dead Muse could mean a new Dark Age."

"My superiors are prepared for such an event." Mendelson continued toward me. "After all, we killed the last one. Burned her at the stake like the witch she was."

The grass was slick under my boots as I edged off the path. The threshold of light gave way to the darkened interior of the park, and I halted, unsure what to do. I had as much as a confession on the voice recorder of my phone. I could make a run for it and hope to get to the street before her.

"Why would you risk a Dark Age?" I stalled, my mind racing.

"If we can't control the Muses," Mendelson said, "we certainly won't allow them to be controlled by anyone else."

One more step and she was within lunging distance.

"What does any of this have to do with Celeste?" I asked.

Mendelson shook her head slightly. "For a goddess vessel, you are disappointingly simple." She paused, studied my face, then answered. "How else were we going to get you back to Portland but for a funeral?"

For a moment, I thought the whole world had gone out from under my feet. Grass and stone, trees and pond, all dropped away like the edges of a crumbling cliff, leaving me adrift in empty space as the shock of her words ripped my world away.

Murdered to bring me home? Celeste killed to lure me to Portland? Celeste.

Mendelson spoke the words so simply. So matter of fact. "Bait," Mendelson said from somewhere in the distance.

I focused on her voice, and all at once, pieces of the Earth snapped back into place. Ground and grass and trees and pond all surfaced and I stood in Laurelhurst Park before Celeste's confessed murderer.

And as my world reassembled, it came together with a granite resolve.

Mendelson lifted her knife. "Your aunt was just a contract—but you I'll enjoy."

343

My feet moved first. My hands, as if controlled by a stranger, shot out and I hurled myself at her smug face. My fingers grabbed her wrists and we lurched together, throwing our weight against one another. We stumbled around the grass until her booted foot stepped behind me and knocked me backward.

I let go as I fell and rolled across the ground. She darted toward me, and I brought my arms up to defend myself, but not fast enough. The curved bronze blade plunged deep into my side.

I screamed. Pain like I'd never known blazed through my body like a flash of white-hot sun. As she jerked the knife free, each detail of the moment was seared into my mind. The slow turn of her lips, the damp rustle of leaves on the grass under my back, the arc as she swung her arm back, droplets of my own blood raining off into the park and spattering into the pond. It was so similar to my vision of Celeste's death.

An urgent need exploded within me. My life thus far flashed in moments of desperate yearning.

My mother held me in her arms, long curly hair bouncing around my small body as she danced with me through rows of vibrant red roses. She smiled and sang and kissed my forehead.

I stood in front of my mother's coffin, her face waxen and cold.

I sat in a school yard, filled with Avian children. They ran around me in circles, laughing and pointing at my wingless back.

Celeste and I drank tea together in the back yard. Then we pressed our hands into the raw cement of a garden stone and set it like a gem amongst the roses.

My first kiss with Liam.

Sybil and I braiding one another's hair as we sat near the surf.

Celeste prodding me to stand before a congregation.

My betrothal promise to Xabien. We were both teenagers.

High school cheerleading tryouts, and the subsequent shame.

So many weekends at college, alone in my dorm.

The moment I saw Liam's face as he bent over me after rescuing me from the subway tracks. Blue eyes branding me all the way to my soul.

Free-fall…

Memories flashed to the surface, too fast to absorb, blurring past incoherently. Yet with this cinematic flood came a renewed sense of strength. A long-forgotten intensity, only hinted at beneath the clutter of cobwebs. A metallic tint filled my mouth. Starlight pulsed in my veins.

There is love.

Yes, love.

This would not be the end of me. It would not be the end of the Muses, or Story, or my life thus far. I finally had something to live for, to fight for. I had love.

Whatever else destiny had planned for me was secondary—because I sure as hell wasn't dying on my fucking wedding day!

Mendelson's arm reached the end of its slow-motion arc and began its descent for a second blow.

I had no idea what mystery waited in the shambles of my memories, but what was unearthed in that hunger for life was a jewel in the deepest core of my belly, as though the very walls of my womb sheltered a power which pulsed with life and the need to live, to create, to make the light of dawn spill over the horizon!

It was bright and powerful, and it frightened me.

But death frightened me more, and so I called upon the power, the pulsing nebula of raw element. I drew it up from my belly and let it fill my whole body as though I were an empty vessel, ready to pour into the vast ocean of space.

It was euphoric. Orgasmic.

Time stopped.

Mendelson's blade froze mid-air, inches from my heart.

The world was still. My limbs throbbed with the heat of a thousand supernovas. The park was lit like a mid-summer's day; the pond mirrored autumn-laden trees, and lush, green grass shone with vibrant shimmers, as though burgeoning fresh from the earth after a long winter.

As I watched, dead leaves began to fall, pushed off the branches by budding new growth. Tulips along the pond sprouted on spindling stems and burst into fireworks of red and yellow, while the rhododendrons bloomed in white and lavender cosmos.

All this, Laurelhurst Park erupting into spring and summer, as Mendelson hovered frozen above me, knife poised for murder. Her face was a twisted mask of focus. She had but one objective, and she intended to complete her mission. She'd murdered Celeste to do it.

I shimmied out from under her body and surveyed the bright summer day in the park. Flowers in a profusion of bloom. Oak trees in leafy splendor.

But it wasn't a summer's day, and there were no children at play on the swings nearby, no picnickers on the lawn near the water—only a crazed fanatic of another faction out to create a new Dark Age, intent on killing me, and destroying all Story.

The second I thought of the possibility of the Dark Age, my grasp on the power slipped. Time resumed. Night blinked, enveloping the park.

Mendelson's knife sank heavily into the earth where my body had been moments before.

Her shoulders sagged. She hissed as she stood, "Sneaky little bitch!"

Power still hummed within my body. I crouched for a fight. But she didn't come toward me; she went for her purse on the bench.

"We'll do this the quick way, then."

I knew, as she was pulling her hand free, that she would have a gun. And not likely a service weapon that could be traced.

I charged her before she could aim and crashed into her body using my weight to throw us both over the wall and into the pond.

Water flooded my sinuses as Mendelson and I wrestled for control. Wave after wave of her empathic power slammed into my body, but my glow from within deflected all her attempts.

"You 'only use *sawyin*," I grunted, "on the bad guys,' huh?"

Soon her *sawyin* turned to fear, and it wafted through the open connection of her link.

She elbowed me in the nose. Blood gushed, and I instinctively clutched my face. She waded back to the wall and climbed up the bank. In the blur of watery eyes, I saw the glint of a revolver sitting on the pavement by her purse.

Shit.

I sloshed to the ledge, crawled over the embankment, and rolled across the ground, ducking behind the bench. She drew aim and fired the first shot. It ricocheted off the cement by my hand.

"Fuck!"

"Stay where you are!" Mendelson screamed.

Her body shook, but her hands remained steady. The barrel was pointed directly at my head as she faced me.

I came up from my crouch, holding my hands up in surrender.

"Using your power like that, you've just given your position away to every creature for a thousand miles. You'll thank me for killing you before you can be torn apart by all the spawn you just summoned."

She pulled the hammer back and I lunged, desperate.

The gun went off as we collided and fell together on the pavement. A bullet ripped through my shoulder. Scalding, explosive pain.

The revolver bounced out of her grasp as we rolled over and over.

I bit her hand. She kneed me in the side where my knife wound bled. Finally, we came to an inglorious stop, my strength finally flagging, her hands around my throat—squeezing the life out of me.

I let go with one hand and patted around where I thought I'd seen the gun, feeling across the grass as I dug deep within myself for the power or light I'd touched before. If I could just draw it back...

I always thought it would be easy to kill in self-defense, believing the line between right and wrong straddled a sea of black and white, and that self-preservation was the obvious, easy truth.

Kill or be killed.

Yet in that moment when someone has their hands around your neck and your windpipe is failing, your hands slapping helplessly at their face, kill or be killed doesn't even cross your mind. Instead, you want only to live. It's not about killing. It's about seeing the face of the man you love. It's about listening to Vivaldi, or tasting honey, or feeling your family in your arms.

It's about one last chance to say "I love you."

Groping to the right, my hand slid along the ground to where the gun landed. My fingernail scraped the grip. I choked on a sob as my pinky slipped helplessly over the cool metal. So close, but it may as well have been the moon.

My lungs burned. The knife wound in my side ached. My entire body was swamped with pain, and I didn't want it to stop. As long as there was pain, I was alive.

In one last surge of adrenaline, I gave up on the gun and wriggled my fingers around the throat of my attacker. I fought for my life. I fought for all that would be destroyed if I died and the world lost the power of Story.

How the hell did my life come to this?

Darkness swallowed my vision. My muscles buckled and my arms dropped to the grass.

I should have told him.

How much of my life have I wasted not knowing the truth?

Then I felt the gunshot. In a moment of delirium, I believed I'd been hit by another bullet. Mendelson swayed, her grip faltering. She opened her mouth and blood poured from her lips onto my face. Then she tipped sideways and collapsed onto her side.

I thought I heard Celeste's voice saying casually, as though over a cup of tea, "Life rarely works out the way you imagine."

Chapter Twenty-Seven

Dawn rises within us all
Say the LightBringers
Each morning they call

It took several gulping breathes for me to comprehend that I hadn't been murdered. And it took Mendelson gurgling on her own blood for me to realize she was still alive, and that she'd been shot. Special Agent Drake of the FBI fell to his knees at my side.

I clutched my bruised throat and gasped a relieved, emotional sigh that dissolved into full-blown relieved sobbing as his hands worked over my body. "You…got my…text."

He touched my bleeding side. "Are you okay?"

I couldn't answer, torn between drinking in deep breaths and choking out sobs of adrenalized relief. He ripped off his jacket and wrapped it around my body as I tried to sit up, then he eased me back down.

I didn't resist. I didn't think I could sit up, anyway. He called dispatch as I rolled my head to see if Mendelson was still alive.

She was.

Her eyes burned with hatred as she fought for air around the gunshot wound to her chest that made a terrible sucking sound as she inhaled. She lay on her side and watched as the man she loved, her own partner, used his handkerchief to staunch my bleeding as he made the call.

"Officer down. Laurelhurst Park. Requesting two ambulances." Drake's voice was miles away. I watched Mendelson's outstretched arm lurch toward the revolver.

"Julius!" I shouted.

Mendelson's fingers gripped the gun. Drake looked up as she brought the barrel to aim. His own weapon was not even in his hands. It had been a choice between his gun and the phone and the bandage. It was written on his face—he'd chosen wrong.

Her expression contorted in a pain-filled smirk.

My hand shot out. I called on the strength I'd harnessed to stop time, hoping I could stop the bullet.

Mendelson pulled the trigger at near point-blank range.

Drake threw his body over mine. His dark hair fell across his eyes, and his mouth made a perfect *O* as the phone fell from his grip. A bullet spiraled in a puff of powder toward us.

I reveled in the effervescent cosmic burst of heat and light as it flooded my body. This time, rather than aimlessly releasing it, I pushed it from my hand, discharging it at Mendelson with all the desperation of wanting to live and desire to protect Drake.

A silver stream of light erupted from my outstretched palm and a low harmonic groan echoed from the earth. The blast of power hit Mendelson in the face and tossed her backwards. She rolled like a tumbleweed across the grass.

Drake landed heavily across my body.

I heard Mendelson groan. Her hair, once long and dark, fanned around her shoulders—a bright sea of white.

Drake moaned, clutching his arm where he'd taken a bullet for me. Though bleeding and bruised, he scrambled on all fours and checked Mendelson's pulse. "She's alive." He leaned against the bench.

The wound in her chest continued to gurgle and the white shock of her hair unnerved me, but I couldn't look away.

"What the fuck just happened, Fable?"

I tried to sit, but the lancing pain in my side and the burning ache in my right shoulder kept me pinned. It hurt to move. Hurt to breathe.

"I shot my own partner, so you'd better tell me what the fuck is going on!"

It even hurt to swallow. "I can't."

"Yes. Yes, you can, and right now! What was that light?"

"Julius," I wheezed.

He crawled closer, leaning in.

The park was becoming alarmingly dark. Then I realized it wasn't affecting him. Only me.

My eyelids drooped. Sleep was so close, such a tempting escape from the agony…

I closed my eyes.

"Stay awake." Drake scooted to me, taking my fingers, slick with blood.

My eyes fluttered open. Everything hurt too much. I just wanted it to stop.

A gust of wind was followed by shadows in the lamplight. Liam landed in the grass. His talons sank deep into the soil. He spread his wings and knelt beside me.

"What the fuck?" Drake yelled, pulling his gun. "Back away from her," he demanded. "Back away now."

"Liam," I said through a fog of pain so thick I didn't recognize my own voice.

"What are you?" Drake asked, climbing to his feet.

Another gust of wind brought two more shadows. Gabe and Zane landed nearby. With Drake on one side of my body and Liam on the other, I thought for a moment Drake might actually shoot.

"My friends, Julius," I grated through a bruised trachea.

Zane crouched, his hawk wings spread for combat, dreadlocks falling over his shoulders.

Gabe raised a lazy eyebrow and crossed his arms. He shrugged. "So this is the FBI agent, huh?" He frowned. "He's not very large."

Liam slowly maneuvered his hands under my body. I cried out in pain and he murmured gently, "I am here."

"Don't touch her!" Drake yelled.

But Liam ignored the man with a gun. He stood, holding me as I bled all over him.

The two men stared at one another, sizing each other up.

"It's okay." I stretched a hand toward Drake.

"She's dying," Liam said. "We must go."

"Take…" I coughed. "Julius…take my phone."

It seemed like forever before Julius finally lowered his gun. He opened his mouth, glanced at each of the three Avians, and sealed his lips.

Hesitantly, Drake stepped up to the man-bird.

"In…right pocket," I said.

Liam remained still as Drake dug into my pocket.

I cried out as my body jostled.

"We must go," Liam said more sharply.

"Got it," Drake replied.

The phone slipped free of my bloody jeans. Who knew if it would even work after being soaked in pond water and blood.

Liam pulled me tight to his body, squatted, and launched up through the small oasis of light in the park, to the darkened sky above. Sirens blared below.

We reached a level altitude and the jarring wing strokes lessened, but I could no longer feel my body. I couldn't feel Liam's warmth or the texture of his skin. Darkness claimed me briefly, and I woke only upon our landing. My eyes closed again.

When I came to, I recognized the café, then the Gate, then the forest of Aria.

At the rich, earthy scent of deep woods, I knew where he was taking me.

In and out of consciousness, I felt him running. The trees grew too close along the path for flight. I tried to hold on, to help him grip, but my arms fell back, slack and useless.

"We are almost there," he said through labored breaths.

We were well over a mile from the Gate, but the Glade may as well have been on the other side of the world. I closed my eyes, contented that if this were the end, at least I was with Liam.

I opened my eyes when warm water surrounded my body and Liam's face hovered nearby, his blond curls hanging down. My dying thoughts moved to the day on the subway platform when he'd saved me from the tracks and I'd only caught a glimpse of him.

Goddess, please never let me lose sight of his beautiful, perfect face again.

"This will take some time, Liam."

I recognized Gwendollyn's voice but couldn't see her. Keeping my eyes open required so much effort. The sparkling waters of the spring flowed over my body, it felt as though the water were carbonated and each bubble kissed my skin and left behind an electric tingle.

The Oak Witch continued speaking to Liam. My eyelids fluttered, but I couldn't stay awake any longer. "You may wish to rest, eat and regain strength," she was saying.

At last, I closed my eyes and fell asleep neck-deep in the tingling source waters of my home.

I heard a familiar giggle, and the voice of the brook said, "Fable, we have something to show you. Tell you. Show you."

I floated, drifting on a current. Blue light shone through my eyelids. I realized I was the water, the rocks, the banks, the tree roots. I opened my eyes and was no longer in my body. I was only consciousness. Immaterial and yet connected to everything. It was freedom on a level I'd never dreamed.

Am I dead?

A soft burbling laugh came from surrounding waters. "Not dead."

What is this?

"Water will show you what is," answered the voice of thousands of tiny bubbles. "Come see your world."

I didn't resist but surrendered to the flow of something I couldn't comprehend, much less control.

"Your kingdom," said the voice. "Your story to tell."

And all at once, Aria opened to me and I saw all things as they happened simultaneously. I was connected to all things.

A mermaid, deep in an underwater city, argued with her mother about her affections for a much lesser noble. Her mother, a dark-haired beauty, refused to listen to her young daughter's pleas. The girl's cries of frustration broke my heart.

We surfaced near a pod of whales, not the creatures of Earth but much larger, smooth, and musical. As if sensing us in the water, they spiraled and danced as we moved past their slick gray bodies.

We followed salmon up a river to a village where centaurs rested near the banks, sharpening their spears for war.

Farther upstream we came to a brook, wherein we traveled to a lake. Around this lake a settlement filled with elk-folk preparing weapons of their own. Their buckskin clothing and rawhide weapons seemed a poor fit for battle.

As we traveled, I witnessed dozens of cultures preparing for war.

Is there a battle coming?

"Yes," the voice replied. "A war of worlds."

What does that mean?

"The fight for the greatest resources of all living creatures begins soon."

Is there a way to stop it?

"Possibly."

Possible how?

"Bring your sisters together. Replenish. Heal. Inspire."

But how do I do that?

The source water declined to answer. We came to a lull in the ground where the sun beat down upon us. After a time, I felt myself being raised, lifted into the air and carried as mist to the other side of the world. I had no concept of time or distance, but it all seemed far, far away.

Then I felt myself joined with the source again as we hovered over high green misty mountains, rich with fertile valleys. Giants roamed the roads, behemoth men with red hair and simple clothes; they, too, prepared wagons full of supplies: shields, swords, and axes.

It's all over Aria. Every place we've been. The Avians, dragons, fairies, dire-wolves, merfolk—even the peaceful nymphs and the nomadic centaur prepare for war.

"Yes, and the deep-sea creatures and desert dwellers, the Oligante, Asiwellians, and Driids."

And minotaur, Gliff, and New Awl.

"What you have not seen, Fable, is what also brews on the world of men."

Earth?

"Yes," the voice said. "Earth prepares for war as well."

We have to stop this!

"Yes."

I awoke in my body, lying in the healing waters of the Glade with sunlight and blue skies and the sound of running water.

I was alive. Page 240 was not my death. The *Prophecy of Crows* had been altered.

"Do not move too quickly," Gwendollyn said.

I rolled my head, swishing hair around my shoulders. Gwendollyn sat on the edge of the embankment. The crown of oak limbs around her head had shed its leaves. Her long legs dangled in the water and her robes were rolled up to her hips.

"How long was I out?" I asked.

"Two days," she replied. "Your wounds were quite extensive, your strength nearly gone."

"I witnessed…"

Gwendollyn smiled "…Aria?"

"How'd you know?"

"I am a foundling child, an Undjinn. Life-bonded to an oak that will never leave this sanctuary." She sighed. "The source waters are my link to the world."

"You can see almost everything from here."

"But touch nothing."

"I'm sorry," I said.

Gwendollyn stood. "There are blessings with such a life." She shook out her robes. "But sacrifices as well."

I sat up slowly, amazed at how great I felt. Energetic. Limber. Starving.

"Where's Liam?"

Gwendollyn pointed to a heap of feathers on a patch of grass near the Oak. "He refused to leave. I finally insisted he rest. He saved your life," she said.

"Again," I agreed. "I've actually lost count how many times he's done that."

A warm glow suffused my belly as I gazed at the dark ridge of his wings.

"I do not mean his journey to deliver you to the healing waters."

I climbed from the pool and sat on the embankment. It didn't matter that I was naked. The sun was deliciously decadent on my skin, and the radiant warmth of the end of autumn hummed in the air.

"What do you mean?" I asked.

"When you both touched the waters," she said, "the source showed me that you two are bonded."

I froze.

"The implications are dire, politically...but the truth is, that one event may be the only reason you were not murdered two nights ago."

I could only gape. "What?"

"With a simple choice, you altered the variables of two destinies...just a fraction." Her long white-blond hair gleamed in the golden afternoon light. "Enough of a fraction, I suspect, to increase your odds of survival during your first true test."

Variables. So it's true.

"They are waiting for you on Earth," Gwendollyn said. "I expect they are quite worried." She waved a hand across the grass, stirring a breeze toward Liam. He roused and sat up. His gaze immediately settled on me. I was acutely aware of my nakedness.

"Your clothes were bloodied and ruined," Gwendollyn said, as though reading my mind. She held out a soft green robe and I wasted no time dressing.

Liam joined us beside the waters. "How do you feel?"

His grin was bright with relief, his eyes a shining, brilliant blue. I couldn't be mad about the free-fall omission; I was too stupidly happy to see him.

"I missed you," I said, wrapping my arms around his neck.

"How could you miss me while you were sleeping?" he teased.

"I don't know how, but I did." Pressing my nose to his neck, I inhaled deeply the scent that was only Liam.

He held me for so long that when I finally looked up, Gwendollyn was stepping into the well of the oak tree. I waved and shouted, "Thank you."

She returned the wave before the sides of the oak groaned and closed as though a pod latched her inside.

"Let's get back to Earth," I said. "Xabien will know I was here."

Liam nodded. Neither of us spoke about the conundrum of my betrothal promise.

"Are you fit to travel?"

"Oddly, yes," I replied.

Liam swept me up, tucking an arm under my legs and another behind my back. He launched skyward. I was amused that he chose to fly us across the Glade—all of five wing-beats to the trail—before landing, a distance I could easily have walked.

My thoughts were a preoccupied tangle of my feelings for Liam, concerns about what I'd witnessed in the source waters, and flashes of memory from my fight with Mendelson and the subsequent awareness of the power within my body.

I am human…and something else.

As we walked down trails thick with leaves, I kept glancing at him in wonder.

How did I get so lucky?

Every few yards, he gazed at me, his eyes asking the same thing.

Despite everything, I wasn't worried. Sure, I had concerns, and obviously I wondered what the hell to do about it all—but I had Liam. After that comforting fact, everything else seemed, well, manageable.

Liam lifted a low-hanging branch for me. I dipped beneath it and came up in the circle of his arms. His wings wrapped around us, cocooning as he drew me in.

"I thought I'd lost you," he whispered in my ear. "Please never do that again."

I desperately wanted to tell him I sure as hell wouldn't. I deeply wanted to promise I would do nothing of the sort. Yet a growing knowledge of the scope of my responsibilities had been building in my mind. With the vast new landscape of pending war and the necessary rescue of my sisters…I could make no such promise.

"I will do my best," I said. "That's as honest as I can make it."

My fingers trailed along his sides as he nuzzled my temple, inhaling my hair.

I didn't want to ruin the mood, but the door was open. "Liam, can we promise right now, always to be open and honest with one another?"

"I have always been honest with you," he said.

"I believe you have been, mostly, but…"

"But what?"

"But what about free-fall?" I took a deep breath and it came out in a rush. "Eleanor said… I mean, are we…you know, married?"

Liam sighed and rested his forehead on mine. Then he took my hand and led me to a fallen tree overcome with moss and growth. He swiped a clean spot and urged me to sit.

"It is complicated," he said.

I stared into his eyes, astonished by my own anxiety that it wasn't a definitive "yes, absolutely, till death do us part."

Make up your fucking mind, Fable!

"I have been carrying this around, just in case." Reaching in to his back pocket, Liam drew out a folded piece of paper. "I had it illuminated."

"Laminated," I corrected.

The plastic-covered paper had been folded dozens of times, read and re-read till the plastic was thin and the permanent creases were dangerously sharp.

"Sybil delivered it to me after you left the first time. I've read it over and over."

Warm light filtered through empty branches, as I spread the note open on the green velvet folds of my robe. Liam settled against a tree nearby, waiting patiently.

The note was in my handwriting on a sheet of paper torn from a notebook.

My Dearest Liam,

I leave tomorrow, but I will only be gone for a year, perhaps two. I know you are angry with me about my treaty with the Northern Reaches and my betrothal pact to Xabien. You have every right to be angry. I would be devastated, were our positions reversed.

I love you.

I glanced up, surprised.

"Keep reading," Liam said.

Please believe me when I say Xabien was not a choice I would have made, were it not for the lives at stake. I cannot protect anyone while I'm under the shield—this pact is the only way of knowing I can help keep you safe while I'm gone. No war will be fought while I am on Earth, so there is no chance you will be called to a front line. It was the only thing I knew to do. I can't ask you to wait for me. That would be too much.

If you love me, if you ever believe we can be together, then I must ask something of you. It is no small thing.

We both know I have duties. My life is not my own. I'm a servant to the Story, a bearer of the source. But you are the one man who makes me feel like I can have something for myself.

My future is unstable. At the risk of sounding melodramatic, I can say my future is fraught with danger and beauty and chaos. I am at peace with that. It's part of the story. But I would also have it full of joy—if you would also wish this future shared with me.

I have seen, if you choose to, one way for us to be together. It is so far in the future, I cannot see the details clearly from the millions of possibilities. But should you choose to have this life with me, there will come a day when I will be a woman and I will want to free-fall with you. That day is foggy when I try to see it better—so much hangs in the balance of so many choices. So I will say to you now, in writing: I wish free-fall with you. When that day comes, please know I chose you years in advance. Do not worry the outcome of my loving you. That is a given.

Should you choose a life with me, I cannot promise what a life it will be.

This one chance will be the only chance we'll get. Like shooting through the eye of a hurricane with a bent arrow toward a moving target.

Whatever my fate holds in the years that I am shielded, I am certain, under all the magic and protective spells and weavings, that my feelings for you will not change. I love you, Liam Odhyn Gunthorson. I put myself in the hands of your choice.

Love, Fable

Liam watched me, intently reading my face.

"I can't believe you kept this letter for 14 years." I folded the laminated paper and mumbled, "I sounded so…different."

"You *were* very different then," Liam agreed. "The shield and your time on Earth changed your voice and the words you use— but it has not changed who you are."

I've really wanted him for half a lifetime? Another younger me, setting up the older me.

The revelation in the letter evaporated any lingering anger I had about the deception. I was a child when I wrote it, but I wasn't wrong in that I'd clearly felt very strongly for him and continued to, even though I couldn't remember all of the reasons why.

"We are married according to the traditions of my people," Liam said as he walked through the leaves toward me, his talons crunching. "I've had many years to think about it, though, and the tradition is that it is always a woman's choice to free-fall." Thumbing a curl off my cheek, he said, "So if you say it never happened, I will support your claim that we are not attached."

"It happened!" I gushed. "Of course it happened."

The flash of relief on Liam's face mirrored my feelings exactly.

How can I possibly want anyone or anything else?

"It happened, and I don't know what we're going to do about the rest of the world—but I wouldn't have done it any other way."

Liam caught me up, lifted me off the tree, and kissed me hard. Then he threw his head back with a shout and swung me around.

For the first time in the memory of my last 14 years, I didn't feel empty or vacant. I wasn't lost or disconnected or alone.

I was truly, deliriously, happy.

Chapter Twenty-Eight

From here to there
By story bridged
Then one tale begins another

Gabe greeted us at the Gate, his long blond dreads tied back with a strand of his own hair. A sharp smile split his scruffy goatee.

"Icarus' wings! There is cause for celebration!"

I smiled, giddy there was so much to be happy about, for once.

Gabe slapped his brother on the back and said to me, "This one here was ready to chew through a Gorgon chain to get you to the Glade. Even the solar wind couldn't keep up with him. What do you call it on Earth…'bat out of hell'?" Gabe grinned. He had the same dimple as his brother.

Liam shook his head. "Perhaps you're just getting slow in your old age, brother."

We'd agreed not to tell anyone about the free-fall until we figured out what to do about Xabien and the Ice Cap Treaty, but I could see in Liam's teasing with his brother that it pained him to keep the secret.

The brothers ribbed at one another as Gabe leaned on the Gate's massive door and pushed. It still amazed me such a thing existed as the gateway. What was purely hypothetical on Earth—essentially a wormhole between worlds—was in fact one umbilicus of many connecting Earth to Aria. A quantum-mechanics work of genius that lesser cultures would take for magic.

How do I know that? Or even understand it?

Knowledge, perhaps memories, perhaps information from the source. It was impossible to tell. But I didn't really care. Pieces were falling into place, and that was a good sign.

The basement of the Glade Café had been cleaned and rearranged. Since my catastrophic entry earlier, when I'd knocked over bags of flour and beans, pots and pans, and bottles of wine, most of the metal shelves had been secured to the walls with brackets.

"We did a little decorating since you came through last time," Gabe said as he nudged me playfully.

My face filled with heat. "I'm really sorry about that."

"It's not to be mentioned," he said. "I hope you find things improved."

Liam reached for a hook that held the binding necklaces. He and Gabe hung similar *yuericks* about their necks. The moment the latches clicked, their wings vanished, their chests seemed an average size, and their talons were hidden by normal human feet.

"Does it hurt?" I wondered

Liam remained silent, but Gabe nodded.

They dressed in boots and T-shirts that were also on a nearby rack. I thought of all the people walking along 23rd Avenue above us, of all the folks in Portland who had no idea that creatures from another world were passing in and out through a Gate under their feet.

"I'm relieved to see you are well, Fable." Gabe ducked his head and grabbed an apron before rushing up the stairs ahead of us. "Eleanor is home waiting for you," he shouted back before disappearing up to the café.

I stood alone with Liam for a moment of silence, resting my head on his chest. We'd talked the rest of the way to the Gate, catching up on each other's lives. I hadn't been able to see him graduate from the Academy, or be recognized by the Council for his work, or be honored with Elite Guard status.

We'd talked like teenagers, catching up on the littlest details and being disgustingly touchy-feely all the way back to the Gate. I hadn't behaved like such a hormonal adolescent, pawing and panting and gazing all dreamy-eyed, since…well, since I actually was a horny teenager.

This feels amazing!

As we stood in the basement, I knew it would be a long time before we'd be able to indulge in such silly reminiscing and fawning.

Up the stairs meant a return to the future that was speeding like a bullet-train bound for destinations unpleasant—and I had a one-way ticket.

I stood on my toes and kissed his beautiful lips. Then I brushed his hair back with one hand and said, "I've got work to do."

He nodded against my forehead and squeezed me one last time.

As we walked up the stairs together, I wasn't afraid. With him, it seemed possible that there was a chance of winning.

The walk home from the café was surprisingly peaceful, truly the first sense of calm since everything began. The trees on Thurman Street were still shedding, and the late-afternoon sun felt like fleece against my skin. Liam's hand in my own as we strolled along almost made it feel like it was any other day for a normal couple. I wanted to capture the image and save it for the days ahead.

Celeste's front yard had recently been groomed, mowed, raked, and pruned for the coming winter. There was scaffolding on the side of the house where the fire had burned most of the fence and scorched the white exterior. Parts of the outer walls had recently been re-painted, and the wooden decorative molding replaced.

They've been busy.

A black-and-white cat followed us up the walk, meowing and rubbing against my legs.

The front door was open. The bustling sounds of cleaning, vacuuming and scrubbing were heard over the chatter of the NaNas. Habitually, I stepped over the front doormat, but was surprised to see there weren't any dead mice to avoid.

"I'm home!" I shouted, relishing the sudden rush of emotion that I could say such a thing and truly mean it. Truly feel it.

Home. I have place. An anchor.

The sliding back door was open, letting air circulate through the house. The furniture had been rearranged, and boxes were strewn about, some empty and others with knickknacks and odds and ends packed inside. One such box had a silver lamp, a folded red blanket, and a stack of books that I didn't recognize. I wondered where it came from.

"Look who's here!" squealed LeeLee as she barreled out of the kitchen. Her hands were all over me in moments, patting, brushing.

"I'm fine," I said. "And I'm happy to see you." And I meant it. I pulled her into a hug.

LeeLee's tall, slender frame reminded me of a stork. Spokes of hair escaped her lavender bandana. She was beautiful to me.

They were all beautiful. As welcome as sunrise after the longest night.

Eleanor and Biddy each wore bandanas and aprons. Biddy's yellow gloves went all the way to her armpits.

"How are you?" Eleanor asked as she angled in for her own hug.

"I'm sorry I had to deceive you," I whispered in her ear.

"Ah, *Cherie*," Eleanor replied with a squeeze, "I was so afraid for you."

"Tell us what happened!" Biddy pushed Eleanor out of the way and wedged herself into my arms.

"It's a long story," I said, "but I intend to tell you everything."

"I'll get the glasses," Eleanor said.

"I'll get the tequila," Biddy joined.

"Limes it is, then!" LeeLee chimed.

And it was like I'd stepped into an oasis. This was *my* Glade, my own sanctuary. This was home, and I planned on staying a while.

"…then while I was in the Glade's healing waters, I joined with the source and went all over Aria," I said as I took another sip of LeeLee's famous margaritas. "Aria is bracing for war, an epic war." I set my glass on the end table.

The NaNas were quiet. Liam stood near the back door, watching Forest Park. A solemn air weighed upon the room.

"I know it sounds bad," I continued, "but there are good things, too." I fought back the urge to look at Liam. "I am remembering pieces of my past…just spastic chunks without context yet, but they are there. And I know now what I need to do."

"That's wonderful!" LeeLee said. "What is it?"

"We must unite the Muses—all of them. Not just find the missing girls, but we must come together." I waited until they were all looking at me before saying, "And I need your help to do it."

"We thought you might say something like that," Eleanor grinned. "That's why we're moving in."

"*What*?" I choked, glancing at Liam.

"If that's okay with you…" LeeLee hesitated.

"We know you have a lot of work to get done, and this house needs constant protection while you do it. So we thought…" Biddy sipped her drink. "Well, I thought it would be good to keep close by…"

It made sense—aside from the sudden disappointment I wouldn't have free reign to maul Liam whenever I felt like it.

Where there's a will…

"It's a great idea," I said. The house was huge. Four of the bedrooms were just walls of books. The attic was unfinished, and two of the guest bedrooms were big enough for queen beds. Not to mention the office, the garage, and the basement. "We'll make this home-base, then, and bring the Muses here to get started."

Biddy's cheeks were flushed. "I call the blue room! It'll be like old times, when we were staking out the Menderillian Compound and we bunked with the diplomat's son…remember, Eleanor?"

"How could I ever forget?" Eleanor said dryly. "I can't wait for the next full moon."

"You're both drunk," LeeLee said disapprovingly.

"You mixed the drinks, Lees," Eleanor accused.

"Stronger than normal, I think," Biddy added.

"Is this what I have to look forward to?" I wondered. But I realized, I actually did look forward to it.

"Full moon," Biddy laughed belatedly. "Get it?"

"Oh, lordy," I murmured.

"If we are to make this the center for collecting and working with Maior," Liam said, "we will need to strengthen it, and lay down better defenses." He hadn't said much in the last hour as I'd recounted the story, omitting the parts involving us.

"That's a good point," LeeLee said.

"I like this one," Biddy winked and pointed her thumb at Liam.

"We've been putting down basic rune defenses and recharging the sigils Celeste left around the property. But you're right. More than one Muse will make a tempting target." Eleanor furrowed her brows. "What did you have in mind, Liam?"

He turned from the window. "It may be costly, but I noted at Skye that the charged ley lines they use for their perimeter and holding cells are running naturally through these hills." Scrubbing a hand through his hair, he said, "It may be wise to use what is naturally here and extend our boundaries of protection wherever we have a natural advantage."

"Ley lines are nearly impossible to manipulate," Biddy said.

"Not if you have someone who knows how to do it," Liam countered.

"Skye," I added. "Skye knows how, and she may help us."

"Like Liam said, that kind of work will be costly," LeeLee warned.

"Wouldn't Celeste want me to use her inheritance for something this important?" I asked.

"Not money kind of costly, Fable," Eleanor said gently, "but *favor* kind of costly."

"Can you really think of another way to protect the Muses?" I wondered. "When are we ever going to need to spend favors more than we need to now?"

We were all quiet for a time. Then Eleanor lifted her margarita to me and said, "Fable Rose Augustine Montgomery, it has been my great privilege to know you for your life—your youth and now as a woman. You are different. You were gone for a few days, and you have returned to us as a young goddess—and I would be honored if you would have me along for the next part of this journey, whatever that may look like."

"And I," said LeeLee.

"Meee, too!" slurred Biddy.

The vacancy left by Celeste's passing grew not smaller but less jagged. Emotion welled up in me and tears overflowed. "Thank you," I said and led the room in a round of inebriated "I-love-you's" and rocking hugs that turned to contented smiles, and then plans for the future.

The bar on Glisan was cramped and poorly lit. I spotted Julius Drake in the back corner, checking his phone. He wore jeans, a T-shirt, and a shoulder sling.

I squeezed between tables packed too tight and eased myself into the seat across from him.

"Hi," I said, catching my balance in the wobbly chair.

Special Agent Drake looked at me as though he didn't know who I was.

"Julius?"

"Don't call me that," he said softly.

His gaze went on uncomfortably long, and I thought for a moment he truly didn't know who I was.

"You should be dead," he said at length.

"Well, nice to see you, too," I said, picking up my purse to leave.

"Why aren't you dead?" he asked, grabbing onto my wrist. "Four days ago you had a bullet wound, a stab wound, purple strangle marks on your neck, and a pint of your blood soaked Laurelhurst Park."

I sat back down. He picked up his whiskey and downed the shot, shaking his head. "I took a bullet, Fable. And I shot my partner for you, and you spewed light out of your hand, and angels came to your rescue—so you'd better have a really good fucking story to go with all of this, or I might just shoot you myself."

His voice carried through the small bar. People turned to look.

I pulled my hand from his grasp and gently touched his arm. "I'll tell you everything. If you really want to know, I'll spare you nothing. But it will be difficult to hear, and once you know everything, there'll be no going back. No safety. You'll be a part of something you'll never be able to escape."

His eyes were bloodshot, his hair mussed. "I'm being investigated for shooting Mendelson. I may be kicked out of the bureau."

"I'm sorry," I said sincerely. "Really."

He chewed the inside of his cheek then said, "You know where the missing girls are, don't you?"

"No, I don't—but I know how to find them. And I guarantee they won't be anywhere near FBI jurisdiction."

"I want to know everything," Drake said. "I'm in."

Later that night, when I returned home, LeeLee met me at the door. The house smelled of baked bread. "So, how'd it go?"

"He's in shock. Obviously I can relate to that." I slipped out of my jacket and slugged off my boots. "I gave him the facts, but I think he's going to need to think on it for a bit before he is going to want to touch proof." I shook my head and smiled. "And I can relate to that, too. I can't really blame him for freaking out a little."

Eleanor walked in from the pantry. "Oh, good, you're home! Is he going to help us?"

"I'm not sure," I admitted. "He's been suspended, pending an investigation; after all, he did shoot his partner to save me, and then I disappeared. He's really pissed."

Eleanor patted my shoulder. "He'll come around."

I paused before delivering the worst part of the news: "Mendelson is still alive."

Eleanor's eyes widened. LeeLee's mouth fell open.

"Apparently, she underwent emergency trauma surgery and survived the collapsed lung. She has been raving and biting and talking in other languages." I exhaled. "Drake says they think she had a psychotic breakdown. Her hair and eyes are all white."

"Oh, honey…" LeeLee began.

"It's all right. I mean, they don't expect her to recover any time soon, but I really wanted her to confess or be charged for Celeste's murder. Drake doesn't know if they'll be able to salvage the recorded data from the phone. Even if they can prove she killed Celeste, they won't be able to prosecute if she's nuts."

"A bullet to the chest and an undiluted blast of pure creative power," Eleanor said. "It's a miracle she survived—but everything she was has likely been wiped clean."

"She's not much more than a ghost, Fable." LeeLee finished. "That will have to be some form of consolation. It's a terrible justice in its own right."

"It will have to be enough for now," I agreed.

The next two days were spent in legal discussions. Mr. Grosskopf, Celeste's lawyer, began the probate process. Any which way you sliced it, Celeste left me millions in book royalties, property, jewelry, deeds, and rights. It boggled my mind.

But the most amazing part was the inheritance she'd kept in trust for my family on Aria: property in the form of buildings and land, and also in trade and labor.

I wasn't sure what most of it was, although, Mr. Grosskopf assured me "labor" didn't mean slavery. He was actually from Aria, one of the many creatures that blended well enough on Earth that he led a double life, working for the Sublime on both sides of the veil.

He was about five and a half feet tall with a bald, bobbly head covered in moles sprouting wiry white hairs. His phone buzzed with a text. Lightning-fast, he tapped out a rapid text response with gnarled, arthritic-looking fingers. "I beg your pardon," he said, as we signed papers in the fading light of the afternoon, "it was my youngest daughter."

"Oh? How old is she?" I ask casually, hoping it would reveal a marker of his age.

"She'll be 96 this winter." He smiled proudly.

My eyes were dry and itchy. I realized I'd been staring far too long without blinking. "Oh, that's cool." My dad was barely 50 and couldn't work the microwave, much less texts or cell phones.

Then Mr. Grosskopf showed me pictures of one of my properties on Aria, a very detailed black and white sketch on thick, yellowed paper. "This was your mother's cottage in West Hartland," Mr. Grosskopf said.

"Why didn't it go to my father?" I wondered. "Clark is still alive."

"Your family's holdings are vast and your lineage ancient. Clark's marriage contract nullifies him from inheriting anything from across the veil."

"My mother agreed to that?" I couldn't believe it. My parents had a pre-nup…or whatever the equivalent was on Aria.

Mr. Grosskopf nodded, his bald head wobbling dangerously on his too-thin neck. "Your mother and father were very much in love,." He patted my hand in a grandfather way. "It was your maternal grandmother's request to have the contract drawn in such a way, and your parents readily agreed."

Shuffling papers, he pushed the drawing closer to me and tapped on the sketch at the top left window of the house, where I could make out the figure of a woman…my mother. "I don't believe they intended to continue living on Aria after you were born, but they wanted you to have your family's holdings."

I lifted the sketch and focused on the image. I remembered the cottage, roses blooming around the outer edge of the low stone wall, birds in the trees, and the hint of an ocean breeze.

"I remember this place."

Mr. Grosskopf was already on to another set of papers, distracted. "That's nice, dear."

By the time I left his office several hours later, I carried a box of paperwork and access to a new account wherein he was wiring funds to begin the immediate and much-needed renovations to Celeste's house.

My last piece of business—a promise to Abra.

Franko welcomed me back to Skye. As we walked through the house toward the library entrance to the prison cells below, Franko extolled me with the details of a play he had been suddenly inspired to write since my visit.

"I never thought of myself as a playwright—truly, I'm more of a performer—but the idea came so suddenly and fully formed, I couldn't sleep until I'd gotten up to start work on it."

I followed behind him, mindful of his excited gesticulating.

"I cannot stop! The idea is pressing out upon the paper as though pouring from a conduit. I will have this play written and performers on the stage by spring."

Stepping into the elevator, I listened to him with half an ear while remembering all those nights when Erik would get out of bed in the dead of darkness to work on his novel. Why Celeste would sometimes write all day, sleep for a handful of hours then she'd rise well before dawn and continue to work.

I wondered if everyone was susceptible to my energy, or power, or whatever it was that seemed to linger—or if it only affected certain people already inclined to story craft. It didn't seem to be inspiring Liam or the NaNas.

What does inspiration from a Muse actually do *to someone? Who does it affect?*

The guard opened Abra's door. I stalled, horrified.

Blood smeared the concrete walls of her cell. Red spatter marked the ceiling and Abra's pale face.

She sat on the floor, a dozen crows and a raven near her feet. Sweat beaded her forehead.

"What have you done to her?" I demanded of the short burly guard. "You can't abuse people already in prison!"

"I ain't touch 'er," he grumbled and closed the door behind us.

Franko covered his nose with his hand. He looked like he might be sick. "I'm sorry. I must wait outside…so much blood…"

I was alone with Abra. She smiled.

"Gets the soft-bellied Gormanders every time." She smirked, using the wall to stand up. "They get restless." She held up an arm where the tattoos had been, revealing blank, bloody skin.

"So I was right," she said. She watched me with the same dark eyes of her birds. Soon the whole murder of crows turned to me, watching as intently as their mistress.

"Look," I began. "I'm good for my word. I'll talk to the Tuatha." I turned to leave. "But if I catch you in my neighborhood, or anywhere near me, my sister Muses, or anyone I care about—I'll do to you what I did to Mendelson, and I won't feel bad about it."

"What did you do to her?" Abra crouched and stroked the head of a bird. It shuffled, little talons scraping the floor.

"Stay out of reach, Abra."

In the hall outside the holding area, Franko was shaky and pale but led me back up through the library, where we met a woman. She was dressed in a soft sage green, medieval gown with wavy red hair down to her hips.

Skye.

"Hello, Skye." I stretched my hand to her, but she only tipped her head.

"She is only a projection to help you feel at ease interfacing with her," Franko said.

Like a ghost? How does one feel at ease with a ghost?

After a pause, I said, "Skye, I deeply appreciate everything you've done for me and mine, and I hope someday to be able to repay you." I straightened my shoulders, then I did something totally alien. "At the risk of burdening your hospitality—I need to ask you for a couple of favors."

Skye smiled, and I remembered what Liam said about the Tuatha DeDannon. Allies so long as it suits them.

But what choice do we have?

She motioned me to take a seat. Franko stood nearby to translate for her, and we began our negotiations.

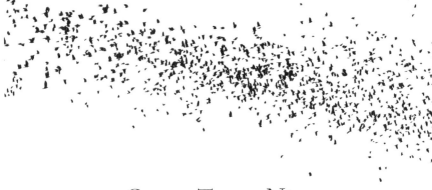

Chapter Twenty-Nine

As one story ends
Another yet begins
Turn the page, Rose
Turn the page

"Beware of Destiny cut loose its tether; Birds of a feather murder together." I read the inky scrawl of my mother's handwriting beneath the watercolor image of a dozen crows in a cherry tree bursting with blossoms.

I closed the large wooden book full of my mother's paintings and ran my fingers over the carving of her name on the cover: Angelica.

"Sacred Nine and Nine Shall Be." was another painting in the book I'd seen, the nine little girls holding hands and dancing around a sapling.

She knew. She tried to warn me in her own way.

Setting the book on the window seat, I glanced out at the back yard. Liam, Gabe, and Zane were all three shirtless in the late-October sun. Silver *yuericks* glinted around their necks and sunlight burnished muscles as they worked to repair the back wall.

Gabe stirred a wheelbarrow of quickset concrete to which he added a pouch of herbs and a vial of red fluid. Zane etched runes into the stones that Liam lifted into place on the wall.

Liam.

Every time I thought about him, my heart raced, and I couldn't wait until we could find a moment alone, and I could run my hands along his—

"Fable?" LeeLee asked.

I shrieked and fell off the window seat. Red-hot guilt throbbed on my face.

"I didn't mean to scare you," LeeLee said, bewildered. She helped me up.

"I'm fine. Just lost in thought," I mumbled.

LeeLee glanced out the window and noted the beautiful half-naked bodies of men out back. "Evidently."

I peeked once more. Biddy walked onto the patio with three cups of lemonade and some cookies. "*Yooo hooo*, bo-oys," Biddy hollered.

"Unbelievable," I groaned. "She's like, a hundred."

"Don't worry about Biddy. She can take care of herself."

"It's not Biddy I worry about."

LeeLee chuckled and glanced around the office. "I really like what you've done with the place."

I'd spent the last few days rearranging Celeste's office to create a space to work. As much as I wanted to keep Celeste's things exactly where they were, it hurt too much to stare around a room that no longer held her spirit, when every knickknack and trinket screamed out her memory.

So I'd started from scratch, keeping only her desk and chair—everything else was new. New white cotton drapes and cushions in the window seat. We'd moved the walls of bookshelves to the hall and replaced them with dark wood armoires and hanging mirrors. Small baskets with found items and things I loved filled little nooks, but for the most part the space was clean, uncluttered, and open.

In time, perhaps, I'd fill it to bursting as Celeste had done, but for the task ahead…I'd need all the space we could manage, to think and work.

"I just popped up to tell you Eleanor and I are headed down to the farmer's market."

I peeked out the window one last time, my gaze fixed on Liam. "Mm hm, okay, have fun."

I didn't hear her leave, I was so engrossed in the marvel of the way he moved, the grace of motion in the fluid shift of his bronze skin. Watching him do something as practical as fixing the stone fence made me so… I shivered.

He was the embodiment of a symphony. Each part working in absolute harmonic perfection. The sun, the slight breeze through the grass, and the bass rumble of his voice as he spoke all made me want to feel and touch and write.

Grabbing my new laptop off the desk, I sat in the window and began typing.

As my fingers hit keys, I wasn't so much in my body as breathing the connection among all living things. Delicious interconnectedness between sun and blades of grass, the draft of wind from a bird's flight; the crinkle of dry leaves in the park. Streams speaking to stones as they burbled by; moss creeping along a rotting tree stump…all of them telling their stories as I wrote.

I was only vaguely aware that at some point day became night and the untouched slices of apples on the desk were removed and replaced with a bowl of soup. Then daylight brought coffee, which I drank with one hand as I typed with the other.

My fingers worked out on the keyboard, a story of war and abduction.

The collapse of a peace treaty and the murder of a great official brought a nation to mourning.

The trance spilled onto my electronic pages.

A forbidden love with a proud people and a child born thrice cursed.
Crows carried messages to faraway lands.
A tower of kept wives plotted rebellion.
Blood-soaked fields and rivers clogged with bodies of the fallen

Tears streamed down my cheeks. And it was not just Aria. I began to realize the war would spill through the veil. I typed in horror.

Portland was razed to the ground, brought to smoldering rubble by a quake.

A desperate famine across the world set neighbors upon one another.

A gold-scaled dragon tore the Chicago L-train in half.

Leviathans wrecked a tanker off the coast of Japan.

Each scene was more terrible than the last. My fingers blurred across the keys, my mind's eye trapped, unable to look away.

Hundreds of beached merfolk dried in the sun.

A small ceramic bowl full of light, cracking the ground with power.

Avians fell from the sky.

Feathers littered the ground, mixed with blood and glass and bodies.

And there in the connection…

Liam's beautiful form, his limbs bent, wing broken. His life-blood spilled across a marble floor.

I screamed and screamed, unable to stop as the vision gripped me hostage to the future while my fingers typed furiously, blurring across the keyboard.

His blond scalp split by a red gash. A spear lodged in his body.

Mercilessly the vision tormented me with the sight of Liam's maimed, twisted body.

A sharp white-hot, pain-filled flash ripped me from the clutches of the prophecy, and I sat on the floor of the office. Liam crouched before me, shaking my shoulders.

"Ohmigod!" I dumped the laptop and threw myself into his arms. He folded me into the safety of his embrace as I wept.

"It's not safe for you to rip her out of a trance like that!" Eleanor snapped from the doorway.

"Can't you see she was terrified?" Biddy said, softly.

"That can't be good," Gabe said, poking his head around the frame.

"Just give us a minute," Liam hissed, smoothing my hair and murmuring, "You're safe. You're home in Portland."

"I think we may have changed something important," I whispered.

"It will be all right. I swear to you."

"No, it won't, Liam." I clung to him. "I saw you."

Tucking his wings around us and pressing his lips to my hair, he rocked me until the light outside the window darkened.

"They are waiting," he whispered.

I nodded, sniffed, and wiped my eyes. "How long was I under this vision?"

"A couple of days," he said.

After printing the total of 200 pages I'd written in two days, I carried the stack of papers downstairs, where the NaNas and Gabe sat around the table. It appeared they'd been fixing dinner but had little appetite. Nearly-full plates crowded the table.

The post-vision hunger gripped me, and my stomach growled.

"Here, sit and eat," LeeLee encouraged, scooping a plate of mashed potatoes and gravy, and her famous Swedish meatballs.

Pulling up a chair, I sat the manuscript on the table and dug in.

"How bad is it?" Gabe asked.

"Gabe…" Liam warned.

"Brother, her eyes rolled back and stars and planets and freakin' *nebulas* filled her eye sockets, and she was screaming as though the Gorgon queen were turning her to stone! It's messed up, and we gotta ask how bad."

"I don't know how bad," I said around a mouthful of potatoes. "I only skimmed over some of the pages as they were coming out of the printer."

"May we?" Eleanor asked, pointing to the stack.

"Sure, maybe you can make sense of it. From what I read, it was all out of order; the scenes seem to have no particular time-line or structure."

Eleanor lifted the papers and returned to her seat. She cleared her throat and began to read as I ate and the others listened.

The reading continued all night and well into the morning. Everyone took turns, as voices became strained and fatigue wore us down. A heavy quiet lingered in the room. Wine flowed into glasses, then coffee and tea. Liam and Gabe took turns pacing, and the NaNas shifted into different positions on the sofa, until daylight cracked through the curtains and LeeLee turned the final page.

All of us sat, laden by the revelations.

Finally, Eleanor said, "I agree with Fable, it's out of order."

"I second that," Biddy nodded. "I'm not sure which part comes first, but I don't think it's linear."

Liam stood quietly near the back window and Gabe watched him with a worried expression.

It hurt to hear the part with Liam. It hurt deep, in many terrifying ways.

"I was thinking about it as you were reading," I said. The black-and-white cat, Sage, slept on my lap. "I think I know what it is."

LeeLee refilled coffee cups and sat back at the bar as she listened. "Go on."

"I think it's an outline," I breathed. "There's no way all that can happen in 200 pages. I think I must have been looking really far into the future at lots of cascading events, and these are just highlight moments of the whole, grand story."

"But how do you know?" Gabe asked.

"I know because it's built like the broad points of an arc. The events are like a bunch of pillars, if you will. But there is no filling, the small choices that make up the conclusion or outcomes of the larger events." I rubbed my eyes. "There are no catalysts for the chain of collapsing events, the small decisions and actions that lead from one pillar to the next. Story cannot happen in a vacuum. So I looked far enough into the future, or maybe some was from the past, that we are only seeing variables of outcomes—and they are subject to change based on the catalysts between."

I continued as they all stared. "If these 200 pages are an outline of what's to come, or what's already happened, I need to put it in the correct order. We need to see which events can be marginally altered and which events I didn't see clearly."

"How do you plan to do that?" Liam asked softly.

"By breaking it down into sections and then focusing on writing each section in vivid, excruciating detail."

"You mean go deeper," Eleanor said.

I nodded. "I've only been brushing the surface of what this power can do. If I go deeper, I might get a better idea of what's really going on."

"Any deeper, and you might end up a vegetable," Biddy mumbled.

I shrugged. "I supposed that's not out of the realm of possibility."

"No," Liam interjected.

"No, what?" I asked.

"No, we can't risk you that way."

"We can't *not* risk me that way," I countered. "And you all know it." Looking around, I met their faces, faces of people I trusted. "We can't be walking around with only parts of the story. We could end up making what seem like really good decisions based on fractions of information, and it could be a total disaster." I stood up and the cat jumped to the floor. I walked to the kitchen and set my mug on the counter. "I feel a surge, and I need to use it while it's strong."

"You need sleep, Fable." Eleanor's eyes pleaded.

"So do you. But this is when it all starts, isn't it?" Glancing around, I realized how tired they all were. "Isn't this what we came here to do? Let me do what I'm built for—I can sleep when I'm dead."

To their credit, they didn't argue but lumbered to their feet and shuffled around. LeeLee put another pot of coffee on to brew.

"I'll take this watch, Liam." Gabe shooed Liam up the stairs with me and took his place by the glass door.

"Where are you going to start?" Eleanor asked as she set about cleaning up the dinner plates from the night before.

"I think the first piece in the outline is the section about Maya," I replied. Talking and walking seemed to take more effort than I remembered.

LeeLee followed us up the steps and watched as I settled into my seat at the desk. Liam folded his wings and stretched out across the window seat, watching me from hooded lids.

"Be careful, Fable," LeeLee whispered. Her tired eyes were lined with worry but also glinted with something else, something warm. "I'm very proud of you, and I know Celeste would be, too."

A month ago, I would have laughed if anyone told me I'd be writing the stories that make up the larger epic of the birth of Muses in our modern world. I'd have screamed lunacy at the thought that I'd marry my childhood sweetheart, a man who also happened to be part eagle.

I'd never in a million years have thought my life would involve conspiracy, murders, abductions, and warring factions of dominant powers—because I was too busy setting TiVo for the next episode of *American Idol* and living paycheck to paycheck to fund my coffee addiction.

Notwithstanding all that, and despite losing my dearest Celeste—I wouldn't go back to what I was. I wouldn't go back to the safety of a dead-end job and a "Mr. Right-now" relationship.

I wanted this. I wanted this crazy new adventure and this grandiose quest. I wouldn't have it any other way.

I believed what LeeLee said. I knew Celeste would have wanted to see me come into my power. I also knew she loved me and would have been happy with my choice, no matter which life I lived.

"Thank you, LeeLee," I said.

It was so unexpected, such a wash of sudden emotion, I smiled. And with a surge of power, my eyes rolled back.

The universe opened up into cosmic dust and spiraling planets. Suns and gases and threads connecting the molecules of all creation spiraled through my eyes, and my fingers flashed across the keyboard.

Chapter Thirty

Maya

Maya leaned against the gargoyle on the edge of the roof. London spread out below in all directions, the Thames a winding ribbon mirroring city lights. Nights were the hardest. The dark hours called up loss like summoned specters, the moment the sun set and the living world slept.

Mom. Dad. Ilyema. Dax.

Rafe. Always Rafe.

Raphael Delaney never stood a chance in this world once he met Maya.

She was a freak. A monster. Everyone around her was doomed to die… And why had she even fallen for Rafe, anyway? She knew better.

No, she wouldn't believe that, because Dax was out there somewhere. But then, maybe Dax was safer away from her, away from the danger Maya inevitably brought with her wherever she went.

Gripping a monstrous marble wing, Maya held on to the statue of a grotesque creature and leaned out over the rooftop. It was easily 70 feet to the pavement.

Maybe they'll think it was an accident.

Just one quick step, and all the nonsense of Muses and other worlds and people she loved being murdered would disappear. No more self-loathing because of her powerlessness to ever prevent anything.

She studied the statue. She'd been climbing up to the roof every day for the past week to write poetry. He comforted her somehow, her gargoyle, ever steady, never complaining when her verse didn't synch or her rhymes were flat.

He was a stone monster, probably the closest thing she had to a friend.

"How pathetic is that?" she wondered, leaning her shoulder against the sculpted curve of his arm. "You know, you're a really good listener." She leaned in and pecked his stone cheek.

Then she held onto his wing and hung over the edge one more time; each time, she knew she wouldn't do it—because Dax still needed her. For no other reason did she pull herself back from the brink but for Dax.

"After little sister is safe, all bets are off," she whispered to the gargoyle. "This other-world Muse shit can go straight to hell, after Dax is home."

A cabbie horn blared beneath the building.

Maya was startled.

Her hand slipped off the wing, and her body tipped forward. For a terrifying moment, she could neither breathe nor scream, as her arms wind-milled for balance.

Then she fell.

Her face sped toward the pavement, wind howling in her ears.

In a horrid blink, she knew she was going to smash onto the roof of the cab. A scream ripped loose from the tangles of her throat and ricocheted off the surrounding buildings.

Just as Maya's heart nearly stopped, there was a tug on her legs, and then she was flying outward, not plummeting.

She swooped with such momentum that her dangling arm hit the waiting taxi and a sharp, urgent pain exploded in her wrist. Clutching it to her chest, eyes closed, she waited for impact.

Nothing.

Wind burned her ears and whipped her long black hair, but she was moving—flying, not falling.

She opened her eyes and stared agape as she flew over the city of London, all lights and streets and echoes of horns. She twisted, peering up.

The gargoyle, her gargoyle, flapped massive, leathery wings. His dark marble body had turned to flesh and supple skin. Her legs were wrapped in his long, ropey tail, the spiked end of which dangled dangerously close to her eyes.

Muscular legs matched huge forearms with ridged fins and meaty fists with claws, but nothing compared to the spiral ram's horns on either side of his bald, angular head.

The creature looked down at her with black, glassy eyes and a wide mouth full of sharp teeth. He thrust his head skyward and howled a guttural bellow.

The sound was rich with the tenor of pending slaughter.

Maya screamed.

About the Author

 *Murder of Crows* is Athena's first published novel. She lives a life of adventure and bliss, rich in friends and family with a spicy dose of chaos. Her passions include; travel, photography, scrapbooking, scotch and storytelling…preferably all with chocolate.

Athena's adventures can be found at www.theblissquest.com

More about the series, *The Pillars of Dawn*, the world of *Aria*, and the progress on the sequel to *Murder of Crows* can be found at www.thepillarsofdawn.com

In honor of all the Kickstarter support and encouragement from friends and family from her beautiful hometown of Valdez, Athena added this prose for the love of Alaska, which is the inspiration for the world *Aria*.

Come Home

By Athena

Come home with me.

I want to show you my Alaska, the place where I grew up. I want to show you my waterfalls, and green temperate forests, my lakes and lush valleys. I want to introduce you to the Sound where I learned to kayak and follow the salmon, and the cliffs where I'd hike to sit and write poetry at two in the morning under the midnight sun.

I want you to meet my glaciers, and hear the sound of the calving ice, like thunderous laughter of gods and smell their winter breath. I want you to swim with me in azure waters so cold we have only each other's bodies for warmth to stay alive. I want you to be welcomed by my purple fields of fireweed where I danced and sang and chased wolves.

Mine was not the childhood of cul-de-sacs and neighborhood barbeques. Mine was a youth full of river rapids, ice and snow and epic mountains, northern lights and bears. My childhood was unsupervised and wild. Civilized only just enough not to be called... feral. I had twigs in my hair, scrapes on my knees and smelled of woods and lichen and sea salt.

And I was happy.

Come home with me. Come taste the low blueberries, the smoked salmon off the rack, and the shrimp fresh from the dock. Come listen to the rivers, and the elder's drums and whale songs. Come dance with me the dance to greet the sun, or linger and watch the aurora slip in emerald and amethyst sand across the sky-bowl. Come taste the air, feel the earth and let me show you the love of my life, let me see it light your eyes and crack open your soul

I want you to see Valdez, so when you peek into my heart, you will understand what lives therein; a vast jewel-hued wilderness ripe with promise, the basis of all my comparisons - then you will know my full meaning when I look you in the eye and tell you, "I love you."